ADAM J. SCHOLTE

Sanctuary

THE RAMULAS CHRONICLES

The Ramulas Chronicles Book 2: Sanctuary

Paperback edition ISBN: 978-1-7638864-2-1
eBook edition ISBN: 978-1-7638864-3-8

Published by Adam J Scholte
www.adamjscholte.com

This second edition: April 2025
First edition: March 2023

A catalogue record for this book is available from the National Library of Australia

Editor: Jason Martin
Design and Typeset: Kristine Joy Magno
Printed in Australia.

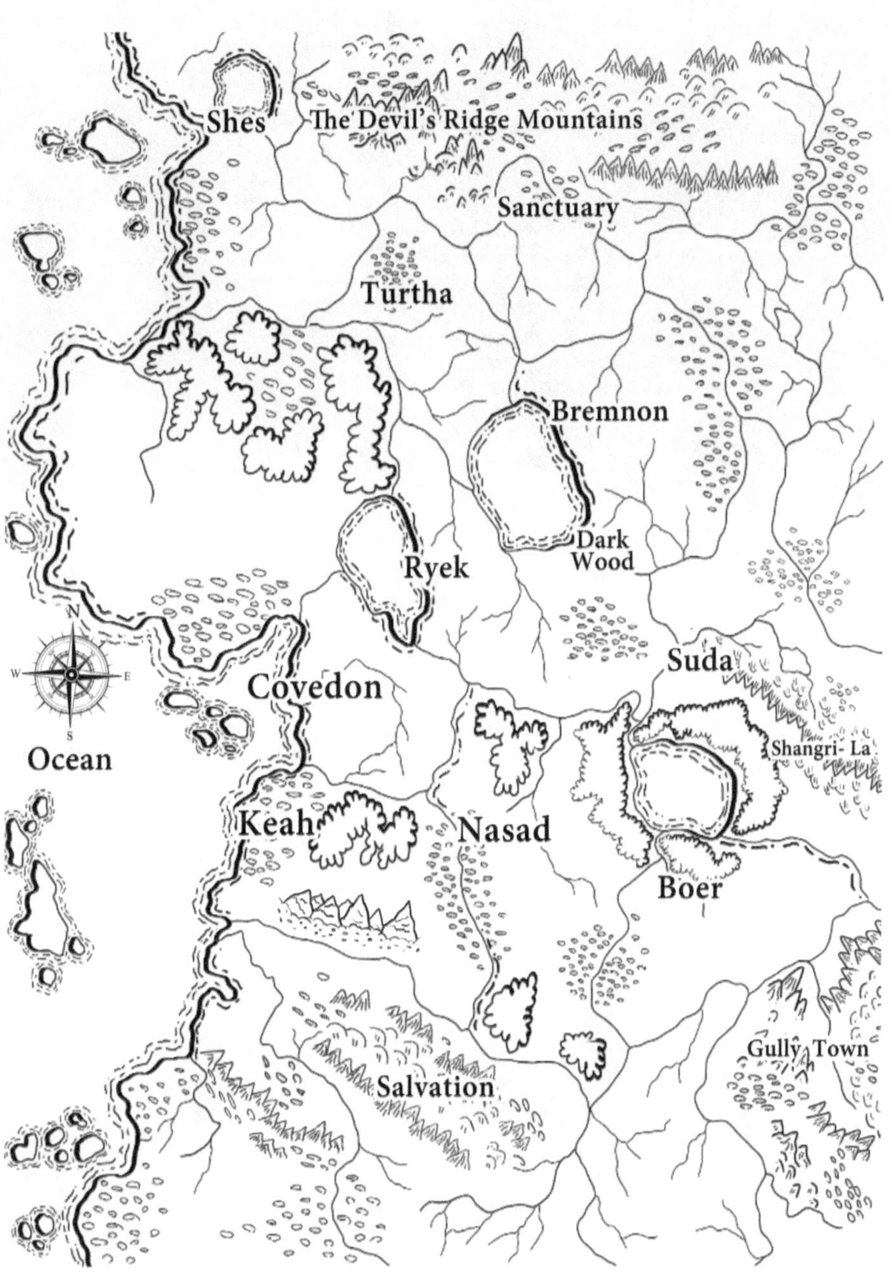

Shes
The Devil's Ridge Mountains
Sanctuary
Turtha
Bremnon
Ryek
Dark Wood
Suda
Covedon
Shangri- La
N
W   E
S
Ocean
Keah
Nasad
Boer
Salvation
Gully Town

Character list

Aleesha—King Zachary's daughter.

Alpha—One of the Warlords chasing Oriel.

Benji—Former thief, friend of Pip and now member of the fallen angels, an elite army with Sanctuary.

Beta—One of the Warlords chasing Oriel.

Captain Aldrich—Member of King Braydon's army.

Declyn—Magician to King Braydon.

Eady—Leader of the Dryads.

Edwin—A dwarf helping dig the tunnel to Oriel.

Emily—An ancient spirit trapped in Sanctuary for hundreds of years.

Fenris—A young Hell hound.

Grace—Daughter of Ramulas, affected by his magic and that of the dryads.

Iguchi—A warrior from across the sea, trainer of the fallen angels.

Jacqueline—Wife of Ramulas.

Jenna—Sister to Pip.

Kate—Eldest daughter of Ramulas, who has unique fighting skills.

K'ayden—Head of the Khilli people.

Lodi—A giant living near Sanctuary.

Lucas—Head of King Zachary's royal guard.

Makayla—Jenna's daughter.

Master of shadows—Head of the thief's guild in Keah.

Michael—Member of the fallen angels.

Miles—Former thief and member of the fallen angels and close friend of Benji.

Nathaniel—Brother of Michael who is trapped near Oriel in the mountain.

Old John—Member of the shadows, thief's guild of Keah.

Omega—One of the Warlords chasing Oriel.

Oriel—A being of pure magic hiding from the Warlords who wish to kill her for her powers.

Owain—Blind archer from Shangri-la.

Patrick—Father of Pip.

Pip—Former member of the shadows and now fighting partner of Ramulas.

Private Anderson—Member of King Zachary's army.

Ramulas—Twin to Remus, leader of Sanctuary and protecter of his people.

Reckoning—A captain of the legion.

Redemption—A caption of the legion.

Retribution—A captain of the legion.

Remus—Twin of Ramulas, head Warlord chasing Oriel.

Royce—Prisoner of Gully town.

Rygar—Dwarf and adoptive father to Lodi.

Rufus—Ramulas' warhorse.

Shayn—Prisoner of Gully town.

Shearok—Young Dragon from Shangri-la.

Shigar—Magician to King Zachary.

Tao—Son of Jenna.

Thomas—Ramulas' friend, part Khilli.

Tilly—Sprite living in Sanctuary's forest.

Valkyrie—Mother Hell hound.

Zachary—Ruler of the Kingdom.

1

Ramulas and Pip rode out of the mountains on the warhorse. They would see the occasional creature duck out of sight or run away as they approached. Pip was alarmed at first, and then she noticed a change in their behaviour.

The Symiaks were weary of the pair and the warhorse; she smiled, knowing this was better than when they first came to these mountains. After a few hours, they arrived at the hut where they found Rufus.

Ramulas was saddle-sore after having encouraged the warhorse to run where possible. He climbed down from Rufus and communicated with him that they would rest. Pip climbed down and did not seem to be as affected as Ramulas from the ride.

'The magician does not appear to be here,' Pip said, looking around.

'I think there is food in the hut for Rufus,' Ramulas said walking towards it.

Pip had reached the edge of the clearing by the time Ramulas opened the hut.

'Hello, my friend,' Shigar said.

Ramulas jumped back as his eyes widened at seeing the king's magician inside the hut. Pip raced to Ramulas' side, holding a throwing knife in each hand; they vanished when she saw Shigar.

'Where did you come from?' she asked.

'I have been waiting for you to return,' Shigar said. 'Was your mission successful?'

'It was and it wasn't,' Ramulas said.

Shigar raised an eyebrow. 'Please explain.'

Ramulas sighed before retelling what Oriel had said to him and how she showed him where Sanctuary was. By the time he had finished, Shigar scratched his beard thoughtfully.

'I see that your journey is not yet finished. Is there any way I could help?'

'We need to travel by the fastest route to the Devil's Ridge Mountains,' Ramulas said. 'Once there, I will need to prepare for the coming of the First Legion. We will not be able to enter the city for supplies; I would be grateful if you could get some for us.'

Shigar clicked his tongue and shook his head. 'Riding is too slow; a ship would be faster.'

'How do we board a ship when the city is locked down and no ships are to leave the harbour?' Pip asked.

A sly smile spread across the magician's face. 'The city of Keah is no longer locked down.'

'What!?' Ramulas and Pip said simultaneously.

Shigar shrugged. 'It was quite simple, really—when the cavalry had returned after their wild goose chase, King Zachary was furious and wanted the city under martial law. Every person was to be locked in their home until the prisoner was found.

'This would mean a city full of angry people locked away indefinitely. Zachary has changed over the last few years; he has forgotten about what it means to be the ruler of his people. He has become paranoid and greedy and allows his daughter to do as she pleases.'

Shigar slowly shook his head. 'If the city was placed under martial law, the people would have eventually risen in revolt, and many would have died. I told Zachary that this would not be necessary; because the prisoner had left the city.'

'How did you convince him that I had gone?' Ramulas asked.

'I brought him up to my chambers and showed him that the crystal and your weapons were gone. He had already witnessed the magical properties of the crystal and knew that no-one but you would take it. Then I told him that I felt your presence leave the city.'

'Is that when he opened the city?' Pip asked.

'No, that took several hours of discussion for Zachary to see reason. I had merchants, the king's council, and advisers talk to the king about the growing tensions within the city. At first light this morning, King Zachary reluctantly opened the gates and harbour of Keah; however, his agents were sent once more to search for you.'

'Then I will have trouble making my way to the Devil's Ridge Mountains with Pip,' Ramulas said.

Shigar laughed. 'The description of you is vague at best. Zachary still thinks you are injured and possess the crystal—those are the two things the king's agents will be looking for.'

Rufus nudged Ramulas from behind and communicated that he wanted food. 'The warhorse is hungry; he tells me there is food in the hut.'

Shigar's eyes widened. 'The warhorse spoke to you?'

Ramulas nodded with a smile.

'Is it just the warhorse, or can you communicate with other animals?'

Ramulas shrugged as he raised an eyebrow.

'This is truly fascinating,' Shigar said as he walked to the hut.

Ramulas and Pip could hear the magician muttering to himself as he moved several large sacks. A few moments later, he dragged one of the sacks out and emptied the contents into a trough. Rufus walked over and began to feed.

'What were those things in the tunnel?' Pip asked.

Shigar gave the thief a sad smile. 'Long ago, a previous magician wanted a secret passageway in and out of the city. He hired workers from the towns of Boer and Nasad. All the workers were expert builders, and they were promised great wealth upon completion of the tunnel; they lived in this grove for months digging from the outside in, and no-one knew of the workers except the magician.

'When the tunnel was completed, the magician was happy with the work they had done. However, he asked the workers one last favour: he wanted doors made of the strongest steel. One for his chambers, and one for the entrance of the tunnel near the hut.

'The doors were soon completed and fitted to both entrances of the tunnel. The magician walked through the tunnel with the men and praised their work. He produced a flask of dragon's blood wine—a very rare drink—and each of the men drank a mouthful and was very grateful.

'When the workers awoke, they found themselves trapped in the tunnel. They had been drugged and their tools had been taken from them. Suddenly, they realised their fate: this tunnel was to be secret, and there could be no witnesses.

'Since that day, they have roamed the tunnel feeding off any living thing they come across.'

'But the doors,' Pip said. 'What about the doors? They could leave anytime they wanted.'

'My, you are a clever thief,' Shigar said. 'The door to my chamber remains, and this door was removed when I began working for King Zachary, yet they refuse to leave the tunnel. That is why I created the potion within the crystal bottle, which keeps them from harming me.'

'What!?' Pip exclaimed. 'Why didn't you tell us about them before we went into the tunnel?'

Shigar shrugged. 'Where is the adventure in life if you know what lies ahead? And it was a test; if you were unable to find your way through the tunnel, you could not have won against the Symiaks that you fought.'

'How did you know we fought with Symiaks?' Ramulas asked. 'We did not tell you.'

'The smell of the creature's blood is very unusual,' Shigar said. 'I can smell it on both of you.'

'How do we go back into the city of Keah?' Ramulas asked, wanting to change the subject.

'Once the warhorse has finished eating, ride him into the city. No-one will question a sergeant and a priestess riding a warhorse. Stay near the docks and I will arrange for a ship to take you to the town of Shes. Keep the warhorse with you—the messenger I send will be able to find you easier that way.'

'How long do we wait by the docks?' Ramulas asked.

'You will be on a ship by nightfall. I must be going; I have things to do.'

'Wait,' Ramulas called to the magician. Ramulas attempted to find the words. He wanted to ask Shigar to pass word on to Jacqueline, but something deep inside questioned how much he should trust the magician. After a brief internal struggle, Ramulas pushed his doubts away.

'Yes?' Shigar replied.

'My family is expecting me to come home any day. I will be unable to tell them what has happened; could you pass a message to them for me?'

'Certainly, my friend,' Shigar said with a warm smile.

Relief flooded through Ramulas at the thought of Shigar sending word. Ramulas gave the magician directions to his farm, along with descriptions of his family. He finished by saying that he would send for them once he was in Sanctuary.

'I will leave first thing tomorrow for Bremnon,' Shigar said. 'But now I must go; there are matters I must attend to.'

Pip and Ramulas watched as Shigar disappeared into the tunnel.

***

Jacqueline smiled as Kate and Grace played amongst the trees with several dryad children. Since Ramulas had gone, everything had seemed to go from bad to worse, but now at least her girls had something to take their minds off what had happened to them.

She looked across the forest towards their farm and sighed. 'Where are you, my love?' she whispered.

Jacqueline had discovered a strength within that she never knew existed since her husband had gone, but she yearned for her family to be whole once more. She wondered what Ramulas would do when he finally returned home to see their farm burnt to the ground. Would he even know where to look for them?

Then an idea came to her; she would take her girls to the farm later in the afternoon and try to leave something to steer Ramulas towards

Matthew's farm. That had been her major concern—Ramulas coming home and not finding them.

***

Shigar sat at his desk focusing on the crystal ball that sat in front of him. He waved his hands over it a few times; each time, his fingers lightly brushed it. Light swirling mists moved within the crystal ball. After a few moments, the mist thickened until Shigar saw only white.

He rested both hands on the desk and waited. The mists within the crystal dissipated and a face peered back at the magician. It was a man with a flat face, almond-shaped eyes that spoke of self-assuredness, olive skin, and short-cropped silver hair. He wore a bright blue silk vest.

The man gave Shigar a curt nod. 'Hello to you, user of magic.'

'Greetings, dancer of death,' Shigar said. 'I need your services. I know of a man who is on a quest. He needs to be taught a lesson.'

A small slightly curved sword appeared in the man's hand. The blade was a foot long, and light played upon its keen edge. Shigar had seen that very blade cut through an oak table as if it was made of butter.

The dancer of death said, 'The lesson I teach will be a painful one.'

Shigar smiled sadly. 'Painful lessons are ones that are not soon forgotten.'

'When do you need me?'

'As soon as possible,' Shigar said. 'When your ship arrives, I will arrange passage on another ship that will take you to the town of Shes. The man I speak of will be travelling east through the forest. You will find him in a town at the base of the Devil's Ridge Mountains.'

The man nodded. 'I will prepare immediately. Tell me, does this man have a pure heart?'

'Yes, he does.'

'That is good. I like using my swords against such a man,' the dancer of death said.

The crystal ball filled with swirling mists for a moment and then became clear. Shigar sighed. Asking for the foreign man's help was not something that he wanted to do; however, he knew that it needed to be done. Now he needed to organise passage on a ship going to Shes for Ramulas and the thief, and then arrange a ship for the dancer of death.

'So much to do in so little time,' Shigar muttered as he walked out of his chambers.

***

Remus stood with the other warlords and red wizards, watching the blue energy strand wind its way through the black hole. The red energy strand had shattered into tiny shards, which were attached to the blue energy strand.

'The crystal has now anchored, my lord,' one of the red wizards said.

'I know,' Remus growled. 'Tell me what you know of its location.'

'There were indications of creatures near the crystal with low levels of intelligence. We removed the restrictions of the crystal, allowing it to move. More magic was sent to the crystal in order to encourage it to be taken to an open area. One of the creatures answered the crystal's call; but instead of moving it where it would benefit us, it was taken into the creature's home,' the red wizard said.

'Where in Oriel's new world is the crystal?' Remus asked as he stepped closer to the red wizard.

The red wizard held his ground, fearing that moving would mean instant death. 'It is within a space ten feet square, a hut made of crude materials that will collapse as soon as the crystal transforms into a doorway.'

'How can you be certain of this? And what lies beyond the walls of this creature's home?'

The red wizard shrugged. 'We are unable to see past the walls of the dwelling.'

Remus glared at the black hole, watching the blue energy strand swim in lazy patterns. It had grown in length by a few inches and had also become thicker. The filament along its side had doubled in length and broken into segments. Now that the crystal had anchored, the blue energy strand would grow at a faster rate.

'Focus all magic on opening the doorway into Oriel's world,' Remus said before walking away.

Remus could feel the anger and frustration building within him. He knew that taking his frustrations out on one of the red wizards would delay them crossing over to Oriel's world. He was not happy with the current situation.

When he had first dropped the crystal on Oriel's world, it had been on a farm; that would have been the perfect place to bring the First Legion through.

Then the crystal had moved for several days; now, it was anchored in a creature's home. When the crystal transformed into the doorway, Remus needed it to be able to break through the structure. He did not want anything to slow their progress in reaching Oriel.

***

Ramulas and Pip rode to the eastern gate of Keah to find a line of people waiting to enter.

Ramulas communicated with Rufus to stop at the end of the line. 'The people would have been here for a while,' he said to Pip. 'I hope we don't have to wait too long.'

Pip groaned behind him. 'You are wearing a sergeant's uniform and riding a warhorse—we can ride straight through the gate. The people will move for us.'

Ramulas nodded while communicating with the warhorse. As they approached the gate, soldiers called for the people to make way for them.

'Avoid eye contact with the soldiers,' Pip whispered to him.

Ramulas held a blank expression as he looked ahead while they rode through the gate. Out of the corner of his eye, Ramulas saw the soldiers snap to attention. He bit down on his tongue to prevent himself from reacting.

Butterflies were rampant in Ramulas' stomach at the thought of entering the city a day after escaping. All they needed now was for him to bring unwanted attention to himself.

Once inside the city, Pip guided Ramulas toward the docks. Most people moved out of the way when they saw the warhorse approaching, but the streets by the gate were filled with people waiting to leave.

The crowds thinned as they came closer to the docks. Few people, including soldiers, gave the pair a second glance as they passed. Within minutes, they had reached the chaos of the docks.

They saw total bedlam: dock workers hurried to load and unload ships and men on the ships and docks were yelling and cursing at one another as boxes and crates were moved on and off ships.

Ramulas watched in amazement as ropes were thrown from the posts on the docks back to the ships, allowing them to leave. A dozen burley dock workers heaved on a large lever. The sound of wood groaning against wood could be heard, and the ship was pushed away from the docks.

As the ship moved away, sails ran up the mast and sailors worked on the rigging. The sails caught wind, and the ship moved out into the harbour.

'Damn,' Pip swore as she hit Ramulas in the back.

'What?' he asked, looking around.

'This is the perfect time for thieving. The young street rats have already started.'

Ramulas looked at the cargo on the docks waiting to be loaded onto a ship. Three boys in their early teens, all wearing plain clothes with caps pulled tightly over their heads, made a beeline toward boxes full of clothing. Ten yards from the boxes, they split. Two went left and one veered to the right. The lone boy walked up to a box and began to rummage through the clothes.

'Hey, you, get away from there!' a soldier shouted.

The boy grabbed a piece of clothing and ran into the crowd.

'Stop! Thief!' the soldier shouted as he gave chase.

Once the soldier had left, the other two boys grabbed an armful of clothes and ran towards Ramulas and Pip.

'No, no, no—go the other way,' Pip whispered behind Ramulas.

The two boys pushed through people on the docks, causing shouts of alarm and curses. This caught the attention of a pair of soldiers nearby who intercepted them. The two boys did not see the soldiers until they ran into them.

'Oh, no,' Pip said as they soldiers took hold of the two boys.

'What will happen to them?' Ramulas asked.

'The dungeons or Gullytown.'

'But they are just children,' Ramulas Protested. 'They should not be punished this way.'

'Well, it happens,' Pip replied.

'Not here; not today,' Ramulas said climbing down from the warhorse. 'Stay with Rufus.'

Ramulas walked over to where the two boys were struggling in the soldier's grasp. 'You found them for me.'

Both soldiers looked at Ramulas in surprise. He reached out and grabbed both boys by the scruff of their necks and pulled them towards him.

'I will deal with them,' Ramulas said before walking away with the boys.

Ramulas kept his eyes forward as he walked to the warhorse, he waited for the soldiers to call out or challenge him, and with each step, he gained confidence. By the time they reached the warhorse, both boys were terrified of him.

Being caught by a sergeant was one thing, but each time they looked at Ramulas his intense focus frightened them. Pip waited until the trio had stopped near the warhorse before removing her hood.

'You stupid boys,' Pip scolded as she stood near Rufus.

Both boys wore expressions that were a mixture of shock and relief; when they had recovered, they dropped their bundles and ran into Pip's arms. She kissed each boy on the head.

'I watched you on the docks, and you ran into the crowd. You did two things wrong: first, you went into the crowd, and second, you brought attention to yourselves. You need more practice. But now I need you to find Old John and tell him where I am.'

Both boys nodded before disappearing into the sea of people.

Pip smile at Ramulas. 'Thank you.'

Ramulas let out a breath. 'That was close. I thought the soldiers would have known I was not a sergeant.'

Pip playfully slapped him on the arm. 'Don't be silly—you did a good job.'

'What do we do now?'

'We wait for Old John. I have business to take care of before we leave.'

***

Old John appeared out of the crowd and made his way over to Pip. 'Nice warhorse. Where did you find him?'

Pip shrugged. 'A friend gave it to us. I have a favour to ask of you.'

'You were not expected to be seen in the city so soon after the events of yesterday, but now you are here, the master of shadows would like to see you.'

Pip shook her head. 'I cannot. We are waiting for a ship. I need you to travel to Bremnon and give my sister a message.'

'What is the message?'

'Look to the stars,' Pip said. 'She will know what that means.'

Old John gave a quick nod. 'I will leave soon. The price on your friend's head has doubled to ten gold coins, and here he is wearing a sergeant's uniform on the docks.'

Pip raised an eyebrow. 'I think we have upset the king; how did the raid go in the castle yesterday?'

A smile crept along Old John's face. 'It went well. The master of shadows was very pleased with your plan—that is why he wishes to see you. And he would like the sergeant's uniform returned.'

'The uniform will be returned once we have boarded the ship,' Ramulas said with a confidence that surprised Pip. 'Someone is coming to find us; once we are on the ship, the uniform will be returned.'

'You have made a good impression,' Old John said. 'First, by escaping the city while the soldiers looked for you, and then when you saved two street rats. You are making quite a name for yourself.'

'I am just doing what I know to be right.'

Old John smiled. 'Have you clothes to change into when you return the uniform?'

Ramulas shook his head.

'I will return with some for you,' Old John said before melting into the crowd.

***

Ramulas and Pip waited by the docks for the messenger. He communicated with Rufus to keep the warhorse calm in the sea of people, but he soon found the warhorse was used to being in crowds.

'I cannot believe how much has changed since Oriel came into my life,' he said to Pip.

She looked up at the former farmer who had left his home on a quest to save this world and had been captured by the king and tortured in the tombs. This had broken Ramulas' spirit and only through rebuilding himself did he change into the powerful, confident man before her.

Ramulas was content watching the loading and unloading of ships. It was a fascinating concept for him; it reminded him of a time he watched ants bring food into their mound.

Occasionally, Pip would turn his attention to the cat-and-mouse game played by thieves and soldiers. She explained that in the sea of people, only two types of people will stay in one place for a long period of time: soldiers and those from the thieves' guild. Both parties knew the other was there, and why they were there. It was just a matter of who was smarter.

Pip had returned with food when a royal page walked up to them. He had been escorted by a soldier, who stood twenty feet away. The page was young and had short, blond, curly hair and a plain, innocent face.

Even without the royal tabard, Pip would know him as one of the royal staff; his bright blue eyes constantly darted from left to right, as if waiting for some unknown enemy to jump out at him.

'I seek Ramulas,' he said, stepping up to them.

Ramulas smiled. 'That is me.'

The page handed Ramulas a scroll that was sealed with wax and a small sack that felt as if it were full of coins. Ramulas broke the wax seal and found several papers. The top piece was a letter from the magician.

> Hello, my friend. I have arranged passage for both of you on the ship *Wave Rider*. It will leave for Shes mid-afternoon. You have papers with the royal mark. They will allow your passage without question. Use the coins to buy a horse and supplies in Shes.
>
> Leave the horse with the page.
>
> Good luck to you my friend,
> Shigar.

Ramulas looked up from the letter to see that Pip had been reading it as well. Her hand reached out for the bag of coins, and Ramulas fought the urge to pull it away from her.

Once she took the sack, opened it, and looked inside, she gasped. 'We have a cabin. The captain of the ship will honour the papers.'

'Let's talk to the harbourmaster to see when the ship leaves.'

He communicated with the warhorse to say they would be parting ways. Rufus was not happy and told Ramulas he did not want to leave him.

You need to go with the page, Ramulas communicated to the warhorse before handing the reins to the young boy.

Ramulas took his weapons and ignored calls from the warhorse as he walked to the harbourmaster with Pip. After some enquiries, they were told the ship would leave in an hour. As they walked to the ship, Old John walked out of the crowd holding a small bundle of clothes.

'I see that your messenger has found you. Come with me to a place where you can change.'

As they followed Old John, Ramulas noticed that both the page and soldier were struggling to move Rufus. Ramulas communicated with the warhorse and told him to go with the page. Rufus' mind was made up; he did not want to leave. Ramulas could see the soldier becoming frustrated. 'Wait here for me,' he said to Pip before making his way to the warhorse.

Ramulas clicked his tongue while sending calming thoughts to the warhorse. 'This horse is a stubborn one,' Ramulas said with a smile to the soldier. 'My ship leaves within an hour. It will be easier to move him after my ship leaves. Wait with the page until I am gone.'

He re-joined Pip and Old John. Ramulas was led to a store filled with piles of rope, nets, and canvas. He was given the clothes and shown to a rear room.

Ramulas removed the clothes and dressed in simple dark leggings and a vest. When he was finished, Ramulas saw that he looked the part of a sailor.

Ramulas took a deep breath and focused on the magical energies that flowed within him. He looked down at the sergeant's breastplate and picked it up with telekinesis. It lifted a few inches off the ground before falling.

Ramulas' reserve was now empty. He knew that he would need to train to regain his magical abilities. He walked out of the small room to find Pip and Old John smiling at him

'You will blend in well,' Pip said.

Ramulas nodded.

'That is good. I will need to return these to their rightful owner,' Old John said, 'then travel to see Pip's sister.'

***

'Girls,' Jacqueline called, 'we are going back to the farm to see what is left.'

She smiled as Kate and Grace ran up to her, excited at the prospect. The girls asked questions as they began their trek, and Jacqueline did her best to answer what she could. The excitement and anticipation grew as they came closer to their home.

Then Grace gasped and reached out to grab Jacqueline by her dress. Her mother looked down and was shocked to see her daughter's eyes glowing a fierce green.

'Grace, what is wrong?'

Grace shook her head. 'We can't go home; there are soldiers waiting for us.'

A cold sensation exploded inside Jacqueline. 'How do you know?'

Grace pointed to the small grove of trees near the burnt-out barn in the distance. 'There is one in the trees and another lying on the grass next to the house. I can see them.'

Both Kate and Jacqueline searched, but could not see anything, before looking at Grace and shrugging. Grace motioned for them to be quiet as she led them in a different direction through thicker foliage toward the farm.

After a few agonising minutes, they crouched behind some bushes where they could see the soldiers Grace had told them about. A sense of helplessness almost overwhelmed Jacqueline as she led the girls away. She truly believed the sheriff would have forgotten about them by now.

How was Ramulas supposed to find them at Matthew's farm, and how could she find a way to warn him of the trap waiting for him when he returned? Jacqueline took the girls back to Matthew's farm, not knowing the next time she would see Ramulas.

***

Ramulas and Pip had shown their papers and boarded the ship. They stood on the deck watching as cargo was loaded. Ramulas communicated with the warhorse and found that it stubbornly waited for him.

As the ship pulled away, Ramulas said goodbye to Rufus, telling him that the ship was leaving.

One hundred yards away, Ramulas saw the warhorse's head turn towards the ships that were docked. He could hear protests as it pushed through the crowd. Ramulas' heart sank as he felt the warhorse's pain of being left behind.

Then Rufus began racing toward his ship. People screamed in alarm as they jumped out of the way. Ramulas communicated with the warhorse, telling it to stop, but to no avail. Rufus wanted to go with him.

The warhorse reached the edge of the docks. Ramulas and Pip watched in amazement as Rufus jumped from the docks to the deck of the ship. The distance was twenty feet, and Rufus landed with a loud bang.

'By the gods!' Pip said. 'That warhorse must really like you.

2

Shigar thought back to the events of the previous day and night, wherein he had eventually convinced King Zachary to open the city of Keah.

Shigar made his way through the halls to Zachary's chambers; the king had called for him. He knew that Zachary would be almost overcome with paranoia.

Shigar thought back to when he first told Zachary that the prisoner had left the city, along with the crystal and his weapons.

The captain of the cavalry had just left Zachary after informing him of the ruse outside the west gate. Zachary called Shigar and his advisers to his chambers, he sat on his throne barely able to contain his rage and frustration.

The king waited for everyone to arrive, with Aleesha seated beside him, before speaking. 'I want every house, store, and building searched in order to find this dangerous prisoner. I want every person in the city locked in their homes until he is found.'

The advisers began to mutter amongst themselves in urgent tones. After a few moments, one of them spoke. 'If everyone is locked in their homes until this man is found, that could take weeks. The people of Keah will not be pleased.'

'I do not care if the people are not pleased,' Aleesha said.

Zachary glared at his daughter, which quickly silenced her, before he spoke. 'This prisoner has a magical artefact that could destroy me and must be found.'

'What if the people of the city do not want to be locked away?' the adviser asked.

Zachary shrugged. 'Put them in the dungeon, and when the dungeon is full send them to Gullytown.'

The adviser gasped in shock. 'The people will revolt. my king. Unrest has been growing across the kingdom with the increase of taxes.'

'Then kill a few,' Zachary said with an absent wave of his hand. 'That will show the people to obey their king. Yes, kill a few and hang their bodies for all to see.'

The adviser was speechless. He opened and closed his mouth a few times before walking to his companions. A cruel smile spread on Aleesha's face.

Shigar looked at the king, wondering where the man he had served had gone to. Before the death of his wife, Zachary was known as a fair and just ruler and—except where the Khilli were involved—he would always listen to reason.

In the past few years, he transformed from a king who would listen to reason to one drunk with power. He abused this by taking too much from the people and punished any who dare question him.

The people within the city of Keah were close to boiling point.

Ramulas had already become a hero to those who had lost everything to Zachary's new ways. Someone escaping the tombs and angering the king gave them something to cheer about for the first time in many months.

Shigar knew that if the city remained locked down for a few days, the people would rebel. This would mean hundreds, even thousands, would die. This would tear the kingdom apart.

Zachary would not see reason, and Shigar knew something needed to be done. He knew that the people of Keah and the kingdom were more than mindless fools who needed to obey the king's every rule.

Shigar needed to defuse the situation before it was too late. 'My king, I have something to say.'

Zachary's head turned to the magician as if seeing him for the first time. 'What do you want?'

'The escaped prisoner has left the city. There will be no need to lock the people in their homes.'

'What!?' Zachary said in shock. 'How do you know this?'

'I think it would be best if we went to my chambers, and then I could show you.'

Zachary quickly dismissed his advisers and called for his royal guards. Shigar was surprised the Zachary had doubled his guard from two to four, and Aleesha had an escort of two Khilli warriors.

'Take me to your chambers,' Zachary ordered before turning to Aleesha. 'You will remain in my chambers until I return.'

There was an uncomfortable silence as the small group walked to Shigar's chambers. The magician remembered a time when he could walk with Zachary and talk about anything; however, those days seemed so long ago.

Shigar let out a sigh of relief when they reached his chambers. He led Zachary to his desk, where the crystal had been placed.

'Where has the crystal gone?' Zachary asked, tapping the spot he had last seen it. 'It was right here.'

'That is what I was saying,' Shigar said. 'I left my chambers, and when I returned, the crystal and the prisoner's weapons were gone.'

'He was here? In the castle?' Zachary asked. 'He still might be here waiting for his chance to attack me. The prisoner might be attacking Aleesha as we speak.' He sent for more guards to watch over his daughter.

Two royal guards raced out of Shigar's chambers, looking for any potential threat and to send word to guard Aleesha.

'The prisoner is not in the castle, nor is he in the city,' Shigar said calmly. 'I felt his faint magical energies as he left the city. Then I lost all trace of him. I have been trying to find him ever since.'

'Where is the prisoner? He must be found,' Zachary said with panic rising in his voice.

'I do not think you need to worry. His magical energies are leaving him, and the prisoner was close to death as he left the city,' Shigar lied. 'He is no longer a threat to anyone.'

'I don't care; I want him found,' Zachary said.

Shigar bowed slightly. 'I will do all I can to find him. But there is a more important matter. If you lock down the city while searching for this prisoner, you will waste valuable resources that could be used elsewhere.'

'You said you have lost all trace of him?' Zachary asked pointing an accusing finger at Shigar. 'How do you know he has not come back into the city?'

'If I were him and suffered as he did, I would not return.'

'But you are not him,' Zachary replied. 'The city will remain locked down until the prisoner is found.'

This started talks between Shigar and Zachary which lasted into the early hours of the morning. By the time they had finished, Shigar had convinced Zachary to open the city, on the condition that Shigar continued to search for the prisoner.

During these conversations, Shigar was careful not to talk about the people of Keah. He focused on how this would benefit Aleesha and Zachary.

***

Shigar received word that Ramulas and his companion had left with the ship, and were heading to Shes. A smile played on the magician's face when he thought of the warhorse jumping from the docks onto the deck of the ship.

Ramulas was a special person, and Shigar would do what he could to help him.

Shigar found himself standing outside Zachary's chambers. The royal guard opened the door and ushered him in, and he walked to the throne where Zachary waited for him.

'You called for me?' Shigar asked as he approached.

'Has there been any word on the escaped prisoner?' Zachary asked.

Inwardly the magician smiled. This would be the excuse he needed to travel to Bremnon to talk to Ramulas' family. 'During my meditations, I have felt very faint magic to the north.'

'Which part of the kingdom?' Zachary asked. 'Is this the prisoner we are looking for?'

'I am unsure of its exact location. However, I believe it is the prisoner we are searching for. I will travel west to find out more.'

Zachary sat in silence for a moment pondering what he had heard. Then he sat straight, his eyes alive with excitement,

'I will send an agent with you. And an escort of ten soldiers.

You will stay with the agent until the prisoner is found,' Shigar's plan began to fall apart before his eyes. With an agent looking over his shoulder, he would be unable to contact Ramulas' family.

'In order to meditate I will need solitude,' Shigar said. 'I will not have that while travelling with an agent and soldiers, I will need a place of my own.'

'Are you saying that you do not want me to send an agent and soldiers to the west?' Zachary asked raising an eyebrow.

'No, not at all,' Shigar replied. 'I think that would be a good idea. I just cannot practise magic when surrounded by people. I will stay on the outskirts of towns and inform the agent when I find something.'

Zachary thought for a few moments. 'Even if it is the smallest thing, I want the agent to know.'

Shigar nodded. 'The smallest detail.'

'When will you leave?'

'Immediately, and hopefully, I will have information by the time the agent arrives,' Shigar said. 'I do not know which town I will go to first. But I will send word when I know something.'

Zachary waved a hand. 'Go now; I will send an agent first thing in the morning.'

Shigar walked to his chambers planning his trip to Bremnon. He needed to hurry in order to stay one step in front of the agent.

***

Ramulas and Pip stood on the bow, watching the ship cut through the waves. They had left the harbour of Keah and were now in the open ocean. Rufus had been brought below with the other livestock. Ramulas was in communication to keep the warhorse calm.

The warhorse had become the talk of the ship, and the crew spoke about Ramulas and Pip being special because of the warhorse. The more Ramulas attempted to play down the situation, the more the respect of the crew grew for him.

For now, Ramulas and Pip kept to themselves.

'Look how far away the land is,' Pip said, pointing to the starboard side.

Ramulas looked out over the ocean and felt his stomach churn as the ship was rocked by waves. 'This is my first time on a ship,' Pip said.

'This is my first time on the water,' Ramulas replied before emptying the contents of his stomach overboard.

Pip hid her amusement while Ramulas experienced his first bout of seasickness. When he had finished, Pip saw that Ramulas had lost the colour in his face.

'Do you feel better now?' she asked, suppressing a smile.

'I think so,' Ramulas said before putting his head over the rail once more.

Some of the sailors had witnessed Ramulas' unease at sea, one of them offered Ramulas a handful of dark green berries. 'Chew on these and they will help you on your journey.'

Ramulas nodded as he accepted the berries. The sailor balked when Ramulas ate all of them. 'I meant only one or two.'

'What will happen now?' Ramulas asked, feeling drowsy.

The sailor shook his head. 'You will sleep a long time.'

Ramulas' eyes rolled back, and he collapsed to the deck.

***

Ramulas had slept on the deck of the ship while Pip had taken the option of the cabin. She came out just after dawn to find they were coming closer to land. Pip saw Ramulas staring across the ocean. She stood next to him for a minute without him noticing.

Pip jabbed him softly in the ribs. 'After two nights, you are finally awake.'

'Two days? We were told it would only take one to reach Shes.'

Pip smiled. 'There was a storm along the coast, and we had to wait out here for it to pass.'

'Did you enjoy your cabin?'

She shrugged. 'I've had better and worse.'

Ramulas laughed. 'You are a mystery. Do you ever tell people what you are feeling inside?'

'You're the one to talk,' Pip said. 'A moment ago, you were on the deck lost in your thoughts. You were in a dangerous place,' she said, tapping the side of her head.

'What do you mean?' Ramulas asked.

'Do not search for something buried in the sands of time; it will only bring you sorrow,' Pip said. 'You were lost thinking about what you had before Oriel came to you. And a part of you wants to return to your old life.'

Ramulas' eyes widened in shock. 'How could you—'

'I am very good at reading people,' Pip said with a sad smile. 'It is a blessing and a curse. It is what makes me very good at what I do—I know when people will do something before they do it. At the same time, I can tell when people will attempt to lie to me.'

Ramulas saw the sadness in Pip's eyes for a fraction of a second, and then her expression hardened. An uncomfortable silence followed. They both looked towards land as the ship came into Shes.

Half an hour later, orders were called out, and the crew raced around the deck and rigging.

Ramulas stared in wonder at the town. It was set on top of a hill. There were a few buildings by the docks, and he could see people walking down the winding road from the town to the docks.

As the ship came closer, Ramulas noticed a few boats at the docks with birds flying overhead. He watched as the captain guided the ship into one of the docks. Workers on the dock caught large ropes that were thrown by the crew. They quickly tied them off and the ship pulled to a halt as the ropes grew taut.

The harbourmaster of Shes had cross-checked the cargo with the documents. All was accounted for, and the crew began unloading with help from Shes dock workers.

Ramulas and Pip went below to collect Rufus and Ramulas' weapons; they said their goodbyes and left the ship. People on the docks stopped what they were doing to look at the warhorse.

Ramulas became very self-conscious with all the attention. Pip did not seem to notice anything wrong. The smell of fish was extremely strong on the docks, and Ramulas saw benches covered in blood.

'Fishermen use the benches to clean the fish when they come back to port,' Pip said.

'Where are the fishermen?' he asked, looking around.

'They are out at sea,' Pip said. 'They leave before dawn and return after midday. All seaside towns are the same.'

They climbed onto Rufus and rode up the hill into the town of Shes. Reaching the top of the hill, they were both surprised at how large Shes was.

From the docks, they were only able to see about a quarter of the town—now they could see the town sprawled out before them. Ramulas reckoned that it was slightly smaller than Bremnon.

The townspeople seemed relaxed until they saw the warhorse coming into town. They would stare and whisper as Ramulas and Pip rode past.

'I don't think the people of this town have seen a warhorse before,' Pip said.

'We need to find supplies for our journey into the mountains and a cart to carry them on,' Ramulas said.

'We need to go there first,' Pip said, pointing to a bakery. 'I am hungry, and I can smell fresh bread.'

Ramulas led Rufus over to the store. Pip jumped from the warhorse and ran into the store before Ramulas had a chance to say anything.

Ramulas communicated with Rufus, telling him to wait while he went inside the store. Ramulas was instantly hungry when he walked into the store.

A small, timid man waited for Pip to order while he fiddled with his apron. It was a small but clean store with various cakes and breads lining the shelves.

'This is a nice town,' Ramulas said to put the man at ease.

'That it is,' the store owner agreed. 'I don't think anyone here has seen a warhorse before.'

Ramulas could feel Rufus' mood change, and knew that something was happening outside, turning to the street he saw a group of local children gathering around Rufus. Ramulas shook his head; all he wanted to do was purchase supplies and leave without any trouble.

'I'll go outside with the children,' Pip said. 'You can order food.'

Ramulas looked at Pip in disbelief before laughing to himself.

'What would you like?' The store owner asked.

Ramulas scanned the shelves, not really knowing how much he should buy. He settled on some pies and a few loaves of bread and pastries. He told the owner of their plans to travel into the Devil Ridge Mountains and their need for supplies and was given directions to a store that would help them.

Ramulas thanked the owner and walked out of the store to find Pip lifting the children onto the warhorse. He communicated with Rufus and found the warhorse enjoyed the attention.

'We have things to do,' he said, handing Pip a pie.

Pip pouted in mock disappointment before waving the children away from the warhorse, Ramulas led Rufus by the reins, and they walked a few hundred yards to a workshop. It reminded Ramulas of Thomas' workshop in Bremnon.

A young, muscular man in a leather apron and short blond hair greeted them as they walked in. 'Welcome, how can I help you?'

'We need a cart fitted to him,' Ramulas said, indicating Rufus outside with his thumb. 'And supplies for mining in the mountains.'

The owner whistled through his teeth as he looked at the warhorse. 'That will take some time; your horse is higher and wider than I am used to. The job will take a few hours.' Ramulas looked at Pip who had been staring intently at the man. She gave Ramulas a quick nod; the man had been honest with them.

'I will leave him with you. Can you feed and water him for me?' Ramulas asked.

'That will cost a bit more.'

'Fine,' Pip said, tossing him a silver coin.

Rufus was led around to the rear of the workshop. Ramulas said he would return when the cart was ready. He chose the cart design and picked the supply items they would need.

Pip watched the owner as he explained what they would need for such a journey. She motioned for Ramulas to get everything the owner mentioned and haggled with the owner for a few moments before they agreed on a price.

Pip offered half immediately and the rest when they returned. Once the deal was done, Ramulas and Pip left the store.

'He was an honest man,' Pip stated. 'He did not try to take advantage of us.'

'Why would anyone want to take advantage of us?' Ramulas asked.

'Because we look nothing like miners. You look like a sailor, and I a priestess.'

Ramulas frowned. 'How many people will try to take advantage of you?'

Pip sighed heavily and rolled her eyes.

A few moments later, they came to a small store at the end of the street. Walking in, Ramulas' senses were assaulted by the smell of burning incense and the sight of different coloured crystals within the store. He saw multi-coloured clothing and a few musical instruments as well.

A young man in a colourful robe smiled at them as they walked in. 'Good day to you both.'

'I was told that you sold maps of these lands,' Ramulas said.

'Yes, we have the finest maps,' the man answered with a sly smile. 'Where do you plan to travel?'

'We are travelling to the Devil's Ridge Mountains.'

The young man looked from Ramulas to Pip and back again, kissed a small amulet hanging on his necklace, and murmured a soft prayer. Pip saw this, pulled her hood over her head, and walked over to look at the crystals.

'Oh, good sir, please do not tell me that you are so brave to be travelling to the Devil Ridge Mountains!' the man said, raising the pitch of his voice.

Ramulas could not understand why this man was behaving so strangely. He looked to Pip, who seemed captivated by the crystals.

An old lady with a shock of white hair came out from the rear of the store. Her robe was the same colour as the young man's. She looked to the floor, and one of her hands reached out slowly for Ramulas.

'Oh, good sir, I have had a vision,' the old lady said. 'You are about to take a dangerous journey where a great evil awaits you. Your only hope is to buy a crystal of protection and keep it close to you.'

The young man looked at Ramulas with wide eyes. 'Do you know what this means? My mother is a seer, and she has seen doom for you both!'

Pip snorted in laughter as she looked at the crystals.

The young man ignored her and continued. 'You must buy a crystal of protection; it is your only hope!'

Ramulas furrowed his brow. How did this old lady know of their journey and the dangers before them?

'Oh no. What will we do?' Pip said in a bored tone. 'We are doomed. Our only hope is to buy a crystal of protection.'

The young man was caught off guard by Pip's attitude, but he quickly recovered. 'Yes, you must listen to your companion. The crystal is the only thing that will save you.'

'Lies!' Pip said as she threw back her hood.

'What!?' the young man said in shock.

Pip sighed. 'We do not need the crystal of protection.'

The young man was at a loss for words. No-one had ever questioned him about the crystals before. Ramulas was confused. How did Pip know about the crystals?

The old lady raised her head and stepped forward. 'My son speaks truthfully. There are no lies about the crystals,' she said, looking defiantly at Pip.

Pip smiled. 'Then tell us of the dangers we face.'

'There are bandits,' the old lady said. 'Rumours of monsters and giants.'

'Lies,' Pip said with a smile.

The old lady straightened and pointed at Pip. 'And who are you to call me a liar?'

Pip opened her cloak to show the array of throwing knives strapped to her body. 'I am Pip. A high-ranking member of the shadows in Keah.'

Both the young man and his mother stepped back and gasped. Ramulas' mouth fell open. Pip winked at him.

The old lady quickly recovered. 'We do not take kindly to thieves in this town. I shall call for the sheriff.'

Pip shrugged. 'When he comes, I will tell him about the crystal of protection. Then he will decide who is a thief.'

The old lady flinched as if slapped.

Pip sighed. 'All we want is a map and we will pay a fair price.'

The old lady turned to her son and gave a slight nod, he disappeared into the back and returned a moment later with a map.

Pip paid for it before they left the store.

'How did you know they were lying?' Ramulas asked.

Pip raised an eyebrow and giggled. 'My father told me long ago, "A fool and his money are easily parted." People in that store prey on people like you.'

3

Ramulas and Pip busied themselves walking through Shes and returned to the workshop just as the cart was hitched to Rufus. The owner's eyes widened when he saw them. Ramulas said it was just luck; he did not want to say that he had been in communication with the warhorse.

The owner showed them the cart filled with supplies for their journey, Ramulas was perplexed at the contents of the cart, but Pip nodded her approval. Once the owner was paid, they headed out of Shes.

They followed the directions on the map, and by late afternoon, Ramulas saw they were coming up to a forest, and he could see the Devil's Ridge Mountains come into view.

'Well, we have two choices,' Pip said, studying the map. 'We can take the road to the right—that will take us around the forest and to the town of Turtha. Or we can follow the track into the forest, but the map does not show what is in the forest.'

'We need to go through the forest. I must look for a sign that will guide us to Sanctuary,' Ramulas said.

Ramulas communicated with Rufus, and they headed into the forest. After a few hundred yards, the road transformed into a little used path, and forest had a foreboding feeling about it as they drew near.

Clusters of trees were so close together that sections of the forest let no sunlight in. Ramulas focused on his magical ability and searched for the surrounding wildlife.

Then he jumped in the seat and gasped. Rufus stopped as he felt Ramulas' shock.

'What's wrong?' Pip asked.

Ramulas' mouth had gone dry. He took a drink from the water skin before speaking. 'I searched the forest for animal life, and then something reached out for me and welcomed me into its home.'

'What is it?' Pip asked.

Ramulas shook his head. 'It has gone. Whatever it was has moved further into the forest.'

'What are we waiting for?' Pip said excitedly.

Ramulas sighed as he communicated with Rufus, and they moved into the forest.

Entering the forest, Ramulas could see shafts of sunlight lancing down through the thick canopy. Often, they found themselves travelling through areas where they could not see the sky.

The forest was alive with the sounds of birds. Only a few could be seen in the trees around them. Ramulas took comfort in knowing that there were no predators nearby.

A few hours later, the surrounding forest began to grow dark as the sun dropped behind the Devil's Ridge Mountains. They soon came to a small grove.

'This will be a good place to rest for the night,' Ramulas said.

'How much further until we reach Sanctuary?' Pip asked.

'I do not know,' Ramulas replied, standing up in the cart to look at the mountain range. 'Oriel will leave a signal to guide us. All we need to do is travel through the forest until I find it.'

They gathered wood and made a small fire as dusk set in. Night had come quickly. Ramulas and Pip sat on opposite sides of the fire, eating from their provisions.

'You can talk to me if you like,' Pip said. 'People do that by fires.'

Ramulas looked up from the fire. 'Sorry, I was thinking about my family. This is all strange to me. Before this journey, I had never been away from my family for more than a day. I want more than anything to be with them, but I know this is something that I need to do. I hope that Shigar will give them comfort when he visits them.'

'I had a message sent to my sister,' Pip said. 'The message was for her to look at the stars. That means I won't see her for a while, and she needs to break the red candles I gave her.'

'Why does she need to break the red candles?'

'Within the candles are stacks of coins, enough to last a few months.'

Ramulas nodded his approval. 'That is clever.'

Pip sighed as she looked over Ramulas' shoulder. 'Here we go again.'

'What is it?' Ramulas said, turning around.

As Ramulas turned, he was engulfed in a thick wall of dense fog.

***

Ramulas' world turned white, and then the fog disappeared, and he found himself in Oriel's cavern. She stood smiling in front of him.

'Hello, Ramulas. I am glad that you have made it this far. You are within a day's ride of Sanctuary.'

Ramulas noticed there was something different about Oriel, but he could not put a finger on it. Then he realised. 'You have changed!' Ramulas exclaimed. 'You look more solid and like a person.'

'I am growing stronger every day, and I do not have to use as much magic because you are closer to me. When you have made your way to Sanctuary, come into the castle, and I will meet you there. But there is something you should know.'

'What is that?'

'Beware the three guardians of Sanctuary. You will meet all three before entering the castle. You and your companion need to remember this: the guardians are not what they appear to be.'

'What does that mean?'

'Listen to your heart,' Oriel said before Ramulas was surrounded in fog once again.

***

When Ramulas' vision returned, he was standing by the fire, and Pip walked up to him.

'What happened?' she asked.

'Oriel said that we will reach Sanctuary tomorrow, and we will meet the three guardians.'

'Who are they?'

Ramulas shrugged. 'I do not know. What I *do* know is that I am tired and need sleep.'

Ramulas threw some logs on the fire before lying down next to it. Within a few moments, he was asleep. Pip studied Ramulas' sleeping form. When she thought she knew what to expect from him, he did something that surprised her.

Pip thought that after Ramulas returned from Oriel, they would both sit and talk for a while; with Ramulas asleep, that would not happen. Pip shrugged and lay opposite Ramulas. In under a minute, she was sleeping as well.

***

Ramulas was in a deep sleep when he heard Oriel calling to him and urging him to wake. 'You have company in your camp.' Rufus entered his thoughts. The warhorse was stressed. Someone was trying to take him.

Ramulas opened his eyes and sat up. He could not believe what he saw before him. It was a creature two feet tall, dressed in a green vest and leggings. He could see that it was female. She had the wings of a butterfly and was using them to lift herself off the ground.

As she rose from the ground, Ramulas noticed that she held the reins of Rufus, trying to lead him out of the grove.

Now fully awake, Ramulas took in his surroundings. It was just before dawn, and he saw Pip had woken. Her eyes were wide in shock. Ramulas motioned for her to stay where she was. He slowly stood and walked to the creature.

'Why do you wish to take my warhorse from me, little creature?'

This startled the creature and she spun to face Ramulas. 'I am not some creature—I am a sprite and welcomed by those of the forest. You have come into my home uninvited; I stake claim on this horse.'

Ramulas stifled a laugh. The sprite could pull on the reins all day and Rufus would not move. He sent calming thoughts to the warhorse.

'I am afraid the warhorse will stay with me, little sprite.'

It released her hold on Rufus and flew towards Ramulas drawing a short sword half her size.

'Do not mock me, traveller, or I will cut you down.'

This brought a smile to Ramulas' face. As Ramulas smiled, the sprite swung her sword at him.

Everything slowed, and Ramulas easily avoided the sword.

'Hey, now!' Ramulas said as he held his hands up. 'There is no need for this; we are not here to hurt you.'

By this stage, Pip was standing and had opened her cloak, revealing her throwing knives. Ramulas quickly shook his head. The sprite's face transformed into a mask of fury as she came at Ramulas again.

Once again, Ramulas used his magical ability to slow everything down as he dodged her strikes.

Ramulas laughed. 'I am sorry for coming into your home, but I was invited.'

'It was not me,' the sprite said with another swipe of her sword.

'You must stop this, or you will hurt yourself,' Ramulas said.

The sprite darted out before charging at Ramulas with her sword. He clapped his hands in front of him, catching the blade between his hands.

The sprite attempted to pull the sword free, but Ramulas interlocked his fingers, increasing the hold. The sprite's wings beat so fast they began to hum. Ramulas saw that she was turning red with the effort of trying to pull her sword free.

Ramulas smiled. 'Would you like your sword returned?'

'Yes, give it to me.' She grunted.

Ramulas released the sword, and the sprite shot back into the bushes behind with her sword flying overhead. Pip giggled. Ramulas shot her a stern look, which only made matters worse.

Ramulas walked over to the sprite as she pulled herself from the bush. 'You should be more careful when trying to steal when you are all alone.'

'What made you think she was by herself?'

Ramulas spun around looking for the speaker but could find no-one. Pip scanned the forest, holding a throwing knife in each hand. After a few seconds, she shook her head. She could not see anything.

'We are at a disadvantage,' Ramulas called out. 'You can see us, but we are unable to see you.'

'Then you must look harder,' the voice said. 'For we are all around you.'

Ramulas gasped and fell back when he saw movement in front of him, Pip let out a squeal next to him.

The trunk of the tree in front of Ramulas formed two green eyes, and below the eyes, Ramulas saw a smile. Slowly the shape of a female formed within the trunk of the tree. A female dryad stepped out of the tree and walked to Ramulas. As she did, Ramulas could see other shapes coming out of the surrounding forest.

'Pip, put your knives away.'

She glared at him and then at the creatures coming out of the trees. Pip growled in frustration before the knives vanished. Ramulas did everything he could to not make it obvious that he was staring at the creatures.

The woman stopped in front of Ramulas, and he marvelled at her appearance. Her hair was reddish-brown, and her skin was rough, dark brown, and covered in vines and small leaves. Small branches protruded from her arms and legs. 'You may touch me if you want to.'

Ramulas was about to answer when he realised that his hand had reached out and was almost touching her. 'I did not mean to—'

She nodded with a smile. 'I can see that you are curious; you have never seen our kind before and want to know about us.'

She reached out and took his hand, placing it on her forearm. Ramulas slowly pulled his hand along her arm and was surprised at the texture of her skin. It was somewhere between human skin and the bark of a tree.

He saw that Pip was also feeling the bodies of the other creatures.

'What are you?' he asked in awe.

'We are dryads,' she replied. 'We are as much a part of the forest as it is a part of us.'

The female smiled. 'We are able to see Grace's magical energy in you.'

'You know of my daughter?' Ramulas asked as his eyes widened.

'Yes, Grace has come to us several times.'

'How has she come all this way from home?'

Eady smiled. 'Grace possesses some of our magic, and is able to walk through trees.'

Ramulas looked at the former thief in shock.

'How long were you watching us in the grove?' Pip asked, changing the subject, as she walked up to Ramulas.

'We felt your presence just before you entered the forest. We have been following you to see if you posed a threat to our home. When Tilly came into your camp'—the female indicated the sprite—'she challenged Grace's father with her sword, yet neither of you drew weapons; you avoided conflict.'

'I am called Ramulas, and this is my companion Pip,' he said by way of introduction. 'There is much I wish to ask you.'

The dryad looked at the warhorse and cart. 'Where are you going, Ramulas? It is a rare thing for people to be in this forest.'

'We are on a journey that must be taken,' Ramulas said before he remembered something Oriel had said. 'Are you the guardians of Sanctuary?'

The dryad shook her head. 'We only care for the forest. I think that you are on more than just a journey, but I will not ask for more than you have given us. You are free to travel through the forest if you respect our home.'

Eady made a motion with her hand. Ramulas and Pip saw the other dryads melt back into the trees. Only Tilly remained in the grove with them.

'I will be watching you, Ramulas and Pip,' the sprite said before flying into the trees.

'But wait!' Ramulas called out. 'There is more that I need to ask of you.'

'For now, all you need to know is that we are here,' Eady said as she came out of a tree behind Ramulas.

Ramulas and Pip jumped in shock. By the time Ramulas had turned around, the dryad had melted into the tree.

'How did she do that?' Pip asked. The dryad had walked into one tree and had come out of another.

All Ramulas could do was shrug.

'What do we do now?' Pip asked.

Ramulas shrugged. 'We pack and go to Sanctuary.'

***

The trees ahead began to open, allowing more sunlight through the canopies. Pip had spent most of that time talking excitedly about Tilly and the dryads. She had travelled to many different places and had heard about the dryads.

They were thought to be creatures of legend, and yet she had seen and spoken to them. Since meeting Ramulas, Pip had seen and experienced things she could never have dreamed of. She was very happy with deciding to stay with Ramulas.

He was thinking about what Oriel had told him about the guardians of Sanctuary. They were not what they seemed to be. What could that mean?

Ramulas had been half-listening to Pip, nodding or grunting whenever she paused. However, the question of the guardians continued to play on his mind.

Pip?' he asked.

'What?'

'Oriel told me something about the guardians that still confuses me,' he said. 'I am to meet the three guardians before entering the castle in Sanctuary, and they are not what they seem. What does that mean?'

'Oh, that's easy,' Pip replied with a smile. 'I might look like a priestess, but I am not—I am a thief. I am not what I seem to be, and neither are you. No-one would think you know how to fight and use magic. You will just have to wait until you find the guardians to know what you are looking for.'

'Thank you for your help,' Ramulas said sarcastically.

Pip laughed while she pulled her hood low and leaned back in her seat.

The trees continued to thin and Ramulas saw the Devil's Ridge Mountains towering to his left. Within half an hour, they walked through grasslands. Ramulas could see another forest ahead; he judged it to be an hour away.

***

At the top of a hundred-foot-tall pine tree, a short, wiry man looked out over the plains; in one hand, he held a looking glass. It was a tube used by sailors to navigate the oceans, but he used it for different reasons.

He had spotted Ramulas and Pip in the cart coming towards his position. He looked down and signalled his companions.

They nodded and readied the ambush; they knew people were coming.

As he climbed down the tree, the man was not worried about swords or bows. As soon as the two on the cart saw their secret weapon, they would give the bandits anything. They waited patiently for Ramulas and Pip to enter the forest.

4

Remus stood in front of the black hole watching the blue energy strand and was fascinated.

The energy strand had grown a few more inches and was thicker; the filaments along the side had doubled in length and formed into tendrils that swam through the air.

Since the crystal had anchored, the energy strand was growing faster than it had before. The red wizards told him that it would still be a few more months before they were able to travel into Oriel's new world.

The energy strand would transform into a doorway within two months. The red wizards and warlords would continue to feed magic into the black hole—this would strengthen the passageway between the two worlds.

Remus knew that without Oriel, he and the other warlords would begin to lose their magical abilities. Oriel was a child of the light. A magical being of pure magic, she had matured early and escaped.

Without Oriel, not only would the warlords lose their magical abilities, but they would also lose their iron grip over their world. The red wizards would then be more powerful than the warlords. Remus would not stand for that.

He knew that this would be all or nothing—there could be no failure. Without Oriel, he and the other warlords were as good as dead. They would only have one chance at crossing over to Oriel's world. Everything needed to be perfect.

***

Shigar walked through the streets of Bremnon. He had ridden for two days with minimal rest. He had memorised the way to Ramulas' farm and would make his way there in an hour, but first, he needed to rest the horse and stretch his legs.

The magician became worried as he heard the rumours of a farmer and his family being hunted by the sheriff. He had a bad feeling that this might involve Ramulas' family when he heard that the two girls had strange abilities.

Shigar rode out of town towards Ramulas' farm, following the directions given to him.

When he arrived at the farm, his worst fears were realised. He came in off the road and led his horse toward a burnt-out shell of a farmhouse. To his right, he saw the remains of a barn.

'Halt! Who goes there?' a soldier cried as he jumped out from behind a tree.

Shigar shook his head. 'What madness is this?'

The soldier was joined by another as one came from behind the barn, both drawing swords.

Anger replaced sadness in Shigar. 'You dare?' he said, pointing to the royal crest on his robes.

Both soldiers paled and backed away.

'Why are you here?' Shigar asked.

Both told of what had happened and said they had been ordered to wait for the family to return. Shigar shook his head and told them he would search for the family and that they were to return to Bremnon.

Once they had left, the magician smiled to himself. He looked east to where he could feel the faint aura of magic. Ramulas' family was right under the soldiers' noses.

***

Shigar found himself at the end of the dirt road which led to Matthew's farm. He was fifty yards from the hut when he saw two young girls. They stopped playing on the porch when they saw him coming and watched him for a moment before disappearing inside

The older girl had blonde hair and appeared to be normal. But the younger girl was different. She was shorter, with dark, curly hair. Her face was chubby and she had bright emerald eyes that radiated magical power.

Shigar stopped his horse ten yards from the dwelling and waited. A few moments later, the girls' mother came out, with the two girls close behind. She wore a plain brown dress, had long red hair, and stood protectively in front of her daughters.

'Why have you come here?' the mother asked, her eyes searching for hidden enemies.

Shigar heard a slight tremor in her voice and knew that he needed to find common ground with this family.

'I will explain once I am off this horse,' Shigar said with a smile before climbing down.

Once off the horse, Shigar sighed in relief. 'Please excuse me; I have been riding for two days, and my body does not agree with it.'

Shigar winced as he hopped from foot to foot trying to bring feeling back to his legs.

'Ah, that's better,' he said after a moment. 'I do hope I am at the right place; I was looking for a friend's farm, but it seems to have burnt down.'

'Do you know my da?' the youngest girl asked as she jumped out from behind her mother.

Shigar smiled. 'Yes I do, but now I need to talk to your mother.'

'What has happened?' Jacqueline asked in a worried tone. 'Where is my husband?'

She froze upon seeing the royal crest on the magician's robes. 'Girls, inside now.'

Shigar held up his hands and smiled. 'Mine is a long and complicated story. I will tell you everything once my horse has been led to water and I am sitting on a comfortable chair.'

The younger girl ran forward and began to wave her arms at his horse while pulling faces.

'Grace, come back here,' Jacqueline said.

'I'm telling the horse to go to the stables,' Grace answered. Then she turned to Shigar. 'I know how to talk to animals; my da taught me. His horse would do what I told it to do.'

A pang of sadness came over Shigar at the mention of Ramulas' horse. A few moments later, Grace had given up on trying to move Shigar's horse.

'Before you come into the hut, I need to know who you are,' Jacqueline said.

'Oh, how silly of me. I am Shigar, the king's magician and friend to your husband.'

Colour drained from Jacqueline's face as Shigar's words sunk in. 'Kate, Grace, take this man's horse to feed off the grass.'

'Are you a real magician?' Grace asked excitedly. 'My da knows magic.'

'Grace!' Jacqueline exclaimed. 'That will be enough.'

'Please do not worry yourself. I know that Ramulas possesses magical abilities,' he said before smiling down at Grace. 'And I know of someone else who has magical abilities as well.'

'Girls, take the horse,' Jacqueline said, trying to change the subject.

Once the girls had led the horse away, Jacqueline looked at the magician with apprehension in her eyes.

'I know of the crystal and why Ramulas needed to take it to the mountains,' Shigar said calmly. 'He has spoken to me. He has also told me of Oriel. Ramulas dropped the crystal in the wrong place. Now he needs to prepare for when the First Legion comes to this world.'

Jacqueline seemed to collapse with each sentence. By the time Shigar had finished, she was feeling light-headed. Shigar walked over to Jacqueline to steady her as she swayed on her feet.

'I think it would be best if we spoke inside.'

Nodding weakly, Jacqueline showed him into the kitchen, and they sat at the table.

'Tell me how you became friends with my Ramulas,' Jacqueline said.

Shigar told of how he first became aware of the crystal and explained that was how he came to know Ramulas. He explained the king's paranoia, which had led to the capture of Ramulas, and then Ramulas' escape from the tombs.

When Shigar talked about Ramulas' time in the tombs, he did not mention the death of the horse or the torture Ramulas endured. Instead, he spoke about the friendships and bonds made by Ramulas.

The girls came inside several times, only to be told by Jacqueline to leave, Shigar told her of the crystal being in the wrong place and Ramulas having to travel to the Devil's Ridge Mountains with Pip.

When Ramulas had settled in Sanctuary, he told her, he would send for his family.

'Ramulas wanted to come home after dropping the crystal,' Shigar said. 'But he needs to train an army to protect you and the people of the kingdom.'

Jacqueline stared at Shigar in disbelief. 'Ramulas know nothing about training armies.'

Shigar nodded. 'I know; he has told me. But as Oriel has told him, people will be drawn to Ramulas to help him in his quest.'

'What did you mean when you said Ramulas will send for his family? Why won't Ramulas come himself?'

'Sanctuary will be your new home, and you will be living in a castle,' Shigar replied.

'Oh, Kate,' Grace said. 'We're going to live in a castle.'

'Sh!'

Jacqueline looked at Shigar in astonishment, and the magician almost jumped out of his skin. Grace's voice had come from next to Shigar, but he could see no-one there. His hand shot inside his robes, only to come back out throwing glittering powder in the air.

Grace sneezed, and then Kate and Grace materialised with a popping sound. Jacqueline's eyes widened in shock as her hand covered her mouth.

'Oh my,' Shigar said with admiration. 'I knew she had magical abilities, but this is truly amazing,' He looked at Grace and smiled. 'Tell me, how did you do that—turn yourself and your sister invisible?'

Grace shrugged. 'I do not know. We just wanted to know where Da was.'

Shigar was both shocked and excited. He had stumbled upon a childhood prodigy of magic. When he had first seen Grace, Shigar saw that she emanated raw magical power. However, he could not have dreamed of her being so powerful.

For Grace to have the ability to make both her and Kate invisible and remain undetected so close to him was high-level magic.

***

Ramulas was lost in his own world, thinking about the three guardians as they entered the second forest. A hundred yards into the forest, he heard a noise in the bushes ahead. Stepping out onto the path in front of the cart were two men. They were dressed in dark leggings and vests. One was tall and broad across the shoulders, and the other was short and wiry—both had short, dark hair. They stopped and both pulled out swords.

Halt! the shorter one called to them. 'What are you doing in our forest?'

'This forest does not belong to you,' Ramulas replied as he communicated for Rufus to stop.

'By the gods,' Pip whispered in a bored tone from underneath the hood of her cloak.

'We will be needing to look inside your cart and take payment for travelling through our forest,' he said, and the taller man nodded.

'You are an idiot,' Pip said loud enough for all to hear.

The two men in front of Rufus were confused at Pip's comment and attitude. They were used to people being afraid at this point. They looked at each other before coming toward the cart.

'Do not come any closer,' Ramulas said.

Ramulas reached into the rear of the cart and held the handle of his war hammer. He felt the weapon transform.

He stood in a fluid motion and held the war hammer before him. Pip touched him lightly on the leg and shook her head.

'I would put that fancy weapon away,' the taller man said.

The shorter man whistled and Ramulas heard something coming through the bushes toward him.

Ramulas almost fell out of the cart when he saw two hell hounds come charging out of the shrubbery. However, these were different from the hell hound that he fought in Bremnon; these hell hounds were larger and had longer spikes.

These were wild hell hounds.

One was much larger than the other, it stood waist-high to the smaller man. The smaller hound seemed to be a pup.

Ramulas felt Pip stiffen next to him, and he cursed himself for being such a fool. He had been worrying so much about the three guardians of Sanctuary that he had forgotten to use his ability to communicate with animals. He should have known about the hell hounds.

'I think we need to teach you a lesson,' the taller man said as he clicked his fingers, and both hell hounds ran at the cart.

Ramulas dropped his war hammer, took a deep breath, and focused. He sent out calming thoughts to both animals. When they felt his presence, the hell hounds both stopped and cocked their heads.

He communicated with them, offering friendship. He found that even though they were wild, they were not full of hate. They had been treated well, and after a few moments of communication, Ramulas found that they were mother and pup. He called both to his cart.

They came forward as Ramulas jumped to the ground to greet them. He squatted, holding out his hands. The mother cautiously sniffed his hands while the pup jumped around barking. Ramulas closed his eyes and communicated with the hell hounds, sending them calming thoughts. After a few seconds, he was patting both of them.

A loud whistle sounded from the trees and both hell hounds looked back to the forest. The pup ran for the trees, only stopping when its mother barked, and it came back to the cart.

'That was not supposed to happen,' the smaller man said. 'They were supposed to come back.'

'I told you we would lose the hell hounds today,' the taller man said.

'We have not lost them yet, Miles,' the short man said, walking to the cart.

He stopped when both hell hounds began to growl at him. This brought a stifled laugh from Pip.

Ramulas saw a third man walk out of the trees. Although he was dressed the same, he was different from the other two—he was tall and broad across the shoulders, walked with grace, and had long, blond hair which came halfway down his back.

The way he carried himself spoke of him being more than just a bandit. There was something strange about this man, but Ramulas could not work out what it was.

'Benji, Miles, what happened to the hell hounds?' the blond man asked.

'I don't know, Michael,' the short one answered. 'I have never seen this before. I will try to get them back.'

'Then you will lose a hand, Benji,' Pip said with a smile.

Benji stopped and looked at the priestess sitting in the cart. Her voice was familiar, but he was unable to see her face beneath the hood.

'If you speak again, I will remove your tongue,' Benji threatened.

Pip slowly pulled back her hood, allowing her purple hair to spill around her shoulders. 'Is that so?' she replied with a mischievous smile.

Benji's mouth fell open and his sword dropped to the ground. 'Pip, is that really you?'

'No, it's your dear old mother, come to give you a spanking,' Pip said before jumping down from the cart and running toward Benji.

He met her halfway and they embraced before holding each other at arm's length.

'What are you doing out here?' Benji asked.

'I am with my friend Ramulas on a quest,' she said, pointing at the cart behind her with her thumb. 'Who are your companions? I have not seen them before.'

Benji introduced Miles, who he had working with for a year, and Michael, who the pair had met a month ago. They had formed as a trio of bandits to rob caravans, and it had been Michael's idea to come into this forest that day.

Michael looked at the hell hounds and patted his thigh. Both hell hounds turned to him for a moment before looking at Ramulas. They had found someone who could communicate with them.

'How are you doing that to them?' Michael asked. 'Why won't they listen to us anymore?'

Ramulas shrugged. 'I have a way with animals.'

'We spent months training them,' Miles said. 'They belong to us; give them back.'

Ramulas shook his head. 'That is where you are wrong. These animals belong to no-one. They are free to choose who they are with.' He turned to Pip. 'We need to go.'

She nodded and said a quick goodbye to Benji before climbing back onto the cart.

'Damn, why did we have to come here?' Miles said. 'I had a vision that we would lose the hounds.'

Then Ramulas remembered what Oriel said about the guardians of Sanctuary. 'Are you the three guardians that I was to meet?'

'Yes, we are,' Benji replied, a little too quickly.

'What are you the guardians of?' Ramulas asked.

'We are the guardians of this road,' Benji said with a smile.

The smile quickly faded when he saw Ramulas' expression of disbelief. Both Miles and Michael berated Benji for his stupidity.

'I have enjoyed meeting you, but we must be leaving,' Ramulas said before focusing on his magical abilities to push Miles and Benji away from the cart. Then he communicated with Rufus and the hell hounds to begin moving into the forest.

Pip smiled. 'Why don't you three join us on our journey?'

Both Miles and Benji shook their heads and stepped back.

Benji pointed at Ramulas. 'He knows magic. He used it to push us away. I don't trust magic after escaping from the druid's labyrinth.'

Pip nodded in understanding. 'Benji, when you are ready, come and find us.'

But Michael saw Ramulas' purple aura expanding and push his two companions back from the cart. He also observed purple energy surrounding the warhorse and hell hounds.

Michael had persuaded Miles and Benji into this forest because he could feel the strange powerful magical energy of Ramulas. If he could feel it, Michael knew that his brother would also feel it and come to Ramulas. Michael knew that this man was the key to finding his lost brother.

5

Shigar sat across the table from Jacqueline, and the girls sat on either side of their mother. When Shigar spoke, all three hung on every word.

'Not only do I see magical energies in Grace, but I am also able to feel magical energy throughout this farm.'

'How can you feel the magic?' Grace asked excitedly.

'I want both of you girls to sit on your hands,' he said.

Shigar smiled as Kate and Grace quickly sat on their hands and looked at him.

After a few moments, he nodded. 'Take your hands out now.'

He laughed when both girls removed their hands and the sensation of pins and needles went into their fingers as the circulation returned. They looked at their hands in astonishment.

'That is what I feel when I am close to magic. And it is very strong in this house. Grace is not the only one with special abilities,' Shigar said. 'I have seen the way Kate moves, and she reminds me of a seasoned fighter. How long has she been training?'

Jacqueline and the girls were stunned at the statement.

'What do you mean when you say "training"?' Jacqueline replied.

Shigar pushed a cup across the table, and it fell off the edge near Kate. She moved quickly and, without thinking, her hand shot out and she caught the cup. Kate's eyes widened in shock.

Shigar nodded at Kate. 'Those reflexes take years to master.'

49

Kate gasped and the cup fell to the floor. Jacqueline looked at both of her daughters in awe.

'I am sorry to have troubled you,' Shigar said. 'I was excited about Grace's magical abilities, and then I saw something special in Kate. I shall take my leave.'

As Shigar stood, Jacqueline reached out for him. 'Wait! When will we hear something about Ramulas?'

'When Ramulas is ready, he will send someone to bring you to him, and that will be soon. One more thing: do not leave this farm until someone from Sanctuary comes for you. The king has sent his agents out searching for Ramulas, and Grace's eyes will bring the wrong kind of attention.'

'You make Ramulas sound like a criminal,' Jacqueline replied.

Shigar smiled sadly. 'He is no criminal, but he is different. That is the only excuse the king needs to hunt him. Stay here and you will be safe.'

Shigar walked away with a heavy heart. The looks of uncertainty by Ramulas' family cut deeply. As he rode back to town, Shigar thought of a story that would keep the agents away from this farm.

***

Ramulas noticed that this part of the forest floor was covered in ferns and bracken along the path. The hell hounds disappeared into the undergrowth and could be heard moving alongside the cart.

As they travelled, Pip told stories of her days with Benji. Ramulas was happy to put a face to the person who had been taken by the druids only to be the first to escape from the druid's labyrinth.

Some parts of this forest seemed even darker than the one they had travelled through the day before. There were places where Ramulas found that there was no animal life, which he thought strange.

It was near midday, and they had followed the paths near the Devil's Ridge Mountains. The only movement around them was that of the two hell hounds moving through the bush. Birds and insects could be heard in the forest.

Then the forest became deathly quiet, and both hell hounds came to the cart.

'Something's not right,' Pip said, looking around at the forest. 'I can feel it.'

'Wait a moment,' Ramulas said.

He took a deep breath and focused on the surrounding wildlife and found they were all hiding. Something they feared was coming, and the hell hounds felt it as well. It was coming towards the cart.

One hundred yards ahead, Ramulas and Pip saw something very much out of place in this forest.

A small girl around Grace's age walked along the path towards them. When saw that Ramulas and Pip had seen her, she waved to them.

She wore a white dress and had light brown hair that came to her shoulders. Both hell hounds disappeared under the cart, and Ramulas could feel they were afraid of the girl, which confused Ramulas.

'What are you doing in the forest?' Ramulas called out to her.

She smiled at him. 'My parents allow me to play in the forest as long as I am not too far from home.'

'Well, then,' Ramulas said, 'how far away is your home?'

The girl turned and pointed down the path behind her. 'An hour walking that way.'

'Isn't that too far away from home?' he asked in a concerned voice.

She shrugged.

'My name is Ramulas, and this is Pip. What is your name?'

'My name is Emily.'

'Do your parents have a small house up the path?'

'No, silly!' the girl said in mock anger. 'We live in a town.'

Ramulas frowned. 'The nearest town is Turtha, and that is a long way from here.'

This brought another giggle from Emily. 'Everyone knows the town where I come from. It is called Sanctuary.'

Oriel had said that Sanctuary had been lying dormant, by which he thought she meant no-one was living there. But Emily said that her parents lived there.

'How many people live in Sanctuary?' he asked Emily.

Emily flinched at the question and shook her head.

'We are on our way to Sanctuary,' Ramulas said. 'Would you like to ride with us? Then I could talk to your parents when we arrive.'

A dark expression crossed Emily's face but was gone as soon as Ramulas saw it.

'I will walk with you,' Emily said before turning back the way she had come.

Ramulas looked at Pip with a smile. 'Do you feel like a walk with Emily and me?'

'Then who will control the cart?' Pip asked.

Ramulas shrugged. 'The hell hounds.'

Ramulas jumped off the cart just in time to avoid a swipe from Pip. He landed with a laugh and walked over to join Emily. When Pip joined the pair, Ramulas communicated with Rufus to pull the cart, and the hell hounds followed.

As they began to walk, the forest came alive again with the sound of wildlife.

Walking down the path alongside Emily and Pip, Ramulas noticed that they were coming closer to the mountain range. He was in awe of how big they really were.

Some peaks were so high that they disappeared into the clouds. Pip and Emily hummed an old children's song as they walked, and Ramulas wondered how much further it was to go.

Emily stopped singing and pointed ahead down the path. 'Sanctuary is not far from here.'

Ramulas looked ahead and saw a shaft of red light shooting into the sky from the mountains. At this moment, Emily raced ahead and vanished into the trees.

Pip made to follow but Ramulas stopped her with a quick shake of his head. The hell hounds gave chase, but he called them back.

A few minutes later, they rounded a bend and the trees opened. Ramulas and Pip saw a clearing before them. On the other side of the clearing was a sight that took Ramulas' breath away.

There was a giant curved wall wedged in between two cliffs. The wall was about eight hundred yards across and fifty yards high. The cliffs on either side towered over the wall itself, shooting into the sky like spear tips.

Ramulas and Pip were drawn in closer to inspect the wall. Most of the wall was covered in moss and lichen, and some parts were cracked and falling apart.

'Look at this,' Pip whispered in awe. 'I have never seen anything like this before.'

'Neither have I,' Ramulas said as they walked to the wall.

They followed a faint path that led to a gate in the middle of the wall. Ramulas reached the gate and looked up at the wall. It appeared as if it had not been cleaned in many years.

After brushing his hand along the lichen, Ramulas turned back to the clearing behind him. He judged it to be about two hundred yards in a semicircle.

'Did you see where Emily went?' he asked Pip.

Pip shook her head. 'Not since she left us.'

'Then let us take a look in Sanctuary. The hell hounds can come with us, and Rufus will wait out here with the cart.' Ramulas communicated with the animals as he and Pip walked through the gate. They found themselves in a passageway with walls twice Ramulas' height and wide enough for three men to walk abreast.

After a while, they came to a junction where they had the choice of turning left or right. Ramulas and Pip looked both ways and saw that they, too, ended in junctions.

'Which way do we go?' Pip asked.

'We will go right, and then turn left,' Ramulas answered.

As they walked through the passageways Ramulas realised they were in a maze. It had fallen into decay; cracks lined the walls, and some sections had holes in the walls the size of a fist. Ramulas and Pip used these holes to look through. They avoided stepping into the puddles of stagnant water as they walked through the maze. Then Ramulas heard the moaning.

A long, woeful moan sounded from somewhere to their right. It was answered by similar moans to their left and ahead of them. Ramulas and Pip looked at each other.

'I don't like the sound of this,' Pip said in a worried tone. 'We need to get out of this maze.'

Ramulas nodded. 'I know. Follow me,' Ramulas said as he began to jog.

Every now and then, Ramulas would look up at the walls to get his bearings. He knew that by moving away from the wall, they would soon arrive in Sanctuary.

Ramulas and Pip came to a courtyard within the maze. It had several other paths leading out of it. A fire burned in the centre of the courtyard. Around the fire crouched six creatures. They looked like people, with mottled, grey skin and long, unkempt black hair.

Ramulas and Pip heard grunts and snorts as the creatures communicated around the fire. A low growl emanated from the younger hell hound. Ramulas looked down to see the spikes rise along its body.

He communicated with both the hell hounds to keep them quiet.

'They know we are here,' Pip said.

Ramulas looked up from the hell hounds to see the creatures staring at them with pure hatred. Ramulas and Pip held their breath, not daring to move.

One of the creatures screamed before racing toward them. It was closely followed by the rest. The moans within the maze changed to answering screams.

'What do we do?' Pip asked as she pulled out throwing knives.

'We fight,' Ramulas replied as he rushed to meet the creatures.

He communicated with the hell hounds, telling them to attack. The pup launched itself at the lead creature and clamped its jaws onto the creature's neck. It went down under the hell hound's weight; the pup shook its head from side to side violently, only stopping when the creature's neck snapped.

The pup joined its mother, attacking the remaining creatures, just as Ramulas and Pip reached the first creature.

Even though the creatures held crude clubs, they were no match for the hell hounds. Ramulas and Pip stood back, watching the hell hounds tossing the creatures around like leaves in the wind.

In a few moments, all of the creatures had been killed. Ramulas communicated with the hell hounds, saying that he was happy with them. They came up to Ramulas and Pip, who rewarded them with a pat.

The screams in the maze sounded as if they were coming closer from all directions, and then they stopped. Ramulas and Pip could only hear the sound of the hell hounds breathing.

'I have a bad feeling about this,' Pip said.

A figure walked out into the opposite side of the courtyard. He looked similar to the creatures, but he was covered in blue tattoos and held a staff.

He smiled at Ramulas and Pip, showing teeth as black as coal. Both hell hounds raced toward him. The creature raised its staff, chanting a few words. The tattoos on his body began to glow, and he brought the staff to the ground.

The sound of breaking glass echoed throughout the courtyard.

The fallen creatures were illuminated with blue light. They were reanimated and picked themselves up from the ground.

Humanoid figures pulled themselves out of puddles, and four much larger creatures came into the courtyard.

'Oh no,' Ramulas whispered.

'I told you I didn't like this feeling,' Pip said.

6

The ship pulled into the docks of Keah. The banner of the ship showed it to be from across the far sea. These ships came once a week importing spices and exotic items for the markets.

As the dock workers unloaded the ship of its cargo, a man stood on the bow of the ship watching the docks. At first glance, anyone from Keah would see him as a foreign trader; upon closer inspection, they would see the subtle differences.

He had olive skin, a flat face with almond-shaped eyes, and short silver hair. He wore a light blue vest and held himself as if he owned the ship.

The man nodded to himself as his horse and luggage were brought to the docks. As he walked, two swords that hung by his hip moved. The swords were slightly curved. The blade of the short one was a foot long, and the other blade was three feet. Both swords were in black, lacquered scabbards.

The man walked onto the docks and stood next to his horse and closed his eyes. To an observer, he may have appeared to have fallen asleep while standing. However, he was quite alert and could feel the people moving around him.

A few minutes later, he felt someone approach and stop six feet from him. The man smiled and opened his eyes.

'Are you Iguchi?' the harbourmaster asked.

Iguchi nodded.

'We have a mutual friend; he has asked me to book your passage on a ship to Shes. But that ship will not leave for a few hours.'

'I trust you will watch my possessions and horse?' Iguchi asked.

The harbourmaster nodded. 'They will be taken care of until they are loaded onto the ship.'

Iguchi gave a curt nod before disappearing into the crowd.

The harbourmaster sighed in relief as Iguchi walked away, Shigar had explained in detail how dangerous this little man could be. He called for two dock workers to watch over Iguchi's things.

Iguchi walked through the streets of Keah and found himself in the market square. Even though it was Iguchi's first time in the city of Keah, he knew that all markets attracted different types of people.

There were traders and merchants selling their wares. Buyers would spend time haggling before a price was agreed upon. Then there were thieves and dishonest people. It was just past midday, and the market was full of moving people and noise.

Iguchi ignored everything except for a six-foot radius surrounding him.

Over the past few minutes, Iguchi had noticed that he was being followed by three men. He pretended not to notice their clumsy attempts at tailing him. Iguchi walked away from the market and felt the three close in behind him.

Iguchi quickly stopped and turned in a fluent movement. The three pursuers almost ran into the dancer of death. They nervously looked at each other and at the nearby crowd. The middle man of the three forced a smile and stepped forward. 'Good day to you, sir. You seem lost. Can we show you the way?' he asked Iguchi.

'I am looking for the docks,' Iguchi replied.

All three men smiled and gave slight nods to one another.

'You would do better waving bright flags and shouting, so people will know of your true intentions,' Iguchi said as he shook a finger at them.

This behaviour confused the men, but they quickly recovered.

'Ah, the quickest way to the docks is through here,' the man who had previously spoken said, pointing down an alleyway. 'We will walk with you to keep you safe.'

'That will not be necessary,' Iguchi replied before walking into the alley.

The three men waited until Iguchi had gone twenty yards before they ran after him.

'Where did he go?' one of them asked as they entered the alley. 'He was just here. He must be an evil spirit.'

'I am not an evil spirit,' Iguchi snapped as he stepped out from a doorway.

The three men all pulled out daggers and surrounded Iguchi.

'How did you tear your pants?' Iguchi asked one with yellow teeth as he looked down.

The bandit looked down only to find the blade of Iguchi's short sword resting on his neck. He dropped his dagger and held his hands up in surrender.

Iguchi heard the shuffle of feet behind him. He reached for the shoulder of the man with yellow teeth and twisted a cluster of nerves. The man screamed and dropped to the ground in pain.

Iguchi spun with a flurry of his swords. After a second, he bent to one knee and pivoted to the left, leading with the point of his short sword.

He stopped when the tip of the sword rested on the inside of the middle man's knee. In a fluid movement, Iguchi whipped the blade up until the tip rested on the man's groin. He looked at Iguchi, eyes filled with terror, his hands out in a pleading gesture.

The man next to him moved forward toward Iguchi. The spinning blades of Iguchi's swords had not touched him, or so he thought.

As he stepped forward, his shirt and leggings fell away from his body. So precise were Iguchi's cuts that only the clothing was cut. The bandit fell to his knees and wept in terror.

Iguchi stood quickly and sheathed both his swords. 'You should be ashamed, preying on a defenceless person such as me,' Iguchi said before walking away.

Iguchi left the alleyway and made his way toward the docks. He would wait there until his ship departed.

***

Ramulas focused and the world around him slowed. He needed to find a way out of this situation. The hell hounds had killed the first lot of creatures without any help; however, the creature with the staff had just brought them back to life. Now four larger creatures and things climbing out of the puddles had joined the fray. The larger creatures were almost twice as big as Ramulas.

To Ramulas, it seemed it did not matter how many were killed, as the creature with the staff would bring them back to life. That creature would need to die first.

Everything returned to normal around Ramulas. 'Pip, the one with the staff.'

Two of her throwing knives spun toward the creature. One of the knives cut its upper arm. It howled and ran back into the passageway. The hell hounds attacked the six original creatures as the four larger ones closed in.

'Damn,' Pip swore, 'he got away.'

'Finish him,' Ramulas said.

Pip raced off into the passageway while Ramulas walked over to one of the larger creatures. To his dismay, Ramulas saw two of the larger creatures follow Pip into the passageway. She had not seen them, and that would be dangerous.

Ramulas communicated with the hell hounds and told the pup to protect Pip. As soon as the pup ran off, Ramulas had to duck a swipe from one of the larger creatures. Ramulas turned and swung both of his weapons. As his war hammer hit the creature in the ribs, Ramulas saw something that almost made him lose focus.

The pup had run up the wrong passageway.

Pip would have to fight on her own.

Ramulas gritted his teeth and followed up with an overhead chop with his battle axe. The axe cut through the side of the creature's neck, sending a fountain of blood spraying over Ramulas. He turned to avoid blood in his eyes.

The remaining large creature was ten feet away and closing in fast. Ramulas quickly glanced at the mother hell hound and saw it take down a third creature. Three remained, and Ramulas knew it would not be able to help Pip.

He looked back as the creature reached down for him.

'I don't have time for this,' Ramulas said as he worried about Pip.

A warm sensation exploded in the pit of Ramulas' stomach and flowed through his body. He stepped inside the creature's reach and dropped his war hammer. He held his battle axe in two hands and swung at the creature with wild abandon.

He struck the creature with alternate right and left chops of the axe. It soon fell to its knees, where Ramulas unleashed his frustrations with overhead chops. Within moments, body parts surrounded Ramulas, who was covered in gore.

Ramulas scooped up his war hammer and raced to help the mother hell hound.

He heard Pip scream in terror before it was cut short.

Ramulas ran for the passageway, knowing he would be too late.

***

Pip raced down the passageway, following the creature with the staff. She saw it disappear around a few corners. After a few moments, Pip caught up to the creature as it came to a dead end. The creature turned to look at Pip with a mix of fear and anger.

It chanted while pointing the spear at Pip. A green ball shot from the staff. Pip ducked, and it flew over her head. The green ball hit the wall behind her and began to sizzle. The smell made Pip gag.

'Ew. That's not nice,' she said, pulling out two throwing knives.

The creature saw the knives and began to chant. Grey smoke rose from the ground near its feet. Pip threw her knives, and as soon as they touched the smoke they fell to the ground.

'Damn,' Pip swore.

Pip needed to get closer to the creature to use her knives. With every step she took closer to the creature, Pip had to dodge another green ball. Finally, when she was within arm's reach, Pip thrust a knife through the smoke and into the creature's heart. The smoke dissipated as it fell to the ground.

Then the two larger creatures rounded the corner, coming up behind Pip. One of the creatures picked her up, causing Pip to scream.

With a low growl, the hell hound pup charged out of a different passage. It ran up the creature's back and bit down on its neck. Pip was dropped as the creature tried to dislodge the hell hound. The other creature stepped in to grab the pup.

The creature was rewarded with spikes from the hell hound piercing its hands. It howled and stepped back to look at its injuries. As if by magic, several throwing knives began to appear in the creature's chest. The creature died wondering where they came from.

The pup shook its head, bringing the other creature to its knees. The hell hound adjusted its grip and shook its head once more. The creature's neck broke with a resounding snap, which echoed around Pip. The pup came up to Pip, wagging its tail.

'Good doggy,' Pip said, scratching the hell hound behind its ears.

At that moment, Ramulas came running around the corner with the other hell hound. He let out a sigh of relief upon seeing that Pip was not hurt.

'I heard you scream and thought I would be too late.'

'No, this one saved me,' Pip said as she continued to pat the hell hound. 'This one needs a name— "pup" does not suit him.'

Ramulas laughed. 'After almost being killed, all you can think of is a name for the pup.'

Pip nodded.

'Let me see,' Ramulas said as he communicated with the hell hounds.

After a few seconds, Ramulas' eyes opened in surprise. 'They were already given names by the three who had them. The pup's name is Fenris, and the mother is Valkyrie.'

'At least these things won't be rising from the dead,' Pip said, pointing to the dead creature with the staff.

'Now, we just need to find …' Ramulas said.

'What?'

'A castle,' Ramulas replied, looking over the walls of the maze. 'We will make our way to the castle.'

After walking through the winding maze, Ramulas and Pip stepped out into a courtyard in front of a ten-storey castle. On either side of the castle were streets lined with houses and buildings.

All of the buildings had been neglected and were in stages of collapse. Lichen and large cracks covered the walls and some walls had even fallen. Ramulas could tell that no-one had lived in the town for many years.

The castle was in better condition than the houses and buildings, but parts of the masonry had fallen and shattered on the ground of the courtyard.

'I don't think anyone has been here for a hundred years,' Ramulas said in a confused tone. 'Emily said that she lived here with her parents. Maybe we will find them in a different part of Sanctuary. Let's look in the castle first.'

They walked across the courtyard toward the castle and Ramulas saw a large puddle at the entrance.

As they approached, something rose out of the water in front of them. Both hell hounds yelped and ran back into the maze.

Standing in front of Ramulas and Pip was a wraith. Its whole body was covered in a fluid dark cloak that flowed up from the puddle.

A memory from Ramulas' old life returned to him. He knew this was a wraith, and that it would feed on their life force. He needed to keep it away from Pip and himself.

'Pip, stay away from the wraith, and don't let it touch you.' Ramulas stepped back and held both weapons before him. As he moved, Pip threw three of her knives at the wraith. The knives passed through the wraith, leaving gaping holes.

The wraith hissed as the holes closed. It reached out a skeletal hand and a jet of water hit Pip in the chest. She screamed in pain before dropping to the ground and fighting for breath.

The wraith disappeared into the puddle, leaving only ripples as evidence of its passing. The puddle then shifted and moved behind Ramulas. The wraith shot out of the water, lashing out at Ramulas with a skeletal hand.

Ramulas turned and blocked with his war hammer. He swung with his battle axe, slicing through the wraith's midsection.

The wraith's body parted like water, only to reform again. Ramulas stared in disbelief; his battle axe did not seem to affect it.

Ramulas spun towards the wraith as he swung his weapons. The wraith was hit three times. Its body exploded with the hits, only to reform again.

The wraith rushed at Ramulas and touched him on the arm. He felt one of the coldest sensations flows through his body. He dropped both weapons and fell to the ground clutching his chest.

He could only watch as the wraith closed in on him. Ramulas held a hand out before him in a pleading gesture.

Then the wraith stopped.

Ramulas could not understand why. He was totally defenceless. Then the wraith slowly moved away from him.

'You leave my friend alone,' Emily said, addressing the wraith as she came up to Ramulas. 'You are mean, and I don't like you.'

Ramulas saw Emily at his side, but there was something different about her. Emily's eyes were completely black, and a primal rage flowed through her. She held Ramulas by the hand and pulled him to his feet. He was amazed at her strength; she had picked him up as if he were just a doll.

The wraith attempted to fall back into the puddle several times but failed.

'I really don't like you,' Emily said as vapours of dark energy rose from her body.

Her hair began to sway, but Ramulas could not feel any wind.

Static energy popped around Ramulas and Emily. Her grip on Ramulas' hand tightened and his bones began to grind together.

'Emily.' He gasped in pain.

Ramulas felt the hairs on his body rise, and he shivered as the dark energies flowed from Emily. The wraith began to shake and tremble. It let out a high-pitched scream before exploding.

Emily released Ramulas' hand, and he looked at her in disbelief, not knowing what to say. He watched as the dark energy surrounding Emily was drawn back into her. She closed her eyes for a second, and when Emily opened them, she appeared to Ramulas as a little girl once more.

So many questions ran through Ramulas' mind as he looked at Emily in a new light. 'Where are your parents, Emily?'

'You both need to go into the castle. There is a nice lady waiting for you,' Emily said, avoiding the question.

Ramulas walked over to Pip and helped her to her feet. Pip hugged her body while her teeth chattered.

'Come into the castle and we will see if we can find something to warm you.'

The hell hounds came racing out of the maze wagging their tails. He communicated with them and found that they were terrified of the wraith.

'Emily?' Pip said.

'What about her?'

'She has gone again.'

Ramulas quickly scanned the courtyard as could not see her, which only brought more questions.

Ramulas shrugged and looked at the castle. 'Let's go inside to see what we can find.'

He communicated with the hell hounds, telling them to wait outside.

7

They walked through the open wooden doors of the castle into a dark hallway. The only source of light came from Ramulas' weapons, which glowed faintly.

After a moment of looking around, Pip asked, 'Where do we go now?'

Ramulas shrugged, and then his eyes widened. 'Did you hear that?'

Pip shook her head.

'Follow me,' Ramulas said.

They turned right and walked down a hallway, passing several open doors. Ramulas was focused on following the voice he could hear inside his mind, but Pip stole quick glances into each room. The small radius of light made by Ramulas' weapons made the shadows dance along the walls. If Pip did not know any better, she would have sworn that there were things moving within the rooms.

As they walked along the hallway, the voice became louder and clearer for Ramulas. He knew it was Oriel. He stopped at a stairway that spiralled upwards, the glow from his weapons only showing the floor above.

'We need to go up,' he said.

After three flights of stairs, Oriel's voice had become clearer. He followed it down the hall to a room with light coming from within.

'She's in there!' Pip said excitedly. 'I can hear her.'

Ramulas and Pip stood outside the room and looked in. Pip gasped in surprise and walked in. As Ramulas followed, he saw that the room was larger than his farmhouse.

A long wooden table filled with lit candles stood in the middle of the room. Tapestries and paintings covered the walls, all depicting men in battle. At one end of the room, Ramulas saw a throne on a raised dais, and on that throne sat Oriel.

'Welcome,' Oriel said with a warm smile as she rose out of the throne and came towards them. 'I see you made it past the three guardians of Sanctuary.'

'There were more than three,' Pip said, referring to the creatures in the maze.

Oriel shook her head as she walked to Pip. 'No, there were only three.

Oriel's hands spread and began to glow as she traced patterns through the air in front of Pip. After a few seconds, Pip sighed as steam began to rise from her wet clothes. When Pip was completely dry, Oriel stepped back.

'Emily was the first of the guardians,' Oriel said as Ramulas and Pip looked at her in shock.

'That is not possible,' Ramulas said.

'You have learned so much in a short period of time,' Oriel said to Ramulas, 'yet there is so much more for you to learn. Of the three guardians, Emily is the most powerful and dangerous.'

'But she is just a girl,' Pip said.

'She was the one who destroyed the wraith after it attacked you,' Oriel said.

Ramulas nodded in agreement. Pip was in a state of disbelief. After the wraith attacked her, she had closed her eyes, fighting for breath; by the time she opened them, the wraith was destroyed, and Pip assumed it was by Ramulas.

'Emily is a very powerful spirit,' Oriel explained. 'She has not crossed over to the other side. Something is holding her here, and until that is resolved Emily will not leave Sanctuary.'

'What of her parents and the other people who used to live here?' Ramulas asked.

'Everyone in Sanctuary died in a war many years ago, and for some reason, Emily chose to stay.'

'How long ago was this war?' Pip asked. 'I have not heard of any such war, and before meeting Ramulas, this place was a myth.'

Oriel smiled sadly. 'The war was five hundred years ago.' Seeing the shocked expressions on Ramulas and Pip, Oriel continued. 'Emily has been wandering these forests and Sanctuary since that time.

She has hidden Sanctuary from travellers who have come through the forests. Besides Grace, you two are the first Emily has chosen to speak to since losing her family.'

'How can you know this if you have come from another world?' Ramulas asked.

Oriel waved a hand behind her, and the wall opened to form a window. As light spilled into the room, Ramulas and Pip saw the mountains outside the castle.

'The mountains speak to me of Sanctuary's history.'

'Emily has been here all this time, but what about the other guardians?' Ramulas asked.

'The creatures within the maze are known as the Nameless. They came down from the mountains when the druids were hunting monsters across the kingdom. Being in the maze helps hide them from the druids. That is where they made their home. Emily did not harm them as long as they stayed out of Sanctuary.'

'What about the wraith?' Ramulas asked.

'The wraith has been a part of Sanctuary since the war in which everyone was killed. It has always avoided trouble with Emily. This time she destroyed it to protect you both.'

'Now that we are here, what do we do?' Ramulas asked.

Oriel smiled and held out both hands, and a glowing purple ball the size of an orange appeared in front of Ramulas. 'Take this to the topmost tower and drop it into the courtyard below.'

Ramulas placed both weapons on the floor and took the glowing ball in his hands. Its warmth flowed through him as he walked out of the room. Pip quickly followed him to the stairway, where they began to climb.

Ramulas found that the glowing ball shone more than his weapons did. He and Pip could see a lot more of the castle. In the hallway behind them, vases and statues shone in the light. They could see the stairs were made of marble; however, they were covered in dust and most of the stairs were cracked.

As they made their way up the stairs, Ramulas and Pip fought the urge to explore each floor. Eventually, they came to the highest tower.

This level only had one room, and it was half the size of Oriel's room. There were four large windows open, facing north, east, south, and west.

They stood at the southern window, and Ramulas heard Pip gasp as she looked over the forest. They could see the town of Sanctuary, into the maze, and finally, over the front wall into the forest.

Ramulas smiled at Pip before dropping the ball out of the window. It seemed to spin through the air before landing. The ball struck the courtyard and exploded, sending a wave of purple energy outwards into the forest. With a rush of wind, another wave shot up engulfing Ramulas and Pip. They both pulled themselves back into the room.

Ramulas watched in amazement as purple dust washed over Pip, mending and cleaning her clothes. He caught her surprised expression when she looked at him. Ramulas saw that the same was happening to him.

Within a few seconds, their clothing was as new as the day they were purchased, and they both felt revitalised. Looking out the window, Ramulas saw the purple wave disappear over the horizon.

'Look at the maze!' Pip exclaimed as she pointed out of the window.

Ramulas looked down and could hardly believe his eyes.

The walls of the maze had begun to move. Unable to take his eyes off the maze, Ramulas watched as the walls moved and opened a pathway from the front gate to the courtyard.

Ramulas blinked a few times to see if his eyes were playing tricks on him, and then he looked at the town. The lichen and moss had gone from the walls, the buildings were free of cracks, and the streets were clean of debris.

Pip pulled Ramulas away from the window. 'Look at the floor!'

Ramulas gasped as he saw the marble floor. It shone beneath their feet as if it had just been polished. Ramulas and Pip could see their reflections smiling back at them.

'That was good magic,' Pip said. 'This room looked old a moment ago.'

'I know,' Ramulas agreed. 'Let's talk with Oriel.'

As they made their way down the stairs, Ramulas and Pip found that the castle had transformed. Light shone in every hallway; doorways were open tempting them to explore. They fought the urge and went straight to Oriel.

***

They were met by Oriel as they walked into the room.

Oriel smiled at the pair. 'Ramulas and Pip, it has begun.'

'What has begun?' Pip asked.

'The glowing ball Ramulas dropped has set off a chain of events that will bring life back into Sanctuary. There are certain people in this world who are able to see and hear things that others cannot, or if I can say it in another way, there are things that happen that people call miracles. Most people do not understand or believe in miracles.

'However, the people who are open to miracles will feel something calling them here. These will be the first people to call Sanctuary their home, and the first to call you "lord", Ramulas.'

'But I am no lord,' Ramulas said.

Oriel smiled. 'This is the true beginning of your journey. Be ready for your people to come in the next few days. They will look to you for guidance.'

'How can they look to me for guidance when I do not know what I am supposed to do?' Ramulas replied.

'Ramulas, you need to have faith and believe in yourself. You will know what to do when the time comes. And you will always find me in this room if you need advice.'

'Where do I start?' Ramulas asked.

'I am sure that you and Pip are curious about the castle and Sanctuary. Please explore and get to know your new home.'

'Talking about a new home,' Pip said, 'which house do I stay in?'

'You will be staying in the castle with Ramulas and his family,' Oriel said.

For a moment Pip could not move. She did not believe what she had just heard. Ramulas and Pip looked at each other.

'Both of your rooms are down the hall. Ramulas has the room at the end of the hall, and Pip's room is next to his,' Oriel said.

Pip ran out of the room with Ramulas close behind. He saw light coming out of the room at the end of the hall. Ramulas overtook Pip halfway to his room; he laughed at her groans of protest.

Ramulas entered his room and stopped almost immediately, he could not believe what he saw. It was not one room, but several. The room he stood in was as big as Oriel's. He walked through the rooms in a dream-like state.

The furniture, chests, and tapestries were some of the finest he had seen. He did not want to touch anything. Ramulas smiled at the thought of his family's reaction to seeing this.

'Let's look at the town,' Pip said, pulling Ramulas out of his reverie.

***

As Ramulas and Pip explored the township of Sanctuary, both hell hounds ran to Ramulas and stopped at his feet. He communicated with them, asking what was wrong. They told him that someone was coming. Emily stepped out of a side street.

'There are people coming,' Emily said before walking to the courtyard.

As they followed Emily, Ramulas recalled the last two hours. After leaving the castle, he communicated with Rufus and told him to come into Sanctuary.

He led the warhorse to the stables behind the castle. Ramulas could not believe how big the stables were; a quick estimation told Ramulas that there were over one hundred stalls.

Ramulas and Pip arrived at the courtyard and saw three figures walking down the newly made passageway from the clearing. Fifty yards from the courtyard, the tallest of the three waved.

'Hello again my friend,' Michael said with a smile. 'It is nice to see you both again, and good to see the hell hounds.'

Michael stopped short of patting the hell hounds when they growled at him.

'Fenris and Valkyrie are happy with me,' Ramulas said.

Ramulas smiled when he saw Michael's reaction to him speaking the hell hounds' names.

Then Ramulas saw Benji twitching nervously and looking back at the maze when he came into the courtyard. Miles attempted to comfort him, but Benji waved him away.

'Benji, what's wrong?' Pip asked.

'The walls near the passageway, I can hear them moving.'

'There is a maze behind the walls of the passageway, and its walls are moving,' Ramulas explained.

'We have to get away from the maze before it opens,' Benji said fearfully as the colour drained from his face.

When no-one moved, Benji became frantic. 'We have to get away from the maze before it opens. If we are this close when it opens, the monsters will come out and attack us.'

Pip walked over to Benji and slapped him hard across the face. Then she took him by the hand and led him to the castle.

After she sat him on the steps of the castle, Pip walked over to a bewildered Ramulas.

'Benji was about to fall into madness once again,' she said with an apologetic shrug. 'It's the only way I know to stop it. After Benji's time in the druid's labyrinth, certain things bring back the horrors that he escaped.'

Ramulas looked at the remaining two. 'Why have you come to Sanctuary?'

Miles nodded at Michael. 'After you left with our hell hounds, we were going to return to Turtha. Then Michael here said that we should follow you for a while, that you would lead us to grand things.' Then Miles looked around at the streets. 'Where are all the people?'

'There are only five of us here,' Ramulas replied. 'I am waiting for more to arrive.'

'What do you mean others?' Miles asked. 'Why are they coming? And why are there no people here?'

Ramulas was about to answer when Michael held up his hand. 'The others he spoke of will come here for the same reason that we did.'

'And what might those reasons be?' Benji asked as he walked over from the castle.

Ramulas looked at the three men, unsure how they would react. He took a deep breath and slowly exhaled before speaking.

'There is an army preparing to come here from another world. The soldiers in this army are unlike any that has been seen in the kingdom. Once this army arrives, it will sweep the lands, raping and killing everything in its path. I must train my own army to be ready for them when they come to Sanctuary.'

'What is Sanctuary?' Miles asked.

Michael slapped his forehead. 'We are standing in Sanctuary now,' Then he looked at Ramulas. 'The more important question would be, why would an army from another world want to come here?'

'I will tell you everything shortly,' Ramulas replied.

'This small army that you are going to train,' Benji said. 'Where are they?'

Ramulas smiled. 'The first three members of my army have just arrived.'

'Where?' Miles said, looking around.

Michael laughed when he saw the expression of disbelief on Ramulas' face. 'Who is your friend?' he asked, indicating behind Ramulas with a nod of his head.

Ramulas turned to find Emily standing behind him.

'Send them in to see Oriel,' Emily said. 'She will tell them what they need to do.'

'Where did she come from?' Benji asked in shock.

Ramulas held up a hand before speaking to Emily. 'Where did you go when Pip and I went into the castle?'

'I was playing in the forest,' Emily said before pointing to the new arrivals. 'They need to see Oriel.'

Ramulas turned back to the trio. 'This is Emily. She lives here in Sanctuary.'

'But how can she live here? You said there were only five of us,' Miles said. 'And who is Oriel?'

Ramulas sighed. 'Come with me into the castle and all of your questions will be answered.'

He led them up to Oriel's room and indicated they should enter. 'I'll return once you have spoken with Oriel,' Ramulas said before walking away with Pip and Emily.

Benji, Miles, and Michael looked at each other before entering the room.

***

Ramulas was in his quarters when Emily came up to him. 'They have finished talking to Oriel. You can see them now.'

Ramulas quickly made his way to Oriel's room where he found Miles, Benji, and Michael in front of Oriel.

Oriel turned to him with a smile. 'Hello, Ramulas. I have met the first three of your army. They are good men, and they believe in the cause that you will be fighting for. Everyone who comes to Sanctuary must come to me. I will tell them what role they are to play in the upcoming battle.'

Oriel gave a slight bow to Ramulas before fading.

'Oriel showed us visions of the First Legion and the warlords,' Miles said in awe. 'Then she showed us what would happen if we did not stop the legion when they came here.'

'And if they take Oriel's powers,' Benji added, 'no-one will be able to stop them.'

Michael held up a small sack filled with coins. This brought a smile from Miles and Benji. 'But the strangest thing was that she knew we had robbed people and caravans along the roads.

'She offered us a bag of coins with a choice. Oriel said that she trusted us to go to Turtha and bring back supplies. We have the choice of returning with supplies and beginning a new life or leaving with the coins.'

'What are you planning to do?' Ramulas asked.

'Go to Turtha and come back with supplies,' Benji replied.

'The three of us are to live in the castle as well,' Miles said. 'But first Oriel said there were weapons and armour for us.'

'Where?' Ramulas asked.

'I'll show you,' Emily said from the doorway.

Pip joined the group as they followed Emily down the stairs. Ramulas wondered what armour might be waiting for him. They reached the ground floor and walked through a series of hallways before coming to a steel door.

The door was solid steel and was covered with intricate patterns of snakes. The only thing missing, Ramulas thought, was a doorhandle.

'Emily, how does the door open?' Ramulas asked.

Emily looked up at him. 'You push it. The door will only open for a person with a pure heart.'

'What if the person who pushes it does not have a pure heart?' Benji asked.

'Then they will die a horrible death,' Emily replied.

Everyone looked at Emily with uncertainty, waiting for her to explain what she had said.

Emily looked at Pip. 'The door will open for you. But when you touch the surface, you do not remove your hand until the door opens.'

'Why me?' Pip asked in shock. 'I am a thief, and if what you said about having a pure heart is true, then I will die a horrible death. Choose Ramulas; he has a pure heart.'

Emily shook her head. 'It must be you. That is what Oriel wants.'

Pip took a deep breath to steady her nerves and carefully reached out and placed her hand on the door. The snakes on the door came to life.

Pip gasped as they slithered towards her hand, but she held it firmly against the door's surface. The snakes felt cold as they covered the back of Pip's hand, and they began to move up her forearm. Pip's willpower was put to the test as she fought against the temptation to pull away.

Then the door swung open.

The snakes pulled away, releasing their grip on Pip. The small group stepped into the room, their eyes widening in awe.

Before them was a room the size of a small warehouse. To their right were rows of chainmail, suits of armour, and breastplates; to the left were weapons and shields lined up in racks.

Miles and Benji ran into the room. They picked up a weapon or piece of armour before putting it back and looking at something else. They shouted to one another what they had found.

Ramulas smiled. It reminded him of the time when he took his girls to Bremnon to buy them candy. Kate and Grace were so excited that they took several moments to work out what they wanted.

Michael slowly walked into the room and walked around without picking anything up. Ramulas found this peculiar.

'You need to find the items with the purple light shining over them,' Michael called out. 'They are the items meant for you.'

'How do you know that?' Ramulas asked.

Michael shrugged. 'I can see purple lights shinning over weapons and armour that would only be suited to me.'

Benji, Miles and Pip made affirmative noises as they followed their lights and ran toward their items.

'I do not see any lights,' Ramulas said as he looked around.

'Then there is nothing here for you in this room,' Michael replied.

'What makes you say that?'

Michael smiled. 'I have heard of places such as this, but there are potions instead of weapons. The potions cure all manner of ailments. The store owner cannot see the lights to give you the potion. You need to find it yourself.'

'Yes!' Pip shouted.

Michael and Ramulas turned to see Pip running excitedly towards them with her left hand hidden beneath her cloak.

Stopping in from of them, Pip smiled as she slowly revealed her left hand. She wore a leather gauntlet with a miniature crossbow attached to the back of her hand. Several crossbow bolts were sewn into the gauntlet.

'That suits you,' Ramulas said.

Pip flashed a smile before running back into the rows of weapons and armour. Ramulas gave in to curiosity and searched the room while the others gathered their items. One thing that struck Ramulas was that every piece of armour and shield had the same symbol.

It was an exact replica of the dragon which was tattooed on his chest.

After a few minutes, Pip and the trio stood before Ramulas proudly, all wearing new armour and holding new weapons. Ramulas felt like someone who had arrived at a feast only to find he was late, and all the food had been eaten.

'Oriel wants to see you,' Emily said from the doorway.

As they walked up the stairs, Ramulas could see a spring in the step of the others.

***

They entered Oriel's room to find her standing in front of her throne.

'I see you have found the armoury,' she said with a smile. 'I see the pride your new items have given you. But in these early days, we must keep the dragon crest hidden.'

Oriel waved to a nearby table where three travel cloaks lay. 'Wear these when you leave on your quests. You each know what you need to do. Gather your horses, and go now.'

'But I did not see them arrive on horses,' Ramulas said.

Michael smiled. 'We left our horses out in the forest. It is an old trick that I learned.'

Michael, Miles and Benji gave a slight bow to Oriel before leaving. Ramulas wanted to ask Michael why he had left the horses in the forest, but Oriel spoke.

'Ramulas, with most of the things you do in Sanctuary, Pip will be by your side.' Then Oriel turned to Pip. 'You will act as a protector for Ramulas and his family. You will also watch over Sanctuary from the rooftops. With so many different people coming into Sanctuary, there is bound to be trouble. You will need to stop any trouble before it begins.'

Pip nodded, unable to speak as her responsibilities sunk in.

'Why did I not have a light showing me my armour in the armoury?' Ramulas asked.

Oriel smiled. 'Because you will be the lord of Sanctuary. You will need to wear something different to everyone else. This armour will mark you as the true leader of Sanctuary.'

'Pip, I will need some time alone with Ramulas. There is an archery range behind the stables; you could test your crossbow.'

Pip's eyes lit up and she raced from the room.

Oriel walked over to the large table and waved her hand over it. Ramulas gasped as several pieces of armour and clothing appeared.

'From this moment on, you will wear these,' Oriel said.

Ramulas walked over to the table to take a closer look at the clothing and armour. The clothing was comprised of a short-sleeved black tunic and a pair of dark leggings. Next to them was a purple breastplate with the symbol of a green dragon.

Ramulas marvelled at the breastplate as he picked it up. The dragon symbol seemed to move as he held it.

He placed it back on the table and looked at Oriel. 'What is this thing?'

Oriel laughed. 'It is a breastplate made from ancient magic. It will enhance your magical abilities slightly. But this will take time. Try your new uniform on.'

Ramulas nodded, removed his vest, and reached for the tunic on the table. Within a few moments, Ramulas had changed into his new outfit. Oriel guided him to a mirror.

Ramulas stood in front of the mirror and looked at a stranger. The man in the mirror did indeed look like someone who could lead an army. The breastplate shimmered with each movement.

Ramulas opened and closed his hands a few times. He was becoming accustomed to his new gauntlets—they were made of a purple material that ran from his elbows to his hands. The top half of Ramulas' fingers were left exposed.

As Ramulas opened and closed his hands, the material would ripple and shift. His knee-high boots were made of the same material; he could feel them move to compensate for any minor move he made.

Ramulas could see that he come a long way since he first met Oriel. That felt like a lifetime ago.

A lifetime ago, was how long it had been since Ramulas had seen his family. A pang of loneliness that he had avoided for so long came back to haunt him.

Oriel walked up to Ramulas, placing a hand on his shoulder. 'Your family will arrive soon.'

'I know,' Ramulas said, fighting back his emotions. 'But I need some time to think.'

'Before you go, I want you to remember that everything you have done is for a purpose. If you stop now, everything you love will suffer.'

8

Remus stood with the warlords and red wizards.

They watched as the blue energy strands swam in patterns through the black hole. Occasionally, it would turn back on itself like an eel in a small bucket.

This would cause brief flashes of bright light, and within the light, they were able to see into Oriel's new world. Remus waved his hand through the air, and the image of Oriel's world hung before them.

From what they saw, Remus knew that the exit doorway would be inside a crude dwelling. The walls comprised a jigsaw of materials—mainly cloth, sticks, and mud. Remus was confident that the doorway's growth would not be hampered by the dwelling.

Remus allowed himself a short feeling of satisfaction before pushing it away. He would not be content until the First Legion had crossed into Oriel's world.

Remus wanted to ensure that once the doorway was opened, the First Legion could walk through immediately. He knew that the magic controlling the passageway was very unstable and wanted the legion on Oriel's world before it collapsed.

Remus walked away from the black hole. He needed to see the legion.

***

He arrived at the training grounds. The legion was formed into squares of ten ranks and ten files, making one hundred soldiers.

These formations were spaced across the grounds into ten columns of ten, making ten thousand of the First Legion that would invade Oriel's world.

'Greetings, my lord.' Redemption's voice came from beside him.

Remus inwardly grimaced. He had not seen or heard Redemption come up to him. Remus looked to the man at his side with grudging respect. Along with Retribution and Reckoning, they made up the three captains of the First Legion.

The three were dressed identically: hooded cloaks with a polished piece of bone across their eyes. A narrow slit had been cut in the bone allowing them to see.

They wore armour plating under their cloaks. Each had a set of weapons that they were proficient with; however, their most impressive feature was their ability to communicate with each other telepathically.

'The portal will be ready shortly,' Remus said. 'How fast can the First Legion be ready to travel?'

Redemption looked down into the training grounds. Reckoning and Retribution walked amongst the legion and clapped once in unison. The First Legion scattered like leaves in the wind. They ran through archways surrounding the training grounds. A few minutes later, they had returned, each with a pack on their back, and returned to their columns. The legion began an orderly march toward the black hole.

Within fifteen minutes, the legion lined the passageway in columns near the black hole, Remus estimated it would take another half an hour for the legion to walk through into Oriel's world.

Remus was satisfied but did not want the legion to become complacent.

'Keep the legion training,' he said to the three captains. 'We need to be ready when the portal opens.'

Without a word, the legion turned and walked back to their training grounds.

***

Ramulas walked through Sanctuary with the hell hounds close behind. For the past few hours, Pip had seen the pain and conflict written across Ramulas' face. She had noticed him in his new armour and wanted to say how good he looked, but then she saw the sadness in his eyes.

Pip approached Ramulas to ask what was wrong. Ramulas replied that he was fine; even though Pip wanted to press the issue, she knew that Ramulas needed some time alone. He would come to her when she was ready.

Doubts and uncertainties had entered Ramulas' thoughts. He was now at Sanctuary waiting for his army, and people who would help him train them, to arrive.

Sanctuary was now his new home; however, Ramulas felt an emptiness within himself being apart from his family. Without his family, nothing felt right.

The sun had begun to drop behind the mountains, throwing shadows over Sanctuary. Ramulas watched these shadows as Emily came up to him.

'I have something to show you,' she said, taking his hand. 'You need to come with me.'

Ramulas wanted to make an excuse as to why he could not come. Then he saw determination in Emily's features—there was something she was not telling him.

'What do you want to show me?' he asked.

'Come with me,' Emily answered as she led him out into the clearing.

Curiosity helped Ramulas' decision as they walked into the forest. Emily released his hand and walked ahead deeper into the trees. Ramulas became confused as they walked away from Sanctuary, his only distraction was the two hell hounds walking by his side.

He asked Emily a few times where they were going—she simply replied that they would arrive soon. The light in the forest had begun to fade, and Ramulas heard a humming sound coming from behind.

He turned to find the forest empty, and the humming had moved to his left. Both hell hounds ran into the trees after the sound. Once they disappeared, Tilly came out of the trees to Ramulas' right.

'Why are you in my home?' The sprite asked.

'Emily wanted to show me something,' Ramulas said with a smile. 'Where are your dryad friends?'

'The dryads are close, and they watch you,' Tilly said before flying away as her wings hummed.

Emily gave the sprite a quick glance before continuing down the path.

'Have you seen that sprite before?' Ramulas asked Emily.

She nodded. 'Tilly lives with the dryads.'

Ramulas wanted to ask more, but then the forest opened before him. As Ramulas walked into the clearing, he saw a pool surrounded by various smooth rocks.

'What is this place?' Ramulas asked.

'This is our sacred place,' a familiar female voice said behind Ramulas.

He quickly turned to see the female dryad he had met when he was camping with Pip. She moved gracefully toward him with a smile on her face.

'It is time for you to meet our family,' she said, waving behind Ramulas. I am known as Eady.'

Ramulas turned to see at least two hundred dryad adults and children step out of the trees, his mouth fell open and his eyes widened. Ramulas had so many questions to ask, but all those questions disappeared as a little girl ran towards him.

'Da!' Grace shouted with a smile on her face.

***

Grace had just helped her mother clean the table after supper when she heard the voices. They were calling for her to come outside.

Grace looked to her mother and Kate to see if they had heard it as well. When they showed no reaction, she was unsure what to do.

After the king's magician had visited them, her mother had been very worried about someone coming to take her away. If Grace went outside, she would get into trouble. The voices called for her again. 'The dryads have come back,' she announced.

'How do you know?' Jacqueline asked in shock.

'I can hear them calling, they want me to come outside to play with them.'

'Let's see what they want,' Jacqueline said. 'Grace, take me to them.'

Grace led Jacqueline and Kate outside, and they were met by two adult dryads. Eady smiled when she saw Grace. 'We have something special for you.'

'What is it?' Grace asked excitedly.

'Your da is near us, and we can take you to him.'

Grace squealed and clapped her hands.

'Where is Ramulas?' Jacqueline asked.

'In our forest at the foot of the Devil's Ridge Mountains.'

'How are you taking Grace to Ramulas? I want to see Ramulas,' Jacqueline said.

Eady slowly shook her head. 'It will not be possible for you to see Ramulas.'

'Why?'

'Grace is a part of us, which means that with our help, she can walk through trees. It would be a very bad thing if we took you into the trees.'

'Then bring Ramulas to us here,' Jacqueline said.

'He would not survive. Therefore, Grace needs to go to him.'

Grace ran up to her mother and jumped around excitedly. 'I want to see Da!'

'No. You are not leaving my side until your father has returned.'

Grace stopped jumping and hung her head in defeat.

'Ramulas needs to train an army before the legion comes to the kingdom,' Eady said. 'But he is losing faith within himself—a visit from Grace will remedy that. If Ramulas loses faith and hope, he will walk away from his quest. Oriel has shown us the horrors of the legion.'

Jacqueline weighed up the importance of Ramulas doing what needed to be done, what Shigar had told her about moving into a castle, and the protective instinct of a mother who wanted to keep her girls close.

'It will only be for a few moments,' the dryad reassured her. 'We know Grace is special to you. We will watch over her.'

Jacqueline was swayed by the dryad's words, and even though she felt uneasy, something inside said that this was the right thing to do.

'Will you be with Grace the whole time?' Jacqueline asked.

Eady nodded. 'Of course. I will not leave her side.'

'Grace, you can go,' Jacqueline said. 'I will wait here with Kate until you return.'

Grace squealed and ran up to the dryads. The female dryad held Grace's hand and knelt in front of her. 'You will need to close your eyes before you enter the tree, can you do that?'

Grace nodded and was taken to the tree. Grace closed her eyes and started walking with the dryad, holding her hand.

Grace felt like she was walking down a very narrow hallway.

Then suddenly, Grace felt open space around her.

'You can open your eyes now.'

Grace opened her eyes and found that she was in the sacred grove with all the dryads.

Then she saw her da.

Grace ran as fast as her legs could carry her.

***

Ramulas fell to his knees and held his arms open while tears of joy streamed down his face. Grace collided with her father and wrapped her arms around his neck so tightly that Ramulas found it hard to breath.

Ramulas did not care. He held onto his daughter, cherishing the moment.

Then Ramulas released Grace and held her at arm's length to look at her. It was then that he noticed something different about his youngest daughter.

Ramulas saw Grace's glowing green eyes.

'Your eyes,' Ramulas said in shock. 'What happened to your eyes?'

Then Ramulas saw that the eyes of all the dryads were glowing green as well. Tilly flew out of the trees to land beside Grace.

'Grace has become one with the forest,' the sprite said.

'What do you mean?'

'She is one of us,' Tilly said before flying back into the forest.

Ramulas turned to Grace, who watched Tilly in amazement.

'Little one, tell me—what happened to your eyes?' Ramulas asked.

'I fell into the mystic pool.'

Eady walked over to Ramulas and explained what had happened since Grace fell into the mystic pool—the dryad children coming to his farm, and the dryads meeting Jacqueline and Kate.

Then Grace said something which filled Ramulas with joy. 'Shigar came to see us. He said we were going to live in a castle. Is that true, Da?'

Ramulas smiled at his youngest girl. 'Yes. I am living in the castle now.'

Grace gasped and her eyes widened.

Eady walked next to Grace. 'We need to bring this one home. Her mother will be worried.'

Ramulas hugged Grace. 'I love you very much and I am so proud of you. I want you to look after your mother and Kate. You are now the boss of the house.'

He watched with a smile as Grace swaggered toward the tree, swelling with pride. Two dryads walked into the tree with her.

Ramulas turned to Eady. 'Can you take me to my family?'

She shook her head. 'I cannot now—you are not one of us. Entering the trees now would mean a painful death. Grace is one of us; that is why she can walk through the trees.'

She waved her hand and the dryads in the clearing began to melt into the trees.

'Do you feel better now that you have seen Grace?'

Ramulas nodded.

'Then have faith,' Eady said before walking into a tree.

He was left in the sacred grove by himself. The mystic pool seemed to shine with magical light as the fish swam through the water. Curious, Ramulas began to walk to the pool.

'It is time to go back to Sanctuary.'

Ramulas turned to Emily and the hell hounds by the edge of the forest. 'Where did you go before?'

'Oriel wants to talk to you.'

Ramulas took one last look around the sacred grove before walking into the forest with Emily and the hell hounds.

***

Ramulas walked into Oriel's room to find her waiting for him. He had been deep in thought about seeing Grace.

'Hello, Ramulas. How are you feeling after seeing Grace?'

'I feel better. Now I want to see Jacqueline and Kate.'

'They will arrive shortly,' Oriel said. 'But there is something that you have forgotten.'

Oriel saw the confused expression and waved her hand. Ramulas' weapons floated before him. Without thinking, he reached out and took both in his hands. Ramulas smiled as they transformed into weapons of silver.

'You will need to train; it is something you did in your old life to build your magic. There is a room directly below this one—you will use that for training.'

Holding his weapons, Ramulas felt the hunger for training return to him. 'Thank you, Oriel.'

She smiled. 'What are you waiting for? Go downstairs and train.'

With a curt nod, Ramulas left and made his way to the training room. He entered the room to find four legion soldiers waiting for him. He knew they were magical animations made from straw, but they were real enough to hurt him.

As Ramulas walked towards them, the legion soldiers looked at him with open hatred and unsheathed their swords. The soldiers knew they were unable to move until Ramulas gave the command.

Ramulas knew the legion soldiers would do their best to kill him. Any mistake by Ramulas could be his last.

He walked over and activated two soldiers.

As they rushed forward, Ramulas spun to his left and twisted his weapons before him. The war hammer blocked a downward stroke by the first soldier, and then the battle axe followed, opening the soldier's stomach and spilling entrails at his feet. Ramulas stepped back, and the remaining soldier rushed in.

The soldier slipped on the blood and entrails, leaving himself open as his arms flailed in the air. Ramulas swung his war hammer, and it crushed the soldier's head and broke his neck with a resounding crack.

As Ramulas looked down at the two bodies, Pip stepped out from behind a curtain.

With a stern expression, she aimed her crossbow at Ramulas' back and fired.

***

Jacqueline felt the anxiety build within her as soon as Grace entered the tree. For the first two minutes, she had put on a brave face for Kate's sake. Now her resolve had begun to crumble. With each moment that passed, she came closer to breaking down.

By the time Grace returned, Jacqueline and Kate were frantic. They both rushed in and almost crushed Grace with their embrace.

After a few moments, Jacqueline released Grace. 'Did you see your father?'

Grace nodded excitedly. 'Da said I had to look after you and Kate. I saw him with the dryads. He lives in a castle.'

Jacqueline was almost overcome with relief. Ramulas was well and had spoken to Grace. Shigar's words—they would be living in a castle— came back to her.

'Da said I have to look after you and Kate, and I am the boss of the house,' Grace said proudly.

Her pride deflated when Jacqueline and Kate laughed.

Jacqueline's worry about Ramulas disappeared as she wondered about their new life in Sanctuary.

***

Ramulas turned when he heard the click of the crossbow. He saw Pip and focused. Everything slowed around him. Ramulas saw the bolt slowly floating towards him and then saw Pip throw four knives his way.

Ramulas ducked under the bolt and came up with both weapons spinning to deflect the knives.

Everything returned to normal, and Pip's hands were a blur as she pulled out more throwing knives.

'Stop!' Ramulas shouted as he used his magical ability.

He pictured a wall pushing into Pip. As Pip threw the knives, she was thrown off her feet, and the knives went wide.

'Hey, that's not fair,' Pip complained.

Ramulas felt anger grow inside of him. 'Why did you attack me?'

'Because Oriel told her to,' Michael said as he stepped out from behind another curtain.

'What are you doing here?' Ramulas asked in shock. 'I thought you had left with Miles and Benji.'

Michael smiled as he walked over to Ramulas. 'I only went with them a short way to ensure they returned with what Sanctuary needs. My quest is different to theirs; I will be leaving tomorrow.'

'What is your quest?' Ramulas asked.

Michael gave a knowing wink. 'It's a secret. I will tell you when I return.'

His answer had thrown Ramulas off balance and did not know how to respond.

Michael saw the confusion and said, 'Oriel sent Pip and me down here to help you train. So, less talking and more training.'

***

The next morning, Ramulas walked into Oriel's room to find her looking out of the window.

She turned to him with a smile. 'Ramulas, I know that you are in need of answers. Come to the window. I wish to show you something.'

He walked over to Oriel who held out her hand. As Ramulas placed his hand in hers, he felt himself rising off the floor. Ramulas looked at

Oriel as they floated out of the window. She gave his hand a reassuring squeeze as they floated to the top of the castle.

'Look down at Sanctuary,' Oriel said. 'Very soon, it will be alive with people. When they arrive, there is much work to be done.'

Ramulas looked down at Sanctuary and, for the first time, noticed a waterfall at the rear of the town. It flowed off the cliff face to feed a small lake. 'That waterfall was not there before.'

'It is one of the things from the Sanctuary of old. This is a sign that Sanctuary is coming back to life,' Oriel said before waving to the mountain in front of them. 'Do you see the light coming from within the mountain?'

Ramulas saw a faint light that seemed to emanate from within the rocks. It was halfway between the waterfall and the maze.

Ramulas nodded. 'What is it?'

'That is where my cavern is. It is where I am trapped. You must dig through the mountain to free me. The rock from within the mountain must be placed into the pit near the north side of the maze. As you place materials into the pit, they will help repair the maze and Sanctuary.'

Ramulas looked over at the maze. Even though the walls were moving, they were crumbling and falling apart. Then Ramulas saw a light shining in the pit.

'The maze is one of Sanctuary's defences. The walls will move to slow any enemy. It is important for the maze to be fixed.'

'I do not know anything about digging into the mountains.'

'People with the proper skills will come to help you do what needs to be done,' Oriel said.

After hearing about the maze, Ramulas remembered what he had seen before. 'After I dropped the purple ball from the top tower, Pip and I saw the maze walls begin to move. What magic is that?'

Oriel smiled. 'Once the maze is fully restored, it will have the ability to move of its own accord. This will separate an invading army and confuse them. It is part of Sanctuary's ancient magic'.

Oriel brought Ramulas back to her room where they found Pip waiting for them.

9

Michael rode out into the clearing; he could feel the ancient magic coming from the maze. It was the kind of magic he had not felt in over one hundred years.

It was an old and very powerful magic.

This made him think of Ramulas and the magical abilities he saw in him. Ramulas knew that he had magical abilities; however, he was unaware of his true potential.

As he rode into the forest, Michael could feel movement all around him. This felt out of place, yet somehow very much part of the forest. Michael stopped his horse and climbed to the ground.

He looked at the trees around him before walking up to an old oak tree. Michael placed his left hand on the trunk and began to massage the surface. After a few seconds, he found what he was looking for.

Michael smiled and slowly pulled at the trunk of the tree. At first, the shape of an arm could be seen. Then the rest of the body followed.

Standing before Michael was a male dryad. Michael released his grip and was rewarded with a smile.

'Well met,' Michael said.

'How did you know of my presence?' the dryad asked.

'Your kind radiates a special magic. I see it as others would see smoke rising from a campfire.'

'Then you know that I am not alone.'

Michael felt movement around him as dryads stepped out from the trees. He counted two score. Michael smiled and held up his hands to show that he did not carry weapons.

The original dryad spoke again. 'As you can see us within the tree, we can also see that you are more than what you appear to be.'

'How much of my true form can you see?'

'We know that you are more than a mortal being, because we cannot be seen by people unless we allow it.'

'You are new to this forest,' Michael said. 'I did not feel you when I came through earlier.'

'We live in this forest and the one south of here. We came in answer to a call.'

Michael nodded. 'So Ramulas' call has been answered by more than just people.'

'We first met Ramulas in the south forest when he travelled to Sanctuary. We felt power within him then.'

'I am able to see his power as well.'

'How many will come to his call?' the dryad asked.

Michael shrugged. 'I cannot be sure. I am on the way to Bremnon for a quest.'

'That will take you a day by horse.'

'Yes, it will,' Michael replied.

'I can make this journey shorter for you,' the dryad said. 'Cover your horse's eyes with a blanket.'

Michael looked at the dryad, waiting for an explanation, but the dryad simply gestured to the horse. Michael placed the blanket on the horse's head, and the dryad stepped closer to him.

'Whatever occurs,' the dryad said, 'do not open your eyes until I tell you. This is how dryads travel. This would bring a painful death to a person, but you are different.'

Michael closed his eyes and felt the rough hand of the dryad on his forearm.

He felt himself being led into the tree. It was as if Michael and his horse were walking down a very narrow tunnel. After a few moments, the tunnel seemed to open once more, and Michael felt the sun on his face.

'We are at the edge of what is called the Darkwood. You may open your eyes,' the dryad said.

As Michael blinked a few times, the words of the dryad sunk in. 'The Darkwood is fifty miles from Sanctuary, how did we come here?'

The dryad smiled. 'This how we travel. We call it tree-walking. Bremnon is two hours to the west.'

The dryad peered into the heart of the Darkwood for a moment. 'There has been a shift in the balance between good and evil. You need to leave this place now.'

As Michael turned to study the Darkwood, the dryad melted into the tree. He felt something dark and evil coming towards him. Michael removed the blanket from the horse's head and felt despair wash over him.

Michael quickly climbed onto the horse and rode.

He raced from the Darkwood, and the feeling of despair became stronger. Hoots and grunts could be heard from the trees, and they were coming closer.

Michael looked back to see six trolls racing towards him. They were tall with bluish-grey skin and had short dark hair and a mouthful of impossibly long teeth.

They let out a hoot when they saw Michael and increased their speed. Michael slapped his horse's rump, willing it to go faster.

The trolls were gaining on him. Michael knew that his horse would tire soon—it had not been trained to run great distances.

The horse increased its speed, but the trolls were still gaining. They were ten feet from his horse when they turned to stone and crumbled to the ground.

Michael pulled his horse to a stop and looked back at the pile of rocks that were previously trolls. It was then that Michael saw a faint blue wall two hundred yards from the Darkwood.

He gazed at the almost translucent wall in front of him, wondering who or what could have placed this here, and for what reason?

***

Riding alone gave Michael time to think. Since coming to this world, he had become accustomed to the loss of most of his powers. All that separated him from people were the gifts of sight and persuasion. Neither of these abilities would have helped if the trolls had caught up with him.

Michael knew that sacrifices needed to be made.

Such was the sacrifice he made in order to find his lost brother, and he accepted the human form he was given.

Michael rode into Bremnon just after midday and knew that he would find another to join him on his journey. Michael ignored the people and noise around him. He focused on a blue shaft of light that shot into the sky.

Within a few moments, Michael stood outside a workshop.

He walked inside to find an array of wagons in different stages of repair.

'Good day to you, sir. How can I help you?' a man called from the rear of the workshop.

Michael saw a short, wiry man whose face was almost invisible under his dark hair and bushy beard. He walked towards Michael, wiping his hands on his overalls.

The man was bathed in blue light.

Michael knew he had found the right person. 'Hello, Thomas. We have a mutual friend who is in need of your help.'

Confusion crossed Thomas' face. 'How do you know my name? And who is this friend?'

'I am talking about Ramulas,' Michael said, coming towards Thomas.

'Ramulas?' Thomas whispered. 'I have not seen him in a while.' Then Thomas' demeanour changed as he became defensive. 'How do I know this is not some trick to hand me over to the king's agents? The sheriff is looking for him and his family.' Thomas crossed his arms and looked defiantly at Michael. 'I will not say another word.'

'I met Ramulas a few days ago; he is safe,' Michael said. 'He is on a quest and needs all the help he can get. Something very bad is coming to this world, and Ramulas is the only one who can stop it. I have come to bring his family to Sanctuary.'

'Sanctuary?'

'It is a town at the foot of the Devil's Ridge Mountains. This is where Ramulas is now living.'

'Why doesn't Ramulas come back here after they stop searching for him?' Thomas asked. 'This is his home.'

Michael shook his head. 'Not anymore. Ramulas needs to train an army. They will be the only hope for this world.'

Michael pulled a red gem out of his cloak and placed it on the counter in front of Thomas. 'Place this in a bowl of water.'

Thomas looked doubtful as he went into the rear of the workshop. A moment later, he returned with a bowl of water. Thomas looked at Michael as he dropped the gem into the water. The water in the bowl instantly began to boil, and steam flowed over the edges and covered the counter. Thomas took a cautious step back but did not take his eyes off the bowl.

After a few seconds, the water in the bowl calmed, and a light shone through the mist.

'It is quite safe to look in the bowl now,' Michael said.

Michael walked over to the bowl and waved his hand. The mist dispersed and the light from the bowl lit up their faces.

The image inside the bowl was of Sanctuary at the base of the mountains. 'This is Sanctuary,' Michael said.

'Where is Ramulas?'

Michael smiled as he moved his hands around the edges of the bowl. The image in the bowl changed with the movement of Michael's hands.

Sanctuary grew larger, and it seemed as if they were moving towards the town. As Sanctuary came closer, Thomas noticed groups of people coming through the forest towards the town.

The image focused on the courtyard in front of the castle. It grew large enough for Thomas to recognise Ramulas in his armour. He gasped when he saw two hell hounds by Ramulas' side.

Ramulas smiled and greeted people as they came into the town.

A young woman in armour and covered in throwing knives always stayed close to Ramulas.

'Those are hell hounds!' Thomas exclaimed.

'They are like Ramulas' pets,' Michael explained. 'He has a way with animals. The girl with the knives is Pip, a former thief from Keah.'

'How is all of this possible?'

'Ramulas is a very special person with magical abilities.'

Thomas remembered the changes he had seen in Ramulas the last time they met; things began to fall into place.

Then then gem vibrated until the bowl broke, sending water across the counter.

'Ramulas needs support. I want you to come with me to Sanctuary and bring his family with us.'

Thomas looked at Michael in shock. 'I cannot leave this store to go to the Devil's Ridge Mountains.'

'If Ramulas is not successful, your workshop, as well as this whole town, will be burnt to the ground. The same thing will happen to all the towns across the kingdom. The people will be killed or enslaved.'

'But we are under the protection of the king and his army,' Thomas argued. 'They will help us.'

Michael slowly shook his head. 'The king's army would not stand a chance against the forces that are coming. Ramulas is the only one with the power to stop them.'

As Michael spoke, he used his powers of persuasion on Thomas. 'Allow me to speak to you in more detail; then you will see why you will need to join us in Sanctuary.'

Thomas' eyes glazed over as Michael spoke. Thomas closed the workshop and began talking with Michael.

***

'I didn't know that you could fly,' Pip said as Oriel and Ramulas came back into the room.

'There are many things that I am capable of,' Oriel said. 'As I become stronger, I will be able to protect Sanctuary.'

'When will more people come?' Pip asked.

'Over one hundred people have heard the call. They make their way to Sanctuary from across the kingdom.'

'One hundred!' Ramulas said in shock. 'That will not be enough to stop the legion. We need more people.'

Oriel smiled. 'For now, one hundred people will suffice. More will follow. If you are to lead an army, you will first need to gain confidence in dealing with people. It will be better for you to start with a small number of people. We only have one chance at beating the legion.'

The enormity of what Ramulas had to do began to weigh on his shoulders. 'I will need people to help me train this army.'

Oriel nodded. 'People will come to help you. But first, you need to have faith and believe in yourself. You must be the one who protects those who are unable to protect themselves.

'You will find that people would rather die fighting for something they believe in, rather than live on their knees. They just need someone to show them the way. That person is you, Ramulas.'

Pip had become bored and tossed a throwing knife from hand to hand. This triggered a question Ramulas wanted to ask.

'Why did you ask Pip to attack me while I was training with the legion soldiers?'

'You need to be aware of attacks from everywhere, not just what you can see. You have become used to fighting the four legion soldiers, but you ignore everything else around you. Pip will help you become ready for these situations.'

'So, are you saying that Pip will attack me again from behind?'

Oriel shook her head. 'No. You and Pip will be fighting the legion soldiers' side-by-side.'

'What!?' Ramulas and Pip said in unison.

'When Pip has spare time, she will train with you.'

'But that will be dangerous,' Ramulas said. 'I could hit her with my weapons. How am I to fight without hitting her?'

'You both will need to learn how to work as a team.'

'When are we to do this?' Pip asked.

'Now would be a good time,' Oriel replied.

***

Michael woke to noises coming from the workshop below. Thomas had invited him to stay for the night. They had stayed awake until the early hours of the morning talking about Ramulas.

He came down to find Thomas fixing two teams of horses to two carts.

'Morning, Thomas. I am glad to see you awake early.'

'I found it hard to sleep after what we talked about last night. I woke up for the first time in my life knowing what I needed to do. If we are to help Ramulas, then he will need supplies. And that is why we need the carts.'

'You seem ready to start your journey, then,' Michael said.

Within ten minutes, they reached the market where vendors were setting up their stalls. Thomas climbed down from his cart and walked over to Michael.

'Stay with the carts while I barter for supplies.'

Michael watched as Thomas spoke to two vendors. In a few moments, both vendors began yelling at each other and Thomas. A sheriff came over to the vendors and Thomas walked away smiling.

'What happened over there?' Michael asked.

Thomas shrugged. 'In exchange for supplies from both vendors, I have promised my store and contents. They are fighting to see who will give me more. That vendor will own more of the workshop.'

'Are you sure this is what you want?'

Thomas looked at Michael with a sad smile. 'My whole life, I have done things to make others happy. I have always felt that something was missing. Now, with what you have told me, I think I will take this opportunity to change my life.'

Michael was amazed at the amount of supplies Thomas received: sacks of wheat, corn, building materials, and countless foodstuffs. When both carts were full, they were covered, and the pair rode out of Bremnon.

Thomas took one last look around the town. He had a feeling it would be the last time he laid eyes on it.

***

Thomas led Michael to a farm outside of Bremnon. They slowed the carts as they approached the house, and Thomas stared at the burned ruins in shock as tears ran down his cheeks.

'I had heard rumours, but I had hoped this had not happened. Where are Jacqueline and the girls?'

Michael scanned the area and soon found the two girls close by. 'The two girls are hiding one hundred yards past the old barn, amongst the crops.'

Thomas jumped onto his seat and called out. 'Kate, Grace! It is Thomas! Come out!'

For a few moments, there was no movement, and then the two girls stood and walked over to the cart warily. They stopped at the edge of the field and gazed fearfully at Michael.

Thomas jumped down from the cart and opened his arms. 'Come to me. Tell us what transpired here.'

He saw their eyes dart to Michael, and he waved them over. 'This is Michael. He is a friend of your father's; he wants to take us to see him.' At the mention of Ramulas, both girls smiled and raced to his cart. 'Take us to your mother so we can talk with her.'

Both girls nodded and turned, pointing behind them. 'We're staying at Matthew's farm,' Kate said. 'We can take you there.'

Thomas followed the girls along an old path with Michael close behind, making their way through groves of trees until they saw an old hut in the distance. The girls ran ahead, calling for their mother. Jacqueline waited for them by the front door when they arrived.

Jacqueline crossed her arms and glared at Michael. 'Hello, Thomas. Who is this you've brought with you?'

Thomas nodded to the other cart. 'This is Michael; he brings news of Ramulas.'

'What news?' Jacqueline asked eagerly as her resolve softened.

Both girls turned to Michael with their mother. Michael smiled when he saw Grace's green eyes and faint purple flames dancing upon her shoulders.

'I have come from a place called Sanctuary, where Ramulas is living. He would like for his family to come to him.' Michael smiled. 'We have come from your farm, and you will have a place to live with your husband.'

Kate and Grace cheered as they jumped up and down, while Jacqueline frowned at the memory of running from the sheriff.

'How do we know that you have been with my husband?'

Michael smiled and removed his travel cloak to reveal his armour. Once the cloak was removed, Grace squealed. 'Da has the same dragon on his clothes!'

Jacqueline allowed her heart to fill with hope. 'Are you sure, Grace?'

Grace quickly nodded. 'Da had a green dragon on his chest when I saw him with the dryads.'

'You know of the dryads?' Michael asked.

'Yep,' Grace said. 'I play with them, and they took me to Da.'

Jacqueline stepped forward and motioned for Grace to be quiet. 'Why doesn't Ramulas come to us?'

'If Ramulas does not train his army, everyone in the kingdom will suffer, and all farms will be burnt to the ground, but Ramulas needs his family to be with him to do these things. Oriel can only help him so much.'

'Ramulas is with Oriel?' Jacqueline asked.

Michael nodded. 'Yes, she is with him every day.'

After a moment, Jacqueline's mind was made up. She had overcome the displeasure of Oriel coming to her home in the fog. Ramulas was only supposed to have been gone for a week to drop the crystal in the mountains before returning home.

Since the visit from Shigar, Jacqueline had heard nothing.

Now Michael stood before her saying Ramulas needed his family.

However, the words which played loudest in Jacqueline's mind, was that Ramulas was spending time with Oriel.

Michael spoke, interrupting her thoughts. 'When the legion come to this world, they will seek you out to use you and your girls as a tool against Ramulas, because he is the one who protects Oriel.'

'What do we need for the journey?' Jacqueline asked, knowing they didn't have many possessions.

'Mainly clothing and anything else you can fit into the carts.'

'When do we leave?'

'As soon as you are ready.'

Jacqueline turned to Grace and Kate. 'Girls, pack your things; we are going to see your father.'

***

Both carts were loaded and items tied down. Jacqueline sat next to Michael in his cart. Her thoughts were a thousand miles away. So much had changed since the fog and Oriel had come into their lives.

She had accepted that Ramulas needed to drop the crystal in the mountains to stop an army from coming to their world, but then he was supposed to come home.

Now, Ramulas was in Sanctuary spending a lot of time with Oriel. Jacqueline wanted to see this Oriel for herself and remind her that Ramulas was her husband.

10

Remus walked swiftly through the hallways following the red wizard. He had just been told of an important development within the black hole. A few moments later, he joined the other warlords and red wizards.

The blue energy strand had grown twice its previous size and was constantly turning back on itself. This continued for a minute, filling the chamber with flashes of bright light.

Then the energy strand began to pulse and swell.

The strand exploded, sending streams of multi-coloured lights shooting out of the black hole. The warlords and red wizards covered their eyes while strong winds buffeted their robes. 'What's happening?!' Remus shouted over the wind.

'I do not know!' the red wizard screamed in reply. 'But this has never been done before!'

Then, as quickly as it started, the wind and streams of energy stopped.

The silence was deafening.

Remus slowly took his arm away from his face to behold what stood before him. The black hole and blue energy stand had vanished. In their place stood a golden archway twice his height and wide enough for four men to walk abreast.

The arch was dark with small white lights dancing within.

'The portal is now open,' the red wizard said. 'We need to reinforce the passageway before we can travel to Oriel.'

'How long will that take?' Remus asked.

The red wizard waved his hands through the air while chanting. A moment later, one of the minute lights from the arch floated towards him and landed on the palm of his hand. A worried expression crossed the red wizard's face, and then he paled.

'Tell me,' Remus ordered.

'The passageway will take longer than we anticipated. The walls are more unstable than we first thought.'

'How long until we are able to walk through?' Remus asked as he stepped closer to the red wizard.

'It will take months before it will be safe to enter the passageway.'

'What!?' Remus said with barely contained rage. 'That is what I was told when Oriel first escaped.'

The red wizard gave a weak shrug. 'If we enter sooner with the First Legion, the portal will close in on itself. This could happen at any stage, and those caught in the passageway will be sent into unknown worlds. We need time to strengthen the portal and passageway.'

While the red wizard spoke, Remus made mental calculations. Oriel would fully mature in about twelve months. He needed to reach Oriel by then in order to consume her magic; however, if they travelled to this world too early, it would jeopardise him finding Oriel.

They only had one chance of successfully going to Oriel's world and capturing her.

Sacrifices would have to be made, but he would need to be patient until the portal was ready.

'Do all that is necessary to open the portal as soon as you can,' Remus said before walking away.

The red wizard breathed a sigh of relief as Remus walked away. He had been certain that he would die for being the bearer of bad news. Then the Alpha, Beta, and Omega surrounded him. His eyes widened in shock as the warlords' hands began to glow.

The red wizard screamed as he burst into flames. The other red wizards looked on as their companion died a painful death. They knew that no more mistakes would be tolerated.

***

Pip dropped to one knee to stab a legion soldier inside his thigh and then stood to open his throat, only to roll away when Ramulas' war hammer hit the soldier in the face. The soldier collapsed to the ground; its face unrecognisable. Pip stood; half her face covered in blood.

'Are you trying to kill me?' she asked Ramulas. 'If I had not moved, you would have hit me.'

'I was only trying to help.'

'Next time, tell me what you are going to do,' Pip said.

They had been fighting the legion soldiers for half an hour. Oriel had given both of them a spell of protection to prevent either of them from being injured or killed.

Without this spell, Ramulas and Pip would have died many times over. Their main goal was to try to fight together as a team. They were both proficient as individual fighters; however, it was another thing to be able to fight alongside someone.

'Oriel wants to see you,' Emily said from the doorway.

Ramulas and Pip were both silently relieved at this interruption as they followed Emily.

'How goes your training?' Oriel asked as they entered the room.

Pip let out an exasperated sigh while pointing to Ramulas. 'He keeps trying to kill me and does not watch where he swings those weapons.'

'She does not stay out of my way,' Ramulas countered.

Oriel laughed and held up her hand. 'There are more important things at hand. People are coming into Sanctuary as we speak.'

Ramulas and Pip looked at each other before turning to Oriel.

'Before you meet them, I think it would be wise not to carry your weapons in your hands. Place them on your back in a cross formation.'

Ramulas was confused but followed her instructions. He flicked both weapons over his shoulders and onto his back. Once the weapons were on his back, Ramulas felt a slight shift in his armour.

'Release your weapons,' Oriel said.

Ramulas' eyes widened as he released his weapons, and they stayed on his back. 'How are they staying there?'

Pip ran behind him and gasped. 'Take your weapons off your back.'

Once they were off, Pip instructed Ramulas to place them on his back once more.

'When your weapons are on your back, part of your armour flows around the handles to hold them there.'

'You will need to greet the people coming into Sanctuary,' Oriel said.

***

Ramulas and Pip walked out into the courtyard in front of the castle and were greeted by the hell hounds. They could see a few groups of people coming down the passageway toward them.

Ramulas could feel both hell hounds becoming excited, especially Fenris. He sent calming thoughts to the hell hounds; the last thing he needed was to scare the new arrivals away. 'Hello, and welcome to Sanctuary,' Ramulas said.

A few of the people looked at the hell hounds with apprehension.

'Do not worry; the hell hounds are quite tame and will not hurt anyone,' he reassured them.

Ramulas counted fourteen people: one family and a few pairs travelling together. They openly looked at the town and castle in wonderment.

'Please make yourselves comfortable. Your housing will be arranged after you speak with Oriel,' Ramulas said.

One of the men stepped forward. 'I have come here for reasons beyond my understanding.' He waved a hand towards the man next to him. 'My brother and I felt something calling us here. We spent the journey from Turtha trying to make sense of this. Now that we are here, I still cannot tell you why.'

Ramulas smiled. 'I am Ramulas, and this is Pip. Since coming here, we have both experienced strange and wonderful things.'

'Oriel will see them in the castle now,' Emily said next to Ramulas.

'This is Emily. She will take you to see Oriel. She will explain why you came to Sanctuary.'

'What of our belongings?' the man asked.

'Your belongings will be safe, and your horses put into the stables.'

Emily took a group into the castle to see Oriel. As they left, they seemed hesitant. After a few minutes, they returned with hope in their eyes and told the others what a wonderful place Sanctuary was.

'We have found our new home,' one of them said as they took their belonging to one of the empty houses.

From that moment forward, there was no more hesitation.

Throughout the day, another twenty people arrived. The butterflies in Ramulas' stomach settled as he greeted more new residents. He was happy dealing with small groups of people but did not know how he would be with hundreds of people.

By the time Ramulas had welcomed the people and spent time in the stables with Rufus and the hell hounds, he was exhausted. By nightfall, he had no trouble falling asleep.

***

With Michael leading the way, both carts made it to the edge of Sanctuary's Forest an hour before sunset. Both girls were extremely excited during the journey. They constantly asked questions about their father and the town of Sanctuary. Thomas sat next to the girls and patiently answered all of their questions.

Jacqueline was focused and quiet. Her eyes were locked on the road ahead. When the Devil's Ridge Mountains came into view, she was transfixed by them. The only time she spoke was when she asked how much further to Sanctuary.

The shadows of the trees spilled out along the grass of the plains, and Michael and Thomas decided to make camp for the night.

***

Michael, Thomas, Jacqueline, and the girls sat around the campfire. They had finished supper and they listened to Michael's stories, and then a humming sound could be heard from the trees.

The sound moved from the left side of the camp to the right and then back again at high speed. Everyone around the campfire searched for the source of the sound.

Tilly burst out of the trees holding her short sword. 'Why do you camp in my home?'

Jacqueline, Kate, and Thomas leaned back with a mixture of surprise and fright. Michael sat silently, knowing the sprite would not harm them.

Grace jumped up excitedly and ran over to Tilly, who hovered just out of her reach. 'Have you come to play?'

'I have not come to play,' Tilly answered with a scowl. 'I have come to chase you from my home.'

'But we are going to Sanctuary to live in a castle with my da,' Grace explained.

Then Michael and Grace both saw the dryads within the trees.

'The dryads are here!' Grace shouted as she ran for the trees.

Two score dryads stepped out of the trees and into the camp.

'Aaaaaaghh! Monsters!' Thomas shouted as he jumped to his feet. He pulled a burning branch from the fire and held it before him. Thomas was on the verge of charging the dryads in sheer panic.

One of the dryads raised a fist towards Thomas and three small darts shot from its knuckles and struck Thomas in the chest.

Thomas gasped once while clutching his chest, and then he fell face-first to the ground. Grace looked up to see the rest of the dryads rush into their camp.

***

The next morning, Ramulas welcomed more people into Sanctuary. He knew that everyone who came to live there would need to re-create themselves and the whole township must work with one purpose if they were to survive.

Sanctuary was coming to life around him. The smells of food being cooked in the mornings, combined with children running around and people talking, gave the feeling of a proper town.

Both hell hounds sat by his side looking intently down the passageway. They communicated that someone was coming.

Ramulas looked to the passageway and saw Emily leading a white horse with several packs tied to it. 'Emily, where did that horse come from?'

'The man from across the sea gave it to me,' Emily replied. 'He is waiting for you to come and see him. He is in the clearing near the trees.'

'Then why does he not come into Sanctuary?'

'The man has something to show you, but you must see him in the clearing, and come alone.'

Ramulas looked at Emily and saw the intensity in her eyes. Ramulas' inner voice said that this man could be important for Sanctuary. Ramulas told the hell hounds to wait for him, and then he walked out into the clearing.

Ramulas walked out of the gate to find a man sitting at the edge of the clearing two hundred yards away. As he moved closer, he saw that the man was dressed in black leggings and a bright blue vest.

His legs were crossed and his head bowed, showing his short silver hair. Halfway across the clearing, Ramulas stopped.

He felt uneasy about the man across from him, but Ramulas was unable to work out why.

As soon as Ramulas stopped, the man raised his head and smiled at him. A cold chill ran through him, and he fought the urge to step back. The man waved for Ramulas to come closer.

'Hello,' Ramulas called as he stood his ground. 'I was told that you wanted to see me.'

'Please, you must come closer,' the man said in a sing-song voice as he waved once more.

Ramulas walked forward, and the man's features became clearer. He understood why Emily said this was a man from across the sea.

He had an olive complexion, a flat face with almond eyes, and wore strange clothes. Ramulas saw a curved sword on the man's lap when he was close and stopped.

'Please, you must come closer,' the man repeated.

Ramulas could not shake the feeling that this man was somehow dangerous. He investigated the forest, searching for anyone who might be there. Then Ramulas communicated with the animals of the forest. The man had come alone.

Ramulas was satisfied that they were alone. The man patted the ground before him and nodded to Ramulas.

'My name is Iguchi; I have come a long way to share valuable knowledge with you.'

'How do you know of me?'

'I have been told of your quest. Now, you must ready your weapons,' Iguchi said as he stood in a fluid motion.

'What are you doing?' Ramulas asked as he stepped back.

Iguchi stood with the point of his sword facing the ground. Ramulas noticed a smaller blade on Iguchi's hip.

'You will need your weapons,' Iguchi said.

Ramulas shook his head. 'There is no need for this.'

Iguchi's sword whipped out, the blade missing Ramulas' nose by a fraction of an inch. Ramulas heard the whistle as the blade cut through the air.

Ramulas took another step back, pulling out his weapons and holding them before him.

Iguchi smiled and stepped forward, kicking a cloud of dust and leaves into Ramulas' face. Ramulas raised both weapons and turned his face away. He realised his mistake when Iguchi rushed toward him.

Ramulas turned back at the last instant, swinging his war hammer to block Iguchi's sword. Ramulas realised he was too late when the flat of Iguchi's sword slapped him on the side of the face.

Iguchi ducked under the war hammer, kicking Ramulas inside his thigh. Ramulas quickly stepped back and struck out with his battle axe. Iguchi followed Ramulas as he stepped back, not giving him any room. He struck Ramulas in the midsection with his shoulder.

Ramulas was pushed back a few feet, and he struggled to breathe.

'You must learn how to fight when your breath is taken from you,' Iguchi said calmly as he watched Ramulas. 'Without control, it is hard to move.'

Ramulas was shocked.

He was able to defeat four legion soldiers in training, yet here was a man smaller than he was, and he was besting him. Frustration built within Ramulas as his breathing returned to normal.

He stepped towards Iguchi while turning his body and spinning his weapons. Ramulas heard steel on steel as Iguchi's sword rang off his weapons. Iguchi slowly backed away into the trees.

He dropped and rolled behind a tree. The tree shook as Ramulas' war hammer hit it.

Iguchi appeared behind Ramulas and punched him in the lower back. By the time Ramulas reacted, Iguchi was behind another tree.

'You need to touch me with your weapons while avoiding mine,' Iguchi said.

Ramulas stepped forward, jabbing his war hammer at Iguchi, who ducked behind a tree and came out of the other side. He slapped Ramulas on the back of his hand with the flat of the sword.

Ramulas turned, but Iguchi had moved behind another tree.

Ramulas ran to the left of the tree and then, at the last moment, twisted to the right, leading with his weapons. Iguchi somersaulted over the weapons as they came in low. He landed on Ramulas' shoulders, pushing down with all of his weight. This took Ramulas by surprise, sending him to his knees.

He turned to find Iguchi calmly waiting for him to pick himself up.

'You are very clumsy. Here you are attacking trees and falling over while I wait for you to fight me. Should I move slower for you?'

Ramulas felt frustration and confusion building within him. He had thought that he was a good fighter after training with the legion soldiers, but the way Iguchi moved made Ramulas feel clumsy.

'I was told you are to lead the people of this town,' Iguchi said with a dismissive snort. 'I think my horse will do a better job. I have not seen him trip over his own feet.'

Ramulas had had enough insults from Iguchi.

He rushed forward swinging both weapons at him. All attacks were parried by Iguchi's sword, or the strange man ducked out of the way.

'You must try harder,' Iguchi said.

Ramulas delivered an overhead chop; Iguchi stepped forward and was inside the swing. He struck Ramulas several times along his arms and body with ridged fingers, and pain shot through Ramulas' body.

Ramulas dropped both weapons and collapsed to the ground. He fought against the muscle spasms running through his body, but he could not move.

Iguchi walked over and stood over him. 'Things are not always what they seem. This lesson has come to an end.'

Iguchi brought his sword above his head. Ramulas watched as the sword came flashing down towards him, and his last thought was that he was unable to protect himself.

***

Michael woke to find it was daytime. Faint wisps of smoke rose from the embers of the previous night's fire. Looking around the camp, he saw that Thomas, Jacqueline, and the girls were starting to stir.

He smiled, remembering Thomas' reaction to the dryads.

Thomas had never seen dryads before and allowed the fear of the unknown to guide his actions. After he was shot and fell to the ground, the dryads removed the darts. They explained that the darts were coated with a sleeping potion.

By the time Thomas woke a few hours later, he discovered the dryads interacting with everyone. Jacqueline explained that the dryads were friends and meant no harm.

Thomas was not immediately convinced about the dryads; it took a while before he eventually let his guard down. Dryad children played with Kate and Grace while the adults spoke with Michael, Thomas, and Jacqueline.

The dryads stayed in the camp until just before dawn and then said their goodbyes and melted into the trees.

Both girls woke and were disappointed to find there were no dryads in the camp. Grace's emerald eyes glowed as she searched the trees. A moment later, Thomas and Jacqueline were awake.

'We will have something to eat,' Michael said. 'Then we will make our way to Sanctuary.'

'How far is it from here?' Jacqueline asked.

'We will arrive today,' Michael answered.

Michael looked toward the Devil's Ridge Mountains thinking about Ramulas. He had very strong magical abilities; all Ramulas needed to do was believe in himself. The lives of many depended on Ramulas becoming a leader, and that was a heavy burden to carry.

Not only did Ramulas need to accept his fate, but he also needed to embrace it.

***

Ramulas heard the sword whistle toward him as it came down. Then he felt a stinging sensation along his left cheek.

'It is done,' Iguchi said as he sheathed his sword. 'Now, are you so rude that you would not invite me into your home?'

Ramulas grunted, still trying to gain control of his muscles.

Iguchi bent down and touched Ramulas behind the left ear. He screamed in pain and curled in a foetal position. A moment later, the pain subsided and Ramulas had control of his body once more.

Ramulas touched his cheek and saw blood on his hand. 'What have you done? I am bleeding.'

'Of course, you are bleeding. I have uncovered something that has always been on your face.'

Ramulas stood and gathered his weapons. He saw that Iguchi looked toward Sanctuary. 'You do not wish to fight anymore?'

Iguchi shook his head. 'I did not fight you. If I had fought, you would be dead. I taught you a lesson.'

'Did I pass that lesson?'

'No. You have a long way to go. You stomp around like some great beast, but with proper training, you will be ready.'

'Who told you of my quest?'

'I have contact with the magician from Keah.'

A sense of relief and understanding came over Ramulas. This was another surprise from the magician. Oriel did say that people would come to help him.

Ramulas attached his weapons to his armour and led Iguchi into Sanctuary. He thought that this small man was one of the strangest people he had ever met.

He still could not believe how easily Iguchi had bested him in combat; he could have killed Ramulas but instead offered advice on training.

As they walked into the courtyard, Pip approached them with a concerned expression. 'Ramulas, what happened to your face?'

'I am fine,' he replied. 'My new friend had been showing me sword skills. I will take him to see Oriel.'

'This will suffice,' Iguchi said, looking up at the castle.

'What will suffice?' Ramulas asked.

'This will be my new home,' Iguchi said waving at the castle. 'It will do for now; then I will need a place to train my men.'

'Who are these men you are going to train?' Ramulas asked.

Iguchi looked around the courtyard. 'I do not see them yet, but when I do, you will be the first to know.'

Ramulas was baffled at Iguchi's strange behaviour, but he knew Oriel would find a role for him in Sanctuary. 'Come and see Oriel.'

'Who is Oriel?'

'She is someone important to Sanctuary,' Ramulas replied.

As they entered the castle, Iguchi saw a descending stairway. 'We need to go down there,' he said pointing to the stairs.

'But Oriel is upstairs,' Ramulas replied.

'Ah,' Iguchi said, pointing to Ramulas. 'But first, we need to tend to the wound on your face. I hear running water down there.'

Ramulas touched his cheek and felt the blood begin to thicken. 'This should have healed by now.'

Oriel had told Ramulas of his enhanced healing abilities, but the cut on his face was not healing. He followed Iguchi down two flights of stairs and wondered what they would find.

They arrived in a dim hallway and Ramulas was about to ask where the water was.

'Shh,' Iguchi said as he placed his hand over Ramulas' eyes. 'Close your eyes and clear your mind. There is too much noise inside your head.'

Ramulas closed his eyes and allowed the thoughts and worries to leave. After a moment, he could hear the trickle of water. Ramulas was amazed that he was able to hear it.

Iguchi removed his hand. 'You must learn to use what is inside of you.'

Ramulas followed Iguchi until they came to a small courtyard. He saw a fountain in the middle. It had water flowing from the mouth of a stone fish that sat on the fountain.

Moss could be seen inside the fountain. Iguchi walked over and took some moss in his hand and beckoned Ramulas to him.

'Leave this on; it will help with the healing,' Iguchi said as he slapped it onto Ramulas' face.

The moss felt cold and damp, it sent a tingling sensation through the wound. But Ramulas was unsure this would help heal his face.

'Where did you hear about moss healing wounds?'

'In my land, some people live in the forests. They have learnt to live with what Mother Earth gives them, and they then teach this skill to others.'

Iguchi removed the moss and pulled out a small metal star, which he handed to Ramulas. Ramulas took the star, and he was able to see his reflection on the surface of the star. A strange symbol had been carved into his cheek.

Ramulas knew that he had seen this symbol somewhere before, but he was unsure where, and the meaning of it was lost to him.

'What is this?' Ramulas asked as he handed back the star.

'Ah, this is a *shuriken*,' Iguchi said. 'Choose one of the flowers.'

Ramulas turned and saw there was a bush covered in purple flowers. 'The top one.'

Iguchi flicked his wrist and sent the shuriken flying. It became embedded in the wall behind the flowers.

'Ah ha!' Ramulas said. 'You missed.'

'Wait and watch closely,' Iguchi replied as he stared at the bush.

After a few moments, the top flower moved and fell.

'"Ah ha" to you,' Iguchi said.

11

Remus stood in front of the archway watching the minute white lights dance within. The red wizard that was killed had been replaced, and this one helped strengthen the passageway to Oriel's new world. Remus motioned for the replacement to come to him.

'Tell me what we can expect when we cross into Oriel's world.'

The red wizard chose his words carefully before speaking. 'From the feedback within the arch, we know that Oriel's world has the same seasonal patterns as our world. By the time we cross, it will be just before winter. The exit portal is situated on the top of a mountain range, and we are unable to feel Oriel's magic. This means she is a long way from the portal. We will search for her when we arrive.'

'This might be a good thing,' Remus said after some thought. 'We do not know what we will be facing. I do not want an army attacking our rear while we attempt to take Oriel. Staying over the winter months will help us to know the locals. If the winters are like ours, we could lose many men if we march through the snow.'

The red wizard sighed in relief; he had expected Remus to lash out and kill him.

'Continue feeding magic into the portal. I want to cross over as soon as possible,' Remus said to the other warlords and red wizards.

As Remus walked away, the red wizard thought about what was said.

The only reason Remus cared about losing men in the snow was that he wanted a large force to take Oriel. Once Remus was close to Oriel, he would waste many lives to get to her.

The red wizard did not want to be nearby when that occurred.

***

Ramulas led Iguchi up to the third floor and then down the hall to Oriel's room. Ramulas saw that Oriel appeared stronger again. He could also see her surrounded by a faint purple aura.

'Hello, Ramulas and Iguchi.'

'You are becoming stronger,' Ramulas said.

'Sanctuary is a place of ancient magic, and with people coming into the town, Sanctuary is returning to its former glory; this is what helps me become stronger.'

'Hello to you, spirit of the dragon,' Iguchi said as he bowed.

The statement, combined with the expression on Ramulas' face, brought a smile to Oriel's face.

'Why did you call her "spirit of the dragon"?' Ramulas asked Iguchi.

'In my homeland, there are stories of people who become possessed by the spirit of the dragon. Like Oriel, they are surrounded by light.'

'When I came into this world,' Oriel said. 'I was told by my father to search for the dragon. That is how I came to you, Ramulas.'

'What has a dragon got to do with me?' Ramulas asked.

'When you were younger and training as a battlemage, you immersed yourself in dragon lore to become stronger. At that time, you worked alongside Remus, who had no interest in dragon lore. The dragon magic was the connection that drew me to you.'

'Does that account for the symbol on my armour?'

'Yes,' Oriel replied. 'Where did the marking on your face come from?'

'Ask him,' Ramulas replied nodding to Iguchi.

'When giving my lesson, I saw the symbol just beneath the skin. I brought the symbol forth.'

Oriel smiled as she looked at Ramulas. 'You are the Avenger; it is you who will bring freedom to the people.'

'I don't understand,' Ramulas said. 'What is the Avenger? I have never heard of it.'

'On the world where you and I come from, there have been rumours of the Avenger,' Oriel said. 'These have been around for generations.'

'What rumours?' Ramulas asked.

'That one day, the Avenger will come to free the people from the warlords' rule. They described his features as being like Remus'. The only difference was the symbol on his face.'

Oriel walked to Ramulas and brushed the symbol on his cheek, and warmth flowed through him.

'When I first saw you, Ramulas, I looked for the magical symbol, and when I did not find it, I dismissed the rumours. But now, things have changed. Everyone from Remus to the beggars on the street of our world will know of the Avenger. The First Legion will hesitate when they see you.'

'It would be wise to strike down your enemy at this time,' Iguchi said.

'What?' Ramulas asked.

'You must learn to attack your opponent within a beat of your heart, with your mind clear of emotion,' Iguchi said.

'Yes, Ramulas,' Oriel added. 'You must take advantage of every opportunity if you are to face the First Legion.'

Oriel turned to Iguchi. 'You have come a long way and must be tired. I will be quick in what I need to show you.'

After Iguchi nodded, Oriel waved her hand to the wall, which turned white. A moment later, an image of the First Legion marching could be seen. Iguchi's swords appeared to jump into his hands.

'This is the First Legion,' Oriel said. 'They will come to this world. They will come for me and kill me.'

'They will do no such thing,' Iguchi stated.

Oriel smiled. 'I see that you have some useful talents. I would ask for you to train a small group in ways that have not been seen in this kingdom. Sanctuary will have its main army trained by others, but your group will be an army within an army. The men you train will be an elite force that will operate separately from the main army.'

'Am I to be a part of this elite group?' Ramulas asked.

Oriel shook her head. 'The people of Sanctuary will need a leader, and you will lead Sanctuary's main army.'

Oriel waved her hand once more and the image vanished from the wall.

'I watched the lesson Iguchi gave you, Ramulas. Why you did not use magic?'

'My magic?' Ramulas replied as he looked down at his hands. 'I did not think about it.'

As soon as Oriel mentioned his magic, Ramulas could feel the energies flowing through his body. He looked at the large table with candles. He focused on the closest candle, and it slid across the table.

Ramulas looked at Oriel, disappointed. 'I should have remembered my magic.'

'Do not be too hard on yourself; true leaders learn from their mistakes.'

'What else does it take to be a leader?' he asked.

'The first lesson is to listen to your people,' Iguchi said.

Oriel looked at Iguchi. 'Thank you for coming to Sanctuary. You will find everything you need in your room. If you need anything, talk to Ramulas.'

'I can show him to his room,' Emily said from the doorway.

Iguchi bowed. 'I must prepare for my men,' he said before following Emily out of the room.

***

'Ramulas, one hundred people have come to Sanctuary, but we will need two thousand if we are to stop the legion.'

'The First Legion has ten thousand soldiers,' Pip said as she walked into the room.

Oriel smiled. 'We have powerful magic on our side.'

Oriel waved her hands in front of Ramulas and Pip and ten multicoloured crystals, the size of apples, appeared in the air. The crystals spun in the air, changing colour from blue to green to purple and then returning to blue.

'These artefacts are to be taken to each of the towns and the city of Keah. Each person who holds the artefact will stay until midnight; the crystal will call out to those who feel oppressed by the king's rule.

'It will offer them a better life in Sanctuary, and a fog will mask their journey out of their towns. Only those who hear the call will be able to see through the fog.

'Talk to those who are here and tell them that sacrifices must be made. Everyone who comes to Sanctuary must be willing to fight for their freedom. Among the people, you will find those willing to take these to the towns and Keah.'

The reality of the situation dawned on Ramulas. 'What of the women and children? Will they be expected to fight as well?'

Oriel nodded. 'All who will come here possess an inner strength that will help Sanctuary.'

'You talk of Sanctuary,' Pip said. 'But what of the other towns, like Bremnon? Who will protect them?'

Oriel smiled sadly. 'Once Remus arrives, he will lead the First Legion to me. I am his reason for coming to this world. Only after he kills me will he go to Keah and the towns of the kingdom.' Turning to Ramulas, Oriel said, 'True freedom requires sacrifice and pain. The people who come will be willing to fight for a better life. Take the artefacts and find nine people to take them.'

'I will go to Bremnon,' Pip said, stepping forward.

Ramulas looked to Oriel while gesturing at Pip.

'You are the one who will hand out the crystals; use your judgement,' Oriel said.

He looked to Pip, whose expression was a mix of eagerness and determination. She thrust out a hand palm facing up waiting for a crystal.

'But you said Pip would be spending time by my side, to protect me and my family.'

'At this early stage, you will be fine without Pip.'

Ramulas smiled as he plucked one out of the air and gave it to Pip. A triumphant smile spread across Pip's face as she placed it in her cloak. Ramulas placed the rest of the crystals inside a pouch Oriel handed him.

'Pip, I need you to do something for me,' Ramulas said. 'Could you ask everyone to meet in the courtyard by mid-afternoon? I will need to talk to them.'

As soon as Pip left, Ramulas placed a hand over his stomach.

'What is wrong?' Oriel asked.

'I have to talk to one hundred people, and I don't know what to say.'

Oriel smiled. 'Take a walk to clear your mind. Return after midday, and I will help you with what needs to be said.'

Ramulas wanted to argue, saying that he was full of doubts and fears about what would happen if he stood in front of the people and could not think of anything to say. Ramulas' mouth became dry, and he could feel his heart quicken.

Ramulas left Oriel's room without knowing what he would do.

***

Ramulas found the two hell hounds waiting for him as he walked out of the castle. Seeing them helped lift his spirits. He walked to the stables where he had found peace.

The handful of people that he saw along the way bowed and referred to him as 'lord'. Ramulas inwardly flinched at the title; however, after trying to correct the first few, Ramulas realised that Oriel had told them he was their lord.

Rufus communicated with Ramulas that he wanted to exercise. He opened the stall and communicated for the warhorse to go into the training grounds.

As Rufus walked out, Iguchi appeared at Ramulas' side. 'Hello, Lord of Sanctuary.'

Ramulas jumped at Iguchi's sudden appearance.

'You are to lead everyone who will come to Sanctuary.'

'I do not know if I will be able to do what is needed,' Ramulas said. 'You bested me in combat, and I had been training.'

'I beat you because you relied on only one style of fighting. Soldiers are taught that if they perfect certain techniques, they will be invincible. But this makes them predictable. In battle, you do not want to be predictable and allow your opponent to know your next move. You need to learn the aspects of different styles; only then will you find your own style in battle.'

'I need to know different styles of fighting?' Ramulas asked.

Iguchi nodded. 'You will also need to know the men who fight with you. A true leader knows the qualities of his men. One man might be a good fighter, but a terrible assassin. You need to know which man will do which task; this is the key to winning battles.'

'How will I learn to be a good leader like this?'

'I have served many leaders, and I see their qualities within you. You surround yourself with people who know things that you do not. You will talk to these people when you need to. I am here to train a special group of men; others will come to help you train your army,' Iguchi said as he patted the hell hounds.

Ramulas thought it was strange that Iguchi was the only one who was not troubled by the hell hounds.

'I must make ready for my men,' Iguchi said before walking to the castle.

Ramulas walked to the training grounds and watched the warhorse run for a while before returning to the courtyard.

***

More people had entered Sanctuary, and Ramulas sent them to see Oriel. Then he saw two large wagons coming down the passageway. He recognised Miles and Benji on the first wagon and a dwarf on the second.

Ramulas had never seen a dwarf. He had heard a few stories about them, but very few came near towns. They were rumoured to live deep within the mountains.

Benji and Miles waved to Ramulas when they saw him.

'Your armour looks good,' Benji called out.

Miles elbowed Benji in the ribs. 'We are to call him "lord".'

Ramulas fought back the urge to correct Miles—he knew it would be pointless.

'This is Edwin, lord,' Miles said as the dwarf's wagon pulled to a stop next to theirs.

The dwarf gave a cheery wave. 'Hello, milord.'

The dwarf had a bushy white beard and wore his long white hair in plaits. He was half the size of Ramulas, and his feet dangled a few feet from the footrest. He wore a dark woollen jumper over his armour.

'We spoke to Edwin about some of the things that needed to be done here. He said that he had a lot of experience in digging tunnels,' Benji explained.

'Over two hundred years of digging tunnels, milord,' Edwin added. 'I am one of the best in these parts.'

'Where have you dug?' Ramulas asked.

'With me clan. North and west of here in the mountains.'

'Where is your clan now?' Ramulas asked, knowing a whole clan would be better than one dwarf.

'Pah,' Edwin said with a wave of his hand. 'The head o' me clan heard a tale of a gem mine a hunnerd miles to the north. They left and I stayed for the taste o' mead in Turtha.'

'What?' Ramulas said in shock. 'You left your clan for mead? How long ago was this?'

Edwin nodded. 'Mead, and other things. They left thirty years ago. When I become bored, I'll go lookin' for me clan.'

Ramulas could not comprehend the dwarf's logic, but he was happy for the dwarf's help.

'Now where did ye want the hole in yer mountain?' Edwin asked.

'Follow me,' Ramulas said as he led them to the cliff face.

They arrived at the cliff to find Emily standing near a large pool of mud where the maze met the mountain.

Emily pointed to the sky. 'Oriel said to follow the light.'

Looking up, Ramulas saw a shaft of light coming from the top of the castle. It shone down on a section of the mountainside.

'Well, I'll be …' Edwin muttered.

Ramulas led the wagons to where the light shone on the rock. They passed several streets of empty houses along the way.

Emily walked over and touched the cliff. The light vanished, leaving the soft glow of a doorway.

Edwin jumped down from his wagon and ran to the wall while pulling out a piece of charcoal. He began to outline the glow, and when it became too high for him, Miles finished the outline. After a moment, the outline faded.

'That was a bit o' luck,' Edwin said. 'Now we know where to start.'

'Everything that you take out of the mountain must be put into the mud pit where Emily was,' Ramulas said.

Edwin looked back the way they came. 'Why would ye want rocks in a mud pit?'

Ramulas smiled. 'When you see Oriel, she will explain everything to you. When can you start digging?'

'I'll be needin' more than just meself, and I'll be needin' a place to put me tools. I could start by morning.'

'You can use space in front of the mine, as well as two of the houses across the way,' Ramulas said.

Edwin was shocked. 'Which ones?'

Ramulas shrugged. 'Take any one; they are all empty.'

Edwin hopped onto his wagon and took it to the nearest house. Miles pulled the other wagon next to it as Iguchi came around the corner.

'Hello to you, Lord of Sanctuary. I have come to you with great news.'

'What great news would that be?'

'I have found the first of my men that I am to train.'

'Where are they?' Ramulas asked, looking around.

'These two,' Iguchi said, pointing to Miles and Benji. 'They must come to me after you have given your great speech to the people. Then they will start their training.'

'What training?' Miles asked.

'You two will be a part of an elite army, better than any soldier of this land. But first, we will join the others for the lord's speech.'

Miles and Benji looked at each other with excitement building between them.

'By the gods!' Miles said, slapping Benji on the back. 'Do you know what we could do with this training?'

Benji smiled. 'Why didn't you see this in one of your visions?'

Miles shrugged. 'I cannot control when they come or what they mean.'

Then Miles' eyes glazed over and his body froze. Benji watched him intently, waiting to see what would happen. He knew that his friend had fallen into a trance, and he was having a vision.

'Arrggghhh!' Miles screamed as he threw himself onto the ground.

Ramulas and Iguchi turned to see what had happened, and Benji gave them an apologetic shrug before helping his friend to his feet.

Ramulas and Iguchi walked toward the castle and Benji looked at Miles. 'What did you see?'

'A giant,' Miles gasped. 'He was standing behind you holding a club.'

Benji saw people walking to the courtyard, and he thought of Miles' vision. Benji knew he would have no chance fighting a giant—he just hoped he would be able to run away.

12

Ramulas paced inside his room feeling nauseous. His mind was blank, his mouth dry, and the butterflies in his stomach made him feel as if he were falling. Ramulas did not know what he was going to say. He made his way to Oriel's room.

Oriel stood by the window when he entered

'Oriel, I cannot do this. I do not know what to say to the people.'

Oriel smiled. 'I know you can do this, Ramulas. I see the strength inside of you. All people wish to be led by a true leader. You will make them feel important and belong to something that is bigger than they are.

'Show them respect, and people will follow you into the depths of hell. The right words have the power to ignite people into a fever pitch that will burn forever. People will forget their old lives to be a part of Sanctuary.

'The king has long ago neglected his people. Show these people that you truly care for them, and they will stand by your side. But most importantly, let them into your heart, and then they would gladly die for your cause.'

Ramulas took a few deep breaths as he heard the people gathering outside the balcony.

'Are you ready for your speech?' Pip asked as she walked into the room.

Ramulas turned to see Pip, Iguchi, Miles, and Benji. 'What are you doing here?'

'Remove fear and failure from your mind,' Iguchi said. 'Replace it with courage. We will stand by you when you talk to the people. It is good to show unity.'

Together with Oriel, they walked out onto the balcony. Ramulas looked down to see the people waiting for him. He took a deep breath and stepped up to the edge of the balcony.

Ramulas raised his hands to the crowd, and they began to cheer for him.

'I welcome you to Sanctuary,' Ramulas said as he felt the butterflies in his stomach calm. 'Everyone here before me came in answer to a call. You people are instrumental in building the foundations of a new beginning in Sanctuary.

'I can offer freedom to any who comes here. We have all suffered in one way or another under King Zachary. Taxes continue to rise while the king's agents spread fear throughout the kingdom.

'For too long we have accepted this way of life, because to question the laws means being sent to Gully Town. If you want freedom, you must be willing to fight for it,' Ramulas said as he punched a fist into the air. The crowd threw their hands up and cheered louder.

Iguchi leaned into Ramulas and whispered, 'Your passion is contagious. Give them something to believe in.'

Ramulas nodded and waited a moment for the people to calm down. 'All of you have spoken to Oriel. She has shown you the First Legion and what they will do when they arrive.'

The wall above Ramulas changed and images of the First Legion marching toward Sanctuary appeared on the wall.

'When the First Legion arrives, we cannot rely on the king's army to protect us. They will come for Oriel to kill her. Once this is done, they will move across the kingdom raping, killing, and enslaving our people.'

The image on the wall changed once again to show lines of slaves walking through the streets. Buildings were aflame and legion soldiers walked alongside the slaves.

Shouts of shock and denial came from the crowd below. In the images they saw loved ones as slaves.

Again, the image changed—this time it showed the people of Sanctuary dressed for battle and waiting for the legion as they came out into the clearing. The people shouted and ran to meet the First Legion.

'A short time ago, I was a simple farmer. When Oriel came to me, she showed me what would happen if I did not leave my home and come here, I know that everyone before me has left their old lives behind in order to come here. I can promise you a life worth fighting for in Sanctuary.'

Ramulas paused for a moment allowing the people to absorb what he had just said.

He raised his hands. 'You have been shown two possible futures. You can wait for the First Legion to arrive and hope the king's army will come to save you. Or you can fight for your freedom. Which future do you want?' Ramulas shouted.

'Freedom!' The crowd roared.

Ramulas took out one of the artefacts and held it up for all to see. He waited for calm before speaking.

'I will need people to take a crystal to each of the towns and Keah. These will help bring more people to join our cause. Who is willing to take one?'

Everyone in the crowd put up their hand.

Ramulas smiled. 'I am happy to see so many willing to help. I will choose people at a later time. This speech has come to an end. But before I leave, I just want to hear what we are all fighting for.'

'Freedom!' The crowd roared.

Ramulas waved to the crowd and stepped back from the edge of the balcony. As the people dispersed, Iguchi came to his side.

'I have found one more to train.'

'Where is this one?'

Iguchi pointed to the rear of the crowd. Ramulas followed his finger and saw two wagons coming through the passageway. Michael was in one of the wagons, and sitting next to him was Jacqueline.

Ramulas' heart skipped a beat.

In the next wagon was Thomas, and next to him were Kate and Grace. Jacqueline and his daughters looked up at Ramulas in awe.

Ramulas could not move. He did not want to take his eyes off his family.

'Ramulas!' Jacqueline shouted.

At that moment, the spell was broken. Ramulas ran down the stairs into the courtyard. As he entered the courtyard, Jacqueline and his girls were running towards him. He was engulfed as all three embraced him.

Ramulas held onto his family while tears of joy rolled down his face. After a moment, he kissed his wife and daughters, still not believing, after all he had been through, that they were here.

Kate and Grace asked so many questions that Ramulas felt dizzy.

'Girls, one question at a time,' Jacqueline said.

Michael walked up to Ramulas, clapping him on the shoulder. 'I told you that I had a quest.'

'Thank you, my friend, but why didn't you tell me?'

'Oriel said that you needed to have your mind on Sanctuary.'

'Are we really going to live in that castle, Da?' Grace asked. 'The sheriff burnt our farm down.'

Ramulas saw Jacqueline and Kate nod sadly, and he felt cold anger running through his body. 'What? When did this happen?'

Jacqueline shook her head. 'We will talk about this after the girls have settled.'

Ramulas took the hint that his wife did not want the subject brought up in front of his girls and would wait until Jacqueline was ready.

'I can show them to their rooms,' Pip said, coming to stand next to Ramulas.

Both girls became excited and looked at Ramulas. 'This is Pip. She is staying in the castle with us.'

After introductions were made, Ramulas allowed his girls to go with Pip into the castle.

Jacqueline kissed him lightly on the cheek. 'You have changed so much. You have lost a lot of weight. And what is that mark on your face?'

'A lot has happened since the last time I saw you. I will go into detail later.'

'Will the girls be safe with Pip?' Jacqueline asked. 'I saw a lot of knives under her cloak.'

Ramulas laughed. 'One of Pip's roles is to protect our family.'

'Do you trust her?'

'She has proven herself to me countless times.'

Jacqueline was shocked by what Ramulas had just said. But before she could say anything, Thomas stepped forward.

'Ramulas, my friend, look at this place,' Thomas said. 'This is wonderful.'

'There is so much for me to show you, Thomas, but that will have to wait.'

'I will take them to Oriel,' Emily said.

'This is Emily,' Ramulas said. 'Go with her to Oriel, and all your questions will be answered. I will talk to you later.'

After Thomas left with Emily, Iguchi walked up to Michael. 'You must come with me.'

Michael looked at Ramulas, who laughed. 'He has a job for you to do. You should go with him.'

Michael left with Iguchi and Jacqueline looked at the wagons,

'We should take our things inside; we can't leave them here.'

Miles and Benji raced up to the wagons. 'Lord, we will take you things in the castle for you,' Benji said.

'But Ramulas,' Jacqueline whispered loudly. 'They look like thieves dressed as soldiers.'

Miles laughed when he heard. 'You have a smart wife, my lord.'

'Do not worry my love,' Ramulas said. 'They used to be thieves, but here in Sanctuary everyone is given a second chance.'

Jacqueline was speechless as Ramulas led her into the castle.

***

Jacqueline, Kate, and Grace had settled into their quarters. The girls were excited to each have their own room. Jacqueline was still in a state of disbelief. She had never seen furnishings of such high quality. Ramulas had said that this would be their new home.

'I want you to meet Oriel,' Ramulas said to Jacqueline.

She looked at her girls, who were in an animated conversation with Pip, before leaving with Ramulas.

Oriel was waiting for them when they entered. 'Hello, Ramulas. I am happy to see that your family have lifted your spirits.'

Ramulas smiled. 'I am relieved to be with them once again. I did not realise how much I missed them. This is my wife, Jacqueline.'

Oriel walked over to Jacqueline and hugged her.

'It's nice to finally meet you,' Jacqueline said as she forced a smile.

'I hope you and your family come to like your new home,' Oriel said.

Jacqueline nodded. 'Our quarters are very nice.'

'Ramulas is the Lord of Sanctuary,' Oriel said. 'The people will see you as the Lady of Sanctuary. Please wear the clothing I have provided in your quarters.'

Jacqueline blushed. 'Oh, but they are far too nice for me.'

'The people in Sanctuary will need someone to look up to. You both will be seen as a king and his queen.'

'But I am not a queen,' Jacqueline protested.

Ramulas placed his hand on his wife's arm. 'My love, just follow me in what I do.'

Jacqueline gave a weak nod.

'Pip has chosen eight others to take the crystals to the towns and Keah. They will leave in the morning.'

'Eight?' Ramulas asked. 'With Pip, that only makes nine crystals. What about the tenth?'

'The last crystal will be for you, Ramulas,' Oriel said with a sad smile. 'The day after tomorrow, you will take yours to Shangri-La.'

'But my family,' Ramulas said in shock. 'They have just arrived. I have not seen them in weeks.'

'Why do you want to take Ramulas from his family again?' Jacqueline asked with a little resentment.

'Ramulas is the only one who will be able to travel to Shangri-La and bring back help.'

The realisation hit Ramulas like a hammer to the body. 'People speak of spirits and dragons in Shangri-La. Before you came to me, I thought dryads and Sanctuary were myths and legends. Now I know them to be real. It is rumoured that the king's army stays away from there. Tell me, Oriel, are there dragons in Shangri-La?'

'Yes, Ramulas, there are several dragons living within the forests of Shangri-La.'

Jacqueline gasped while grabbing Ramulas by his arm. Ramulas looked at his wife and saw pure terror.

'No,' Jacqueline said. 'I will not let you take him; he has left his family once to help you. I will not let it happen again.'

Oriel saw the determined expression in Jacqueline and knew she would have to win her over. Oriel waved her hand at the wall behind her. An image of the First Legion marching through Bremnon was shown. They burned buildings and cut down people who stood in their way.

Jacqueline gasped and turned her head away from the grizzly scene, burying her face in Ramulas' breastplate. He looked ahead at the now-familiar picture with an arm around his wife.

'You must watch, Jacqueline,' Oriel said softly. 'This is the army coming to your world. If we do not do everything possible to stop them, they will cross the kingdom unhindered.'

Jacqueline slowly raised her head to see the First Legion marching columns of slaves out of Bremnon. She gripped Ramulas tighter as she witnessed people devoid of hope placed into the slave pens. Oriel waved her hand and dismissed the image.

'I showed Ramulas the same images. That is why he chose to leave your farm with the crystal. I would not ask him to go to Shangri-La if it were not important.

'Ramulas has a dragon spirit within him. This should help him with the dragons. Sanctuary will only have two thousand people against ten thousand of the First Legion. Ramulas will return safely to you.'

Jacqueline nodded. 'I wish to return to my quarters.'

Oriel gestured for Ramulas to take his wife out of her room.

Once Ramulas and Jacqueline had left, Oriel thought of the tension she felt from Jacqueline after saying that Ramulas needed to go to Shangri-La. She felt resentment from her.

Oriel needed to find a way to show Jacqueline that she was not the enemy.

***

On the way back to their quarters, Ramulas heard clicking on the floor behind them. He focused and found that the hell hounds were following them.

'Wait here and close your eyes,' he said to Jacqueline.

Ramulas waited until her eyes were closed before communicating with the hell hounds to sit in front of Jacqueline and himself.

Once they were sitting Ramulas said, 'Open your eyes.'

Jacqueline gasped when she saw the hell hounds and quickly stepped behind Ramulas.

'Fenris, Valkyrie; come here,' Ramulas said, snapping his fingers.

Both hell hounds came to sit at his feet. Ramulas leaned over and scratched both hell hounds behind the ears. 'You have nothing to worry about. These two are quite harmless.'

'But they are hell hounds,' Jacqueline said in disbelief. 'Like the one that attacked you in Bremnon.'

Ramulas smiled. 'The only thing you need to fear is being licked to death.'

Ramulas looked at his wife and saw uncertainty. 'Come next to me and let them get to know you.'

Jacqueline slowly walked to Ramulas' side and looked down at the hell hounds, who wagged their tails.

'Now offer them the back of your hand,' Ramulas said softly. 'And remember: they will not hurt you.'

Jacqueline held her hand out and both hell hounds sniffed it. Fenris gave it a lick.

'Now slowly scratch them behind the ears.'

As Jacqueline scratched them, Ramulas could see that Fenris was about to jump. He communicated for them to stay calm. Ramulas watched for a few moments for Jacqueline to accept the hell hounds.

He spoke when she smiled. 'I think after the first shock, the girls would like them.'

'Oh no,' Jacqueline said. 'They would be too scared. I think we should wait.'

'It's too late for that,' Ramulas said.

Jacqueline looked up to see both girls frozen in terror. Fenris and Valkyrie turned and began walking towards the girls with their tails wagging.

'Sit,' Ramulas said.

Both hell hounds immediately sat, and Ramulas communicated for them to lie on the floor. As both hell hounds dropped, Ramulas looked at his girls. Grace was rooted to the spot, and Kate slowly stepped back towards their quarters.

Ramulas smiled. 'Girls, these hell hounds are friendly. Even your mother has patted them.'

Seeing that both girls were still unsure, Ramulas motioned for Jacqueline to move forward with him. They both walked over to the hell hounds and patted them.

Both hell hounds wagged their tails, happy with the attention. Fenris rolled over and communicated that he wanted his belly scratched.

'See,' Ramulas said. 'They won't hurt you.'

Both girls watched their parents with uncertainty. Ramulas was unsure if they would come.

Then Grace took a step forward.

Kate followed, and soon they had joined their parents in patting the hell hounds. After a few moments, Ramulas saw that his daughters were still a bit uneasy.

'That's enough for now,' he said as he stood.

When Jacqueline, Kate, and Grace stood, Ramulas told the hell hounds to go to the stables.

***

After the hell hounds had gone, Ramulas took his family back to their quarters. Pip stepped out of the door as Kate was about to enter. In mirrored movements, Pip and Kate moved around one another.

Pip's eyes widened when she saw the way Kate carried herself. Pip stepped toward Kate, thrusting two ridged fingers into her stomach. Pip smiled when Kate stepped to the side while deflecting the blow.

Pip quickly pulled out two of her knives and sent a dizzying combination at Kate, whose hands seemed to move independently, slapping Pip's hands.

'Pip, what are you doing?' Ramulas asked.

'Look at the way Kate is moving,' Pip said as she returned the knives. 'She moves like a fighter.'

Ramulas shook his head in annoyance. 'Don't be silly,' he replied, missing the knowing glances between Grace and Jacqueline.

'But—'

'Not now, Pip. My family has just arrived. We will talk about this later.'

Once in the quarters, Ramulas encouraged the girls to try on the new clothes in their chests. This seemed to lighten the mood of his family.

Then Benji appeared at the door fighting for breath, the colour drained from his face and his eyes full of terror.

'What has happened?' Ramulas asked.

'My lord,' Miles said as he came next to Benji, 'you need to come into the courtyard quickly.'

'Why?'

'Druids have come into Sanctuary. They wait for you in the courtyard,' Miles replied.

Ramulas was hit by a bolt of cold energy at the thought of the druids. He told Benji to watch over his family while Miles and Pip walked out with him.

Thoughts raced through Ramulas' mind; he had had two encounters with the druids, and both times he was almost taken into the druid's labyrinth.

The only person he knew who had escaped from there was Benji. Parents used stories of the druids to scare their children.

People still went missing, and it was said they were taken to the labyrinth.

Now they were here in Sanctuary.

***

Shigar worked in his chambers, deep in thought. It had been a week since he had seen Ramulas. He received word from the harbourmaster that Iguchi had come into Keah and had gone onto Shes.

Shigar knew that Ramulas would need all the help in training his army, Iguchi had grown up in a land of warring factions that had been in conflict for hundreds of years.

His meeting with Ramulas' family had far exceeded his expectations. Even though Ramulas' wife was not happy with him being away, she understood that her husband was safe and that she would join him soon.

The biggest surprise for Shigar was that Grace had magical abilities. It first shocked him, and then Shigar was excited to have found a child prodigy. He had heard of a few magicians whose powers develop early.

However, Shigar never thought he would encounter someone like her. Grace had so much raw untapped power. The best place for her would be with other magicians, so they could guide Grace through her abilities.

He had returned to Bremnon after talking to Ramulas' family, Shigar was met by one of Zachary's agents and a score of soldiers. They waited for any news that Shigar had found the escaped prisoner.

Shigar knew and disliked this agent, who had the reputation of knowing when people lied, so Shigar decided to dance around the truth without actually lying. He would not elevate the agent's status by allowing him to catch him in a lie.

'Hello, magician,' the agent called out as Shigar rode into Bremnon. 'What news have you?'

'There is no trace of the escaped prisoner. His magical energies are nowhere to be found.'

The agent watched Shigar closely as he answered. 'Why, out of all the northern towns, did you choose Bremnon? What was your business in this town?' He asked slyly.

'I did not just come to Bremnon,' Shigar said, pointing a finger at the agent. 'I also stopped at Nasad, where I found no trace of the prisoner. I do not like your tone; you are supposed to support me, not accuse me.'

'I was accusing no-one,' the agent said innocently. 'One would only think that if they were trying to hide something. Are you hiding something, magician?'

'How dare you?' Shigar exploded. 'I told the king why I came out west, and he is the only one I will answer to. If you ask me one more question, I will turn you into the toad that you are.'

Shigar turned away and walked to his horse. As he rode past the agent, Shigar glared at him, daring him to say a word.

***

Two days later, Shigar returned to the city of Keah. He informed Zachary that the prisoner could not be found.

Aleesha sat by her father's side, and Shigar did not want to talk in front of her.

Zachary absently waved a hand at his daughter. 'Do not worry, magician. I have told Aleesha about the escaped prisoner and the crystal.'

Shigar balked as Aleesha gave him a smug smile.

'My daughter will rule these lands one day, and she needs to know everything. And I will not let Aleesha out of my sight until the prisoner is found. Do you have a problem with her being here?'

Shigar shook his head while thinking, *Zachary you have created a monster. She will treat the people worse than you.*

Shigar wanted to change the subject. 'Something needs to be done about your agents. They are causing resentment among the people. The raising of taxes made people complain, but the agents are pushing them too far.'

'My agents have a duty to find this prisoner,' Zachary said. 'This prisoner could come back to harm Aleesha or me.'

Not for the first time, Shigar thought, *What has happened to you, my friend? A few years ago, you were the people's king. The death of your wife has destroyed your soul. You used to care for the people, but now they are nothing to you.*

Your greed for more coins in your coffers consumes you, and you are constantly worried about people plotting against you. Zachary, you are turning everyone against you, especially those who were once close friends.

'The people give all that they are able,' Shigar tried to explain.

'The collector of tax and my agents tell me differently,' Zachary retorted. 'Who are you to question me?'

'I thought that I was one of your trusted advisers,' Shigar replied. 'I am to give you advice when you need it.'

'No!' Zachary said. 'You are to support the decisions that I make.'

'I apologise, my king,' Shigar said with a bow. 'I was wrong to doubt you. I will return to my chambers and continue my search for the prisoner.'

'Next time, learn your place, magician,' Aleesha said with a sneer. 'Kneel before your king and princess.'

Shigar looked at Zachary in shock while the king patted his daughter's hand. Zachary gave a slight nod to the magician. Shigar fell to one knee before quickly leaving.

Shigar walked back to his chambers and lamented the lost friendship that he had with Zachary. He even felt out of place within his own chambers. All Shigar wanted to do was find a place where he truly belonged.

Aleesha was hungry for power, Shigar could see this in her eyes; this made her extremely dangerous. Shigar knew that he would need to watch himself around her.

13

Miles led Ramulas and Pip down the stairs and into the courtyard. No-one spoke, each lost in their own thoughts.

They stopped in the courtyard and Ramulas counted twelve druids Standing before them.

Michael and Iguchi stood near the druids. They spoke to each other in soft tones and did not seem alarmed. They were more curious.

The same could not be said about the other people in Sanctuary. They stood at the edge of the courtyard, watching from behind buildings and pillars.

Ramulas saw something different about the druids. At first, he could not figure it out, and then it came to him. They wore green robes.

The last two times Ramulas had encountered them, the druids wore black hooded robes. Everything Ramulas had ever heard about the druids confirmed this.

Then as one, the twelve druids turned to face him.

A cold chill ran through Ramulas' body, but he ignored it and took a step towards the druids. Ramulas could see no visible part of their bodies and knew that was part of the reason people feared them.

'Why have you come to Sanctuary?' Ramulas asked them.

One of the druids removed its hood. The crowd gasped when the druid's hands came out of its robes; the druid's skin was green and scaly, its fingers ending in black talons. Once the hood was removed, everyone took a step back.

The druid was completely bald. Its head and face were completely covered in green scales and there were two slits where the nose should be. Eyes of pure blackness greeted Ramulas. He fought back his anxiety, as he knew that he needed to set an example to the others. He took a slow breath and nodded at the druid.

'We have come in answer to a call that was heard in the Darkwood,' the druid hissed.

Ramulas looked at Pip. 'Oriel,' they said simultaneously.

Ramulas stepped forward and offered his hand to the druid, the druid's hand snaked forward and gripped Ramulas'. The hand felt cold and clammy, but Ramulas gripped it tightly as he met the druid's gaze unflinchingly.

'Welcome to Sanctuary. I would like to take your group into the castle to see Oriel.'

The druid nodded, and the group followed him into the castle. Michael, Iguchi, Pip, and Miles walked behind the druids until they arrived at Oriel's room.

'Hello, Ramulas, and welcome, druids,' Oriel said as they entered the room. 'I had hoped you would come.'

'What!?' Pip said in shock.

'Pip you need to listen to the druids and why they have come to Sanctuary.'

'But they're druids,' Pip said. 'They kill people and take them to the—'

Oriel held up her hand and gave Pip a look that silenced her. 'Let them speak.'

One of the druids hissed something, and they all removed their hoods. Everyone in the room looked at the druids in a mixture of fascination and horror.

One of the druids stepped forward. 'We can understand your fear of us. But we are not the ones that you need to fear. It has been our fellow druids who have been performing foul deeds across the kingdom, and we suffer from that reputation.

Many years ago, we were all summoned to the king of Keah to rid the kingdom of monsters. We left our home in Suda and told the king what this would do to us.'

The druid paused to gesture to his face. 'The king promised to repay us for our work. However, when we were finished, we were chased out of every town and Keah. After several weeks of travel, we found ourselves in the Darkwood.

'Our leader wanted to repay the people of the kingdom, by showing them terror. This would be done by randomly taking one person and placing them within the Druids' Labyrinth.

'Our group of twelve chose not to follow this path. We stayed true to our beliefs and did not seek vengeance. We are here today because we were called.'

'Then why didn't you stop the other druids from taking people?' Pip asked.

'We attempted to reason with them. But they did not listen, and we could do no more. We are prohibited from harming our fellow druids.'

'You stood by and did nothing,' Pip argued. 'And now you are here, how will that stop the druids?'

'Pip, we have a bigger problem,' Oriel said. 'And these druids will be able to help us.'

'The people of Sanctuary will not be happy to have druids walking around the town,' Ramulas said.

'I know,' Oriel replied. 'For now, they will stay in the upper levels of the castle. I will talk with them. If the druids are not good for Sanctuary, I will send them away.'

'I will show the druids to their quarters,' Emily said from the doorway.

After the druids had gone, everyone except for Ramulas left Oriel's room. He felt a light throbbing behind his eyes, and a wave of mental fatigue washed over him.

'You need to trust me with the druids, Ramulas,' Oriel said. 'The people of Sanctuary will come to accept them over time.'

'But people have feared them for generations. They will find this hard to forget.'

'The druids will prove themselves,' Oriel said. 'You have more important issues. People will leave with the artefacts tomorrow, and the day after, you will go to Shangri-La. You need to spend time with your family.'

The realisation hit Ramulas like a bucket of cold water. He had not spent much time with his family since they had arrived.

***

The next morning, Ramulas met Pip and the eight others who were to leave. They waited in the courtyard with a horse and provisions.

'These are the men who will take the artefacts,' Pip said.

Ramulas took out an artefact and held it up so it caught the light. It changed colours and glinted in the sunlight.

'Oriel has given me ten of these artefacts. Each of you will take one to your destination.'

Ramulas handed an artefact to each of the men. He smiled seeing the men's faces light up as they received one.

'This is an important mission that we are about to undertake. You will travel to your chosen place and wait until midnight. The artefact will cover the area in a thick fog.

It will call out to those who feel oppressed by the king and offer a better life at Sanctuary. These people will come to you, and the fog will protect you until the morning. You will need to lead the people to Sanctuary.'

One of the men counted those holding an artefact. 'Lord, there are only nine here. Who will take the tenth?'

'I will take it. Why would I ask you to do something if I would not do it myself?'

'Where are you going, my lord?' the same man asked.

With a serious tone, Ramulas said, 'Shangri-La.'

'What!?' Pip said in shock.

The respect the men already had for Ramulas increased tenfold at the thought of their lord going to such a dangerous place.

'I will be leaving for Shangri-La tomorrow,' Ramulas said. 'I will be going to ask for help in facing the First Legion. Please follow me—I wish to show you something.'

Ramulas led the men and Pip into the forest by the edge of the clearing. Once in the forest Ramulas turned and held up his hand.

'What you are about to see will seem strange, but no harm will come to you,' Ramulas said before looking at the trees. 'I am ready.'

All of the men jumped in their saddles as dryads stepped out of the trees. Several hands dropped to their swords.

'Easy, men. These are dryads, and they are friends of Sanctuary,' Ramulas said as the eight dryads gave slight nods. 'As I said before, Sanctuary will need all the help it can. So, ride and return with more people for Sanctuary.'

After the dryads melted back into the trees, the men rode away with a sense of awe at seeing the mythical creatures.

***

Ramulas returned to his quarters to find Jacqueline and his girls waiting for him. All three were dressed in matching red silk robes; his wife looked radiant, and his girl's eyes shone with confidence.

'I have been so busy since you arrived,' Ramulas said. 'I have not had the time to show you Sanctuary. Let's walk as a family as we look at our new home.'

Ramulas took Jacqueline's hand and led his family out into the courtyard, where they were greeted by the hell hounds, the girls hid behind Ramulas, while he communicated with them to walk with his family.

'Do not worry, they will not harm you,' Ramulas assured them as the hell hounds walked by his side.

As they walked through the streets, the people addressed Ramulas and Jacqueline as 'my lord' and 'my lady'. At first, Jacqueline was uneasy, but Ramulas gave her hand a reassuring squeeze.

After a few moments, Ramulas could hear Grace giggling behind him. He turned to see what had happened, and Grace gave him a guilty expression. Fenris walked away from Grace to Ramulas' side.

Ramulas continued to walk while greeting people throughout Sanctuary. He heard Grace giggle a few more times, and out of the corner of his eye, Ramulas saw that both hell hounds had left his side.

Then Kate could be heard giggling as well. Ramulas took another step and looked over his shoulder. Fenris walked alongside Grace. She offered the hell hound her hand and he licked it; she pulled her hand away while giggling.

Ramulas stopped and turned around. 'What's going on?'

Both Kate and Grace looked guilty as they hid their hands behind their backs. Ramulas communicated to the hell hounds that he was not happy that they had left his side. Fenris hid behind Grace and Valkyrie behind Kate.

Ramulas saw that both his girls stood protectively in front of the hell hounds. 'I see you have made some new friends.'

Both girls nodded silently while Ramulas communicated with the hell hounds. *Watch over my daughters, and let no harm come to them.*

'Look at that,' Jacqueline said in awe, watching the hell hounds with the girls.

'I don't think the hell hounds will stray far from the girls,' Ramulas said with a smile.

Emily walked around the corner, and Grace squealed, running up and giving her friend a hug.

'Da, can we play with Emily?'

Ramulas nodded, and both girls left with Emily.

'Will the girls be safe?' Jacqueline asked.

Ramulas nodded. 'With Emily and the hell hounds, they could not be safer. Now that the girls have gone, I would like some time alone with you.'

Ramulas lay on the king-sized bed. Jacqueline was in his arms with her head resting on his shoulder. For the past few minutes, they had not spoken; for Ramulas, nothing could surpass the feeling of holding his wife and listening to her breath. He wanted this to last forever.

'Rami, is this a dream?' Jacqueline asked.

'No, this is all very real,' he replied. 'In a few weeks, Sanctuary will be filled with people. They will look to us for protection.'

'When this is finished and you defeat the First Legion, will we be going back to our farm?' Jacqueline asked.

'Would you really want to?'

Jacqueline let out a long sigh. 'I don't think I will be able to. The girls are so happy here, it would take a lot to remove them.' Jacqueline traced lines along Ramulas' chest. 'I don't want you to go to Shangri-La tomorrow.'

'I need to,' Ramulas said as he played with her hair. 'Oriel said only I could go there.'

'You seem very close to her, letting Oriel take you from your family.'

'I don't want to talk about Oriel now. I am alone with you, and that is all I want to think about.'

Ramulas kissed Jacqueline on the lips, and she returned it passionately. Ramulas' heartbeat began to quicken as their combined passion intensified.

It seemed like a lifetime ago since he had been close with his wife. It was something where Ramulas felt connected to his wife in an emotional and physical sense.

Jacqueline had begun to undress when the girls could be heard talking as they entered their quarters. Jacqueline untangled herself from Ramulas' arms as the girls entered the room.

'We will finish this tonight,' she whispered.

The girls came up to the bed talking excitedly about Sanctuary, and the hell hounds followed them in.

Ramulas covered his face with his hands and gave a mock moan of frustration.

'What's wrong, Da?'

'He has a headache,' Jacqueline said. 'See if you can make him feel better.'

Kate and Grace smiled at each other before climbing on the bed and jumping around. Ramulas did not have the chance to say no before Fenris joined the girls on the bed.

***

Just before dawn, Ramulas lay in bed with Jacqueline asleep in his arms. He had been awake for a while listening to her murmur in her sleep.

Light began to come through the window when Ramulas made the decision to leave. As he pulled his arm out from under Jacqueline, she woke.

'Hm. Don't go. I want you to stay with me.'

Ramulas leaned in and kissed her. 'I need to do this. I will be back in a few days.'

He kissed her one last time before moving away from the bed. Within moments, Ramulas was dressed and holding his weapons.

Ramulas walked into Grace's room to find her asleep with Fenris lying on the end of her bed. The hell hound's head rose as he entered, and its tail began to wag.

Ramulas communicated with the hell hound to stay with Grace and protect her. After kissing Grace on the forehead, he went into Kate's room. Ramulas saw Valkyrie and communicated the same message of protection. After kissing Kate, he walked into Oriel's room.

***

Ramulas walked in to see Oriel standing by the throne.

'Hello, Ramulas. Are you ready for your journey to Shangri- La?'

'As ready as I will be,' Ramulas answered. 'It will be a long ride.'

Oriel shook her head. 'You will not be taking your warhorse or your weapons.'

'What!?' Ramulas said in shock. 'It will take a week to walk there, and how do I defend myself without my weapons?'

'The dryads will help you get to Shangri-La, and it will be seen as a threat if you bring your weapons.'

'But I cannot go into the trees with the dryads. When I saw Grace in the sacred grove, I asked to be taken to my family. That dryad said that I was not one of them and entering the trees would mean a painful death.'

Oriel smiled. 'Both Sanctuary and the forests surrounding Shangri-La are places of magic, which has now infused with your magic. This will help you travel, but it cannot be done all of the time.'

'How do you know this?' he asked.

'I am in the mountains, and they have shared the history of the surrounding lands with me. They have told me about the people in Shangri-La.'

'Will the dryads bring me back?'

Oriel shook her head. 'No, you must find your own way back.'

'How?'

'A way will be shown to you.'

Ramulas placed his weapons near the throne.

'Did you know that this is your throne?' Oriel asked. After Ramulas shook his head, she continued. 'Once you return, you will hold meetings and address issues here.'

Ramulas was dumbstruck. Even though he had accepted people calling him 'lord', he had never thought of sitting on a throne.

***

Ramulas walked into the forest and waited a few moments, and then a dryad appeared before him.

'I need to go to Shangri-La; can you take me there?'

'We are not welcome in that forest, but I can take you to a place nearby. You must make your way from there.'

The dryad walked up to Ramulas and placed a hand over his eyes. 'As we travel, you must keep your eyes closed.'

Ramulas nodded and allowed the dryad to lead him into the tree. He felt the sensation of the tree closing around him for a few moments. Then everything opened up, and he could breathe again.

The dryad removed his hand and Ramulas was pushed forward. He opened his eyes to see that he was two miles from Shangri-La.

The first thing Ramulas noticed was that the trees of Shangri-La were huge. Even from this distance, they were bigger than he could have imagined. The legends of Shangri-La told of large trees; however, he never expected this.

Ramulas made his way to the edge of the giant forest and fought back the fear building within him. He could not tear his eyes away from the trees. The trunks of the trees were so wide that Ramulas would be able to fit his farmhouse inside one of them.

The trees themselves seemed to rise into the clouds above. The forest was deathly quiet as Ramulas took the first few cautious steps into the trees. He focused on his ability to contact the surrounding wildlife and found they were hiding from something big.

Three hundred yards into the forest, Ramulas came upon a grisly sight: in a small clearing, he saw skeletons dressed in old armour on pikes. He counted twenty in all. The warning was clear: it was a message not to enter.

As much as he wanted to turn back, Ramulas knew that it was important for Sanctuary for him to contact the people of Shangri-La.

For what seemed hours, Ramulas walked deeper into the forest without seeing any signs of people. The forest was quiet and Ramulas had lost all sense of direction.

Ramulas walked into a clearing and saw a man standing in the centre. He was dressed in patchwork greens, his head was bowed, and he held a nocked arrow, which was aimed at Ramulas.

'Did you not see the warning at the edge of the forest?' he asked Ramulas.

'I was told to come here,' Ramulas said. 'We are in need of your help.'

'And who would ask you to give your life away so freely by coming here?' the man asked as he looked up.

Ramulas gasped. 'Your eyes—they are white. You cannot see. How do you hold that bow?'

The man smiled. 'I can see without the use of my eyes. My body makes up for my loss of sight. Come with me.'

The man motioned for Ramulas to take the path on the left. With Ramulas in the lead, they walked through the forest. 'You will meet with the council, and they will decide your fate.'

'But I have done nothing wrong,' Ramulas replied. 'I have only come here asking for help.'

'That does not concern me. No outsider has come into Shangri- La in over one hundred years and lived to tell the tale.'

Anxiety within Ramulas began to build and he panicked. He took one last look at the forest around him before running into the trees to his right.

Ramulas ducked and weaved as he saw arrows flying overhead. This encouraged him to increase his speed. After a couple of minutes, Ramulas looked back and saw that he had lost the blind man. He slowed down and tried to work out where he was.

Ramulas was startled when a huge shape flew overhead. By the time Ramulas looked up, it had disappeared. Ramulas quickly walked until he came to a large clearing. He stopped and looked around, deciding where to go.

The huge shape flew over him once more. Ramulas raced across the clearing, trying to hide in the trees. When Ramulas was halfway across the clearing, a green dragon landed in front of him.

Ramulas skidded to a stop twenty yards from the dragon. The creature's head reminded Ramulas of that of a horse, and it was bigger than his body; the dragon stretched its wings before folding them along its back. Ramulas guessed the wingspan to be about fifty feet.

The green scales shone in the sunlight and its claws were dug into the ground as it readied to pounce, but the most terrifying part of the dragon was its mouth. It was filled with sharp teeth that were like white, curved swords. The dragon opened its mouth and raised its head before rushing at Ramulas.

14

Pip walked through the streets of Bremnon feeling a strange sense of detachment. After leaving her horse in the main stables, Pip headed to Jenna's dwelling. She hugged her sister Pip and wrestled with the twins.

'Pippa, is there something wrong?' Jenna asked.

Pip cringed at the name. She allowed no-one else except for her sister to call her by her birth name. It brought back too many memories of their parents, who were taken to Gullytown.

'Nothing is wrong. You need to pack. We are leaving here tonight.'

'Why? Have you angered the master of shadows?' Jenna asked, referring to the head of the thieves' guild in Keah.

'No. I have found us a better place to live,' Pip said. 'And we leave tonight.'

'Where are we going?'

'We are going to a place where we can live a better life.'

Jenna saw the expression of defiance in her younger sister and knew that the conversation was finished.

'Did Old John come with my message?' Pip asked.

Jenna nodded, and Pip asked for the rest of the coins that were hidden in the candles.

Pip purchased a cart that would be hitched to her horse. She walked the streets of Bremnon and had the feeling that she would not return after that night. She had one hand inside her cloak, playing with the artefact. Pip hoped it would work the way it was supposed to.

It was a few hours after sunset, and Pip stared intently at the artefact that she held in her hand; she wondered why nothing had happened as she paced the small living room.

Then the artefact began to glow softly. Pip gasped and brought it closer to her face just before the artefact exploded in a ball of white light. Dropping the artefact, Pip fell to her knees and covered her eyes.

The pain from the light felt like two hot needles had been thrust into her eyes. A few moments later, the throbbing subsided, and Pip removed her hands. She blinked a few times and was relieved when she could see.

Fog streamed from the artefact and flowed out of the open window. A few seconds later Jenna walked into the room with a surprised expression.

'I felt it,' she told Pip excitedly. 'Something has promised me a better life in a place of peace and harmony.'

'That's where I have been,' Pip said with a smile. 'And we leave as soon as the others arrive.'

They woke the twins and dressed them for the journey. Pip was glad that they had packed earlier. Soon they were outside sitting in the cart watching people come towards them in the fog.

Pip hopped down from the cart and greeted each person, explaining that they would leave soon. Within an hour, Pip felt a click in the artefact and the fog around them dissipated. She knew it was time to go to Sanctuary.

Pip had arranged the horses, carts, and wagons in a column with her leading, standing up on her cart. Pip took one last look back at those who answered the call and, with a wave of her hand, Pip signalled that they were leaving.

As the column left Bremnon in the middle of the night, Pip held the artefact tightly in her hand, she knew that the spell of the fog would dissipate by morning and the several hundred people she led would be seen. The sheriff would be told, and questions would need to be answered. Pip knew her main priority was to bring these people to Sanctuary without incident.

For someone like Pip, Sanctuary was around six hours away. However, leading this many people, she knew it would take Adam: take them how long to reach sanctuary?

Once there, Pip would have them visit Oriel, who would show them the First Legion, and then they would be given instrumental roles within Sanctuary.

Looking across at Jenna, Pip saw uncertainty on her sister's face. She gave her a reassuring smile; it was all she could think to offer. Once they arrived at the castle, Pip would show Jenna her new life.

Pip had never led a column of people anywhere before. If she was experienced, Pip would have known to occasionally ride to the rear of the column to check on everyone; if Pip had done this, she would have noticed the sand and gravel on the highway shifting.

All traces of the column's passing had been covered. The best tracker in the kingdom would say that several hundred people had vanished into thin air.

***

The dragon shot forward so quickly that Ramulas had no time to react. Its front claws opened and engulfed his breastplate. Before Ramulas had a chance to blink, he was pinned to the forest floor with the dragon above him.

Ramulas dared not move as he fought to overcome the fear exploding inside him. The dragon's head snaked down to be within a few feet of Ramulas'. It tilted its head to look at Ramulas with its left eye.

Then he recalled his ability to communicate with animals.

Ramulas focused and sent calming thoughts to the dragon and offered his friendship. The dragon's head twitched and moved a few feet away from him, and then Ramulas saw something that chilled him to the bone.

The dragon looked at him with a level of intelligence that surpassed most people, and then the dragon's expression changed to one of hunger. Its mouth opened, and its head came down towards Ramulas.

Panic overwhelmed Ramulas and his muscles refused to obey his commands.

'Why do you think I allowed you to run?' The blind man asked as he walked into the clearing.

Ramulas turned toward the voice, and the dragon's teeth stopped a foot from his face.

'I could have struck you at any time with one of my arrows,' he said with a smile. 'Now we will take you to the council.'

Walking up to the dragon without concern, the man shouldered his bow and mounted the creature as one would mount a horse. He gave a shrill whistle, and Ramulas' stomach lurched as he was lifted into the air.

Ramulas held onto the dragon's claws for dear life as they rapidly ascended above the trees. He turned to see the ground far below and regretted it instantly.

Ramulas' head swam as a cold sensation ran throughout his body; he focused on watching the dragon beat its wings. They reminded Ramulas of the sails of a ship as they beat through the air.

Ramulas felt the dragon slow its wings, and they began to descend. He saw the gigantic trees come into view again and, a few moments later, Ramulas was dropped from the dragon's claws. He landed on the forest floor with a thud, and the air was knocked out of his lungs.

Ramulas rolled around on the ground, fighting for breath. He saw that he was in a clearing about the size of Sanctuary. There were huts scattered throughout the clearing and dwellings built high up amongst the trees.

Narrow walkways connected the dwellings in the trees and spiral stairs could be seen winding up the thick trunks.

The blind man walked over and helped Ramulas to his feet as people began to appear. Ramulas saw at least a few hundred.

'What is this place?' Ramulas wheezed.

'We now stand in the heart of Shangri-La,' the man said. 'Now tell me what name I shall call you.'

'Ramulas.'

'I am Owain. You will remain in this clearing until the council decides your fate.'

'I have only come here to ask for help,' Ramulas protested.

'That is not my concern. The council will decide your fate.'

Ramulas looked around at the people and saw that they all wore patchwork clothing. The men wore different shades of green and the women wore shades of green, blue, purple, and red. The men's hair was short while the women wore theirs long, with colourful ribbons weaved into their hair.

Owain led Ramulas to one of the larger huts. As they entered, Ramulas saw that the floor descended into a large oval room. In the middle of the room was a table with ten men seated in chairs. They stared at Ramulas.

'Who is this man, Owain?' asked the man at the head of the table.

Owain turned to Ramulas. 'He will give us a good reason as to why we do not feed him to the dragons.'

Owain's smile and tone of voice sent chills through Ramulas.

Ramulas took a deep breath and walked to the table and place the artefact on its edge. At first, nothing happened, and Ramulas felt his anxiety rise within him as the men watched him.

Then small cracks appeared along the surface of the artefact, sending out shafts of light. The men around the table were transfixed by the light show.

Then the artefact broke, flooding the room with light; as one, the men at the table covered their eyes just before they were engulfed by the light. When the light subsided, the men blinked in wonderment.

'I did not know this would happen,' Ramulas said.

'Is what we saw true?' The head of the council asked Ramulas.

'What did you see?' Ramulas asked.

The man looked at the others at the table and saw that they all wore the same grim expression.

'The magic within the light told me of Oriel coming to this world, and the First Legion that will come for her,' he paused to see if the others had experienced the same thing.

He continued when they nodded. 'After taking Oriel's power, they will move from town to town like locusts, killing and burning everything in their path. You are the first person to come to Shangri-La in many years. You bring us news that does not concern Shangri-La or its people.'

Ramulas' jaw fell open in shock.

'How can you say this does not concern you?' Ramulas asked. 'After the legion has taken Keah and all of the towns, they will come here.'

The head of the council shook his head. 'Long have we separated ourselves from the affairs of the kingdom. We have no wish to become involved. Our dragons will protect us if the legion comes here.'

'The warlords who will come with the legion use magic, and after they kill Oriel, their magic will be stronger,' Ramulas said as frustration built up within him. 'We must stand together.'

The head of the council pounded his fist on the table. 'You are in no position to tell us what to do. Now take your leave.'

Owain stepped forward and took Ramulas by the arm. 'Come outside with me.'

Once outside, Owain closed the door. The people in Shangri-La stopped what they were doing and stared at Ramulas.

Owain appeared to look around before speaking. 'This man awaits the council's judgement,' he said in a loud voice. 'He will remain here until judgement has been passed.'

Owain walked back into the hut, leaving Ramulas with the people of Shangri-La. For a few seconds, people continued to stare at him, making Ramulas feel self-conscious, and then they returned to their tasks.

Feeling out of place, Ramulas attempted to introduce himself, or start a few conversations. The response was always the same: the person would smile politely and walk away without speaking.

He approached groups of people in conversation, but they fell silent and walked away when he came near.

To the children of Shangri-La, Ramulas was a novelty; they would run up to Ramulas and point at the dragon on his breastplate before running away.

The day was coming to an end when Ramulas saw several pits filled with wood and set alight, large iron pots were placed over the fires, and the smell of food cooking made his stomach growl.

Ramulas walked around trying to ignore the hunger pangs as he saw the food being served. A few moments later, an old lady walked up to Ramulas with a bowl of steaming stew. Ramulas smiled gratefully as he took the bowl. 'Thank you.'

'You are to stay in there until someone comes for you,' she said, pointing to a small hut behind Ramulas.

Ramulas was in shock. He had spent hours walking among the people without anyone speaking to him. By the time he had recovered, she had walked away.

Ramulas walked to the hut, inhaling the aroma of the stew. He entered the hut and began to eat. Once he was finished, Ramulas lay on the cot by the wall, which was the only piece of furniture in the hut.

He soon began to feel drowsy as the hut started to spin around him. Ramulas' last thought was that his food had been drugged.

***

The sun rose behind the column Pip was leading. They were halfway to the forest outside of Sanctuary. The Devil's Ridge Mountains began to appear in the light as the fog lifted.

Gasps could be heard as the people saw how close they were to the mountains and their new home. Pip looked across at Jenna and smiled. Her sister's mouth hung open and her eyes were wide.

'The mountains are beautiful, aren't they?' Pip asked as the cart came to a stop.

Pip tousled Makayla's and Tao's hair before standing up in the cart and facing back to the column.

'By the end of the day, we will be in Sanctuary,' Pip called out. 'There you will find your new homes and a better life.'

A cheer came from the column as Pip returned to her seat and they began to move forward again.

After several hours, they arrived at the forest. Pip looked at the trees on both sides of the road. Every now and then, Pip would see dryads move through the trees as they followed the column.

She hoped they would show themselves before the people arrived at Sanctuary.

***

Pip led the column into the clearing in front of Sanctuary's wall. The excitement had built up within the group of refugees. Makayla and Tao were ready to jump out of the cart when they saw the wall.

Gasps of wonderment could be heard as people looked upon the wall of Sanctuary. Excited conversations began throughout the column as Pip led them into the town.

Pip stood on her cart in the courtyard, facing the column. She organised the people into a semicircle as they entered. The news spread quickly, and the people of Sanctuary came to greet the newcomers.

'This is Sanctuary, your new home,' Pip called out. 'Before you do anything, you must go into the castle and talk to Oriel. She will tell you where you live and what you will need to do here.'

Then Pip saw the expressions of the people turn from fascination to horror. She looked down to see Jenna trying to pull Makayla and Tao into the rear of the cart.

Pip slowly turned and saw Kate and Grace walking out of the castle, each with a hell hound, Jacqueline followed close by with her head held high. All three wore matching purple robes.

'This is the Lady of Sanctuary and her daughters,' Pip said. 'The hell hounds will not harm you.'

Grace looked down at Fenris. 'Go inside.'

Fenris sat at her feet, and no matter what Grace did, the hell hound did not move from her side. Then Emily came out of the castle.

'I will take them to see Oriel,' Emily said, pointing to a group of people.

'This is Emily,' Pip called out. 'She will take you in small groups to see Oriel. Leave your belongings here until you have seen Oriel. They will be safe.'

'Hello, Pip,' Jacqueline said as she walked to the cart. 'Is this your family?'

Pip nodded and made introductions before asking, 'Has Ramulas returned?'

'No, we are still waiting for him,' Jacqueline replied. 'That is why we have come to greet the people.'

Pip watched as Jacqueline made her way around the newcomers, she greeted each person with genuine warmth and spoke a few words that left them smiling.

Pip turned to her sister. 'Come into the castle, Jenna. I will show you where we are staying.'

Kate and Grace raced over to help the twins from the cart. Makayla and Tao were taken into the castle before Jenna could react. Pip lightly touched Jenna's arm and gave her a reassuring look.

Kate carried Makayla, but Grace struggled to lift Tao. Pip took Tao's hand and led him inside, with Fenris close behind.

Pip was happy that the first of the townspeople had arrived.

***

Ramulas woke in the darkness to find a hand clamped over his mouth; he gripped the hand and began to struggle.

'Quiet. It is time for us to leave,' he heard Owain say.

At the sound of Owain's voice Ramulas relaxed and Owain removed his hand. 'Where are we going?'

'I am going with you to Sanctuary.'

'Just you?' Ramulas said in disbelief. 'We need more people.'

'Come with me and all will be explained.'

Ramulas was led out of the hut just before dawn. No-one from Shangri-La could be seen. Owain took Ramulas to a clearing away from the people.

Ramulas was shocked to find a green dragon waiting for them. Several packages lay near the dragon.

'The council spoke about you, and the army that will come. It was decided that we would not involve ourselves in such matters.'

'What!?' Ramulas said in shock. 'If we do not stop the First Legion at Sanctuary, they will kill Oriel. When they have her magic, they will rape and pillage across the kingdom.'

'The council knows this. But they have grown comfortable with the knowledge that dragons protect Shangri-La, and they have for generations.'

'Then why are you here?' Ramulas asked.

'I wish to see this First Legion, and help you be ready for them.'

'I thought that you could not see?' Ramulas asked.

'I cannot, but I still wish to be there.'

'But you said that the council did not want to help. Why did they send you?'

'They did not send me to go to Sanctuary. I was sent to kill you.'

Ramulas stepped back with both hands before him and Owain laughed. 'We do not have much time. We need to ride the dragons before they realise that you are not dead.'

'Will the council be angry at your decision?'

'The council is not always right,' Owain said as he walked to the dragon. 'But now we must leave.'

Owain whistled once as he tied the packages to his dragon. Another smaller green dragon dropped into the clearing in front of Ramulas, who jumped back in fright.

This dragon had made no noise as it dropped from the sky, and it was twice the size of his warhorse.

The smaller dragon walked over to Ramulas, and again he could see the intelligence in its eyes. It stared at him for a moment.

You will suffer much pain along the road you must travel, a voice said inside his head.

Ramulas saw amusement in the dragon's eyes as his eyes widened in shock. *Hello, human. I can communicate with you. You will find pain on the path you travel. However, do not alter this path, for if you do, greater pain will be felt by those close to you.*

'What!?' Ramulas said, falling back. 'How do you know of my path?'

I can feel the spirit of the dragon within you. I can see both of the futures before you. It will take great strength to walk the right path.

Ramulas stood and looked at Owain, who had finished tying packages to the dragon. 'The dragon spoke to me.'

Owain nodded. 'Yes. I heard you talking to Shearok. You must be special. Very few people are able to communicate with dragons.'

'Was something done to my food last night?' Ramulas asked.

Owain nodded. 'Yes. It was to prevent you from leaving. If you were seen by the dragons of the forest, they would have eaten you.' Ramulas looked at the dragon near him nervously.

'You will need to ride Shearok,' Owain said, waving to the dragon near Ramulas.

'How do I do that? I do not know anything about dragons.'

'It's like riding a horse,' Owain said with a smile. 'But these horses fly. The dragon will obey your commands. All you need is confidence. Come, we must go.'

Ramulas watched as Owain climbed onto the larger dragon and hold onto two large scales at the base of its neck. Then the dragon shot into the air with a beat of its wings.

Shearok crawled to within six feet of Ramulas and lowered its body to the ground. Ramulas looked at the dragon hesitantly and then looked up at Owain flying above.

With a sigh, Ramulas climbed onto Shearok and held on. 'What do I do now?'

Hold on, the dragon replied.

With a beat of its wings, they rose into the air. Ramulas gripped the scales tightly and squeezed his legs against the dragon. With a few more beats of its wings, Shearok brought Ramulas above the trees.

Looking down, Ramulas almost brought up the contents of his stomach. Thoughts raced through his head as he focused on keeping his balance. Owain's dragon circled fifty feet above Ramulas.

Calm your thoughts, Shearok said. *Think of me as a horse you can ride through the clouds.*

Ramulas thought of riding Rufus, and then with a beat of its wings, Shearok flew above the trees. Owain followed on his dragon, still above them. Ramulas thought about being that high and immediately he shot up to fly next to Owain.

A sense of joy and elation spread through Ramulas. His mouth began to ache as his smile grew, and his heart beat like a drum in his chest.

Both dragons sped south until they left Shangri-La. Ramulas was in awe as he looked down at the fields in the early morning light. They were hundreds of feet in the air. Ramulas wondered what it would be like to fly closer to the ground, and Shearok descended into a steep dive.

'Whooooohoooo!' Ramulas screamed as he held onto the dragon. Thirty feet from the ground Shearok levelled out. Trees flashed by at incredible speeds. An idea came to Ramulas.

He found that by slightly moving to the left or right, he could turn the dragon. He gripped Shearok tightly and weaved in and out through the trees. As they came out of the trees Ramulas heard Shearok in his mind.

We move to the mountains now.

They rose into the sky, and Ramulas saw Owain several hundred yards away. Within a few moments, both dragons flew side by side. The Devil's Ridge Mountains could be seen in the distance.

All sense of time was lost to Ramulas as he flew. They reached the mountains and turned south, following the mountains until they reached the forest, and then before too long, Ramulas saw Sanctuary in the distance.

'We must land,' Owain called to him.

Ramulas nodded as he fought back disappointment. As both dragons landed in a small clearing, Owain climbed down and began to untie the packages from his dragon.

With a heavy sigh, Ramulas climbed down from Shearok, his feet felt heavy and cumbersome as he walked around. After a few moments, Owain had the packages on the ground, and Ramulas' feet had returned to normal.

Then, without warning, both dragons shot into the air and flew back towards Shangri-La.

'Where are the dragons going?' Ramulas asked.

'They have served their purpose and will return home,' Owain replied.

'Will they return when the legion comes?'

Owain shook his head. 'No, they will only fight to protect Shangri-La. They will not be needed here.'

'But with the dragons, Sanctuary will beat the First Legion,' Ramulas protested. 'You said the dragons would help.'

'That is not correct,' Owain said with a smile. 'I said that *I* would help, and I brought this.'

Owain unwrapped a cloth from something on one of the packages. When he was finished, he held it up for Ramulas to see.

Ramulas saw a shiny black oval shield half his height. 'What can one shield do to help?'

'This is not a shield,' Owain said, it is a dragon's scale. And within this scale is the spirit of a black dragon.'

Ramulas moved closer to the scale and could see something swimming through the murky blackness. His heart skipped a beat as the dragon's spirit became aware of his presence. The image within the scale formed a giant eye devoid of emotion. A chill ran through Ramulas as he stepped away.

'How does it work?' Ramulas asked.

'When the scale is struck with force, the dragon will be released. But this can only happen once.'

'This will give the legion a good surprise when the dragon comes,' Ramulas said.

'Man is always afraid of the unknown,' Owain said. 'You will need to play on that fear and use it to your advantage.'

Ramulas looked at the packages and saw that Owain and himself would be able to carry them. 'We are close to Sanctuary. If we leave now, we will arrive soon.'

After they strapped the packages to their backs, Ramulas led the way, and then he heard Owain clicking with his tongue as he walked.

'What are you making that noise for?'

Owain smiled. 'When I click my tongue, I hear echoes of everything around me.'

Ramulas snorted in disbelief.

Owain clicked a few times before looking directly at Ramulas. 'There are two large trees, taller than the rest,' Owain said pointing to his right. 'The third branch up on both trees has fallen.'

Ramulas was amazed as Owain described both trees. He could not help but believe what Owain had told him. They continued to walk and reached Sanctuary within the hour.

15

In the courtyard, they were met by Iguchi, Miles, Michael, Benji, and five other men Ramulas did not recognise.

'Welcome to you, Lord of Sanctuary,' Iguchi said with a deep bow. 'I have found more to join my group. I will begin their training.'

Ramulas watched as the group left, and then he turned to see Jacqueline come out of the castle. His breath was taken away by how radiant she looked in her purple robes. He stood for a moment with his mouth open as she ran towards him.

Coming out of his trance, Ramulas dropped his package and ran to meet her. He embraced Jacqueline and kissed her passionately.

'So, you *have* missed me,' Ramulas said.

'Of course, and so have the girls.'

'Where are they?' Ramulas asked as he looked around the courtyard.

'They are in the castle playing with Pip's family.'

'Pip brought her family here?'

Jacqueline nodded. 'Yes. They came with the people from Bremnon yesterday. And the people of Turtha came later in the day.'

Looking across the courtyard, Ramulas could see that there were a lot more people than before he left. 'They need to see Oriel.'

'Everyone has seen Oriel. Pip and Emily helped when the people came.'

A warm sense of pride washed over Ramulas as he looked at his wife. The Jacqueline he knew would have been too shy with this amount of new people. Looking at his wife, Ramulas saw a woman of confidence.

'I am so proud of what you have done. How are the girls with the hell hounds?'

A smile grew on Jacqueline's face. 'The hell hounds do not leave the girl's side, and the girls are very happy.'

Emily came out of the castle and looked at Owain. 'Ramulas, Oriel wants you to bring the man from Shangri-La to her.'

Owain nodded while shouldering his bow and a quiver full of arrows. Ramulas gave Jacqueline a hug. 'I need to go. I will be back soon.'

Jacqueline watched Ramulas walk away with Owain and Emily. She continued to feel resentment towards Oriel. Ramulas had just returned from Shangri-La and she wanted to spend time with him. But Ramulas ran to Oriel whenever she called him.

***

Ramulas and Owain entered the room to find Oriel waiting by the window. 'Hello, Ramulas. I am happy that you have returned safely. Did you find the help we needed from Shangri-La?'

'This is Owain. He was the only one who was willing to come.'

Oriel smiled. 'I wonder what help a blind man could offer Sanctuary.'

Owain sniffed the air around him and then clicked his tongue a few times while turning his head. 'There are several candles on a large table in the middle of the room. Choose one, Ramulas,' Ramulas became curious as he walked over to the nearest candle holder. There were five candles on it in a pyramid formation. Ramulas tapped the middle one.

'Now move away from the table,' Owain said.

As Ramulas moved away, Owain removed the bow from his shoulder. His upper body blurred as he shot four arrows in rapid succession. Every candle had been struck, except for the one in the middle.

Ramulas stared in amazement, the candle he chose had not been touched.

'I can teach people how to use a bow,' Owain said. 'I need people who are willing to learn.'

Oriel waved her hands in front of Owain, and he was soon covered in sparkling dust. He stiffened for a moment, and then the dust was gone.

Owain smiled at Oriel. 'I will do what I can to prepare the people for the First Legion.'

'I will take him,' Emily said from the doorway.

'What just happened?' Ramulas asked.

Oriel opened her arms. 'I have gained more magical powers. All new arrivals are covered in magical dust. This serves two purposes: the first is that it tells my story and the coming of the legion. What the legion plans to do here after they kill me, and what needs to be done in Sanctuary to stop them. All of that in a moment. And secondly, I can see into their souls, and know where they need to go in Sanctuary.'

'That will make things easier,' Ramulas said.

'I have done this with the druids,' Oriel said.

Ramulas slapped his forehead. 'I had forgotten about them. What role will the druids play?'

'They have a unique set of magical abilities which will help Sanctuary. But before that can happen, the people of Sanctuary must come to accept them, and this will be hard.

'I read the souls of the druids, and I could see generations of fear against the druids. I have spoken to the druids and together we have come up with a plan to break the ice.'

Oriel waved her hand and Ramulas' weapons floated towards him. He reached out to take them and looked at Oriel.

'You will need your weapons,' Oriel said.

Ramulas was about to ask why when the twelve druids appeared out of nowhere and surrounded him with wands drawn. Ramulas shouted in alarm as he held his weapons before him.

'Do not allow the bubbles to touch you,' one of the druids said.

Ramulas focused and everything around him slowed. Streams of bubbles slowly shot out of the druids' wands. Focusing again, Ramulas sent the bubble towards the druids on the right. They backed away and ceased using their wands.

Then everything returned to normal and Ramulas lost the power of telekinesis. Bubbles came at him from all sides. They were green and varied in size. Some were as small as grapes, while others were the size of oranges.

Ramulas dodged the first few bubbles before using his weapons. As his war hammer hit the first cluster, the bubbles popped, sending out webs of sticky green goo.

Movement became almost impossible, and Ramulas' right eye was sealed shut. The druids lowered their weapons, and the bubbles vanished. They stood watching Ramulas struggle.

After a few seconds, the sticky goo covering Ramulas, and his weapons dissolved, and he was free to move once more.

'At full strength, one bubble can hold a person for a minute,' one of the druids hissed. 'The more bubbles on a person, the longer they are held. We can weaken the bubbles so they dissolve on contact. This will bring amusement to the children of Sanctuary. Once we gain the children's confidence, their parents will follow.'

Ramulas thought on this for a few moments, thinking of Kate and Grace's reaction to the bubbles.

Then he smiled. 'Take things slow with the children.'

The druids nodded and left the room.

'That was handled like a true leader,' Oriel said. 'That was a hard decision to allow the druids to interact with the people of Sanctuary, but it needed to be done. The druids—along with Iguchi, Owain, and the others—are instrumental to defeating the First Legion.'

Oriel paused before continuing. 'People from Bremnon and Turtha have been placed in houses amongst one another. This will help them become like family.

'After midday, people from other towns will begin to arrive, and you will be very busy. I can feel tension coming from Jacqueline. I think she resents the time you spend with me.'

Ramulas shook his head. 'No, Jacqueline is very understanding. She would tell me if something was wrong.'

'Has Jacqueline ever said to you, "If you don't know what's wrong, I am not going to tell you"?'

'Oh no,' Ramulas said, realising that he had not seen the signs that Jacqueline was upset.

'After today, time with your family will be hard to come by. Spend time with your wife now. I know of a place where she would be happy.'

Oriel waved her hand and an image appeared in front of Ramulas. It showed Sanctuary and the mountains behind. The image moved south along the paths in the forest before winding up the mountain. Ramulas knew that Jacqueline would be happy there

'Now go,' Oriel said before she disappeared.

***

Ramulas raced down the hall to his quarters. He ran into Thomas and asked him to watch his girls, grabbed Jacqueline by the hand, and took her to the stables. He ignored all of her questions as he pulled her up onto the warhorse with him.

Ramulas rode Rufus out of Sanctuary and into the forest. Jacqueline's tight grip on him as they rode brought a smile to his face.

Within ten minutes, they had arrived at the base of the mountain, where the track wound upwards. Ramulas climbed down before helping Jacqueline off the warhorse.

'What are we doing here?' she asked.

'I have something to show you,' Ramulas replied.

He communicated with Rufus to wait in the clearing before taking Jacqueline by the hand and leading her up the path.

Ferns and bracken on either side of the track came up to Ramulas' waist.

'It is not far from here,' he said, giving her hand a light squeeze.

The incline of the path became slightly steeper as it wound up the mountain. After one hundred yards they could hear running water and more light filtered through the canopy as the trees thinned out.

The sound of running water became louder, and then a small, shaded grove opened up before them. A small waterfall fed a rocky pool in the middle of the grove.

Stepping into the grove, Ramulas felt the temperature drop as clouds of mists sprayed over Jacqueline and him.

'This ... This is beautiful,' Jacqueline stammered. 'How do you know of this place?'

'Oriel showed it to me,' Ramulas replied. 'She said that you would like it.'

Jacqueline had tears in her eyes as Ramulas led her to a patch of grass by the pool. She was overwhelmed by this romantic gesture by her husband. Since arriving in Sanctuary, Jacqueline had felt neglected every time Ramulas went to see Oriel.

'We can only stay a short while,' Ramulas said.

Jacqueline silenced him with a passionate kiss as she pushed him onto the grass.

***

Ramulas had led Jacqueline further up the path, and they had walked past the waterfall until the path became too steep for Jacqueline. As Ramulas looked down into the forest, he saw multiple paths running up the mountain.

Then something caught his eye. Facing toward Sanctuary, Ramulas saw Iguchi leading his men along an almost invisible path. After a few moments, the group disappeared into the ferns.

Looking closer, Ramulas saw a network of paths leading toward Sanctuary, and then Iguchi's group reappeared running along another path.

A buzzing sound filled the air and Tilly came out of the trees. 'You need to return to Sanctuary. More people come.'

They arrived at Sanctuary just before another group of people came from Shes. Ramulas sent Rufus to the stables while Jacqueline brought the girls into the courtyard. Pip joined them in the courtyard and help organise the newcomers.

Ramulas walked into the courtyard with Jacqueline by his side. He welcomed back the man who had brought the people to Sanctuary.

'Before you stand the Lord and Lady of Sanctuary!' Pip shouted from behind him.

All eyes focused on Ramulas and Jacqueline.

'Welcome to Sanctuary,' Ramulas said in a voice that carried across the courtyard. 'You have come in answer to a call from a magical artefact. Here in Sanctuary, you will find freedom from the oppressive lives you have lived under King Zachary.

'You will have a chance to start a new life where you will belong to something that matters, but this life does not come freely. We must be prepared to fight for our freedom.

'I know that each one of you has given up your old life to come here. This shows that you have something that separates you from other people. This will help you defend the land from the dark forces that will soon arrive.

'Each of you will see Oriel inside the castle. She will show more of what is to come and your role in Sanctuary. After speaking to Oriel, you will be given housing.'

Emily came out of the castle and escorted a small group in to see Oriel. People of Sanctuary came forth to welcome the newcomers.

After the last group from Turtha had seen Oriel, a group arrived from Rylek. Ramulas and Jacqueline greeted this new group, and he repeated his speech.

Ramulas was astonished at how quickly the town around him was coming to life. As more and more people came, Sanctuary became more vibrant and full of activity.

A rider came racing through the gates and into the courtyard. Ramulas recognised him as one of the men sent out with an artefact. Ramulas waved in greeting as the man pulled up in front of him.

'My lord, the people of Nasad will arrive shortly.'

'Thank you,' Ramulas said.

Oriel was correct, Ramulas thought—his life was becoming busy. He looked back to see that Jacqueline had seen the exchange. Walking up to her, he gave his wife a kiss.

'Here we go again,' he sighed.

***

The next morning, Oriel sent for Ramulas and Pip. They entered the room to find Edwin and two druids with Oriel. The dwarf wore a grim expression and stole occasional glances at the druids.

Ramulas heard a sharp intake of breath as Pip saw the druids, and she stepped behind him.

'Hello Ramulas and Pip,' Oriel said. 'Pip, I need you to bring two more to Sanctuary. They are very shy and need someone like you to accompany them here.'

Oriel waved her hand and sent a fine purple mist over Pip.

Once Pip was covered in the mist, she knew which path she needed to take. Pip felt the pair's loneliness and their desire to be in a place where they belonged.

The mist dissipated and Pip smiled at Oriel. 'I will bring them here. Look after my family until I return.'

As Pip left the room, Ramulas thought of her family. Since Jenna had arrived in Sanctuary, Jacqueline had taken her under her wing. Kate and Grace were constantly playing with Makayla and Tao, with the hell hounds close by. Pip's family would be safe while she was gone.

'Milord,' Edwin said as he stepped forward. 'We have a problem with the tunnel. We have been digging for days, and we are only ten feet deep. The mountain has lots of granite through it.'

'That is why I have brought the druids,' Oriel said. 'They will help with the tunnel.'

Both druids nodded before leaving the room.

'Where are they going?' Ramulas asked.

'They will bring people to help dig into the mountain faster,' Oriel said.

'What?' Edwin said. 'Tell me who can dig tunnels faster than a dwarf.'

Oriel smiled while Edwin crossed his arms defiantly and looked at her while tapping his foot.

'My good dwarf,' Oriel said softly. 'These are very special people.'

'Edwin,' Ramulas said, 'come and show me the progress of the tunnel.'

***

Pip rode north through the forest, always keeping the mountain range to her left. She searched for a small valley within the mountains. Pip came to a small clearing and knew that she was close to the valley.

But looking around, she could see no sign of the entrance, and then out of the corner of her eye, Pip saw a flash of light. Climbing down from her horse, Pip walked to the cliff face and saw a small opening.

The opening seemed small, but Pip decided to investigate. As she came closer Pip saw a path to her left, which led into the valley.

Pip walked back to her horse and led it inside. She stood at the edge of the valley and saw it was only one hundred and fifty yards long and narrow. The cliffs on either side were covered in vines.

Leaving the horse behind, Pip walked to the far end of the valley. She looked for a way to climb up, but most of the vines were rotten or too weak to support her weight. However, Pip soon found a way and started to climb.

She made her way up the wall until reaching the edge of the cliff. A strong smell filled her nostrils, followed by a shadow that fell over her. Pip looked up and her mouth fell open as a yeti reached down to grab her.

Pip screamed as she was pulled up.

She was thrown across the rough ground, rolling a few times before stopping. Pip moaned as she saw two yetis closing in on her.

They were slightly taller than she was and covered in shaggy brown hair. They had elongated arms, which brought their hands past their knees, and a mouthful of canine teeth.

Pain shot through Pip's body as she threw two knives at the closest yeti. Its eyes widened in surprise as the knives entered its chest, killing it instantly.

As it fell to the ground, the other yeti became enraged and attacked Pip. The yeti moved too fast for her to react. All Pip could do was hold her hands up to ward off the blows.

The yeti's fists rained down on Pip like a pair of sledgehammers. Then Pip was picked up and slammed to the ground. The air was knocked out of Pip and stars filled her vision.

When the stars cleared, Pip saw the yeti's hands rise again, but she was too weak to defend herself. Then she saw something out of the corner of her eye. The yeti was thrown into a tree with a bone-shattering thud.

A giant stepped in front of Pip. He was twice the height of Ramulas and carried a huge club with ease. He smiled leaning over her.

'I have founds my supper,' it said in a gravelly voice.

As the giant reached for Pip, she fell into the safety of darkness.

16

Ramulas had been inspecting the progress of the tunnel with Edwin. He had told the people helping the dwarf that help was on the way.

Emily came around the corner. 'Ramulas, Oriel needs you.'

Ramulas followed Emily into Oriel's room, where he found Iguchi, Miles Michael, and Benji all wearing grim expressions; however, what shocked Ramulas was seeing Jacqueline standing next to Oriel with tears in her eyes.

'What's wrong?' he asked Jacqueline.

'Ramulas, we have a problem,' Oriel said. 'The group from Keah is in trouble.'

Oriel waved her hand at the wall, causing it to shimmer. A moment later, an image appeared. Jacqueline turned away as the image came into focus.

Ramulas saw six wagons, several carts, and several hundred people being chased by Zachary's soldiers and cavalry. The soldiers fired arrows into the group and attacked those who could not defend themselves.

Women and children screamed. While the men did their best to fend off attacks, it would not be long until the people of Keah were overwhelmed.

'They are five hours west of Bremnon,' Oriel said. 'A soldier has ridden back for reinforcements. They need your help. Go through this doorway and help them.'

Oriel waved her hands through the air and a doorway of flame appeared before the image. Ramulas looked at, Michael, Miles, and

Benji. They held their weapons ready. Iguchi appeared calm; however, his eyes betrayed his impassive demeanour by blazing with intense fury.

Jacqueline turned to him. 'Go, and bring them back safe.'

'Sanctuary!' Ramulas yelled as he led the men into the doorway.

***

Ramulas and his four followers stepped through the portal into a cloud of dust as the majority of the caravan escaped into the trees. As the dust settled, they found themselves facing a tense sight.

Two carriages and an old farm cart had stopped, surrounded by a group of soldiers on horseback.

It was chaos.

The drivers of both carriages had attempted to defend their passengers, but their bloody bodies lay on the ground. The black and grey horses were not as large as Rufus, but they seemed very aggressive.

Ramulas focused and attempted to communicate with the horses. If he could sway them, the battle would end quickly. However, there was something interfering, and Ramulas could not communicate with them.

One of the riders had dismounted and was in the process of laying his boot into an old man. The captain's horse, regaled in blue, was also without rider. However, Ramulas could not see where the captain was.

From the second carriage came the sound of a woman's scream, which was silenced by a slap.

The outrage which flowed through Ramulas caused him to throw caution to the wind.

With a cry that surprised even him, Ramulas said, 'Halt, in the name of Sanctuary!'

The twelve remaining horsemen turned at the sound, shocked until they saw the small band that had interrupted their entertainment.

'Oh, mighty lord,' a blond private said with a laugh. 'Has your small army come to protect these people?'

The other soldiers laughed. Perhaps they had a right to laugh, Ramulas thought as he noticed how awkwardly Miles, Michael, and Benji held their swords. But Ramulas had to do what was right.

'I am Lord Ramulas, and I demand that you release these people of Sanctuary at once,' he said, taking his battle axe in both hands.

The now-familiar transformation of his weapon gave him confidence. Michael, Miles, and Benji fanned out to Ramulas' right, and Iguchi stepped to his left.

The young private, arrogantly oblivious to the magic before him, saw nothing to fear. 'Oh, captain,' he called out in a sing-song voice, 'a group of entertainers have come to perform for you.'

The door to the second carriage crashed open. Out stepped the massive captain, adjusting his belt around his rotund form with a curse. The carriage rocked as he stepped onto the ground.

'Who dares disturb the work of King Zachary!' he roared, waddling forward.

'A foreigner?' The captain scoffed as he saw Iguchi, and then he saw Miles and Benji. 'You two look like the thieves from Turtha that we have been searching for.'

The captain, eager to return to the woman in the carriage, waved his hand. 'Just kill them, and do it quickly.'

The private smiled. 'With pleasure, captain.'

The private was eager to impress his comrades. He drew his sword and kicked his horse forward, straight for Ramulas.

The former farmer planted his feet, lowered his battle axe, and waited. He focused once again, trying to communicate with the horse, but to no avail.

Just before the horse reached Ramulas, he whispered, 'I am so sorry.'

With a mighty swing upwards, the blade of the battle axe sliced through the thick neck of the charging horse, felling it immediately.

The horse's body slammed to the side, pinning the private beneath it. As the bones in his legs shattered, the private screamed once before fainting.

A moment of horrified awe passed through all that was present.

Then all hell broke loose.

With a great cry, three horsemen rushed forward. Benji and Miles sprang into action. They ran at the horses, cutting into them. Two horses collapsed, throwing their riders, who were dispatched by Iguchi's deadly blades.

Unable to change course, the surviving rider crashed forward. Ramulas swung with his battle axe and cut into the side of the horse. It fell awkwardly, throwing its rider to the ground. Ramulas turned to finish off the soldier.

As he did, Michael noticed that some of the soldiers had held back. One of them held a lethal-looking crossbow and had it aimed at Ramulas. With lightning speed, Iguchi launched one of his throwing stars; he had seen the danger as well.

The star was embedded in the forehead of the bowman.

But it was too late.

The bolt flew across the field and the Lord of Sanctuary went down. In a rage, Iguchi drew his swords again and attacked the remaining soldiers on horseback.

Benji, Miles, and Michael were close behind. 'Sanctuary!' the trio shouted.

With a leap, Iguchi kicked a rider in the chest. As the chest cavity, collapsed Iguchi pivoted, cutting down another soldier before landing like a cat.

Michael, Miles, and Benji attacked the left flank with such fury that the soldiers were caught unaware. Iguchi pushed in towards the left, hemming the soldiers in.

Try as they might, the kingdom soldiers were no match for the angry men of Sanctuary.

Two soldiers away from the battle looked at each other before quickly turning their horses and racing for Bremnon. Iguchi took the throwing star from the dead bowman and flung it at the riders.

The rider on the left cried out before falling from his horse. This only encouraged the remaining soldier to spur his horse on as he lowered himself in the saddle.

Iguchi turned to Michael, Miles, and Benji with a mixture of rage and sadness in his eyes. Benji and Miles looked behind him in disbelief.

As he turned, Iguchi gasped in surprise. Standing unsteadily on his feet was Ramulas. Iguchi was speechless.

Ramulas reached up to rub his head. 'Oh, I am going to have a headache tomorrow.'

Ramulas turned, and caught in between his war hammer and armour was the crossbow bolt. Iguchi ran up to remove the bolt and show Ramulas.

'That was a lucky shot,' Ramulas said.

Iguchi nodded. 'The goddess of luck was smiling down on us this day.'

'Where is the captain?' Ramulas asked.

'Over here,' a voice called from the other side of the carriage.

The captain stood by the carriage with someone holding his arm. Ramulas smiled as Shigar stepped out from behind the carriage and pushed the captain towards the men of Sanctuary.

***

A whip cracked in the distance followed by a scream. Royce stood and looked across the valley. He wiped the sweat from his forehead with the back of his hand and focused on the prisoner who was being punished.

'What happened?'

He turned to see his friend Shayn, who had also stopped digging. Shayn had arrived in Gullytown a month before Royce, and they had formed a friendship—first out of necessity, for a person could not survive on their own in this living hell, and then they found they had much in common.

They had both stood by their principles and refused to pay inflating taxes; for this, they were charged with stealing from the king and sent to Gullytown. Their sentence was five years; they had not known anyone to live past four years.

'That was Patrick,' Royce replied. 'He has not been faring well since the death of his wife last week.'

Shayn shook his head. 'If he is not careful, he will join her.'

Royce looked at his friend, who was very different from him. Shayn was shorter by half a foot and broad across the shoulders, with a mop of fair hair, whereas Royce was lean and tall with dark hair that mostly hung in front of his eyes.

'Are there any guards or dogs looking this way?' Shayn asked.

Royce quickly scanned the valley and shook his head, and then he scurried to Shayn's hole.

Another crack of the whip was followed by Patrick's scream.

'We have been here almost two years and nothing changes,' Shayn said.

Royce smiled. 'Nothing out here, anyway. But still, we look for a way out of this valley.'

'We cannot climb the walls or walk out. Our only choice is the dig through the rock.'

They both saw the dog walk away from Patrick's hole with a smug smile as the guard followed. Dogs were former prisoners; they were given privileges in return for informing. For this, they were despised by the other prisoners.

Royce and Shayn spent most of their time planning a way out of Gullytown. The valley was three miles long and half a mile wide, and sheer wall enclosed the valley. There was only one entrance, which was heavily guarded, and several tunnels lined the walls.

All excavations were taken out through the mouth of the valley, the only way in or out. Their chances of passing the twenty guards were slim at best. Even if the several hundred prisoners charged the entrance, they were too weak from lack of food and harsh working conditions.

The prisoners of Gullytown resembled the walking dead, their bodies were thin and covered in layers of dust. This did not hide the numerous scars on their backs from being whipped.

Their eyes were void of emotion, and the sense of hope had been replaced with despair.

However, Royce and Shayn were the exceptions.

***

'You have been slow in your work today,' a dog said, walking up to Shayn's hole. 'And why is he out of his hole?' the dog asked, pointing to Royce.

Shayn shrugged while holding up a pick. 'Well, I have not stopped working.'

'Still, you are very slow,' the dog said as Royce ran back to his hole. 'And you both need to show me respect.'

The dog fondled a red rag that hung by his side. He looked down at Shayn who fought to control his anger. All prisoners knew that when the dog lifted the red rag, guards would come and beat them without mercy.

'Dog!' Royce called out from his hole.

The dog forgot about Shayn as he searched for the perpetrator. 'Who said that?'

When no reply came, the dog walked away with murder in his eyes.

***

The end of the day came quickly, and the pair walked to the tunnels to hand in their tools. After the tools were returned, the call came for the prisoners to be locked in their tunnels.

As the prisoners walked into the tunnel, they were given a chunk of stale bread and a bowl of cold broth. All the prisoners began to file into the tunnel, except for one man.

Patrick stood outside the tunnel with desperation in his eyes. 'My daughters. I must return home; they need me. Jenna and Pippa need me.'

The guards stepped forward, pulling out their swords. Patrick stood his ground, gripping his pick.

Royce walked to the entrance of the tunnel when Shayn grabbed him by the arm and shook his head.

'They will kill him,' Royce whispered.

'Him and anyone else involved,' Shayn replied.

'Into the tunnel, prisoner,' the dog ordered.

Patrick shook his head. 'Jenna and Pippa need me to come home,' he cried with building hysteria.

The dog walked up and slapped Patrick hard across the face. Patrick screamed and swung his pick, which was embedded in the top of the dog's head. The dog collapsed dead to the ground, and the guards hacked at Patrick with their swords.

Patrick took the first few blows before falling. But still, the guards did not relent in their slaughter. Royce and Shayn forced themselves to watch as everyone else looked away. The guards stopped after a few seconds and seemed to revel in butchering Patrick.

The steel barred door was locked to the tunnel, and a torch was set near the entrance where the prisoners huddled around the light. Royce and Shayn walked several hundred yards into the darkness of the tunnel, where they came to their sleeping pallets.

While the rest of the prisoners gathered around the torchlight, Royce and Shayn spent time in pitch darkness discussing their escape.

Shayn ran his finger along the tunnel floor, leaving a trail of heat residue, he outlaid a map of the tunnel system they were in. Royce sat and watched the drawing on the floor, and he saw Shayn's glowing red eyes.

Infra-red vision.

Something had begun to happen to the pair a year ago. As the friends moved deeper into the tunnels, one of those things was the ability to see in the dark.

'By my thinking, we can start a vertical shaft on this branch of the tunnel,' Shayn said as he tapped a section of the map. 'We could reach the surface within a month.'

'Ha, now why are you in such a hurry to leave our cosy home?' Royce asked. 'The guards take our tools from us, and they think that we cannot dig.'

Shayn grunted in agreement, around the time they could see in the dark, the two friends found that they were able to pull small pieces of rock from the tunnel walls. For short periods of time, they were able to shape the rock with their hands.

The pair worked until the early hours of the morning before they were overcome with fatigue.

***

Royce and Shayn sat on the valley floor eating their morning meal.

A dog walked up to them with a smile. 'Since the man who caused a disturbance last night was your friend, it will be your job to bury him.'

Patrick's mutilated body still lay where it had been the night before. The friends smelled the first signs of decay as the sun rose, and flies gathered around the corpse.

Standing behind the dog were two guards waiting for an excuse to whip Royce and Shayn. The friends brought Patrick's body into the burial tunnel near the entrance of the valley.

Close to midday, both were ready to collapse from exhaustion. The dog watched closely as they buried Patrick. He waited for any reason to pull out his red rag. Royce came out of the tunnel carrying a basket of rocks. He looked towards the entrance. What he saw caused him to drop the basket.

Two druids had appeared at the entrance of the valley.

***

Four guards huddled together in a small circle. A pair of knucklebones fell in the middle of the group; the result brought curses from three of the guards and a shout of triumph from the fourth.

Coins were handed to the winner, who quickly placed them in his pouch. Looking up the guard saw two druids standing before him.

'In the name of the gods!' he shouted, falling back.

The other three guards turned to face the druids in shock.

'We have come to warn you of a storm,' one of the druids hissed.

'What storm?' one of the guards asked as he pulled out his sword. 'How did you come here without us seeing you?'

The guards looked past the two druids to see their horses, and behind them were miles of open plains, making it impossible for anyone to approach Gullytown without being seen.

'We have come from Sanctuary with a warning,' one of the druids hissed. The druid opened his arms wide; the guards fell back in shock as they saw the green scaly skin and taloned hands.

A ball of light grew in front of the druid as he chanted in a soft voice. The ball turned from white to purple before shooting in the air. The sound of rolling thunder filled the valley as the ball of light filled the vortex.

'What madness is this?' one of the guards shouted over the noise.

The guards gained confidence as reinforcements came running from the valley.

'You did not heed our warning,' One of the druids said as he threw a handful of stones into the air.

The guards' mouths opened in shock as the stones transformed into wasps, which attacked them. The druids were quickly forgotten as the guards ran from the wasps.

The rain fell as the sky grew dark and lightning shot from the clouds. The rain made it impossible to see more than ten feet.

The first druid reached into his robes and pulled out a fist-sized blue crystal. He held it towards the prisoners in the valley. He closed his eye and squeezed the crystal, and a wave of blue light shot across the valley.

'Now we wait for the ones Oriel sent us here for.'

***

Royce and Shayn watched the druids talking to the guards in awe. Like everyone in the kingdom, they knew of and feared druids. Neither of them had seen one before.

'What do you think is going on there?' Shayn asked.

'I don't know. But I think something is about to happen.'

'Get back to work, you two,' the dog snapped at them from behind. 'Or should I call the guards?'

The friends turned, and Shayn said, 'We were just—'

'I'll teach you to disrespect me,' the dog said as he pulled out the red rag and waved it above his head.

Looking at the entrance, Royce saw the guards running around, frantically waving their arms about. He reached out and pulled Shayn close.

Then heavy rain fell, which limited their vision, accompanied by the rolling of thunder.

'I told you something was happening,' Royce shouted over the downpour.

'What do we do now?' Shayn shouted back.

At that moment, a wave of light washed over them, and the friends looked at each other in shock.

'Did you hear that?' Shayne shouted.

Royce nodded.

'Those looking for Sanctuary come forth.'

The dog stepped closer to the friends. 'I will make sure you are both beaten!' he shouted.

'Shut up,' Shayn shouted as he delivered a backhand to the dog, causing him to fall into the mud.

Both friends ran through the rapidly forming puddles toward the entrance. They headed towards the glowing blue crystal. A few moments later, the friends stood in front of the druids.

Feelings of awe and excitement overrode generations of fear of the druids.

One of the druids held out the blue crystal. 'Sanctuary lies within this light. Touch the crystal and be free.'

The two friends looked at each other for a fraction of a second before simultaneously reaching for it.

The druids looked down at the crystal to see it was a darker shade of blue. The men who had come forth were now inside the crystal.

'We have what we came for,' one of the druids said. 'It is time for us to return.'

As they rode away from Gullytown, the druids remembered how the dryads had helped them. They were taken to a grove of trees ten miles away from Gullytown.

However, they would have no help returning to Sanctuary. They had days of riding ahead of them.

17

Pip woke to a world of pain as she regained consciousness. Every muscle in her body burned in agony. She groaned as a dizzy spell came over her.

Something warm and damp fell over her face, Pip groaned once more as she attempted to move her arm. She winced as the movement sent pain throughout her body.

The damp cloth was roughly pulled from her face, sending waves of agony through her, Pip opened her eyes to see a giant leaning over her wearing a lop-sided grin.

'Aaaargh,' Pip croaked.

The giant straightened and covered its mouth with its hands while looking around fearfully.

'Git yerself away from the lass,' a dwarf called as he came into view.

The dwarf slapped him on the leg, and an expression of pure terror crossed the giant's features as he jumped away from Pip.

'I—I didn't do it,' the giant said clasping his boulder-sized fists in front of him. 'She was awake, and I took to looking.'

The dwarf stomped on the giant's foot, which brought a yelp from him, and then the dwarf shook his finger at the giant. 'If ye have undone any o' me work, there will be hell to pay.'

The giant went to the corner of the room and hid behind his massive hands. It was at least four times larger than the dwarf, and yet he was terrified of him. The dwarf walked away from Pip to a steaming pot hanging over a fire.

Pip looked around and saw that she was in a hut with a very high ceiling. The dwarf returned with a steaming bowl and placed it on the table next to Pip.

'Don't ye worry yerself about Lodi,' the dwarf said, waving to the giant. 'Ye must be hungry, let me sit you up.'

The dwarf gently wrapped his stocky arms around Pip and Brought her into a sitting position. 'Where am I?' Pip asked.

'About a mile from where the yeti attacked ye. It was lucky that Lodi heard the fightin'.'

'I did a good thing, Rygar,' the giant said as he nodded eagerly.

The dwarf shot the giant a look before picking up the bowl.

'How long have I been here?' Pip asked.

'A day and a night,' Rygar said. 'And I'm thinkin' you be needin' some rest. I have dressed all yer wounds.'

It was then that Pip realised that her cloak and throwing knives were missing. She saw that her body had been wrapped in bandages and her belongings were at the end of the bed.

'I need to return to Sanctuary,' Pip said.

Rygar sighed as he pulled on his long black beard before smiling down at Pip. 'I know we seem a strange sight, a giant and dwarf together. We are supposed to be enemies, but I found meself stuck with Lodi. I am Rygar, what is your name?'

'Pip.'

'Well met, Pip. I'm thinkin' to give ye some broth an' tell ye why Lodi and meself will be comin' to Sanctuary with ye.'

'What broth is this?' Pip asked.

Rygar smiled. 'Yeti broth.'

'I squished 'em good,' Lodi said with a grin from the corner.

Rygar looked at Lodi. 'Why don't ye go down to the stream and catch some fish for our new friend?'

'I can get lots of fishes,' the giant said before stomping out of the hut.

'He will be gone for a while; Lodi's forgot the net again,' Rygar said. 'I think ye should be knowin' about Lodi an' meself.' A sad smile crossed Rygar's features as he gave Pip some broth. 'Ten years past, me clan were digging tunnels twenty miles from 'ere. We found an old set of tunnels an' set off to see where it would lead us. After a while, we hear fightin'. The sounds of giants fightin'.

'There's nothin' that excites a dwarf more than stompin' a giant. Fifty o' me clan ran until we came out to an opening. We were surprised to see the giants attacking one of their own—it was Lodi.

'There were three giants that attacked Lodi. Bein' that giants and dwarves are mortal enemies, we charged out o' the tunnel and attacked the giants.

'By the time the giants knew we were there, it was too late. Their knees were bashed with hammers and calves cut with axes. In a short time, me clan killed the three who were attacking Lodi.'

A sad smile crossed Rygar's face as he let out a short laugh and shook his head.

'After watching how we killed the other giants, Lodi stood with a stupid smile and thanked us for helpin' him. He asked if me clan could be his friends. The head o' me clan, Grundle McGregor, stepped forward with his axe over his shoulder.

'He asked Lodi to bend down a bit so he could look at his new friend. As Lodi bent down with a smile, Grundle shifted his feet and readied his axe.

'The dolt had stuck his face right in front of Grundle and smiled as the axe came down.

'Somethin' happened inside o' meself as I rushed in an' put me shield in front of Lodi, blocking the killin' blow. I knew at that moment that I had chosen Lodi over me clan. I stood me ground in between Lodi an' me clan without sayin' a word.

'I put meself on the side of a dwarf's enemy. Me clan did not look at me as they walked back into the tunnel. The message was clear: I was no longer part of me clan.

'I stood for a while after me clan had left, when Lodi asked if I could be his friend. I came to realise that Lodi was not all there with his thinkin'.

'His giant kin saw him as a weak link, and they set out to kill him. At times, I give him a swipe o' me axe, but now I see him as me own boy. He would not last a week if meself left him.'

Then Pip saw a sparkle in the dwarf's eyes.

'About a week ago, we heard a call to come to Sanctuary, and then Lodi an' meself saw a lot o' people movin' through the forest. What greetin' would Lodi have if we came down from the mountain?

'Oh, I'm thinkin' there won't be too many smiles or dancing girls to greet us. No, that's when Lodi brought you 'ere. I was thinkin' ye could talk on our behalf.'

'You could have come before,' Pip said. 'We have even accepted a group of druids.'

'Well, we can take ye to Sanctuary when yer well enough. Lodi can find others to bother, and he won't be trippin' over me feet all the time.'

Despite the dwarf's gruff demeanour, Pip knew he had the best intentions for the giant.

'Do ye and meself have a deal?' Rygar asked.

Pip nodded weakly. 'I will talk to the Lord of Sanctuary for you both.'

***

'My, look how far you have come, my friend,' Shigar said as he released the captain.

The magician pulled out a wand and tapped it on the captain's head. This brought screams of panic from the captain as he fell to the ground.

'Help me! I have gone blind! I cannot see,' the captain wailed.

Shigar walked away from the carriage with a smile on his face. He clapped Ramulas on the shoulder and nodded to the other men of Sanctuary. A moan caught everyone's attention. They looked at the pile of bodies on the ground.

One of the bodies began to move. Iguchi stepped in raising his sword.

'No!' Ramulas said, stopping the downward swing. 'Bring that one here.'

Iguchi reached down and pulled the soldier up by his hair, which caused him to scream. He was brought to stand before Ramulas. The Lord of Sanctuary quickly assessed the man's injuries—apart from a broken arm and some scratches, he seemed fine.

'Why were you harming my people?' Ramulas asked quietly.

The soldier looked around to see that only he and the captain were still alive; one moment they were all having fun, and then everything fell apart.

'They were on the king's road without papers.'

'What!?' Ramulas said in disbelief. 'When was this made law?'

The soldier shrugged, not having an answer. Ramulas looked at the captain who still cried on his knees.

'How do you stop him from crying?' Ramulas asked Shigar.

Shigar tapped the fat man on his head, causing him to gasp. 'I can see!'

'Stand up,' Ramulas ordered.

As the captain stood, he attempted to regain some dignity as he came to Ramulas.

'I hope you know that King Zachary will not be pleased with you killing his soldiers,' the captain said with a false sense of bravado.

Ramulas saw that the people of the caravan began to come out of the trees. Michael, Miles, and Benji were encouraging them to re-join the caravan.

'What you need to worry about now is that *I* am not pleased, but you and your soldier are free to leave. These are the people of Sanctuary, and they are under my protection. I am showing you more mercy than you deserve.'

The captain's face went through a series of emotions as Ramulas spoke, and then he gasped in shock. 'You're him! The one who escaped from the tombs. The one who killed James then vanished.'

Now it was Ramulas' turn to be shocked. He did not think someone would be able to recognise him; however, he quickly regained his composure.

'You have one chance—leave now, and I will allow you to live,' Ramulas said before turning to Iguchi. 'I need this caravan on its way to Sanctuary as soon as possible.'

As his men moved into action, Ramulas saw that the captain was still there. 'We will need horses,' he said to Ramulas haughtily.

A bitter laugh escaped Ramulas. 'The horses stay; you go.'

The colour drained from the captain's face when he saw Ramulas' expression. He motioned for the soldier before quickly walking toward Bremnon.

Iguchi walked up to Ramulas and whispered something to him. Ramulas' eyes widened before nodding.

'Michael, Miles, and Benji, we are heading south. We lead this caravan to the Darkwood,' Ramulas shouted loud enough for the captain and soldier to hear.

Within ten minutes, the caravan had begun its journey south. The men of Sanctuary rode the king's horses; Ramulas rode the captain's horse. Ramulas and Shigar led the caravan, while the men of Sanctuary ensured everyone was calm.

After travelling half an hour south, Ramulas stopped and held up his hand. He slowly rode past the people while speaking loudly.

'King Zachary will soon hear about what happened to his soldiers. He will discover that you have left Keah. People from across the lands have made Sanctuary their home; Zachary will know of this as well.

'The king will come looking for us—that I do not doubt. That is why his captain will tell him we have gone into the Darkwood. Now, we turn north and to the Devil's Ridge Mountains and Sanctuary. There you will find a place of acceptance, where you can begin a new life.'

The people gave a cheer, and then a woman with a small child on her lap spoke. 'Is it true?'

'Is what true?' Ramulas asked.

'Are you the one who escaped from the tombs, and made the soldiers look like bumbling fools?'

'I—Uh—' Ramulas stammered.

'That he is!' Shigar called out. 'He is the only person to escape from the tombs.'

Excited murmuring broke out along the caravan, and Ramulas felt extremely self-conscious at the attention.

At that moment, Michael rode up to Ramulas and said there was something he should see at the rear of the caravan; Ramulas told Miles and Benji to help Shigar lead the people to Sanctuary.

Iguchi followed the pair as they reached the rear of the caravan. What Ramulas saw almost caused him to fall from his horse.

The soil behind the last wagon was churning. Looking further down the road, Ramulas could see no sign that anyone had passed that way.

'By the gods,' Ramulas said in awe. 'What does this mean?'

'It is good magic,' Iguchi said. 'Those who will come for us have no tracks to follow, so they will not know where Sanctuary is.'

'This will give us time,' Ramulas said. 'Let's get these people to Sanctuary.'

***

By late afternoon, the caravan had travelled through the forest and made it to the wall of Sanctuary. Ramulas stopped just before the gate to look back at the people. He smiled seeing their expressions of awe.

'Welcome to Sanctuary,' Ramulas called out. 'Welcome home.'

He led the people into the courtyard, where he found his family and the hell hounds waiting for him, Ramulas climbed down from his horse to have Jacqueline engulf him in a hug, both his girls soon joined in.

'I was so worried,' Jacqueline said with tears in her eyes.

'Then you worried for nothing,' he said, wiping the tears from her cheeks. 'Everyone has come home safely.'

Michael, Miles, Benji, and Iguchi arranged the newcomers in the courtyard, and Emily came out to stand by Ramulas' side. Ramulas disentangled himself and stepped forward to make his welcoming speech.

After the speech, Emily took the people in to see Oriel while other people of Sanctuary welcomed the newcomers. But something was missing, Ramulas thought.

Not something, *someone*.

'Where is Pip?' he asked Jacqueline.

'She has not returned yet.'

Ramulas thought that strange, as she had left days earlier. He would speak to Oriel once she had spoken to the newcomers.

***

One of Zachary's agents boldly walked past the two guards and into the king's chambers, Zachary was in deep conversation with his councillors. Aleesha sat by her father's side wearing a bored expression.

The agent stopped before the throne and cleared his throat. Zachary looked up and saw that the agent held a small silver tube; Zachary waved the councillors away, he knew the silver tube was a message via pigeon.

He took the tube from the agent and unrolled the letter within.

Zachary looked at the agent. 'Find Shigar and bring him to me now.'

The agent quickly left the chambers and Zachary re-read the letter before handing it to Aleesha. It was from the captain who had chased the group from Keah and encountered the men from Sanctuary. Two things from the letter hit Zachary like a boot to the stomach.

The first was that the prisoner who escaped from the tombs was calling himself the Lord of Sanctuary—Zachary had never heard of the place. The men from Sanctuary attacked and killed kingdom soldiers and then led the people into the Darkwood.

The second thing was that Shigar had taken the side of the escaped prisoner and ridden off with him onto the Darkwood.

'Father,' Aleesha said. 'Why did you send the agent to find Shigar? The letter said that he was with the escaped prisoner.'

'I am hoping that the information about my magician was wrong.'

'What if he has gone with the prisoner?'

Zachary scowled. 'Then I will punish Shigar.'

A sadistic smile grew on Aleesha's face. 'I want to see him punished.'

'Why?' Zachary asked as he turned to his daughter.

'A few weeks ago, he struck me. Shigar said that if I told anyone, he would kill me.'

Anger and confusion clouded Zachary's thoughts, whether Shigar was in the castle or not, Zachary would see him suffer. Then the thought of people leaving Keah for Sanctuary angered him even more.

Why would hundreds of people leave the city of Keah and travel to a place Zachary had never heard of?

The agent returned to Zachary's chambers with a grim expression. 'Shigar is not in his chambers or the castle. Some of his books and scrolls are missing.'

'Show me,' Zachary ordered as his face flushed with anger.

Aleesha quickly followed her father.

They arrived at Shigar's chambers with an escort of six royal guards, Zachary walked in and saw that items had been removed from the shelves, and the table that was always covered in scrolls and potions was now empty. The agent informed Zachary that Shigar had not been seen since a dense fog a few nights ago.

Zachary burned inside as he felt a deep sense of betrayal. First, the prisoner with magical abilities escapes from the tombs, and now Shigar had formed an alliance with him. Zachary shook his head, not wanting to accept that fact.

Zachary wanted answers and wanted both the prisoner and Shigar in chains before him. 'Send word to the captain in Bremnon. I shall meet him in Nasad. Ready two hundred soldiers. We leave within the hour. We will track down Shigar the traitor.'

The agent nodded before leaving. Zachary looked around Shigar's chambers. He wanted to burn everything, but that could wait until he returned with the magician. A cruel smile spread across Zachary's face thinking of Shigar watching his life's work destroyed.

'Aleesha, you will stay here until I return,' Zachary said in a tone that left no room for argument.

***

Lucas discussed the logistics of travelling to Nasad and then onto the Darkwood. They would arrive in Nasad after nightfall. It would take time to organise provisions, horses, and men.

The captain of the royal guard left to prepare, and a squire helped Zachary don his armour. The agent returned and held out his hand showing three small silver tubes, Zachary waved the squire away and read the three letters.

A cold sensation flowed through his body as he read the letters, they were from the towns of Rylek, Turtha, and Shes. The letters were almost identical, after a night-time fog hundreds of people had gone missing from the towns.

What happened in Keah was now happening across the land. Were all these people going to Sanctuary?

'You can't have all of these people go missing in my kingdom, without it coming to my attention,' Zachary said to the agent. 'I want this Lord of Sanctuary found.'

18

Pip was fit enough to walk with Rygar's help, and Lodi and his adopted father had gathered their possessions and were ready to travel to Sanctuary.

After a mile of walking, Pip began to limp severely. Lodi picked her up without a word and carried Pip as if she was a baby.

They reached the valley where Pip encountered the yeti, and Rygar sighed as he looked back. 'I'll be missin' me home, but it's time fer movin'.'

Lodi climbed down into the valley, and Pip noticed that her horse was gone. She watched Rygar climb down and thought it odd for the dwarf to have his shield and axe underneath his pack. If they were attacked, it would take the dwarf too long to retrieve his weapon.

But then Pip looked up at Lodi, realising that Rygar did not have to worry while he was with the giant.

The trio made their way into the forest and followed the mountains south toward Sanctuary, and within half an hour they had reached their destination.

Lodi stood in the clearing with Pip in his arms. Rygar stood next to the giant. They were greeted by Ramulas with his hell hounds, Iguchi, Miles, Benji, Michael, and twenty other men in armour.

Each person was well-armed and wore a stern expression.

'I telled ye lassi—plenty o' smiles,' Rygar grumbled.

'Put her down gently,' Ramulas called out.

As Pip was placed on the ground, she winced and waved to Ramulas. 'I'm fine. These two are friends and they saved me from yetis. They nursed me back to health and want to join Sanctuary.'

Lodi nodded in agreement and was quickly stopped by a glare from Rygar. Ramulas made a slight gesture. Michael, Miles, and Benji helped Pip into Sanctuary.

As Pip passed Ramulas, she said. 'They mean no harm. Bring them to Oriel.'

Ramulas looked at the pair. 'I think it would be best if you came into the castle and spoke to Oriel.'

Ramulas waved for the dwarf and giant to follow him. Iguchi and the rest of the men came into Sanctuary behind them.

As they entered the town, the people stopped and stared at Lodi with wide eyes and open mouths. The people of Sanctuary were mesmerised by the sight of the giant.

Lodi and Rygar were led to Oriel's room to find her waiting for them with a smile. 'Welcome to Sanctuary. Please tell me why you have come.'

Rygar retold the same story that he had told Pip. During the story, Oriel waved her hand and Pip was covered in a fine white dust.

Pip glowed for a few seconds before it subsided. Then she smiled while moving her body. 'I'm better. A little stiff, but nothing hurts.'

Ramulas looked at Lodi, who towered over him. Luckily, the castle had high ceilings. The giant was nervous and avoided eye contact with everyone in the room.

'I want to hear his side of the story,' Ramulas said, pointing to Lodi.

Lodi's eyes went wide as he covered his mouth with his hands. He reminded Ramulas of the time Grace was caught taking something from the larder.

'Oh, don't be worryin' yerself bout Lodi. I'll be watchin' over him.'

An expression of relief crossed the giant's features, and then Ramulas spoke once more. 'I know you will look after him, but I want to hear his story.'

'My boy is dumber than a sack o' rocks and would confuse everyone,' Rygar said.

At this statement, Lodi began to laugh and covered his face trying to hide the fact. The more Lodi tried to stop laughing, the louder he was.

Rygar slapped Lodi across the leg. 'Stop yer laughin' or yer goin' to feel me boot.'

Lodi's eyes widened in terror. 'I—I never was laughin'. Ye said I was in a sack o' rocks. I will live in a cave and bring ye no more trouble.'

'Bah, ye wouldn't last a week without me watchin' yer every step,' Rygar said with another slap. 'Ye can see that my boy is harmless.'

'I agree,' Ramulas said.

Everyone in the room turned when Oriel waved her hand. Lodi and Rygar were covered in a faint purple glow. Lodi let out a yelp and jumped before a calmness washed over him.

After a few moments, the glow faded. The dwarf and giant both wore determined expressions.

'These two will be a great help to Sanctuary,' Oriel said. 'They will do everything they can in our fight against the First Legion.'

Lodi swung his boulder-sized fists through the air. 'Why they want hurt pretty lady? I will crush them.'

'Ye will wait till they come,' Rygar said before turning to Ramulas. 'I'm led to be thinkin' that meself can help train yer people fer this legion.'

'What do you know about training people?' Ramulas asked.

'Me clan have been smashin' monsters' heads for hunnerds o' years,' Rygar said with a wink. 'I'll be teachin' yer people a few dirty tricks.'

'I will show them where to stay,' Emily said from the door.

After they left with Emily, Oriel vanished, and the room exploded into excited conversation about having a giant in Sanctuary.

'You saw a giant in one of your visions,' Benji said to Miles. 'Was that the one?'

Miles nodded, unable to talk.

***

Ramulas and Jacqueline walked the streets of Sanctuary ensuring people had settled in, and after a few minutes they heard children squealing and the hell hounds barking. Ramulas communicated with the hell hounds and discovered that Grace, Kate, Jenna's children, and the hell hounds were under attack.

Ramulas gripped Jacqueline's hand and quickened his pace toward the sound. When they rounded the corner, Ramulas stopped at the sight before him.

A druid stood in the middle of the street holding a wand, Kate, Grace, Makayla, Tao, and the hell hounds were jumping around in front of him.

The air was filled with green bubbles. The children laughed and squealed as they jumped to hit the bubbles. When they burst, streams of sticky goo covered the children and hell hounds. The goo disappeared as soon as it touched them.

Looking past the four children and the hell hounds, Ramulas saw several other children watching the spectacle; they were eager to join, but were held back by their parents. Ramulas released Jacqueline's hand and walked to the closest set of parents and children in the crowd.

'Does that look like fun?' Ramulas asked two boys that were close to Grace's age.

They both nodded vigorously.

Ramulas made eye contact with the parents. 'Do you know that they are my daughters?' he said as he nodded toward Kate and Grace. 'I would not let them near the druids if it were not safe.'

Hesitation crossed the mother's face at the thought of letting her boys be close to the druid, and then she looked from Kate and Grace to Ramulas' calm smile and back again.

'Play with the bubbles,' she said to her boys. 'But don't go too close to the druid.'

She released her boys and they rushed into the fray, jumping and laughing with the others.

Over the next few moments, other children were allowed to join the fun with the druid.

'Isn't it wonderful?' Jacqueline whispered as she came up to Ramulas.

'Yes, it is. I hope this is the beginning of people accepting the druids.'

'Hello to you, Lord of Sanctuary,' Iguchi said as he appeared next to Ramulas. 'We must begin training.'

Ramulas kissed Jacqueline before leaving with Iguchi.

***

Iguchi led Ramulas to the training grounds where Michael, Miles, and Benji waited with a group of others in matching uniforms. A quick count told Ramulas there were fifty in Iguchi's group.

'These are my Fallen Angels,' Iguchi boasted proudly. 'I have found the number that I was looking for.'

'Why are they called "Fallen Angels"?' Ramulas asked.

'That is a secret,' Iguchi said with a sly wink. 'You will understand later, but now, you will learn to fight from your warhorse.'

Ramulas looked at the Fallen Angels standing proudly in their uniforms and holding their swords and shields. They had been the only ones in Sanctuary to be given armour and weapons.

Oriel had said to Ramulas that Iguchi's group needed to feel a different sense of belonging than the rest of Sanctuary. They were to be an elite force within Sanctuary's army.

A feeling came over Ramulas, and he called out, 'Fallen Angels, kneel before me.'

They obeyed at once, forming a line in front of Ramulas, and fell to their knees. Beginning from the left, Ramulas walked past each one, grasping a shoulder plate as he passed. Purple smoke rose from the armour where he lay his hand.

To each one, Ramulas murmured, 'You are the guardians of Sanctuary. May Oriel guide and watch over you.'

Ramulas saw each of the Angels swell with pride as a mark was left by their lord. When he had finished, Iguchi gave a nod of approval.

Rufus was brought to Ramulas. Once he climbed on, Ramulas saw ten of the Fallen Angels holding quarter staves. Among them were Michael, Miles, and Benji.

'Lord of Sanctuary,' Iguchi said, 'you will need to pass through the Fallen Angels and reach the other side. Use your weapons to fend off attacks.'

Ramulas saw the serious expressions worn by the Fallen Angels as he climbed onto the warhorse and readied his weapons.

Ramulas communicated with Rufus to charge the Angels, who waited fifty feet away. The five Angels on the right lowered their staffs while those on the left directed theirs at Ramulas.

Ramulas would focus on the left as he charged through.

The Angels separated into two groups, leaving Ramulas a gap to ride through. As Ramulas came to within ten feet of the Angels, he leaned to the left, lowering his war hammer.

The Angels on the left stepped back, avoiding Ramulas' weapon. Already committed to the move, Ramulas was surprised when Benji dropped his staff and rushed forward to grab his wrist.

Simultaneously, Michael and Miles lifted Ramulas' right foot out of the stirrup. With a great push, the Lord of Sanctuary came crashing to the ground.

Air exploded from Ramulas' lungs, and he lost the grip of his war hammer as he hit the ground. Michael and Miles ran to Ramulas and delivered overhead strikes with their staves.

Ramulas lifted his battle axe too slowly. Two cracks sounded as the quarterstaff struck his breastplate. The rest of the Fallen Angels stood back watching.

'You were close,' Iguchi said as he walked over. 'But it was wrong.'

Iguchi reached Ramulas and helped him to his feet. 'Taking the Lord of Sanctuary was good. It was not perfect; we will need to practise.'

In a blur of movement, Iguchi dropped and spun, hooking his leg behind Ramulas' ankles. For the second time, Ramulas found himself lying on the ground.

In the blink of an eye, Iguchi stood over him holding a quarterstaff. 'You must look for a quick kill,' Iguchi said as he thrust the end of the staff into the side of Ramulas' neck. 'Strike here, here, and here,' Iguchi said, moving the staff to Ramulas' armpit and then under his ribs.

'The inside of the upper arm and leg have major veins,' Iguchi said, lightly tapping on Ramulas with his quarterstaff.

Dropping the staff, Iguchi helped Ramulas to his feet once more. 'It is wise to know your opponent's strengths and weaknesses. Now we will look at the weaknesses.'

Looking across the training field, Ramulas saw Rygar and Lodi watching with interest. Twenty people near the giant watched as well.

Iguchi motioned for Ramulas to climb onto Rufus again.

'Oh, Lord of Sanctuary,' Iguchi said with a smile. 'Never affix your eyes on one Angel. In battle, you must always take quick glances at all that surrounds you. In this way, you will see everything.'

Ramulas brought Rufus around for another charge at the Fallen Angels.

***

Zachary arrived in the town of Nasad an hour after sunset. He was accompanied by two hundred soldiers, and a cordon of royal guard led the column with their king.

The captain who had met Ramulas and the men from Sanctuary waited with the mayor of Nasad. They were surrounded by several men holding torches and met their king at the edge of town.

'Welcome my king,' the thin, balding mayor said with a bow. 'I have been informed of your arrival, and my town is at your disposal.'

Zachary ordered that his soldiers and royal guard were fed and shown to their quarters and the horses seen to. While the soldiers were taken into town, Zachary and five of the royal guard were taken to a luxurious house.

The fat captain had shown them the way and continued to fawn over Zachary. He kept apologising for what had happened. Trays of meat, bread, cheese, and fruit adorned the large table at the end of the room. Three serving girls waited silently for instructions.

'Lucas,' Zachary said to the captain of the royal guard. 'This is too much food. Set aside a small portion for us and give the rest to the men.'

Orders were given to the serving girls, and they hurried to deliver food to the soldiers.

'That was wise, my king,' Lucas whispered.

Zachary smiled. 'The carrot and the stick, Lucas. I need the men in high spirits when we meet Shigar. Most of them fear the magician.'

Once the allocated food was taken, Zachary and the royal guard sat with the fat captain.

Zachary forced a smile as he looked at the captain filling his mouth with food. 'Please tell me everything that happened. Start from the beginning, and do not leave anything out.'

The captain told of how his small company came across a few hundred people from Keah, who ignored all calls for them to stop and explain where they were going. The captain had ordered his men to stop the caravan. Then the men of Sanctuary had appeared and attacked his soldiers. All of the soldiers except for one had been killed.

The fat captain fished the story by telling of his heroics and how he faced the men of Sanctuary on his own, and that he had heard them say they were headed for the Darkwood.

'Please tell me,' Zachary said calmly, 'from which direction did the men of Sanctuary come?'

The fat captain opened his mouth, searching for something that would confirm his story.

'I … I … Uh, was holding a dangerous person down with my sword in a carriage when they arrived.'

'Were you using the sword in your pants?' Lucas asked.

The expression on the fat captain's face was all Zachary needed. 'Tell the men to be ready at dawn,' he said with a dismissive wave to the captain. 'If I find that you were away from your post when you were attacked, you will be sent to Gullytown.'

The fat captain paled before leaving the room.

Lucas smiled at Zachary. 'He was having his way with one of the women when the men from Sanctuary came, and I think the fight went differently than how he told it. The injured private is still in Bremnon, we will talk to him tomorrow.'

Zachary nodded as he tried to piece together the story he was told. He knew there were pieces missing, and they would soon fall into place. He was sure the private in Bremnon would help.

***

Zachary led the soldiers into Bremnon just after midday. They had left before dawn and ridden hard the whole way. The mayor of Bremnon and the injured private waited for their king.

The soldiers were told to see to their horses and get some rest. They would be leaving shortly.

Zachary, Lucas, and the mayor sat in his office with the injured private. Zachary saw that his arm was in a sling and the left side of his face was covered in bandages. He waited for food and drink to be placed on the table before speaking.

'Tell me your name, private,' Zachary said.

'Private Anderson.'

'Now, tell me of the caravan and what happened with the men of Sanctuary.'

Private Anderson told the same story as the fat captain, up to when they saw the caravan outside of Bremnon. From the moment they intercepted the caravan, the private's story was different to the captain's.

'When the caravan did not stop, the captain ordered his men to attack the people. Many people ran into the trees as the soldiers attacked. After a few people were killed, the captain saw a woman in one of the carriages.

'A few moments after he entered the carriage with the woman, the men of Sanctuary walked out from a doorway of light.

'None of the soldiers took them seriously. The Lord of Sanctuary ordered us to release the people. The captain came out of the carriage and ordered us to attack—that is when the men from Sanctuary began killing us.

'The Lord of Sanctuary led the people toward the Darkwood. Only one other soldier escaped and has not been seen since.'

'Sergeant Anderson,' Zachary said. 'Are you well enough to show us where you saw the men of Sanctuary?'

'Why—What?' Anderson stammered. 'I am a private.'

Zachary shook his head. 'No, you showed great courage, and you are promoted.'

Anderson swelled with pride. 'I will show you, my king. It is not far from this town.'

'That is what I was hoping to hear,' Zachary said.

***

A few hours later, Sergeant Anderson rode alongside King Zachary to where the bodies of soldiers still lay. A score of ravens that were feasting on the bodies took flight as the column came close. Caws of protest could be heard as they flew for the trees.

The sight of bloating bodies, combined with the smell of rotting flesh, was almost enough to make Sergeant Anderson turn away.

Almost.

But he held his resolve, fixing his gaze on a tree beyond the carnage. The soldiers' horses had been taken, but their armour and weapons remained.

'The horses have been taken, my king,' Sergeant Anderson said.

'I can see that,' Zachary replied. 'But taken where? I see no tracks, and a few hundred people with wagons and carts would leave some trace.'

Lucas climbed down from his black stallion and inspected the ground near the dead soldiers. He looked back the way they had come and then south to the Darkwood.

'As we came to this position, I saw the tracks of horses and wagons,' Lucas said. 'But from here, it is as if the ground has swallowed them.'

'Magic,' Zachary said through clenched teeth. 'I would expect nothing less from Shigar the Traitor.'

Frustration built within Zachary, and he saw the fat captain fidgeting. 'You!' Zachary said, pointing to the captain. 'You will remain with four soldiers to bury these men. If it is not done by the time I return, you will go to Gullytown.'

Looking away from the fat captain, Zachary ordered the column north.

***

Zachary had led the column to within half a mile of the Darkwood. Hooting and growling could be heard coming from the forest. He could feel the tension in the air as fear began to build in his men. He would lead by example.

They continued to within one hundred yards of the Darkwood. The hoots and growling became louder and more frantic. This added to the soldiers' trepidation, fuelled by childhood stories of monsters that filled the foreboding forest.

Zachary looked to Sergeant Anderson and spoke in a bored tone. 'Sergeant, lead the men to the edge of the trees. See if there is any sign of the people from Keah or Sanctuary.'

Sergeant Anderson moved away from his king before barking out orders. The soldiers broke into three sections: the middle section of fifty men rode for the trees while the other two sections followed on the left and right sides.

This was the only manoeuvre the former private knew; he just hoped that it would work.

Fifty yards from the tree line, the soldiers stopped as the Darkwood grew deathly quiet. Sergeant Anderson called for the soldiers to move forward; the soldiers moved ten yards before chaos erupted.

Hordes of tall, lanky trolls burst out of the trees; within seconds, they had reached the first line of soldiers. Hoots and grunts mixed with men screaming as the two races clashed.

The two flanking positions had not moved to help or retreat—they were caught in the same frozen terror as Sergeant Anderson, who only wanted to escape.

Kicking his heels into his horse, Anderson tried to turn away from the trolls in terror, but he only had the use of one arm, and his horse bolted toward the trolls. He screamed in a mix of terror and pain as his life flashed before his eyes.

The soldiers in the rear flanks took this as a signal to attack. The charge of men and horses tipped the tide of the battle, which allowed Sergeant Anderson to call a safe retreat.

As one, the soldiers turned their horses and raced back to their king. The trolls hooted and gave chase.

After ten yards, a few trolls in the front line suddenly turned to stone before collapsing. More ran into the barrier and turned to stone.

The remaining trolls stood their ground and let out tormented howls. They knew they could go no further.

Zachary looked on without interest, wishing Shigar was here to help with the trolls. As soon as the thought entered his mind, Zachary felt bile build in the back of his throat. The feeling of betrayal was still raw.

They had lost a handful of men and horses. Zachary knew the caravan had not passed the Darkwood. He needed answers about Sanctuary and where the people of the kingdom have been going to.

He looked at Lucas. 'We will find nothing here. Let's return to Keah and plan our next move.'

Lucas turned and gave orders to return to Keah. Zachary could have sworn that he heard a collective sigh of relief.

19

Ramulas and Pip stood side by side in front of four legion soldiers. They looked at Ramulas and Pip with open hatred. The pair had been fighting together over the last couple of days, whenever they found the time.

'Are you ready?' Ramulas asked calmly.

Pip nodded while loading a bolt into her small crossbow.

'Begin,' Ramulas said to the first two soldiers.

The soldiers burst into motion as Ramulas focused and everything around him slowed. The legion soldier in front of him led with a thrust with his red-bladed sword.

Ramulas spun, flicking the battle axe to deflect the sword. He followed with his war hammer, crushing the soldier's armoured shoulder and sending him onto his companion.

Then, in the blink of an eye, time returned to normal. Ramulas heard the clash of armour as the two legion soldiers collided and fell to the floor. Pip cursed and jumped back.

Ramulas rushed in with his battle axe raised. Pip shot one soldier with her crossbow and threw two knives into the other.

'What was that?' Ramulas asked in disbelief.

Pip shrugged while smiling at Ramulas. 'A woman's work is never done. We are always cleaning up after men.'

'I was about to finish that one,' Ramulas said incredulously.

'And I was fine with them,' Pip said, retrieving her knives and crossbow bolt.

She wiped her knives on the tunic of the dead legion soldier. The two soldiers who had not been activated were watching the exchange with open hatred.

'Are you saying that you are able to fight two by yourself?' Ramulas asked.

Pip crossed her arms and gave a slight nod.

By this stage, the two legion soldiers had repaired themselves and stood ready to fight. Ramulas saw the eagerness in their eyes.

'We shall see,' he said, activating both.

Ramulas quickly spun to the left while using his weapons to parry attacks from his opponent. He moved away from Pip to grant her wish.

Pip danced in between the two soldiers with a knife in each hand.

She would use her knives to tap the red blades of the swords just enough to keep them at bay. Pip danced in the middle playing with the two, which frustrated Ramulas.

Pip seemed bored as she danced between the two soldiers. She kicked one in the stomach, sending him sprawling. The other soldier delivered a backhand swing with its sword, which Pip ducked.

As the blade passed, Pip stood and kissed the legion soldier on the lips. The legion soldier dropped its sword in shock and Pip slit his throat.

The legion soldier dropped like a puppet whose strings were cut, and a fountain of blood sprayed from the soldier's neck. Pip hopped away from the blood and gave a bow to Ramulas.

He saw that the remaining soldier had recovered and had come up behind Pip with his sword raised. Ramulas did not want to throw his weapons for fear of hitting Pip.

'Behind you,' he called out while using his magical ability.

The red blade flashed down and stopped an inch from Pip's neck. Ramulas gritted his teeth under the strain of holding the sword with his magical ability.

Pip rolled forward and came up in a fluid motion, sending a throwing knife into the soldier's eye. The knife was thrown with such force that the soldier's head snapped back.

'By the gods!' Ramulas exclaimed. 'What were you thinking? You could have been killed.'

'I knew that you would help,' Pip said, tossing her hair.

'Aaaaaargh!' Ramulas said before storming out.

A few moments after Pip left, Iguchi stepped out of the shadows. He was joined by Michael, Miles, and Benji.

'They make a good fighting team,' Iguchi said, nodding in approval. 'Her fighting style angers him, and the angrier he is, the more focused he becomes.'

'Is that not dangerous?' Miles asked. 'Becoming mad during a battle?'

'In most people it is dangerous,' Iguchi answered. 'But the Lord of Sanctuary is different—his power comes from his emotions.'

***

Miles and Benji walked through the hallways of the castle. Twenty yards from Oriel's room, a druid stepped out into the hall in front of them.

Benji gasped while stepping back. Miles stood his ground, unsure of what he should do, and then he heard a sharp intake of breath from Benji. Miles turned to see another druid in the hall behind them.

Benji was frozen in fear, with eyes as wide as saucers. The druid behind them took a step towards Benji.

This broke the spell on Benji. With a shaky hand, Benji reached for the sword on his hip. 'You will not take me back to the druid's labyrinth,' he said softly.

Both druids stood impassively, not moving a muscle. Since they had come to Sanctuary and begun to play with the children, Benji had avoided them. This was the first time he had encountered them in such a confined space.

Now Benji felt trapped. There was nowhere for him to escape. Thoughts of his torments in the labyrinth flooded back. He would not let them take him again. He began to slowly draw his sword.

'Benji, stay your hand,' Ramulas commanded.

Benji snapped his head around to look at Ramulas at Oriel's door while sheathing his sword.

'Benji, Miles, come into the room.'

The two druids stepped away to allow Benji and miles room. By the time Benji made it into Oriel's room he was visibly shaken. Ramulas brought them both to Oriel.

'What happened out there?' Ramulas asked.

'We were on our way here,' Miles said. 'Then the druids came into the hall. Benji thought they would take him again.'

Oriel looked at Benji, who had the expression of a rabbit caught in a trap, his eyes darting fearfully around the room.

Oriel began to chant while waving her hands through the air. Within a second, Benji was bathed in a soft white light. All traces of fear left Benji, replaced with a look of peace.

Of all the people in Sanctuary, Benji is the only one who has yet to accept the druids,' Oriel said. 'I sense a great fear of the druids within him. They have made him experience horrors that he will not recover from.

'I will help him along that path. I cannot fully remove his fear of the druids, but I can remove enough so that he only feels discomfort around them.'

With a wave of her hand, the light disappeared. Benji looked calm and relaxed.

Oriel smiled at him. 'Benji, there are two druids outside. Could you ask them to come in please?'

Benji smiled and walked into the hallway, Miles stood in shock, not understanding what had happened.

'He will not remember his encounter with the druids,' Oriel explained. 'If I had not helped him, his fear of the druids would have spread throughout Sanctuary. The people would lose morale, and we would lose when the legion comes.'

Miles nodded as Benji returned with the two druids.

'Welcome, druids,' Oriel said, 'We have need of your talents. Together with Shigar, you will need to teach someone the aspects of magic.'

***

Shigar walked into Ramulas' quarters and smiled at Jacqueline in greeting. 'Hello again. I trust you have settled into your new home? I spoke to you at your farm about Grace's magical ability and her need for teaching.'

A stern expression crossed Jacqueline's features. 'And I told you that Grace will not be going across the sea.'

Shigar smiled. 'Circumstances have changed. Oriel, the druids, and I will guide Grace in the way of magic.'

'When was this decision made? And why was I not asked?'

'The decision was made a short while ago with Ramulas.'

'Well, I am Grace's mother. And I would like to know these things.'

Without another word, Jacqueline brushed past Shigar and into the hallway. By the time she entered Oriel's room, Jacqueline's anger had built up. Ramulas, Rygar, and Lodi were talking with Oriel.

'How dare you,' she said with a tremor in her voice.

All eyes in the room turned to her in surprise.

'Grace is my daughter, and you made plans for her to learn magic without talking to me.'

'Oh, no,' Ramulas sighed. 'I had forgotten to talk to you about it. I had been so busy that it slipped my mind.'

Jacqueline walked over to Ramulas full of determination. Lodi saw her expression and quickly hid behind the throne.

'You discussed our daughter with her,' Jacqueline said, stabbing a finger at Oriel. 'But not with me. Sometimes I think you enjoy being with her more than me.'

Ramulas' mouth opened in shock, and he was at a loss for words. Rygar did not want any part of this—he excused himself and took Lodi with him.

'It is not what you think,' Ramulas said, reaching for Jacqueline.

'Then tell me what is going on,' she said pulling away from him.

'If Grace is not mentored in magic,' Oriel said softly, 'she will hurt herself and those close to her. Like allowing a small child to play with fire. Ramulas is doing things normal people could not dream of. The lives of everyone in the kingdom lie in his hands.'

Jacqueline's demeanour softened as Oriel's words sunk in, and then she began to feel embarrassed. Jacqueline had come into Oriel's room and made a fool of herself.

Ramulas stepped in to hold his wife in his arms and looked her in the eyes. 'Everything I do is for you and the girls,' he said, kissing her on the forehead. 'Grace will be practising magic in this room. She will be safe here. Is that fine with you?'

Jacqueline nodded feeling foolish. 'I am sorry to come here angry.'

Ramulas laughed. 'Do not be sorry. This shows that you care for the girls.'

***

Shigar sat on the floor in Oriel's room, and Grace sat opposite him with her legs crossed. He had told her that she was going to learn how to use magic.

Grace waited; eagerness showed as she found it hard to sit still. Fenris wagged his tail as he sat by her side.

'When magic first came into the universe,' Shigar said, 'it began as something very small. The tiniest of sparks within a dark void. Then it slowly grew. Like this.'

Shigar held his hands out in front of him, a shoulder width apart, with his palms facing one another. He took a few slow deep breaths, and then a small light the size of a grain of rice appeared between his hands.

Grace gasped in fascination, and her eyes widened as it appeared and began to grow. As the light grew, small tendrils of energy reached out for Shigar's palms. Within a few moments, the light had grown to a quarter of an inch across. Arcs of blue energy danced between Shigar's hands.

Grace reached for the ball of light impulsively—too fast for the magician to act. By the time Shigar said, 'No,' Grace had taken the ball of light away from him.

Grace held her hands apart in the same fashion as Shigar had done. She giggled as the arcs of energy tickled her hands. The magician sat watching in shock.

'Doesn't that hurt?' he whispered.

'It tickles,' she replied.

Shigar clapped his hands and the ball disappeared. Grace dropped her hands and pouted.

***

Oriel watched the pair with amusement. Grace showed more magical ability than Shigar had thought possible. Grace was eager to learn as much as she could, and Shigar was attempting to slow her learning process.

After an hour, the magician said that the lesson had finished. Grace protested and begged for just a few minutes more.

This brought back fond memories of when Oriel was a child of the light. Her father Antok had seen her mature rapidly in the magical arts and attempted to hide how advanced Oriel had become.

Anger and bitterness flooded through Oriel as she remembered her father's sacrifice—he had been killed by Remus, giving her time to escape. That moment played over and over in her mind.

Oriel pushed those thoughts away, not wanting to cloud her mind. She, above everyone in Sanctuary, needed to focus and plan for when the First Legion came. The smallest mistake would mean the death of everyone in Sanctuary and the kingdom.

***

As Ramulas walked through the streets of Sanctuary alongside Pip, he noticed people whispering in hushed tones while pointing at him. He saw a sense of awe and fascination written on their faces. Pip smiled as she walked with a spring in her step.

219

Near the waterfall at the rear of Sanctuary, a group of four men approached Ramulas.

'Lord, are the stories true?' The stocky spokesman asked.

'What stories?' Ramulas asked.

'That you escaped from the tombs,' the stocky man said.

'And that you bested four soldiers with your bare hands after killing James, the king's giant?' Another eagerly added.

Ramulas shook his head. 'No, that did not—'

'It was six soldiers,' Pip said, interrupting and opening her arms in a dramatic display. 'And the Lord of Sanctuary snapped one of the swords in half with his bare hands. Then the rest of the soldiers fled in terror.'

The men were mesmerised by Pip's account of Ramulas' escape. They looked at him in new-found admiration and awe. The men were unsure how to act in the presence of such a person. They gave a few awkward bows before vanishing in the crowds.

Ramulas looked down at Pip in shock. 'In the name of the gods, why did you say that?'

'Oh, what could you ever mean, my lord?' Pip said with a sly smile. 'I only spoke the truth.'

Ramulas was stunned by what Pip said. 'You know that is not what happened.'

Pip gave a slight shrug. 'I have been telling these people what they needed to hear.'

A bolt of cold shot through Ramulas. 'What do you mean?'

'These people need a leader they can respect and look up to. If I told them that you escaped in a cart of rotting fruit, as weak as a kitten, they would see you as a normal man.'

'But that is the truth,' Ramulas protested.

Pip sighed. 'Sometimes people do not want to hear the truth. They would rather hear a story that gives them hope and a cause to believe in. These people look to you with hope, and that is a powerful thing.'

'When did you become so grown up?' Ramulas asked.

A look of sadness crossed Pip's face. 'The day the king sent my parents to Gullytown and I had to look after Jenna.'

'When did you tell these stories?'

'The day the people of Keah arrived; they were telling rumours of you escaping from the tombs. I fanned the flames of those rumours by telling different stories to separate groups,' Pip said with a smile. 'Come with me; I want to show you something.'

***

Ramulas walked through the streets of Sanctuary with Pip; he wore a hooded cloak, which Pip said he needed to hide his identity. She led him to the area that acted as the marketplace of Sanctuary.

A group of about fifty people had gathered around a tall lanky man with short dark hair, he stood on a crate and gestured to the people.

'I was there, I tell you,' He shouted to the crowd. 'I witnessed our lord's escape from the tombs and the city of Keah.'

Pip led Ramulas through the crowd as the man continued.

'It was at the west gate,' the man shouted before pausing for dramatic effect. The crowd waited in anticipation.

'The city was locked down. No-one was allowed in or out. I was walking past the western gate when I heard fighting. I turned to see a beast of a man, his clothes filthy from the tombs, and his eyes ablaze with fury. He fought five soldiers with his bare hands.'

'I thought it was six,' Ramulas whispered.

Pip elbowed him in the ribs, which silenced him.

'Our lord threw the soldiers around like they were sacks of wheat. Then he bent to pick something from the ground.' The man lowered his voice. 'I could not believe my eyes when I saw our lord pick up the cell door which held him in the tombs,' the man said, raising his voice once more.

'Our lord lifted the door with ease as he ran for the western gate. Arrows came down from the wall to hit the door he held above him. But when he arrived at the gate,' the man said in hushed tones, 'a soldier sitting on a warhorse pointed a crossbow at our lord.'

The man paused once more and looked at the faces of the people who hung on every word.

'I ran up and knocked that soldier from the warhorse and helped our lord climb on. As he rode out of the gate, I held back the soldiers who tried to chase him.'

Pip walked behind Ramulas and pulled away his cloak in one swift movement. The crowd gasped as one when they saw Ramulas amongst them.

The man who had been telling the story was frozen in fear. He knew that he had been caught out. Ramulas knew that he, Pip, and the man knew the story to be a lie. He understood that uncovering the lie would break the morale of the crowd.

'My lord! I … uh, was only—' the man stammered.

Ramulas raised his hand with a smile and the man fell silent. 'I thank you for your help,' Ramulas said as he walked over and clapped the man on the shoulder.

The group exploded into excited conversation as Ramulas and Pip walked away.

Rygar appeared from a side street and gave a low bow, which dragged his beard on the ground. 'Good day, milord. I'll be startin' to train small groups, and I'll be thinkin' to start with that one.'

Ramulas saw that the dwarf pointed to the group he and Pip had just left.

20

The two druids rode into Sanctuary mid-morning. They had spent the last few days riding from Gullytown. When they entered Oriel's room, they found Oriel, Ramulas, and Pip waiting for them.

'Welcome,' Oriel said. 'The dryads told us of your coming. Did your journey fare well?'

One of the druids reached into his robe and pulled out the blue crystal. He threw it to the ground where it shattered, sending white smoke into the air. Blue light grew within the smoke and formed two figures.

A moment later, the light and smoke disappeared to show Royce and Shayn. They both blinked a few times and then looked at their new surroundings in awe. They felt out of place in their dirty and tattered clothes.

'Hello, and welcome to Sanctuary. I am Oriel.'

'Where is Sanctuary?' Shayn asked.

'You have been brought to the base of the Devil's Ridge Mountains,' Oriel said. 'We are in need of your unusual talents.'

'And what talents might they be?' Royce asked evasively.

Oriel waved her hand and the pair were covered in a nimbus of white light. Shayn and Royce were shown the coming of the First Legion and what they would do to the people of the kingdom after killing Oriel; lastly, they were shown what they could do in Sanctuary.

The light faded and Oriel spoke. 'Now that you have arrived in Sanctuary, I will offer you a choice. You stay and help, or you are free to walk out of here free men.'

The two friends looked at each other and then at Oriel, smiling.

'We would be happy to stay and help,' Shayn said. 'We have spent many years in Gullytown, and neither of us has a family to go to.'

Pip rushed forward; eagerness written over her face as she approached the two. 'Have you seen my parents?' she asked. 'They were sent to Gullytown three years ago. My father's name is Patrick, and my mother's name is Janice.'

Ramulas laughed. 'Pip, allow them to answer one question at a time.'

'Pippa,' Royce whispered in shock.

Pip's head snapped towards Royce, and she walked up to him. 'Besides Jenna, only my parents called me Pippa. Did you know them well?'

A flicker of pain mixed with regret flashed across Royce's face. It lasted only a second. However, Pip still saw it.

'What?' Pip said, grabbing Royce by the shirt.

'Your … father …' Royce said, avoiding eye contact with Pip

'Your father spoke of you often,' Shayn said as he forced a smile. 'The last we saw of him, he was well.'

Pip saw through the lie in Shayn's body language. In the blink of an eye, Pip grabbed Royce by the hair and a knife appeared in her hand. The point of the blade rested just below Royce's eye.

'Be truthful,' Pip snarled. 'Tell me of my father.'

Royce held up his hands and was frozen to the spot. 'Your father was killed by the guards the night before the druids came for us.'

Pip seemed to sag as her knees weakened. 'What of my mother?'

'Life in Gullytown was hard on her,' Shayn said. 'She died shortly before your father.'

Pip released Royce and collapsed to the ground. A mournful cry escaped her lips. Her body began to shake as she sobbed uncontrollably. Royce and Shayn stepped back, unsure what to do. Ramulas came and knelt by Pip, placing a comforting hand on her shoulder.

Ramulas felt a sense of helplessness as Pip's body shook with each sob; gone was the confident young woman he knew. Before him was a person with shattered dreams and a broken heart. Ramulas felt a lump growing in his throat, and his eyes filled with tears.

'I am sorry,' he whispered to her.

Pip looked up at Ramulas, her face a mask of agony. Ramulas saw a side of Pip that cut him deeply.

'It's not fair,' she said in a voice that was barely audible. 'My parents did not do anything wrong, and they were sent to Gullytown to die.' Then a look of fierce determination crossed her features. 'The king will pay for this.'

Oriel stepped forward. 'Let me ease your pain.'

'How?' Pip said as she stood.

'I can take this painful memory from you.'

Pip quickly shook her head. 'No. I want to remember everything about my parents. I need time alone.'

Ramulas removed his hand from Pip's shoulder as she walked over to Royce and Shayn. 'I am sorry for my actions,' she said before walking to the door.

The pair from Gullytown nodded in understanding, and then Shayn looked at Pip before she walked out of the door.

'Pippa,' Shayn called, causing Pip to stop and turn. 'Your parents spoke of you and Jenna every day. Just before your father died, he said that he had to go home to his girls.'

Pip's face grew taut as she struggled to control her emotions. Tears flooded her eyes as she nodded her thanks before walking away.

***

Once Pip had left, Ramulas turned to the pair from Gullytown, 'Please forgive Pip. She had hoped to see her parents again.'

'There is nothing to forgive,' Royce said. 'We have seen a lot worse in Gullytown.'

'We need your help digging into the mountain,' Oriel said. 'I need to be free before Remus arrives. If he finds me in my cavern, he will kill me for my powers.'

'We will do what we can,' Shayn said.

'Come with me and I will show you the tunnel and introduce you to Edwin,' Ramulas said. 'Then you can look around Sanctuary.'

The duo was curious about the tunnel that led to Oriel. They looked at the castle and town of Sanctuary in wonderment. When they arrived at the tunnel, Edwin came out to meet them.

'Now, these two are lookin' like miners,' the dwarf said, waving at their clothes. 'Now come inside.'

Edwin led them past workers pushing carts of rubble from the tunnel. The sound of multiple tools hitting rocks could be heard. The sound grew louder as they walked into the tunnel.

After thirty feet, they came to the end of the tunnel, where five people covered in dust chipped at the wall.

'This is wrong,' Royce said, running his hand along the wall.

'What do ye mean "wrong"?' Edwin asked in a defensive tone.

Shayn smiled as he walked to the end of the tunnel where the workers had stopped. He ensured the dwarf watched as he massaged the wall. After a few moments, Shayn's fingers sank into the stone. Edwin's mouth fell open as Shayn pulled out a chunk of granite.

The five workers gathered around the hand-shaped hole in amazement.

'The mountain is talking to us,' Royce said. 'You need to increase your angle slightly. Then you will reach Oriel.'

Ramulas laughed. 'I think I will show you to your housing.'

'If it is fine with you, we would rather stay in the tunnel,' Royce said.

'But there are plenty of houses,' Ramulas protested.

Shayn shook his head. 'We will be happier in here.'

***

Pip had been missing for half the day. Since she found out about her parents the previous day, Ramulas had been worried about her.

Ramulas spoke to Oriel about his concerns and was told that Pip was in the forest. Tilly would show him the way. Ramulas walked out into the clearing and found the sprite waiting for him.

'Your friend is in the trees,' Tilly said before flying off into the forest.

Ramulas ran to keep up with the sprite, and after a few minutes, he came across Pip in one of the trees. She was straddling a branch ten feet off the ground.

Pip was holding Owain's bow and a quiver full of arrows was hanging from her shoulder. She didn't seem to notice Ramulas as he walked over to her. Pip nocked an arrow and sent it flying at a tree one hundred yards away.

Ramulas stood below Pip and smiled up at her. 'It is not nice to take what does not belong to you,' he said, referring to Owain's bow. 'You have your throwing knives and crossbow.'

Pip nocked another arrow without acknowledging Ramulas. After letting that arrow fly, she spoke without looking at him. 'I will return the bow and arrows when I am finished,' Pip said in a voice thick with emotion.

'I know that you are in pain,' Ramulas said.

Pip slowly turned to look at Ramulas. He winced at her expression, which was a mix of pain and defiance. 'You know nothing of my pain.' Pip held Ramulas' gaze while she nocked another arrow. 'I wish to be alone,' she said, releasing the arrow.

Ramulas walked away knowing that Pip would not be alone; the dryads would watch over her.

***

Zachary sat brooding on his throne. The combination of the prisoner escaping from the tombs, Shigar joining him after the men of Sanctuary attacked his soldiers, and the thousands of people who had disappeared across the kingdom spelled conspiracy to him.

He softly cursed to himself; Zachary should have had the prisoner killed when he first came into Keah. *Now he calls himself the Lord of Sanctuary. And he has won the alliance of Shigar.* The king was certain that his disappearance had something to do with this.

An agent entered his chambers, and Zachary waved him forward after he was shown a small silver tube. The agent gave the silver tube to his king and said it had come from Gullytown.

Zachary unrolled the note and began to read. By the time Zachary had finished, he was overwhelmed with disbelief and confusion.

'Two druids attacked the guards of Gullytown and helped two prisoners escape,' he said in astonishment.

The agent already knew. He always made a point of reading everything the Avery sent out.

However, the agent feigned surprise at the news.

The note from Gullytown was the tipping point for Zachary. He thought for a moment. The druids had mentioned that they had come from Sanctuary. This added a level of uncertainty to this situation. The druids were last seen riding west from Gullytown, and the nearest town was Suda.

'Why are the druids working with the people of Sanctuary?' Zachary asked. 'Druids come in the middle of the night and take people away. Since being banished, they have never attacked soldiers.'

The agent shrugged.

Zachary's eyes widened as he thought of Shangri-La. Since the days of his grandfather, there have been rumours of dragons there. The kingdom soldiers hadn't gone there for generations. Could this be where Sanctuary was?

'This problem must be solved,' he said to the agent. 'I want all agents to be accompanied by a score of soldiers and four Khilli warriors. I want these people of Sanctuary found. I do not care what needs to be done. They must know the price for plotting against their king.'

'I will have every part of the kingdom searched, my king.'

***

Iguchi had been taking the Fallen Angels out for the last few days. They would leave just before dawn and return after dark exhausted. The Angels carried large packs on their backs filled with stones and soil.

The packs were dropped at the training grounds. The Angels slept, ate, and went straight to sleep, only to wake the next morning to start again.

'This isn't fun,' Benji said as he struggled to feed himself.

The Fallen Angels sat at a long table eating supper. Benji's whole body shook as he brought a spoon up to his mouth.

'Pain is your friend,' Iguchi said walking up to Benji. 'Your body is rejoicing to be alive.'

'But I thought this was going to be fun,' Benji complained.

'Sh,' Michael said.

Benji looked across at Michael with curiosity. He was the only Fallen Angel who did not seem affected by the rigorous training.

'You must train with determination, as if you were a weapon made from the finest steel,' Iguchi said.

'But we are flesh and bone, not steel,' Benji replied.

'That is where you are wrong,' Iguchi said, holding up his middle finger and forefinger.

In a blur of motion, Iguchi thrust his fingers through the surface of the table. The Fallen Angels gasped in shock.

Iguchi pulled his fingers away from the table to reveal he had punched a hole through the inch of solid wood. His fingers did not have any marks or scratches on them.

'Through training of the mind and body, you will become a weapon,' Iguchi said.

'How long will it take us to do that?' Miles asked eagerly.

'With hard training and dedication, it will take ten years. This means you will need to train harder for the legion.'

A collective moan sounded along the table; again, Benji looked across at Michael in confusion. He was the only Fallen Angel who did not seem to mind training harder.

***

Remus stood with the other warlords and red wizards in front of the golden arch. They looked into the dark tunnel which had minute white lights dancing within.

One of the red wizards held up a dull silver ball which softly hummed. 'This will show us the true nature of the passageway.' He tossed the ball into the arch, causing the white lights to gather around it.

With a soft click, the tunnel disappeared. In its place was an image of a passageway made of mist. The walls, floor, and ceiling constantly moved as if a strong wind blew down the passageway.

Gaping holes dotted the wall where mists were pulled into the darkness. Long, dark shapes swam along the walls just below the mist.

'My warlord,' said a red wizard who held a red-bladed sword. 'I will throw this into the golden arch. Using your magical power, lead this to Oriel's world and stop it from entering the holes.'

Remus walked up to the red wizard and took the sword from him. If anyone was to throw it into the arch, it would be him. He threw the sword into the arch; it wavered in mid-air for a moment before appearing in the passageway of mist.

The pressure Remus felt was instantaneous as he fought to hold the sword in place. He grunted with effort, attempting to keep the sword from being pulled into one of the dark holes. The other warlords used their magic to assist Remus.

Despite their combined efforts, the sword was pulled into one of the holes within a few seconds.

Remus gasped as the sword was pulled from his magical hold, and then one of the long dark shapes emerged from the mist. It looked like a giant snake with rows of impossibly long teeth.

The image wavered before returning to a dark passage with dancing minute lights.

Remus, Alpha, Omega, and Beta staggered slightly as they fought against the loss of vertigo when they recovered a red wizard stepped forward.

'We need to seal the dark holes before we are able to travel to Oriel's world,' he said to Remus. 'They lead into unknown worlds. The First

Legion will be separated as they walk through the passageway. This will take time.'

Remus nodded as he looked at the golden arch. He understood that this was an unforeseen problem and would need to be rectified.

'What of the creatures within the mist?' Remus asked.

'Once the dark holes have been closed, they will be trapped underneath the mist.'

'How did Oriel travel through the passageway unaffected?' Remus asked.

'By keeping her dragon form, Oriel would have been too fast and strong for the effects of the passageway.'

Remus looked at the golden arch. He wanted more than anything to wield Oriel's power.

***

Royce and Shayn worked in harmony with Edwin, making progress into the mountain; even though they had the ability to mould rocks and pull sections out, they were unable to do this for long periods of time. When their ability was almost exhausted, they would place their hands on the wall and focus; minute hairline fractures would spread across the surface like spiderwebs. This allowed the workers to continue.

One thing bothered the dwarf about the duo since they had arrived. Royce and Shayn had not left the tunnel and refused all offers of food and housing. He also noticed something as they made their way deeper into the tunnel that he needed to show to Ramulas. He sent one of the workers to bring him into the tunnel.

A short time later, Ramulas walked into the tunnel. 'Hello, Edwin. I was told you had something to show me.'

'Yes, my lord. Follow me.'

As they walked along the tunnel, Ramulas noticed that the walls were wide enough for three men to walk abreast and the ceiling was just over six feet high, but the most stunning detail was that the surface was as smooth as marble.

'Me an' me kin have no use o' these when we're digging,' Edwin said, waving to the torch on the wall. 'Dwarves can see in the darkest o' tunnels. One o' the signs is that our eyes shine red in the dark.'

As they walked over to the torch, Ramulas could see Royce and Shayn working on the wall, Edwin dropped the torch into a barrel of water, engulfing the tunnel in darkness. Ramulas' mouth dropped when he saw two pairs of red eyes staring back at him from the duo.

'Now, I'm thinkin' that these two are a bit too big to be dwarves.'

***

'No, ye done it wrong,' Rygar said to the two groups.

He waved the two lots of ten people apart. Each person was dressed in armour and carried a shield and a curved sword. He had been training them for almost a week. He could tell it was the first time they had trained or had even held weapons.

'When ye see a shield comin', lift yer shield to block and then strike with yer own sword.'

The dwarf glanced over to where Lodi was standing and waved him over, Rygar and the giant demonstrated the aspects of attack and defence, he shooed Lodi away and turned to the groups. 'Now we'll try this again until we get it right.'

He allowed himself a small smile by the end of the day as he saw the movements of the people becoming more natural. Oriel had shown everyone images of the First Legion, and Rygar knew that even the kingdom soldiers would be hard-pressed against them. Proper training would take years; time that they did not have, but once the basic moves were learnt the real training would begin.

***

In the clearing outside the wall, Owain paced in front of eight archery targets made from straw, standing fifty yards from him were two hundred soldiers of Sanctuary, each holding a bow and quiver with twenty arrows.

'First group, ready your bows,' he said, looking at the group with his milky white eyes and clicking his tongue a few times.

Ten stepped forward, nocking arrows to their bows, and Owain nodded when he knew they were ready. 'Shoot the target.'

Owain tilted his head and listened as the arrows took flight. Soft thuds sounded as four hit the targets. The other arrows flew too high or wide. The archers who hit the targets congratulated each other while the others sighed in disappointment.

Owain shook his head. 'All of you missed the target; the middle has been dyed the size of my hand. No-one hit the dye.'

One of the archers stepped forward. 'How do you know none hit the mark?'

'The sound of an arrow hitting the dye is different than striking straw,' Owain said as he walked over to a target and felt its surface, before returning and picking up a bow. He reached over to a quiver and nocked the bow; a hush fell over the archers as they watched the blind bowman click his tongue while pulling the bow taut.

'Take a deep breath before letting it out slowly, and then you may release your arrow.'

His arrow flew across the clearing and hit the very centre of the target. The archers gathered around and murmured in astonishment. He handed the bow to the nearest archer and told them to shoot as he had done. A smile played on his lips as he heard the collective intake and release of breath as they shot at the targets.

This time nine arrows hit their targets, and Owain's smile grew as he heard the gasps of surprise. He moved through the different groups throughout the day. He needed them to be able to perform this task without thinking, and then they would move on to more difficult tasks.

21

After another session of training, Ramulas and Pip walked along the halls of the castle. He gazed out at the night-time sky as they passed windows admiring the stars. Then they heard music and singing; they looked at each other before quickly going to an open balcony. The sight below brought a smile to Ramulas' face, and he noticed Pip's demeanour had brightened, which was rare these days.

The people of Sanctuary had come out into the streets; laughing singing and dancing. 'Would you look at that,' he said in disbelief.

For the first time in his life, Ramulas felt a sense of contentment. People from across the kingdom had come together as a community. He raised an eyebrow at Pip. 'Let's bring our families out; they are missing the fun.'

They quickly made their way to the chambers to find them empty. Ramulas groaned inwardly, realising that they would have heard the noise and joined the people. He had been so busy preparing for the coming of the legion that he had neglected his family.

The pair quickly made their way outside to find their loved ones in the courtyard. Kate and Grace ran to Ramulas while Jacqueline smiled at him. He held his daughters as Pip ran to her sister, and then he made his way to his wife.

He held her close. 'Just for tonight, I want to think about us; for too long my mind has been occupied.'

She smiled and led him through the streets; groups sang folk songs while others cooked from open fires in the streets, and then it hit

Ramulas—this was the summer festival. He had always taken his family to the celebrations in Bremnon.

Time had passed so quickly since Oriel had come to him. Ramulas and Jacqueline locked eyes, and he wanted this moment to last forever. It seemed like a lifetime ago when he had been this close to his family. Ramulas promised himself that nothing would happen to his family. He didn't know how he could live without them.

***

The archers lined the wall as Owain paced behind them. They were each ten yards apart watching four carts with mounted targets. The carts were attached to pullies to move them across the clearing, and Iguchi came out to stand in front of them.

'Remember to breathe and time your shots,' Owain called out. 'Aim slightly in front of the moving targets. Each set will release two arrows in order starting from group one.'

The blind archer waved a hand above his head and the carts proceeded to move across the field. The first wave of arrows rained down onto the field, most of them hitting targets, closely followed by the second group of arrows.

One of the arrows flew straight at Iguchi, who stood calmly watching as it came toward him. At the last moment, he twisted his body and it missed him by an inch. Iguchi flew into motion, running up and down the clearing pulling arrows out of the ground, ducking and weaving. The small man easily avoided the rain of projectiles.

This unnerved some of the archers whose shots flew too wide or high, after two minutes, Iguchi whistled and the arrows stopped; over half of the arrows had hit the targets, but far too many had missed the mark. Iguchi raced through the gate, making his way up to the archers.

Owain smiled as he felt the small man creep up behind him. 'Greetings, Iguchi. How did my archer's fare?'

'How could you know of my presence? I move as silently as the breeze.'

'I didn't hear you. I listened to those around me making way as you approached.'

'That is good. They performed well. Only a few were distracted by my presence in the field. But still, they have a lot more training before they can become the best archers. That is what we will need when the legion comes.'

Owain nodded, knowing that to be the best would take them years of training—years that they did not have.

***

Grace sat on the floor in front of six druids, who formed a semicircle kneeling with their hands on their thighs. They had been mentoring her over the last few weeks and were impressed that Grace had absorbed everything so quickly.

Today, they had something different in mind for her.

The druid opposite her held out a slim wand in from of him. A green bubble formed on its tip, which caused Grace to smile.

'Do not allow the bubbles to touch the ground,' the druid hissed, waving his wand.

Grace's smile grew as bubbles of various sizes appeared above her and slowly floated down.

Grace opened her hands in front of her while looking at the bubbles. She gently waved at the air. A few bubbles joined to form a larger one, and then she sent other bubbles into it. It grew to form a bubble as big as a cart and floated ten feet above her.

Grace giggled at the expressions of fear she saw on the druids. She clicked her fingers and the bubble popped, sending a web of sticky green goo over the druids, covering them from head to toe. Grace was the only one who was unaffected. The goo flowed from her like water on a duck's back.

Grace laughed at how funny the druids looked.

'That is not very funny, Grace,' Oriel said.

Grace clapped her hands and the goo turned to mist, which rose into the air.

'How did you do that?' One of the druids asked. 'How did you know to form the bubbles into one?'

Grace shrugged. 'I like big bubbles.'

'Why did none of the goo stick to you like it did with us?'

'I didn't want to get my clothes dirty.'

The druids were astounded by her casual response. What Grace had demonstrated with ease would make her the envy of any magic user.

One of the druids took a handful of small stones from his pouch and tossed them into the air. They transformed into a dozen stone wasps, which hovered above Grace. Her face lit up as she witnessed the change.

'Do not stand,' one of the druids warned. 'They will sting if you stand. You need to move them first.'

With a squeal of delight, Grace jumped into a standing position and held her hands out to the wasps.

They began to buzz angrily, becoming agitated, the druids gasped thinking that Grace would be stung.

Grace opened and closed her chubby hands enthusiastically while she whispered to the stone wasps. One of them dropped onto her hand. A small flash of white light burst from Grace's palm when the wasp touched her.

Then out of the flash flew a wasp with yellow and black stripes. The druids fell back in shock, realising that Grace had magically transformed the stone wasp into a living creature.

Then the rest of the stone wasps landed on her outstretched hands; a succession of flashes heralded the transformation of the wasps; a wave of dizziness came over Grace as the wasps crawled over her.

She fainted and was caught by the druids.

Oriel rushed over and waved her hands above her. Grace was soon covered in a faint purple nimbus of light.

'She has exhausted herself,' Oriel explained. 'She will sleep for now. When Grace awakens, we will teach her the lower levels of magic. She shows the magical ability of someone who has trained for years.'

Oriel looked down at Grace's sleeping form with a sad smile. Grace's magical ability was growing faster than her ability to control it. She was on a dangerous road; however, Oriel knew how she felt. At Grace's age, she had been schooled in the arts of magic by her father. She had learnt at a pace far quicker than the previous students.

Now that Oriel had matured, she understood why her father had wanted her to slow down. She knew that one day Grace's magical ability would consume her if she was not given guidance. If that happened, Grace's magic would control her, and then Grace would be beyond any help.

***

Kate walked into her quarters to find her father and Iguchi deep in conversation. They both stopped and looked at her, and she felt self-conscious.

Iguchi picked up an apple from the table and tossed it at Kate. Without thinking, she reached out and caught it.

Then Iguchi rushed at her with a wooden staff. He performed a series of thrusts and twirls at Kate, each of which she easily avoided. With each move, he came gradually closer.

Then, suddenly, Kate kicked Iguchi in the stomach, took the staff from him, and stepped back in a defensive stance.

Iguchi smiled as he looked back at Ramulas. 'I told you, this one is a natural fighter. I will need to train her.'

Kate's demeanour changed, and she dropped the staff. 'Father, I do not want to be a fighter. I want to be a lady, like Mother.'

Ramulas was shocked. 'But look at what you can do …'

'That is enough,' Jacqueline said entering the room. 'If Kate does not want to learn, then she does not have to.'

Ramulas turned to Iguchi for support, and the small man bowed to Jacqueline. 'Hello to you, Lady of Sanctuary. Your daughter will make a fine lady of this castle. She should not train to fight.'

Ramulas flinched as if slapped. One moment he and Iguchi were discussing how much Kate needed to be trained like Grace, and the next, he is siding with Jacqueline. By the time he had recovered, Ramulas found Pip waving to him from the doorway. Iguchi, Jacqueline, and Kate had gone.

Ramulas and Pip stood in front of the four animated soldiers in the training chambers. The legion soldiers glared at the duo with open hatred, Ramulas heard a yawn and turned to see Pip smile and wink at him.

He held back a retort, knowing that Pip wanted to anger him and the soldiers. Since Pip found out her parents had died in Gullytown, she had become dark, angry, and brooding.

Over several weeks, she had slowly returned to the Pip that Ramulas knew; every so often he would see a pained expression, and then it would vanish in the blink of an eye, he knew these were times Pip wished to be alone.

The subject of the king always brought out her anger. Three times in the first week, Oriel and Ramulas had to prevent her from travelling to Keah and killing the king.

Even though Pip seemed her normal self, Ramulas could still see an undercurrent of anger in everything she did.

'Are you ready?' he asked.

Pip nodded with a determined smile.

'Since we have been fighting them, they know our moves and are learning from them,' Ramulas said.

'Then, let's teach them a lesson,' Pip said.

The four soldiers burst into action as the duo came near, two came for Ramulas, and the other two for Pip. They had become used to Ramulas and Pip moving away from each other.

This time, things were different.

Ramulas and Pip moved into each other and turned so they were back-to-back.

The soldiers were surprised and hesitated for a fraction of a second, two of the soldiers raised their swords at Ramulas, who swung his battle axe, the blade biting through the knee of one of them.

With a tight spin, he positioned himself behind the injured soldier. With an overhead chop, he put the axe through the soldier's spine, sending him sprawling to the ground.

The remaining soldier jumped over its companion and struck out with a combination of thrusts and slashes. All Ramulas could do was block and parry with his weapons.

Then he heard Pip gasp before cursing. He took a quick look behind and saw Pip was in trouble. The soldier he had killed had lost a lot of blood. She had stepped into the growing pool and slipped. A soldier lunged at her with his sword.

As Ramulas turned, he swung his battle axe at his opponent's head. The soldier brought its shield up to block. Ramulas smiled as he kicked him in the stomach, sending him sprawling.

He let out a scream of rage as he threw his battle axe at Pip's opponent. The axe spun toward the startled soldier but he turned, and the axe flew harmlessly by.

The expression of relief was wiped away when Pip thrust one of her knives into the soldier's groin with a high-pitched scream. He grabbed his privates and pitched forward.

'Ramulas!' Pip shouted in warning.

As Ramulas turned, he let the war hammer swing to the ground. The soldier rushed at him with an overhead strike. Ramulas gripped his war hammer with both hands and swung it into the soldier's breastplate, lifting the soldier a few inches.

Two throwing knives and a crossbow bolt appeared in the soldier's body, and he was dead before hitting the ground.

Then a wave of dizziness came over Ramulas as he dropped his weapon. He sat on the floor with his hands on his knees. All energy had left him.

Pip stood before him with a smile. 'Rest a while. Then we can fight them again.'

Ramulas shook his head. 'That is enough for me.'

'But you are the hero who escaped the tombs,' Pip said in mock admiration. 'The way that people talk, you pulled down the castle of Keah.'

Ramulas smiled weakly. 'You will be the death of me. Some people say I got this scar on my face when the king tried to take my eye.'

'I was there,' Pip said with a wink. 'That's what I saw.'

Ramulas sighed and shook his head.

***

The Fallen Angels raced through the trees. Each carried a sack full of heavy rocks. They had been running for an hour, and Benji had begun to feel sore. He looked across at Miles and Michael. Miles struggled for breath, and yet Michael did not seem affected.

He thought back to when they had first started training—Benji could only last a few minutes carrying the sack. Since then, all of the Angels had become stronger and faster under Iguchi's training.

They returned to a small clearing, where they found their swords and shields waiting for them. The Fallen Angels dropped their packs and picked up their weapons and shields before running back the way they had come.

Arriving back at camp, they found Iguchi's tent torn apart and his swords on the ground. There were signs of a struggle, and Iguchi was nowhere to be seen.

Michael made hand signals and the Angels formed a semicircle in the clearing. Hidden in the trees above, Iguchi watched as they slowly moved into the camp.

He waited until Miles was below him before he flicked a pebble at Benji's shield. Miles turned at the sound as Iguchi dropped from the tree. He landed on Miles' shoulders before kicking away.

Miles was pushed to his hands and knees while Iguchi landed next to Benji, delivering a punch to his stomach. With fluid movements, Iguchi sent two more Angels into the trees.

This all happened in under two seconds. It was only then that the Fallen Angels reacted to the threat.

Iguchi held up his hand. 'You are all lazy. You fell for an old trick, running into the camp without looking.'

There were a few murmurs of how they were all tired, which was the reason for their mistake.

'Your enemy will not stop to ask if you are well,' Iguchi scolded. 'You saw what I wanted you to see, and you ran into the camp blindly, stomping your feet. Where are the Fallen Angels who I taught so much?'

Iguchi smiled inwardly as he saw the expressions of disappointment. This showed that they all wanted to improve.

Iguchi sat at the base of a large elm tree, and the Fallen Angels gathered around him. Every one of the Angels had their armour and shield at their feet.

Iguchi swept his arm in a tight arc. 'Look around you in this forest. You will all need to become one with the trees, and then you will be invisible, and the enemy will not see you.'

He held up a few differently shaped leaves—one from a fern, an elm, and an oak tree. 'These leaves will help you to become invisible and blend with the trees.'

He took a pinch of green powder from a small clay pot in front of him and placed it in his mouth. He chewed before spraying the shield in a few places. He then used the three leaves and added shades of black and brown.

When he was finished, Iguchi held the shield up for the Fallen Angels to see.

The Angels immediately began to coat their armour and shields with dye. Before too long, the branches were filled with camouflaged armour and shields.

'We must run,' Iguchi said. 'You are becoming lazy.'

He led the Fallen Angels through the forest until they came to the clearing where the sacks waited for them. They shouldered the sacks and ran through the trees at a fast pace.

Suddenly, Iguchi stopped and held up a hand, and the Angels stopped behind him.

'Tell me what you see,' he said.

He looked around and saw blank expressions. Iguchi picked up a stone and threw it into the forest, where it bounced off an invisible wall with a clang, Iguchi walked a few feet and picked up one of the breastplates hanging from a tree.

'If you cannot see your own armour and shields, how will the soldiers of the legion see you?'

An expression of astonishment, followed by understanding, flowed through the Angels. Iguchi motioned for them to collect their armour.

Once they were ready, Iguchi called Benji to him. He held three clay pots. Iguchi dipped his fingers into the pots and smeared lines of green, black, and grey onto Benji's face until it was completely covered.

'You must all cover your faces like this,' Iguchi said.

The Fallen Angels stepped forward, dipping their fingers into the clay pots. Within minutes, all the Fallen Angels had their faces covered.

'Where have my Fallen Angels gone?' Iguchi asked with a smile.

The Angels looked at each other, and all that could be seen was the white of their teeth and eyes.

'This is the new look of the Fallen Angels,' Iguchi said. 'Wear your colours with pride.'

22

The king's agent had heard rumours from the towns of Bremnon and Turtha of people coming to purchase supplies by the wagonload before disappearing north. Outside of both towns, the tracks of the wagons vanished. The agent questioned small hamlets and farms outside of the towns, but to no avail. Either people did not know anything, or they were hiding something.

Then the agent noticed a pattern. When he searched the town of Bremnon, there would be reports of the wagons in Turtha, and when he searched Turtha, the wagons would be seen in Bremnon. This game of cat and mouse had gone on for too long, and the agent was becoming frustrated.

Then he decided to change his tactics. The agent sent his escort away with word to wait for his call. He then wore old robes to hide his identity.

After a few days, he saw the wagons in Turtha. He followed from a distance as they headed north until they entered the forest. He rode back to Turtha as fast as he could and sent word for his escort to return.

A week later, the agent and his small group arrived at the edge of Sanctuary's Forest. It had been many weeks since the Lord of Sanctuary attacked the king's soldiers outside of Bremnon. It had been weeks of hoping and searching for this agent. He looked into the trees; confident he had found Sanctuary.

***

Tilly had been following the agent's small group for an hour as they moved deeper into the forest. Several times, she had wanted to challenge the newcomers. She knew they were different from the people of Sanctuary—their eyes were hard and cold.

Each time she wanted to challenge, a nearby dryad would motion for her to stay back. Over one hundred dryads watched from the trees as the agent led the group towards Sanctuary.

'Ramulas must be told,' Eady said to Tilly.

Tilly buzzed her wings and disappeared into the trunk of a tree, followed by Eady.

A moment later, they came out at the edge of the clearing near Sanctuary. Tilly flew through the gate and into the courtyard. Men, women, and children gathered around the sprite in awe as she hovered just out of reach. They spoke in excited tones. Most of them had never seen a creature like Tilly before.

'I must speak to Ramulas,' the Sprite said.

She refused to acknowledge anyone until Ramulas and Pip came out of the castle.

'What has happened?' Ramulas asked, coming up to Tilly.

'The king's men are in the forest and are coming this way.'

The colour drained from Ramulas' face. 'Where are they?'

'The dryads will show you,' Tilly said before flying out into the clearing.

Ramulas scanned the faces around him and found Rygar. He made his way to the dwarf. 'Ready the people for battle. We may have some company.'

Rygar nodded as Ramulas and Pip headed outside into the clearing, where six dryads waited for them.

He looked at Eady. 'Show me where they are.'

She smiled and stepped forward holding out her hands for him. 'Close your eyes. I will take you into the trees.'

She held Ramulas' hands and led him to the trunk of a large oak tree, and he felt himself being pulled along a narrow passage before coming out into the open air once more. Eady released Ramulas' hands and he opened his eyes. He found they were in a different part of the forest.

Eady pointed to the right and Ramulas saw the agent leading the group along a path. Ramulas focused on the animal life within the forest and soon found that this was the only group to enter the forest.

Ramulas walked out onto the path fifty yards from the agent. The sight of someone coming out of the trees startled the agent, and he stopped his horse.

'Why have you come into this forest?' Ramulas asked.

The agent forced a smile while his mind raced. 'We look for a place called Sanctuary and also the Lord of Sanctuary. Could you be him?'

Ramulas was in a state of shock. *How had this group found Sanctuary? There should be no way for anyone to find it.* He quickly pushed those thoughts away.

'Leave this forest now, and no trouble will come for you.'

He noticed the agent whisper to his soldiers while making slight hand signals. As they moved on their horses, Ramulas saw the four Khilli soldiers—among them was K'ayden. His heart soared at seeing his friend once more.

Then he saw two of the soldiers slowly removing bows from their pommels.

Ramulas' instincts saved his life. As he ran back into the trees, an arrow hit the ground where he was standing.

'Take me to Iguchi and the Angels,' he said to Eady.

***

The agent gasped as Ramulas stepped out onto the path. From the descriptions he had been given, he knew that Ramulas was the person he was seeking.

He whispered for the soldiers to shoot while trying to keep Ramulas occupied, and then the Lord of Sanctuary raced into the forest, where the agent quickly gave chase.

The agent ran into the trees where Ramulas had gone, but there was no trace of him. It was as if the forest itself had swallowed him up. After all the weeks of searching, he had hoped to be the one who found Sanctuary. It would give him so much favour with the king. He could not let his dreams of power vanish.

He decided to follow the path and hoped it led to Sanctuary.

***

Ramulas stepped out of a tree at the base of the Devil's Ridge Mountains. He saw Iguchi instructing the Fallen Angels through fighting drills.

The small man smiled when he saw Ramulas. 'Hello to you, Lord of Sanctuary,' he said with a bow.

'I need the Angels back at Sanctuary,' Ramulas said with a sense of urgency. 'The king's men are in the forest.'

Iguchi's smile disappeared as he listened to Ramulas' encounter with the agent. He also told Iguchi that if there was a battle, the four Khilli were not to be killed. Iguchi nodded before giving orders to the Fallen Angels.

Looking to his right, Ramulas saw that Sanctuary was a mile away. He motioned for Eady to take him home.

Ramulas quickly made his way into the courtyard. He found Rygar, Owain, and Pip waiting for him.

'One of the king's agents is in the forest and heading this way. He has a score of soldiers on horses and four Khilli warriors. I hope to turn them away, but if I don't, I want the Khilli left to the Fallen Angels.'

The three nodded and Ramulas continued. 'Owain, I need your archers on the wall as a show of force. I do not want them to shoot arrows unless I give the command.'

Owain looked at him with his milky white eyes. 'They will not release until I tell them, my lord.'

Ramulas heard Owain clicking as he walked away, and he turned to the dwarf. 'Rygar, I want everyone in the courtyard dressed for battle. Wait until I am on Rufus, and I will lead you out.'

Then Ramulas saw Lodi peeking from behind a corner. 'Is there a way Lodi could come out and give them a scare?'

Rygar smiled. 'Don't ye be worryin' bout him. Lodi will give 'em a good fright.'

Rygar walked away shouting orders and Ramulas turned to Pip.

'What about me?' she asked.

'I want you to be by my side, but for now, let's see our families.'

As the pair walked into the castle, Ramulas was surprised at how natural it felt giving orders. More fragmented memories came back to him of his past. But as quickly as they came to him, they were gone. He wished that he could remember more of his previous life. He knew that it would help when the legion came.

Inside the castle, they told their families what was happening and told them the safest place would be in the throne room. Ramulas was happy to see Emily playing with Grace. Oriel had said that Emily was the most powerful of all the guardians.

Walking into the throne room, Ramulas saw Oriel, Shigar, and the druids.

'Welcome, Ramulas,' Oriel said. 'The first of your trials is coming. How you deal with this will affect the people of Sanctuary. This is also a test for the people under you.'

Ramulas looked around and was comforted by the fact that Oriel, Shigar, and the druids were there. He asked that they protect the families. He kissed Jacqueline and his girls before calling the hell hounds and leaving with Pip.

***

Ramulas sat on Rufus in the courtyard with Pip and the hell hounds by his side. To the left and right were the people of Sanctuary lined in columns. They wore armour and held curved swords and shields at the ready. Lodi stood by Rygar swinging his huge club and looking truly terrifying.

A signal from the top of the wall told Ramulas that the agent had arrived.

'Let's go,' Ramulas said as he led the people out into the clearing.

Ramulas rode out of the gate to see the agent and his party near the tree line. He stopped Rufus halfway across the clearing as the people of Sanctuary lined in columns along the base of the curved wall.

The agent and the soldiers pulled back in shock as Lodi came roaring out of the gate swinging his club.

When Lodi stopped, Ramulas called out to the agent. 'You need to come away from the trees; it is not safe for you there.'

The agent turned on his horse to see Iguchi and fifty Fallen Angels in camouflage step out from the forest. Their swords and shields were held casually by their sides and their faces showed no emotion. They fanned out behind the kingdom party with Iguchi in the middle.

The agent moved his horse forward, motioning for the rest to follow. His mind raced with how to make the best of this situation. When he was twenty yards away, Ramulas held up his hand. The agent looked warily at the hell hounds.

'That is far enough. Why have you come to Sanctuary?'

The agent puffed out his chest and tried to appear dignified. 'Your people attacked and killed several kingdom soldiers outside Bremnon. For that, you will stand trial. You are also wanted for plotting against the king,' he said, pointing at Ramulas.

'My people were attacked by the kingdom soldiers; they were killed in defending the people of Sanctuary. You have your answers—now leave Sanctuary and never return.'

The agent grew red in the face as he attempted to control his anger. 'You dare speak to an emissary of the king in this way?'

The soldiers pulled out their swords, and two nocked bows. Ramulas saw the agent flinch as the two hundred archers on the wall aimed their bows at his group. The Fallen Angels silently closed in around the kingdom party.

'Do not be foolish,' Ramulas warned. 'Leave now and your lives will be spared. Send word to the king that we are not to be troubled here anymore.'

The agent's face was a mask of fury as his mouth opened and closed. Ramulas communicated with the Khilli's horses, causing them to run left, straight into a line of Fallen Angels.

'Shoot him!' the agent shouted, pointing at Ramulas.

The two archers loosed their arrows at Ramulas. Their eyes widened in shock as their arrows veered away from the Lord of Sanctuary. Ramulas smiled as his magical ability protected him.

Then everything went to hell.

A shower of arrows came down from the wall into the mounted soldiers. Both men and horses screamed as arrows pierced their bodies.

Eight soldiers were dead or injured and another five were thrown when arrows hit their horses. The agent hit the ground and rolled away from his dead horse.

The people of Sanctuary screamed in outrage when arrows were fired at their lord. The columns broke apart as they ran to defend Ramulas. The sound of rolling thunder caused Ramulas and Pip to turn.

Lodi with his long-running strides quickly overtook the people. Before Ramulas could say anything, the giant was past him, swinging his huge club.

The broken bodies of four soldiers and three horses flew; the hell hounds, who had raced into attack, narrowly avoided being struck.

***

As the Khilli's horses veered to the left, the Fallen Angels dropped their swords. The Khilli kicked and slashed at the Angels with their throwing disks. These blows were blocked by the upraised shields of the Fallen Angels.

They pulled the Khilli to the ground, where they were pummelled into unconsciousness. Iguchi rushed in to stop the onslaught and bind the hands and feet of the four warriors.

***

'Stop!' Ramulas shouted.

From Lodi to the archers on the wall, everyone stopped and looked at him. Ramulas looked around and saw that his people were angry and eager to fight. Rygar had finally caught up and pushed through the crowd.

'Back into yer formations!' the dwarf shouted before he turned to the giant. 'Ye almost hit our lord! Stand yerself against the wall.'

The people of Sanctuary re-formed their columns against the wall, and Lodi walked with his head hung in shame.

With the Khilli bound, the Fallen Angels picked up their disks. Then they surrounded the agent and remaining soldiers.

The agent stood defiant, looking at Ramulas. 'The king will hear of this treason.'

'I know he will,' Ramulas said with a sigh. 'But you ordered your men to shoot—that is why your men lie dead. Lay down your weapons, take your survivors, and you will be escorted from here.'

'What of the soldiers you killed, and the Khilli?' The agent asked.

'The Khilli will be killed and your dead buried.'

'What!?' The agent gasped in shock. 'You dare?'

Ramulas ignored the agent and turned to Rygar. 'They will need an escort.'

Forty people escorted the agent and the survivors toward Bremnon through the forest. Only after they left did Ramulas go to the Khilli. They were all conscious, looking at him blankly.

'Hello, my friend,' Ramulas said to K'ayden. 'You are now free.'

'It does not seem that way,' K'ayden said, holding up his bound wrists.

Ramulas nodded to Iguchi, whose sword blurred through the air as it cut the bonds of the Khilli.

'Send the people back inside,' Ramulas said to the dwarf.

The Khilli stood warily as the Fallen Angels still surrounded them. Their faces were bloodied and swollen.

'Now that the agent thinks you dead, your families will not suffer. Come inside and we will talk about the future of your people.'

As they walked into Sanctuary, Iguchi came up to Ramulas. 'This was unexpected. We are training the people for the legion, and I think we have made another enemy. We must train the people harder.'

Ramulas shook his head. 'I warned them to leave us alone, but they would not listen.'

Iguchi shrugged. 'If a spider knows that a bird is near and wants to eat it, the spider knows it needs to hide, but if a fly becomes entangled in its web, the spider will rush out to eat the fly. The bird is soon forgotten. Some men are the same—they will ignore danger if their pride becomes injured. The king's agent is such a man.'

23

L odi stood with his back to the wall looking from side to side. When he saw that there were no people this late at night, he ran to the shadows of another building. The giant repeated this until he arrived at the training ground.

He looked around once more before entering the stables. Lodi had seen the people of Sanctuary train with the horses, and he wanted to do the same.

Pip watched Lodi from the roof of the barracks, she had been following him for several minutes, jumping from roof to roof. Even if Lodi had looked up, he would not have seen the former thief, who was adept at blending in with the shadows.

She watched as the giant led a horse out into the middle of the training grounds and tethered it to a post. Lodi then took ten steps back before running at the horse. Pip gasped in shock as she realised what was about to happen, and then Lodi launched himself into the air.

The horse screamed as it was crushed beneath Lodi's weight.

Lodi quickly jumped up, his face full of panic, and looked around, before running back into the stables. He came out a moment later with arms full of straw, which he used to cover the dead animal. After it was covered, Lodi shook his head, pulled the horse out, and carried it away.

Pip followed him to the pit where rocks from the tunnel were placed and reused in the maze, Lodi threw the horse into the pit before running away.

Pip ran to the barracks where the Fallen Angels were sleeping. She quietly woke Benji and Miles and explained what Lodi had done and what they needed to do. The three of them pulled the corpse out just before it was sucked into the pit. She thanked the two Angels.

Pip felt sorry for the giant. Ramulas would have to be told what had happened.

***

An hour after dawn, Rygar and Lodi were called to the throne room. As they entered, the duo saw an image of the dead horse floating in front of Ramulas, Oriel, and Pip.

Lodi flinched when he saw the image. 'I … I didn't do it. He was sick when I seen him.'

Rygar exploded. 'What in the nine hells have ye done this time?' the dwarf said as he took a swipe at Lodi.

'Calm yourself, good dwarf,' Shigar said, entering the chambers. 'You should listen to what Pip has to say.'

Rygar calmed himself as Pip recounted the story. When she had finished, Lodi opened and closed his mouth a few times.

Rygar looked at him with a pained expression. 'This was our chance to be with the people, and ye killed one o' their horses.'

'I—I can go back to the mountains,' Lodi said, nodding. 'And bring no more trouble.'

The dwarf waved a hand at the giant. 'Bah. I'm stuck with ye, and ye knows it.'

'A moment, dwarf,' Ramulas said as he walked over to Lodi. 'Everything that goes into that pit is sucked into the ground and used to rebuild the maze. Do you know what would have happened if the horse was sucked into the pit?'

Lodi shook his head.

'It would have turned into a stone horse and run through the maze.'

Lodi slowly nodded not quite comprehending what a stone horse looked like.

Shigar's eyes widened in surprise as an idea came to him. 'That would be amazing—a stone horse in the maze.'

Everyone looked at the magician.

Shigar smiled at Ramulas. 'I need a horse and cart for a few days.'

Ramulas nodded and Shigar raced from the room.

'I did the good thing?' Lodi said, smiling.

'No, you did a bad thing,' Ramulas said. 'And we need to make sure something like this does not happen again.'

Lodi cowered and hid behind his hands while Rygar stood protectively in front of his adopted son.

'I know why you did that to the horse,' Ramulas said softly. 'But there are things that a giant cannot do. With everyone training, we have forgotten about you. Do you want to train?'

Lodi nodded. 'I can be the good soldier.'

'Rygar, you will need to train Lodi with the people; can you manage that?'

The dwarf smiled as tears filled his eyes. 'I can, and thanks, milord. He doesn't mean any harm.'

'We knew that when we first met him.'

***

The agent and his party arrived in Bremnon; he sent a short note to the king via pigeon of what happened. He purposefully left out major details, and only stated that he will be in Keah with a couple of days.

He knew that King Zachary would want to ride out and meet with him and then be shown the way to Sanctuary. But that would be unsafe unless the kingdom army came, and that would take time to organise. The agent also walked a thin line, saying he would ignore any reply from the king.

The agent knew that much planning was needed before returning to Sanctuary. He knew that once Zachary found out all of the details, he would want to tear Sanctuary to the ground.

He smiled to himself, knowing that he held power over the king. He would plan to move himself very close to the king after this. After all, it was he, above all the other agents, who had found Sanctuary.

***

Ramulas sat with the four Khilli in the throne room; with help from Oriel's magic, all their wounds were healed, and they were told that Sanctuary was a place of freedom for them. The king would think them dead, and no punishment would await their families.

K'ayden had become the unofficial speaker for the group. He looked up at Ramulas. 'Why did you have us beaten and brought here?'

'When the king receives word that you are dead, no harm will come to your families. You saved my life in the tombs, and you are here so that I can return the favour.'

'But what of the rest of my people?' K'ayden asked.

'After you told me of your people's plight, I swore to myself that if I could ever help you, I would. Now I think that time is near.'

'You cannot bring your army to Keah to save my people,' K'ayden said. 'When the king knows of your intentions, he will kill our families.'

Ramulas shook his head with a smile. 'We won't do that. But tell me one thing—when the agent returns to the king and tells him of what happened, what will he do?'

'The king will become angry. He will come here with his soldiers and Khilli warriors.'

Ramulas nodded. Shigar had said the same thing. Ramulas did not want a fight with the kingdom soldiers—the people of Sanctuary were training to fight the legion.

However, if the king brought his soldiers and Khilli to his new home, it would be the perfect opportunity to free the Khilli people. Shigar had told Ramulas of a way into the city of Keah unknown to anyone else.

Ramulas told the four warriors of his plan and how it counted on the king coming to Sanctuary with the Khilli warriors. It was a risky plan, but if it was timed correctly, the Khilli people would be free.

The four Khilli spoke amongst themselves for a few moments before agreeing to the plan. Ramulas called Iguchi, Rygar and Owain to join the Khilli.

Once they arrived, discussions were held over the king's tactics and army training. Every now and then, Rygar, Iguchi, or Ramulas would ask a question.

At the end of the discussion, Rygar spoke. 'The people of Sanctuary won't be ready if the king brings his army straight away.'

Iguchi nodded. 'The people need to train harder.'

They were right, Ramulas thought, as the burden of responsibility weighed heavily on his shoulders.

He just hoped they would be ready in time.

***

The Fallen Angels waited at one end of the training grounds. At the other end stood two hundred of Sanctuary's archers. They each had five blunt arrows, made for bruising, not killing. The people of Sanctuary sought every available vantage point to watch the upcoming spectacle.

Everyone had been told that the king may be coming with his army, and this training would help the archers fire under pressure.

The archers were separated into two groups. Each group had half of the archers kneeling at the front line—these were to release arrows first. As they reloaded, the archers behind would follow. This would be repeated, sending wave after wave of arrows at the Fallen Angels.

On Iguchi's signal, the Angels would rush toward the archers. The Angels would only fall if struck by three arrows.

Iguchi raised his hand and held it for a few seconds before dropping it.

The Fallen Angels ran screaming with shields before them across the training ground.

The first wave of arrows flew. Half were harmlessly deflected by shields—the rest were too high or wide. Only twenty Angels were struck, and still they came.

The second wave of arrows flew.

This time, thirty of the Angels were struck as they spread their formation, but none had been hit three times. They had covered a quarter of the distance and picked up speed.

The archers fumbled loading the third wave of arrows; only half were fired, most going wide, the Fallen Angels were halfway, and order among the archers vanished as they fired at will.

The Fallen Angels closed the gap. With only three falling from triple hits, they rolled over the first row of archers and into the second. The Fallen Angels whipped their shields back and forth, hitting archer's arms, legs and bodies. Some archers attempted to use their bows as weapons, but to no avail.

Once every archer had been struck, Iguchi whistled, and the Fallen Angels stopped and helped the archers to their feet.

Rygar came storming up to the archers. 'Now, what happened to ye? I've seen ye shoot arrows at targets. But when the targets run at ye, ye fall apart.'

He waited for the words to sink in. 'Knowin' what ye needed to be doin' is one thing, but knowin' when an' how ye should be doin' it is another thing. The hardest part o' any battle is just before it starts,' he said loudly, for all to hear.

'Battle plans will always fall apart,' Iguchi said, joining in. 'And when they do, you will need to know what to do. That will take lots of training. I saw fear in your hearts when the Fallen Angels ran at you.'

'How do we stop the fear from entering our hearts?' one of the archers asked.

Iguchi smiled. 'You must train until the fear leaves you.'

He motioned for the Fallen Angels and archers to take their positions again. Iguchi raised his hand and dropped it when he heard the archers moan.

***

Rygar had positioned two groups opposite each other in the training ground. Because he knew time was against them, the dwarf wanted the people to perfect the basic fighting moves. It would be better than teaching them more moves and not performing them properly.

Rygar called out and the first group attacked with a combination of a right, left, and a thrust to the stomach and then stepped back and defended as the second group copied the manoeuvre.

The two groups moved back and forth until their arms felt like lead and they could not lift their swords and shields.

Then Rygar would place ten people from one group in the middle of the training ground. He chose forty from the other group to surround them. Both groups only had their shields.

The smaller group were told that they needed to do anything necessary to break through the circle, and they needed to do this as a whole group, not leaving anyone behind.

As the dwarf watched different groups go through the same test, he thought to himself, *It looks messy and painful, but it's the only way to teach teamwork.* He had seen too many people become separated in battles and killed; the people of Sanctuary needed to learn through pain.

Rygar trained the people for days until their movements became natural. He saw Lodi in the background imitating every move.

***

Iguchi spoke with Ramulas in the throne room. 'If your king comes with his army, you must defeat them in such a way that they will never want to attack again; then he will tell others what to expect if they wish to come here.'

Ramulas sighed. 'When I first came here, Oriel told me that I needed to train an army to fight the First Legion—evil soldiers who would come here and do terrible things to the people of the kingdom. But if King Zachary comes here with his army, we will be fighting our own people.'

Iguchi laughed bitterly. 'I have travelled to many lands, and some people fight and kill in the name of their god or beliefs—they each believe that their ways are just. They want other people to worship and believe in the way they do. You are fighting for something greater: the freedom of your people. Believe in this, and you will not lose any battle.'

Ramulas nodded, as the words made sense to him.

'Now come with me,' Iguchi said. 'I wish to show you something.'

Ramulas followed the small man to one of the many kitchens in the castle. This one was empty of people. Iguchi motioned for Ramulas to be seated while he prepared food.

After a few minutes, he sat opposite Ramulas, and each had a bowl of steaming broth with noodles and vegetables. Iguchi pulled out two thin wooden sticks which he used to eat and smiled at Ramulas.

'Where I come from, these bowls warn others of my abilities.'

'What do you mean?' Ramulas asked, looking down at his bowl.

'The way everything is presented shows my skill with my swords.' He saw that Ramulas did not understand. 'To become an expert with killing, one must have a way to hone their skills.'

As Iguchi spoke, his sticks danced in his hand as he stabbed the air above his bowl. 'Even the way we write our symbols tells how skilful a warrior is with the short sword.'

He motioned for Ramulas to stand away from the table and handed him one of the thin sticks.

'This is the symbol for war,' Iguchi said as he waved his stick in patterns through the air. 'Now hold up your sword and I will show you how the symbol is used for fighting.'

Ramulas held up his thin stick and was instantly mesmerised by how Iguchi's stick danced before him, and then his stick went flying and Iguchi struck him in the throat.

The small man smiled. 'This is why only warriors cook the best noodles.'

Ramulas shook his head. How many more secrets did Iguchi have?

24

The agent walked into the king's chambers escorted by two royal guards. The surviving soldiers from his party had been sent to the dungeons for questioning. Zachary rolled a small silver tube in between his thumb and forefinger.

Then he stopped and opened the tube, took out the letter, and read out loud. '*My king, I have found Sanctuary, lost men. Await my return. I will not respond.*'

Zachary looked at the agent with an amused expression. '"Await my return"? I thought, as king, I was the one who gave orders. Pray tell me, agent, are you planning to take my place as king? Are you planning to take my place as Aleesha's father?' he said, gesturing to his daughter who sat by his side.

The agent smiled, shaking his head.

'Sir agent,' Zachary said with a cold smile, 'what reason do you have to smile? At this very moment, the men you returned with are being questioned. If your story differs from theirs, you will suffer.'

The agent continued to smile. The king's paranoia had deepened— this would make him easier to manipulate. He knew that Aleesha would be no problem either.

'I sent you out with four Khilli,' Zachary said. 'They did not return. Where are they?'

'The Khilli are dead,' the agent said bluntly.

Zachary recoiled as if slapped. 'Start from the beginning, and tell me what happened at Sanctuary.'

The agent outlined his tale, from following the wagons into the forest and meeting the Lord of Sanctuary to the battle outside Sanctuary and the message to the king.

'A giant?' Zachary asked in shock. 'They have not been seen in generations.'

'This giant killed several men with one swing of its club.'

Zachary leaned forward on his throne. 'Did you see the Khilli die?'

The agent shook his head. 'No, but they were bloodied and very still when I last saw them.'

Zachary shook his head. 'This sounds like Shangri-La all over again. Did you see any dragons?'

'There were no dragons.'

'You may leave,' Zachary said with an absent wave of his hand. 'I will have the captain of the royal guard talk to you about Sanctuary.'

As the agent walked away, Zachary thought of an old book he had read as a child. It was written decades ago by his grandfather, and it told of the failed attempt to bring Shangri-La back under the kingdom's rule. Shangri-La had declared itself a separate nation.

Rumours of dragons and dark magic had kept the kingdom soldiers, and everyone else, away from the forbidden place for all this time. Now Sanctuary wanted separation from the kingdom as well.

'I cannot allow this to happen,' Zachary said as he stood.

'What will you do, father?' Aleesha asked.

'This Lord of Sanctuary needs to be punished. Wait here until I return,' he said before walking to the library.

He walked into the large, well-lit room and was astounded at the number of books his family had collected over generations. He did not visit the library often—he left reading and studying to others. The library was twice as large as his throne room, with dark wooden shelves filled with books from floor to ceiling.

Zachary found the section that he wanted and ran his finger along the leather-bound books until he came across the one he was looking for.

Dust had gathered along the spine; however, the gold lettering was still visible. The book felt heavy as he pulled it from the shelf, yet it was one of the smallest in the library. He found a seat near a window and began to read.

Shangri-La
Entry for King Braydon on Midsummers Day.

Five weeks past, I had received word that small groups of people have been seen leaving the city of Keah and towns across the kingdom. After several weeks of searching, my agents have informed me that these people are living in the great forest.

The people had renamed this place Shangri-La.

When word came to me of this, I sent the collector of taxes with two sheriffs, ten knights on their warhorses, and ten lance riders to collect taxes.

Two weeks had passed without word from the party. Ten days was the expected time of their return. No word had been received by pigeon or any other means.

One week later, I was called to the north gate of the city. The sight that awaited me was far more than I could ever imagine.

A dirty, haggard figure lay on the floor of the guardhouse. I could not see the importance, but then something caught my attention. I saw the outline of a red eagle on his torn vest. I brought myself closer to the man and saw that it was one of the sheriffs who went to Shangri-La.

He was covered in dirt, his beard unkempt and hair a wild mess, but this wretch was the sheriff.

'What happened, man?' I asked. 'Tell me now.'

The sheriff did not seem to hear my words or see me standing before him. I snapped my fingers in front of his face and only then did he realise that he was not alone. Looking at me through the eyes of a madman, he reached up and grabbed my tunic.

'Dragons,' he whispered as the madness grew in his eyes.

'What dragons?' I asked.

The sheriff answered with a high-pitched scream as he looked over my shoulder and pointed. I quickly turned, pulling my sword free. All I saw were the soldiers of the guard house looking sadly at the sheriff.

'I am sorry, my lord,' the sergeant said. 'He has been that way since we found him a short while ago.'

I fetched a priest to come and heal the sheriff and then asked for the sheriff to be taken into the castle.

When the sheriff was better, the priest called for me, and when I arrived the sheriff began his tale of the march on Shangri-La.

The group had travelled to the towns of Suda and Nasad before turning east. They had made good time, reaching the border of Shangri-La's Forest in five days.

After an hour's travel into the trees, they were met by a lone man, who informed them that they would die if they did not leave. The group laughed at the man and continued deeper into the forest, where they saw a green dragon.

This was the moment when the sheriff began to scream hysterically. His body shook uncontrollably for a few moments before he lay still and quiet. The priest checked the sheriff before looking at me and shaking his head. The sheriff had passed.

I was both shocked and intrigued by what I had witnessed, so I decided to organise a larger party and see Shangri-La for myself. The sheriff's talk of a dragon had me worried. It would take countless men and many machines of war to slay this beast. With this thought, I went to see my magician, Declyn.

I arrived at his chambers and told him of Shangri-La and the sheriff, and that I wanted to see this place for myself. Declyn smiled as he placed a small wooden box in front of me. He opened it and pulled out a crystal ball the size of an orange.

He held it up for me to see. The crystal seemed to be alive as dark mists swirled within. 'This holds a black dragon,'

Declyn said. 'They are the strongest of all the dragons—we will not have a problem in Shangri-La.'

I was stunned that my magician held such a spell without my knowledge, but also relieved that we had such a powerful card up our sleeve.

'But what if the other dragon is also black?' I asked.

Declyn smiled and shrugged. 'Then we wait until the fight is finished before we kill the survivor.'

Declyn and I rode in a carriage to Shangri-La. With us on this journey were one hundred knights on their warhorses and twenty-five royal archers who could hit a bird in flight from two hundred yards.

Declyn spent his time buried within his books, studying, and preparing for the battle. On the fifth morning, a shout brought the carriage to a stop, and Captain Aldrich opened the carriage.

'My lord, we are in sight of Shangri-La.'

Stepping out of the carriage, I looked past the knights on horseback to gaze upon Shangri-La. We had ten miles to travel, and I was taken by how big the trees were. The forest of Shangri-La towered over everything else. By my estimation, the trees were over one hundred yards tall.

'Captain, my horse,' I called, stepping down from the carriage.

Looking back at Declyn, I saw him wave me away with a smile. He would study for as long as he was able. Captain Aldrich handed the reigns of my black steed. I nodded to the captain as I mounted, and he called for the party to move forward. I rode alongside Aldrich, leading the column.

Within a short time, we reached the border of Shangri-La. We were met by a sight that turned my stomach—the path into the forest was lined with large spikes. Impaled on those spikes were the rotting corpses of the men I had sent before.

A murder of crows feasted on the decaying bodies. An arrow flew passed me, hitting one of the black birds. The rest took flight, cawing their displeasure.

Turning, I saw the stern expression of a royal archer. All the men had gathered behind me. I ordered three of the closest to stay behind and bury those on the pikes, and I led the rest into Shangri-La.

Captain Aldrich and a few men rode up to scout the trail. Two minutes later, they returned.

'My king,' Aldrich said, 'the path is covered in roots, and the horses are sure to break a leg. We will need to walk.'

I nodded and the captain gave orders for the men to travel by foot and carry some supplies.

As the men tethered their horses, I looked deep into the forest and was awestruck at how wide some of the trees were. They grew even larger toward the middle of the forest.

Within minutes, knights and archers returned on foot, each carrying a small pack. A scout was sent forward as we moved deeper into Shangri-La. Declyn walked by my side holding the crystal ball which contained the black dragon. The only dangers were the thick twisting roots on the forest floor.

Captain Aldrich held up his hand, and the column came to a stop. Declyn was breathing heavily, not being used to strenuous exercise. I was thankful for my combat training, which had prepared me for this long walk.

'Can you hear that sound?' Aldrich asked.

I shook my head.

'Exactly,' he replied. 'This forest should be alive with the sounds of wildlife—birds and the like. The forest has fallen silent. Something is going to happen; I can feel it.'

My heartbeat began to quicken with excitement. 'What makes you say that?'

'I sent a scout ahead and he has not returned. He should have been here half an hour ago.'

The revelation of the scout not returning was a shock to me. What could this mean? There was a small clearing one hundred yards ahead. Captain Aldrich sent two groups of archers to flank either side of the clearing.

The captain turned to me. 'My king, the archers will be waiting for us by the time we are in the clearing. We will have the advantage of surprise.'

We stopped at the edge of the clearing and the captain signalled that he would go in by himself. When he was halfway across, Aldrich made hand signals and the archers emerged from the trees.

We seemed alone in the clearing, as well as the whole of Shangri-La. The captain dropped to one knee and began digging in the soil. After a short moment, he pulled out a small smouldering piece of wood.

'Whoever filled this fire pit knows we are here. We are close to finding the mystery of this place.'

There were two paths ahead of us. Aldrich sent a scout down each of the trails and waited a few minutes, the scout from the right path returned and Aldrich smiled saying that we need to go down the left path.

'Why do we take the left path?' I asked.

He smiled coldly. 'Because that scout did not return—that means we are very close.'

We made our way down the path for a short while before a large clearing opened before us. We found a small village built in and around the trees.

Yet there was not a soul to be seen.

Captain Aldrich, Declyn, and I walked into the village while the rest of our men fanned out behind us. Declyn held the crystal ball in front of him while constantly looking at the sky.

'You are not welcome here,' a voice called out of nowhere. 'Leave now or die.'

We all looked for the speaker, but he could not be seen.

'Show yourself,' Captain Aldrich called out.

The tension increased as we waited for the speaker to appear. A man stepped out from behind one of the buildings. He was dressed in simple green leggings and a green vest. He stepped in front of Aldrich and smiled with confidence.

'Did you not see our warning?'

Captain Aldrich exploded. 'They were my men.'

He grabbed the man's vest and struck him across the face. Blood poured from his nose and mouth, but the man's smile chilled me to the bone.

'You will all die screaming.'

He whistled loudly, and a huge shadow swept across the clearing. At this moment, Declyn gripped my arm tightly. I saw him looking upward in terror, and I followed his gaze to see a green dragon drop into the clearing.

Declyn gave a shout, pushing me aside and smashing the crystal ball onto the ground. The crystal ball exploded into a dark, swirling mist that grew rapidly. Within the mist, I saw the shape of a dragon forming.

'How do we control it?' I asked Declyn.

'Oh no. Do not say that,' Declyn said as he cowered away from me.

'You do not control me!' the black dragon boomed.

Its giant head snaked down to be level with mine. I felt a cold shiver run through me. The head was twice the size of my body; I was lost for words to pacify the dragon.

At that moment, a stream of flame shot over the black dragon, and it turned to find the green dragon.

With a mighty roar, the black took flight after the green. We all watched in fascination as the two creatures battled above us. The black was almost twice the size of the green. Another line of flame struck the black in the chest.

It accepted this as it crashed into the green, clamping its jaws around the green's neck.

The black turned in the air, shaking its head from side to side. The green appeared helpless as it was thrown around like a doll. The black opened its maw, releasing a stream of acid coating the green's wings.

Steam rose from the green's wings and, with a roar of protest, it fell to the ground.

Suddenly, more large shadows raced across the ground. I looked up to see several greens dropping from the sky. Two greens landed on the body of the black, it beat its powerful wings and almost dislodged the threat.

Almost, but not quite.

Twenty yards in the air, the three fought. The black snapped its head back and forth attempting to bite the greens. But the greens flew off the black, sending streams of flame onto the creature.

The back rolled through the air as it dodged the flame. It quickly caught up to the greens. Using its teeth and claws, the black began tearing into the greens. The black had the upper hand and was sure to win.

Then three more green dragons dropped from the sky and how the tide turned—the black was sorely outmatched and attempted to fly away from the greens.

The greens darted in and out, biting, tearing, and slashing. After a few moments, the black fell to the ground, its body burnt and bloody. The greens landed on the black and tore it to pieces. They stopped when it was dead and looked hungrily at the kingdom forces.

'You were told to leave,' said the man in green.

His voice broke the spell that had fallen over my men when the greens fell from the sky—royal archers let fly with their arrows, which bounced harmlessly off the shining green scales.

One of the green dragons sent a stream of flame into the archers, burning five, and their screams cut through me like a rusted knife. The knights ran into the trees.

'Hold your positions!' Aldrich called.

A green dragon turned its head and grabbed the captain in its jaws. He screamed as he was tossed into the air. At this sight, the men ran faster for the trees.

Declyn raised his hands, casting a spell and sending a blast of ice into the face of one of the greens.

'Attack!' the man in green shouted.

People swarmed out of the houses, armed with swords and spears. The hatred on their faces was absolute. They followed the dragons, who chased my men into the trees.

The dragon hit with the ice spell shook its head, causing shards of ice to fall around Declyn and me. Declyn pulled out a dark amulet hanging from a slender chain around his neck.

A thick fog flowed from the amulet and, within seconds, I could not see a thing. My breath quickened as I heard the fearful screams of men dying and dragons roaring.

'Come with me,' Declyn said.

He grabbed my arm and pulled me along and found the fog had cleared somewhat. We followed a path that led away from the village and, after a while, we found ourselves in a clearing.

As we entered, several knights crashed through the trees. I was about to call them to us when two green dragons flew overhead. The knights were covered in streams of flame. I will never forget the sounds of the knights as they were cooked in their own armour.

More of my men, archers, and knights ran through the clearing, chased by the people of Shangri-La. Glowing arrows were fired at my men. Somehow, the arrows had the power to melt through armour sand knights and archers were sent screaming back into the trees.

Declyn's hand tightened on my arm as he guided me around the outside of the clearing. As we moved, both man and beast stepped away from our protective fog.

As we made our way back to the carriage and horses, the sounds of fighting and screaming all but stopped. I wondered how we could have suffered such a bitter defeat and where all of those green dragons had come from.

It seemed to take hours to reach the carriage but, when we did, the men were dead. They had been placed on pikes alongside the other bodies. The horses had been torn apart and the carriage smashed beyond use.

Declyn waved his hand and the fog surrounding us vanished. 'We had best start walking.'

I looked at him in disbelief; however, I knew he was right. To stay near Shangri-La would mean death. We walked until we were both exhausted and had blisters on our feet. We found shelter within a small grove of trees. Feeling weary, we fell asleep.

We woke sore, hungry, and thirsty, and if I appeared anything like Declyn did in his dirty state, we were both in need of a bath and clothing.

Setting off as the sun rose, we came across a small farmhouse. After realising who we were, the farmer and his wife invited us in. They did not have anything I was accustomed to; however, they gladly shared what little they had.

Early the next morning, our clothes were washed, we were bathed, and two horses were provided for us. We made haste to Suda. Arriving there, Declyn and I spoke to the sheriff and told him of Shangri-La.

At once, he offered to ride with two hundred soldiers to Shangri-La, seeking vengeance for his king. Smiling, I declined his offer, for I knew firsthand that one thousand men would not be enough. He was instead ordered to pass the word that no-one was to go anywhere near Shangri-La.

Within two days, an escort of three hundred soldiers had brought me safely home to Keah. I called for a meeting with my council and outlined the doomed march on Shangri-La. When I had finished my tale, all agreed with my decision.

What if the dragons attacked the towns and Keah itself? How many lives would be lost? No, it would be better to leave that place alone entirely.

Zachary closed the book, thinking that the agent did not mention any dragons. He would gather his army and march on Sanctuary. They had a giant, but he had a machine of war that would deal with the problem.

The agent and survivors would be questioned on every aspect of their encounter. When he arrived at Sanctuary, Zachary wanted no surprises.

25

The First Legion had grown restless. They had been training every day since Oriel escaped and knew that they would soon be travelling to another world to destroy any opposition. However, the three captains—Redemption, Reckoning, and Retribution—saw morale falling.

As captains of the First Legion, they knew that bad morale could become contagious. The soldiers of the First Legion needed to be reminded of battle.

Remus stood on a small hill two hundred yards from the town. It was an hour after dawn. He had travelled with the legion through half of the night. They stood with the warlord, watching the quiet scene below.

'The people know we are here,' Reckoning said dryly.

'I want them to know fear before they die,' Remus said.

The town had five thousand people—half the amount of the legion. Normally the legion could kill everyone in the town without any problems, but Remus wanted the legion to be challenged.

They were stripped of their armour, swords, and shields. They would turn their bodies into weapons.

Remus looked down at the pile of branches before him. The legion knew that the signal to attack would be when it was lit, and when the fire went out the attack would cease.

Some of the townspeople gathered at the top of the wall, watching, and waiting. They knew they would face death, but did not know why.

Remus did not need a reason.

With an absent click of his fingers, the branches were alight. The First Legion ran towards the wall. Arrows and rocks came down from those on the wall. Only a few legion soldiers fell before the columns reached the base of the wall.

Grappling hooks attached to ropes were thrown, and soldiers scaled the wall like ants to find people running at them with swords.

The townspeople did not stand a chance.

The soldiers formed small wedges and ran along the wall. People were knocked off both sides. A group of soldiers dropped behind the wall to open the gate.

The townspeople ran to the gate, knowing that if it was opened, they would all die, more soldiers dropped down to ward off the people.

Once the solid timber bar was removed, the gate swung open and the legion poured in like a flood, pushing the townspeople back.

They formed crude lines of defence as the legion came into their town. People were swept away like leaves in the wind. Controlled chaos ruled as small groups of soldiers chased down screaming men, women, and children. The fire at Remus' feet began to die. He clicked his fingers, and the fire was brought back to life.

After several minutes, the screaming had almost stopped. The town was now being searched for those in hiding. With a wave of his hand, Remus killed the small fire at his feet. The legion left the town and form up in front of Remus. From what he could see, only a handful suffered minor injuries.

More importantly, the legion had tasted blood. They would be eager to find Oriel.

***

Shigar returned to Sanctuary and was met in the courtyard by Ramulas and Pip.

'Welcome back,' Ramulas said with a smile. 'I trust your journey went well?'

'Hello, my friend. I have collected far more than I thought possible,' the magician said, waving to the cart filled with clay pots of various sizes. 'These will help with the battles to come.'

'How do pots help in a battle?' Pip asked.

Shigar laughed. 'It's what I have in the pots. Come with me to the pit and I will show you.'

The trio arrived at the pit in time to see a cart full of stone dumped into it. The rocks were slowly sucked into the whirlpool to be reused in building the maze.

Shigar climbed down and held a pot. He waited for Ramulas and Pip to come closer before opening the lid.

He laughed as Ramulas, and Pip jumped back in shock as a tentacle slithered out.

'These are octopuses,' he said, tossing the clay pot into the pit.

The pot broke, and the octopus was sucked into the centre.

'Can you imagine our enemies walking through the maze filled with stone octopuses? I have seen them open large clams—just think what an octopus made of stone could do to armour.'

'By the gods,' Ramulas whispered. 'But the people of Sanctuary will need to stay out of the maze, or they will be harmed.'

Shigar shook his head. 'Octopuses are territorial. They will protect the people of Sanctuary from outsiders.'

'I cannot wait to see the looks on the faces of the king's soldiers in the maze,' Pip said.

For the next few minutes, all the pots were thrown into the pit except for one, which Shigar put aside.

'Why did you not throw that one in?' Ramulas asked.

Shigar smiled. 'This is a special trick for when the legion comes.'

***

Ramulas walked past Oriel's room and noticed Thomas talking with the four Khilli. He had seen his friend from Bremnon around the warriors since they came to Sanctuary.

He walked into the room, and the five men turned to him and smiled.

K'ayden opened his arms. 'Today is a good day, my friend.'

Ramulas was confused. 'In what way? What has happened?'

K'ayden came close to Thomas, clapping him on the shoulder. 'Another lost child wants to return home.'

Ramulas was speechless and could not understand what was happening. He knew that Thomas had some Khilli blood in him, but what was going on?

Thomas smiled with tears in his eyes. 'Ramulas, I thought I found a new home when I came here. I have always longed for a place where I belonged. But when my brothers arrived, I heard the singing of our people and knew I had to return home.'

Ramulas was in shock as K'ayden continued. 'Many of our people have left the plains of our homeland before we were taken prisoner. It has always been our desire for them and their children to come home. Thomas is the first to hear the calling. He must be born again and learn the ways of our people. When we are united once more, we will, as a tribe, accept our brother into our family.'

Ramulas was overcome with a range of emotions—disbelief, happiness, and confusion. 'What happens now?' he asked.

'Thomas will stay with us and learn the old ways, and then he will know how to prove his worth to the Khilli people.'

'How do you prove your worth?'

'By doing what you have done, Ramulas—show that you have the heart of a warrior.'

Ramulas left the room and seemed to float as he adjusted to what he had experienced. Just when he thought Sanctuary had shown him everything, there was always something else.

***

Edwin saw Ramulas outside the tunnel and asked him to look at the progress they had made. Walking inside, he saw many people covered in dust working on the walls.

Ramulas was amazed to see the tunnel went one hundred yards into the mountain. The tunnel had been widened so a wagon could pass through with ease. At the end, he saw the two friends from Gullytown. They were sitting against the wall deep in conversation.

Since coming to Sanctuary, they had still not come out of the tunnel, eaten, or drank. They had built a small alcove where they rested.

What Ramulas found strange was that Emily stood near the duo. She seemed to look through the wall of the tunnel. She turned when Ramulas and the dwarf approached.

'We are coming closer,' she said.

'Can you see how far Oriel is?' Ramulas asked.

Emily shook her head. 'Not Oriel. We are coming closer to them.'

'Them?' Ramulas asked. 'Are there other people in the mountain with Oriel?'

'There are things in the mountain, they know we are coming.'

'What are these things?'

Emily smiled up at Ramulas. 'You will soon see.'

Ramulas was lost for words when Emily walked away. He was about to question her further, but she faded away into the darkness.

'I will ask Oriel if she knows what Emily means,' Ramulas said before turning to Royce and Shayn. 'The digging is going well. You have the freedom to walk around Sanctuary if you like. I have not seen you out of the tunnel.'

Royce smiled. 'We are happy here. This mountain feels like home, and it talks to us. Deep within the stone, something is calling to us.'

Ramulas nodded as he looked at the duo from Gullytown. While everyone else who worked in the tunnel was covered in dust, the greyness seemed to be a part of them. Even the whites of their eyes had begun to darken.

Royce and Shayn were changing, but into what, Ramulas did not know.

***

Iguchi stood near the bank of the river watching the Fallen Angels wade across the river holding large rocks above their heads. In the last two days, they had only slept six hours. He wanted them to train with as little sleep as possible and not knowing when their next meal would be.

He saw the Angels begin to tire. The river was fifty yards wide and five feet at its deepest point. This was where Benji struggled with the two crossings. The first time, he dropped his rock and took a minute recovering it; the second time, Michael and Miles walked with him for support.

Iguchi was proud of his Fallen Angels. He had pushed their minds and bodies past what they thought was possible. He had taught them to ignore the pain in their bodies. It was their minds that were weak—their bodies would survive.

Michael was the only Fallen Angel who did not seem affected by the rigorous training. Iguchi knew that Michael was different from the others, and he knew that Michael would show his true form soon.

As the Fallen Angels came out of the river and dumped their rocks into a pile, Iguchi tossed several stones at them. His smile grew when the Angels' hands snapped out to catch them without thought.

'You are all clumsy,' Iguchi called, walking toward them. 'You have fallen into the river, and now you are wet. You will need to run until your clothes are dry.'

Without a word of complaint, the Fallen Angels gathered their swords and shields. Benji ran ahead to scout and Michael and Miles took flanking positions. The rest ran in lines of two through the trees.

Even though it was a month past summer, it was still warm, and Angels' clothes would soon dry.

Once they were dry, Iguchi gave them food and taught them the rules of war.

'The best defence is to elude all attacks from your enemy. But Sanctuary is at the base of a mountain—this will make eluding difficult. We will need to engage the enemy as they come through the forest.

The enemy will then show us their defence. We must hit them hard and then disappear into the forest and elude them until we find a weakness.'

He paused, letting the words sink in.

'When running from the enemy, they will expect you to run as far as possible. They will chase you. We must do what they do not expect. We will hide among the trees and, when they are close enough, jump out to strike at them. Then we will run away once more.'

The Fallen Angels all responded with tired nods; he had seen a great improvement with the Fallen Angels in the past few months.

Iguchi wanted a few more years training them, and then they would be men of iron. He hoped and prayed that this training would be enough when the fighting began.

***

Ramulas walked into his throne room to find Oriel waiting for him. 'Hello, Ramulas.'

'Hello, Oriel. I have come from the tunnel and wish to ask you some questions.'

Oriel nodded with a smile.

'Emily was in the tunnel and told me that we were close to *them*. There are things in the tunnel that know we are coming. Do you know what she is talking about?'

'Somewhere within the mountain close to me, I feel the presence of another. The things Emily spoke of are magical items. He thinks they will set him free from his prison, so he calls for them.'

Ramulas gasped in shock. 'Is there someone else in there with you? We must find them after we release you.'

Oriel shook her head and smiled sadly. 'He has been trapped within a different dimension in the mountain for a very long time. This has made him extremely angry. If we find him, I do not think it wise to free him.'

'But you have magical abilities,' Ramulas replied.

'I sense powerful magic around this one—magic that is strange to me.'

Ramulas was at loss for words. Another magical being trapped in the mountain with Oriel. What could this mean for Sanctuary?

'What else did you want to ask?' Oriel said.

'The two from Gullytown—there is something different about them. They are beginning to change.'

'My powers have slowly been returning, and the ancient magic of Sanctuary has come to life with people in the streets once more. This magic has joined with mine, allowing me to see things. Royce and Shayn are becoming earth elementals. I saw this in them when they first arrived.'

'What are earth elementals?'

'They are beings who are one with the earth. Royce and Shayn will soon become things of living stone.'

'What!?' Ramulas said in disbelief.

'But this is the life they have chosen. And you have other matters to attend to,' she said, looking at the door.

Ramulas turned to see K'ayden walking toward him.

'Hello, my friend,' the Khilli said. 'You have a beautiful home here, and we have enjoyed time with your family, and Thomas has returned to his people. Now I understand where your strength comes from.'

'Thank you,' Ramulas said as he noticed a troubled expression on his friend. 'What is wrong?'

'We enjoy the freedom of walking around Sanctuary and the forest, but we yearn for our families. We are two days travel from our homeland, but we cannot go because, if we are seen, our families will suffer. You have freed us, but inside we are slowly dying.'

Ramulas gripped K'ayden by his shoulders. 'I know how you must feel. When I was locked in the tombs and tortured, I thought I would never see my family again. You helped me keep that hope alive—now I am asking you to trust me. You will be with your families soon enough.'

The Khilli nodded. 'Thank you, my friend. I have something to show you so you can understand us better. Come into the clearing an hour after sunset.'

***

It was dark when Ramulas walked out into the clearing, but not dark enough that he could not see the outline of the trees. The clear night sky was full of stars and a crescent moon. The four Khilli stood with Thomas by the trees. The whites of their teeth showed as they smiled. Ramulas noticed a subtle change within Thomas, something he could not define. He seemed to hold himself with more purpose.

'Hello my friend,' K'ayden said. 'Come with us.'

Ramulas followed the Khilli through the forest until they came to a clearing.

K'ayden tilted his head up toward the mountain. 'Look to the sky for five bright stars surrounding a bright red star.'

Ramulas followed the Khilli's gaze and soon found the cluster.

'The red star is where we talk to our families when we are away from them. They also look to this star. Our people know that when we pass, our bodies are a gift to the earth mother, but our spirits join our ancestors in the red star.

'We always look to the red star and ask our ancestors to watch over our families when we are away and to give them strength until we return.'

Ramulas fought back tears and the lump in his throat as he felt K'ayden's pain.

'It is not until you have lost all that you hold dear that you learn to see through different eyes. It is normal to want to survive. But we must have more if we want to truly feel alive. Thomas is starting to feel as we do.'

At that instant, out in the clearing, Ramulas knew that he would do everything in his power to help unite the Khilli people.

***

Lodi walked out of the barracks into the training grounds. He was dressed in silver armour, which shone in the sunlight, and held a ten-foot broad sword and a shield the size of a man.

The group that was training stopped to look at the giant. At that moment, another group rushed in to knock them to the ground.

'Why in the nine hells did I train ye for, if yer lookin' the wrong way?' Rygar shouted.

The people picked themselves up and dusted off the dirt. Rygar nodded, and they were attacked once more from behind. This time they were warier getting up.

Rygar motioned for them to stand. 'I'll show yer a dirty trick.'

The dwarf motioned for one of the soldiers to come to him. When he was close enough, Rygar fell back as if he was hit. As soon as he was on the ground, Rygar rolled towards the soldier and swiped at his legs with his axe.

The soldier jumped back, and Rygar rolled to his knees while stabbing at the soldier's stomach, causing him to jump again.

Then, in a fluid movement, the dwarf was on his feet. 'Never let yer enemy rest, even when yer on the ground. Keep 'em jumpin' around. Then they'll be too busy to kill ye.'

For the rest of the day, the people took turns fighting from the ground.

***

Iguchi stood in the clearing outside Sanctuary holding a kite. Attached to the kite was a ten-foot red ribbon.

He looked up at the archers along the top of the wall. 'You have improved greatly with moving targets. Now, I want you to hit the ribbon. As you fire your arrows, the Fallen Angels will gather them from the ground. Do not think of them—only think of the ribbon.'

Iguchi ran, tossing the kite into the air. The wind caught the kite, and it lifted into the air. Every so often, Iguchi would pull at the string, causing the kite to weave through the air, sending the ribbon in spiralling patterns.

Owain clicked his tongue a few times before calling out group numbers. Arrows began to rain down into the clearing. While several came close, none of the arrows hit the ribbon.

Iguchi nodded and the Fallen Angels ran out from the trees and began gathering arrows. They occasionally twisted their bodies to avoid being

284

hit. Iguchi nodded to himself, happy with the way the Angels moved; however, he would never admit this.

The small man shouted up at the archers. 'You must not look at where the ribbon is. Look to where it will be—only then will you hit the ribbon.'

After an hour of running, Iguchi felt a tug as the first arrow hit the ribbon. This brought a cheer from those on the wall.

Iguchi stopped and looked at the arrow and then the archers. 'You have done well. But this is only one arrow from two hundred. When all of you hit the ribbon, then it will be time to cheer.'

***

Pip walked into the forest with Ramulas until they came to the dryad's sacred grove. When they arrived, all the dryads were waiting for them. Every one of them smiled at Pip when they saw her.

She looked around the grove in awe. 'I have never seen so many in one place.' Then Pip turned to Ramulas. 'You still haven't told me why you brought me here.'

'Welcome, Lord of Sanctuary,' Eady said. 'Is this the one who is in need of our help?'

Ramulas nodded, thinking of the discussion he'd had with Oriel. She had told him that Sanctuary needed every advantage for when the legion came. One of those would involve bringing Pip to the dryads—for what reason, he was not told.

Eady smiled at Pip as she gestured to the grass. 'Lie upon your back and we will show you the way.'

Pip looked at Ramulas with uncertainty, and he gave her a reassuring smile. 'This will be fine.'

Still slightly unsure, Pip fought against her judgement and lay on the grass. She saw a circle of smiling dryads above her and was shocked when vines came out of the ground, binding her wrists and ankles and then her whole body so she was unable to move.

Pip fought the fear building within her as smaller vines ran over her face to hold open her eyes.

'Ramulas,' she whispered.

Ramulas was stunned as he looked at Eady. 'What are you doing to her?'

Eady smiled down at Pip. 'Do not struggle. This will finish soon.'

She stood over Pip holding a handful of leaves, squeezing her hand. Small drops of green liquid fell into Pip's eyes. She screamed in pain and struggled against the vines. Ramulas stepped forward but was held back by the dryads.

'This is the only way,' Eady said.

The vines released their hold, and Pip curled into a foetal position and cried as she covered her eyes.

The dryads released Ramulas, and he rushed to her side, holding the former thief in his arms.

'The pain will leave soon,' Eady said. 'Then she will see through new eyes.'

After a few moments, Pip stopped crying and took her hands away from her face. Then she gasped. 'By the gods, I can see everything.'

Ramulas said. 'You could see before.'

Pip turned to face him and Ramulas gasped in shock. Her eyes had been brown before—now they were green and glowing brightly.

Pip smiled at him. 'I was blind before, and now I can truly see a whole new world. Everything that was once hidden is now open to me.'

Ramulas looked at her in confusion. 'What do you mean?'

Pip pointed to a tree thick with leaves, describing the location of all the animals within. Ramulas could not see them, but he used his magical ability to communicate with animals and was stunned to find Pip was correct.

She continued pointing out animals within bushes and even underground before saying there were dryads within the trees.

She turned to Ramulas with power emanating from her eyes. 'You are on fire. When I first saw you in Bremnon, you had flames dancing on your shoulders—now your power has become much stronger.'

'In what way?' Ramulas asked.

Pip looked at Ramulas through her new sight and saw the energy burning within him, as if someone had placed a lantern inside a scarecrow. Every part of Ramulas radiated power.

'I don't think I could find the words to tell you.'

26

Ramulas quickly made his way to the tunnel. He had received word that Edwin had found something. He arrived to find a very excited dwarf.

'Milord, there is something very strange inside. See yerself.'

He led Ramulas toward the end of the tunnel, where he saw a group of people gathered around an opening to the left. Edwin clapped his hands and shooed them away.

Ramulas followed the dwarf through the opening, where he saw a small network of tunnels. A faint light shone from one of them. Ramulas felt something calling softly to him. He felt compelled to walk towards the light.

After fifty yards, he found himself in a small cave, where saw Emily, Royce, and Shayn waiting for him. Near them, Ramulas saw something that caused his mouth to hang open.

Floating in the air and surrounded by light was a sword in a blue scabbard and a silver gauntlet.

'What are these?' He asked.

Emily smiled while waving at the items. 'These are the things I told you about. They are calling for him.'

'Calling for who?' Ramulas asked.

Emily pointed to the rear wall of the cave. 'He is in there, and he calls for them.'

'There is something you need to know about them,' Royce said. 'Reach out and touch them.'

Ramulas walked over to the sword and reached out for it. Blue mist fell from the scabbard and the air around the sword turned extremely cold. He quickly pulled his hand away after touching the mist.

Ramulas looked back at the others. 'By the gods, that's so cold.'

Ramulas shook his hand, trying to bring feeling to it once again.

Shayn smiled. 'Try the gauntlet.'

Ramulas prepared himself for another blast of cold. However, he was totally unprepared for what happened. He reached out to grab the gauntlet, and it flowed through his fingers like sand, again, and again he tried, but it always seemed to melt in his hand.

'They don't want you,' Emily said. 'They want him—their owner.'

Ramulas was puzzled. 'Who is the owner?'

'He is my brother.'

Everyone turned in shock to see Michael standing at the entrance of the cave. He was covered in a nimbus of white light.

'Who is your brother?' Ramulas asked. 'And why are these here?'

Michael smiled sadly. 'All I can say is that we need to leave here. My brother will be very upset if someone takes his weapons.

That was not enough for Ramulas—he needed answers. 'Who is your brother, and who are you?'

A strong, bitterly cold wind came from nowhere and buffeted everyone in the cave and then, just as suddenly as it appeared, it was gone.

'We must leave before my brother becomes angrier,' Michael said.

Ramulas led them out of the cave. His mind was reeling from what he had experienced. He looked at Michael in a new light. Ramulas thought that he knew the Fallen Angel, but things had changed.

'We will talk of this later,' Michael promised.

***

Nathaniel watched in curiosity as the humans and the dwarf entered the cave where his weapons were. He saw that they had magical abilities— the young girl was the by far the strongest.

They had each tried to take his weapons, but the sword and gauntlet still called for him and wanted no-one else.

Then he saw Michael, and a surge of pure anger flowed through him. His brother was one of the figures responsible for placing him in this prison.

Nathaniel knew that he would not be able to leave this prison, but since he felt Oriel's presence nearby, his powers had slowly begun to return.

Nathaniel spread his wings and beat them, sending a gale into the cave, and he was relieved when they left.

Then he felt a mix of emotions; he had been here for several hundred years. Just before his banishment, Michael had lain bleeding from a mortal wound delivered by Nathaniel. Why was he here?

Nathaniel shook those thoughts away. With his power growing, he would soon have his freedom, weapons, and revenge; very soon.

Beware the rage of a fallen angel.

***

Zachary sat at the head of the long table in his chambers. A score of others filled the chairs—these included his agent, captain of the royal guard, and counsellors.

They had gone over the agent's information thoroughly three times—a small group of soldiers could reach Sanctuary within four days; however, Zachary would bring three thousand royal lancers, cavalry, infantry, knights, and all of the Khilli warriors.

They would need to bring supply wagons and machines of war; this would make progress slow.

In order to save time, one thousand soldiers would travel by ship to the town of Covedon. The rest would travel with the supply wagons and meet them there, and then the whole force will move to Turtha. Zachary will acquire more men at these two towns.

Then the agent would lead the way to Sanctuary. They would arrive within two weeks with almost four thousand men.

From what the agent had told them, Sanctuary only had around one thousand men, but they did not show discipline. They were brave when facing forty kingdom soldiers, but how would they react when facing the might of the kingdom army?

The city of Keah would be left with less than one hundred soldiers, which would not be enough to defend the city if it came under attack. Zachary could not think of anyone who would attack his city. Keah's main problem was the Symiaks, and they did not cause trouble until winter.

News of Sanctuary had now spread across the land, and Zachary needed to make an example of them. He was confident leaving his daughter in the castle while they marched on Sanctuary—she would be safer there than in the battle. It was time for him to talk to the Khilli.

***

Zachary was escorted to the wing where the Khilli were housed. Over the past week, word had been sent out for all Khilli warriors to return to Keah. For the first time in generations, all the Khilli were together once more.

The warriors knew that if they did not do what was asked of them, their families would suffer. Zachary could hear the excited chatter as he came closer to them. He could not understand the crying each time a warrior was reunited with his family.

Forty royal archers lined the balcony above them as Zachary walked out among them.

'Warriors,' he called.

The chattering ceased, and the Khilli looked up at him.

Zachary smiled down at them. 'It has been far too long since you have all been together. Cherish this moment, for come tomorrow your warriors will march alongside my army to Sanctuary. Your families will stay until your return.'

The Khilli erupted in protest, they were still mourning the loss of four warriors and knew that marching on Sanctuary would cost them many more lives.

Zachary allowed them to continue for a few moments before raising his hand. The royal archer nocked their bows and aimed into the crowd. Protests were replaced by gasps of shock.

'Ah,' Zachary said. 'I see that I have your attention. We march at dawn tomorrow. Enjoy time with your families. While you march, they will be taken care of.'

Zachary walked away and was followed by the archers. The Khilli were furious—they knew many would not return.

Some of the younger warriors wanted to attack the king's men and return to their homeland. However, the older warriors forbade such talk—even more would die, including their women and children.

They would wait for an opportunity to escape from the king another time.

***

In the early morning light, people lined the streets of Keah. Word had spread that Zachary had found the person who escaped from the tombs, along with those who had vanished across the land.

Trumpets sounded as the soldiers marched from the castle to the docks, where they boarded ships for Covedon, and then more trumpets sounded when royal lancers, with their shining lances pointing to the sky, led the column on their horses.

They were followed by a company of knights riding one hundred warhorses. Then came the cavalry, Zachary and his royal guard, royal archers, supply wagons, engines of war, and lastly, the Khilli warriors.

The procession took an hour to leave the city out of the western gate.

***

Ramulas walked into the throne room to find Oriel waiting for him. 'Ramulas, you seem worried. What is the matter?'

293

'There have been too many changes with the people around me. You told me to take Pip to the dryads, and now she sees things that others do not.'

'Pip now sees the real world; she can see inside people's souls. This allows her to read more into what people's intentions are.'

'But she went through so much pain when it happened to her.'

Oriel smiled. 'There can be no great change without pain, and I do not think Pip would want to change back to the way she was.'

'I found the things in the tunnel Emily spoke about, and who they belong to,' Ramulas said.

'What did you find?'

He told her of the magical sword and gauntlet and then explained the light surrounding Michael, and that the items belonged to Michael's brother. Ramulas was now unsure of the Fallen Angel.

Oriel smiled. 'I knew that Michael was different when he first came.'

'What is he?'

'I cannot tell you; he will show you when he is ready. What I can say is that Michael is needed here, and he has a good heart.'

'I want you to tell me now,' Ramulas insisted.

Oriel shook her head. 'There are more important things for you to worry about.'

'Like what?'

Oriel waved her arm and the wall behind her transformed into the image of the city of Keah. Five ships were leaving the harbour filled with soldiers. The rest of the army and Khilli marched from the west gate. She waved her hand once more, and the image vanished.

'The king is coming with his army. They will arrive soon; the people of Sanctuary must prepare for battle.'

Thoughts of Michael and Pip disappeared as Ramulas' mouth became dry. The people would be facing the king's army. He needed to talk with Iguchi, Owain, and Rygar.

Then he thought of his family.

If the people of Sanctuary were not successful, what would become of his family? But Ramulas knew this was bigger than his family.

People across the land would suffer if the First Legion were not stopped. One battle would be hard enough, but fighting two battles seemed impossible.

'This is not fair.'

'There is not much in life that is fair. You need to do what you can for the freedom of the people.'

A sense of determination came over Ramulas as Oriel spoke. He nodded once before walking from the room.

The first test for his people was coming.

***

The Fallen Angels ran through the trees with stone-laden packs strapped to their backs. Iguchi ran with them, impressed with their improvement over the months of rigorous training.

He told them they were headed to a cave at the base of the mountains. He ensured they all knew of its location.

Then Iguchi stumbled and fell, hitting the ground hard.

The Angels stopped immediately, gathering around their fallen leader.

'Iguchi, what happened?' Benji asked leaning forward.

'I have been shot by the enemy,' Iguchi said, grimacing in pain and holding his stomach.

The Fallen Angels instinctively fanned out around Iguchi, facing outwards, swords and shields at the ready. There was no sign of anyone else in the forest.

'We must reach the cave before the enemy returns,' Iguchi said. 'Who will lead us?'

'Michael,' Several Angels said.

In a fluid movement, Iguchi rose and struck Michael in the stomach before dropping to the ground. As Michael collapsed, the Angels looked at each other in shock. They had thought Iguchi had been struck by an enemy—now this had changed things.

'Michael has also been struck by the enemy,' Iguchi said. 'Now who will lead us?'

After witnessing what happened to Michael, none of the Angels spoke.

Iguchi pointed a finger at the Angels. 'Each of you must learn to lead the group. Two of us have been injured. We must reach the cave before the enemy comes; a true leader will know what to do. Who will lead us?'

The Fallen Angels understood what Iguchi meant—without a leader, there is no direction.

'I will lead,' Miles said, stepping forward.

He ordered four Angels to each carry Michael and Iguchi, a scout was sent ahead, and two flanked the group while one covered the rear. The rest created a protective circle around Iguchi and Michael.

Arriving at the cave, Miles ensured that the area was safe before entering. Once Iguchi and Michael were inside, a barrier was built at the entrance.

Iguchi stood. 'You have done well, my Angels. If a battle is bad, we could lose many Angels. All of you have the strength to lead this group. If one falls, another must quickly take their place. Without a leader, all groups will scatter.

'This is what we will do in this battle—take their leaders.'

***

Grace sat opposite Oriel in the throne room. Oriel had been impressed with Grace's progress; however, she was amused at how impatient Grace was with learning magic.

Grace acquired the knowledge of spells almost as quickly as she was shown and was eager for the next. As soon as the young girl was shown a simple spell, she would replicate it with ease and ask for something more difficult.

Oriel opened her hand, palm facing upward. She chanted softly for a few seconds, and then a fireball the size of an orange floated just above her hand.

Grace's eyes widened as she squealed in delight trying to reach for the fireball.

Oriel laughed softly as the fireball floated away from Grace. She tried a few more times, but each time it danced out of reach.

'Make it stop,' Grace said. 'I want to touch it.'

'No, Grace. If you want a fireball, you need to learn how to make one yourself.'

Grace grunted in concentration as she held out both hands. The fireball ceased moving, seeming to freeze above Oriel's palm. Grace slowly pulled her hands closer to herself. The fireball moved two inches away from Oriel's palm. She gasped at the magical energies and pulled the fireball back.

'You cannot have this one, Grace; you need to make your own.'

Grace frowned for a moment before her eyes lit up and she clapped her hands once. The fireball above Oriel's hand shot out a pea-sized flame toward Grace.

Oriel was shocked at what she had seen and felt and, before she could do anything, the smaller fireball was above Grace's outstretched hand. She gently blew on it until it grew as large as Oriel's.

Grace smiled at Oriel proudly. 'Now we each have one.'

'How did you do that?'

Grace shrugged. 'I have seen fire do that when Da makes big fires—small fires jump out of the big one. I thought of that when I saw your fire.'

Oriel held back her sense of excitement as Grace spoke. The young girl still suffered bouts of tiredness when using magic; however, she was becoming more powerful with each passing day.

What excited Oriel the most was that Grace could make objects appear by just thinking about them—not even Oriel had that ability when she was Grace's age.

She wondered how strong Grace's magical ability would be when the Legion arrived.

***

Pip watched the interaction between Oriel and Grace from behind a tapestry. She had found a network of hidden tunnels in the castle; Pip saw a whole new world since the dryads had changed her.

Out of everyone in Sanctuary, Grace was the happiest about the colour change in Pip's eyes. She told anyone that would listen that she and Pip were magical sisters.

With her new-found vision, Pip was able to see inside Oriel and Grace.

Oriel's true form was that of a green dragon sitting on its haunches, with its wings folded along its back, and head lowered so it could fit under the fourteen-foot ceiling. At the centre of the dragon was an intense light in the shape of Oriel.

As Grace's energy glowed from within, Pip saw a juvenile purple dragon with minute wings and a short tail. When Grace attempted to take the fireball, the dragon's image grew slightly. And when Grace stopped using magic, the dragon returned to its normal size.

She saw Grace's dragon curl up ready for sleep as Grace yawned. Pip wondered how much Grace's magic would come into play when the legion arrived.

27

Ramulas walked the hallways of the castle deep in thought, and he narrowly avoided colliding with a Khilli warrior. He looked up to say something and stepped back in shock—before him stood Thomas wearing only a pair of loose pants. His bushy black beard was gone, his hair was trimmed in the traditional Khilli fashion, and his eyes shone with inner peace.

'Hello, Ramulas. I have taken the next step to joining my people.' Thomas tapped the side of his head. 'I can hear our ancestors calling me. I have always ignored them before, but since my brothers arrived, I now know my true calling.'

Ramulas was overwhelmed with joy for his friend. He had seen Thomas change since coming to Sanctuary, but never believed that this could be possible. 'I am happy for you, my friend.'

Thomas nodded. 'I now need to show my people that I have the heart of a warrior. K'ayden said that I will know of that time when it comes.'

Ramulas sighed. 'So much has happened since Oriel came into my life, my friend. I never dreamed of anything like this happening. Now look at you, my good friend—another good thing to celebrate.'

'I am going to talk with my brothers. Please come join us.'

Ramulas nodded and the two friends walked out into the forest.

***

Zachary was relieved when they arrived at the town of Covedon. He had spent the previous night sleeping rough on the road, and he looked forward to finding a comfortable bed. He knew there would be many more days on the road.

The thousand infantry that came by ship were waiting in the town and had set up camp outside the walls. The kingdom army expanded the camp, swiftly erecting tents and pens for the horses.

Only Zachary and the royal guard were to stay in Covedon. He did not need to worry about the Khilli warriors—they would not try to escape, as they knew their family's lives depended on it.

A score of soldiers that came by ship returned from neighbouring towns with horses and supplies.

Zachary and the royal guard were invited to dine with the mayor and sheriff. The king fought to control himself as platters of meats, fruit, breads, and cheeses were placed on several long tables in the dining room.

His recent diet had consisted of salted meat and hard travel bread. Once the servants stepped away, Zachary placed a few small items of food on his plate. A part of him wanted to have his plate overflowing, but that would not show leadership, he thought.

Then he signalled for everyone else to eat.

The mayor turned to Zachary next to him. 'My king, I trust you had a pleasant journey.'

Zachary inwardly sneered at the fat man with his pudgy fingers and the high-pitched voice of a girl. But he forced a smile when he spoke. 'Thank you. We will be staying the night and leaving on the morrow.'

The mayor breathed a sigh of relief. 'The people of this town have become excited since your men arrived by ship. But now that the rest of the kingdom army is here, people have become worried. It has been many years since we have seen war.'

A seething rage threatened to explode from within Zachary, and it took all that he had to maintain composure.

He looked at the mayor. 'You snivelling fool—your role is to lead your people, not to question your king. Pray that my march goes well, for if I return unhappy, you will go to Gullytown.'

The mayor gasped as his eyes bulged, and a hand absently held his heart.

Zachary smiled. 'Now tell me, how many of Covedon's soldiers will be marching alongside the kingdom army?'

'One hundred and fifty, my king.'

'Is that all?' Zachary asked, feigning surprise. 'I thought Covedon had at least double that number.'

The mayor shrank in his chair while his eye darted around nervously. 'My king, Covedon has over three hundred soldiers, but I wanted to keep some here in case of attack.'

Zachary fought the rage that threatened to explode from within. Once he regained his composure, he forced a smile. 'I understand. Now I wish time alone with my men.'

The mayor nodded and quickly signalled for everyone to leave and was glad to absent himself as well.

Zachary drank his wine, wanting to rid himself of the foul taste the mayor had given him. He needed to have the appearance of showing courtesy—he would need help with marching on Sanctuary.

He turned to the captain of the royal guard. 'Lucas, I want the soldiers of Covedon to be the first thrown at the wall of Sanctuary, and when we return, the fat pig of a mayor will be sent to Gullytown.'

A smile grew on Lucas' face while several others laughed. After the laughter died down, he turned to the king. 'The journey from here to Turtha will bring us near the Khilli's homeland. That might bring trouble from the warriors.'

Zachary thought for a moment. 'Yes, I can see your point. We will take the road to the Darkwood and ten miles from the forest, we turn to Turtha.'

'That will be an extra day of travelling.'

Zachary cradled his elbow in his left hand and tapped his lip with a forefinger. He pondered a few seconds before replying. 'It is the best course for us to take.'

***

Ramulas stood in front of the image of the kingdom Oriel had projected on the long table in the throne room; with him stood Pip, Shigar, Iguchi, Rygar, Owain, and K'ayden.

A column of white light rose from the town of Covedon.

'Your king and his army are here,' Oriel said. 'I am only able to see when they enter the towns. To track his army all day is draining on my magic.'

'Do not worry, we are thankful for this,' Ramulas said.

Iguchi nodded. 'It is good to know where your enemy is.'

'We'll be knowin' when they're comin',' the dwarf said.

Ramulas looked at K'ayden and thought of the Khilli women and children. It brought back memories of when he was held in the tombs.

'Shigar, are we still able to access your secret entrance into the castle? This is the time for us to rescue the families,' Ramulas said.

The magician nodded. 'We can leave when you are ready.'

'No,' K'ayden said, stepping forward. 'Soldiers from the castle will send pigeons with messages to the king. He will kill the Khilli warriors when he finds out.'

'Then we wait until the army leaves Turtha,' Pip said, as if it was obvious.

Ramulas nodded. 'I want everyone in Sanctuary ready by the time Zachary arrives with his army.'

'Then we will have games of war,' Iguchi said. 'Split the people into two groups, and have one attack Sanctuary. This will prepare them for what is to come.'

'How does this work?' Ramulas asked.

Iguchi smiled as he spread his arms. In each hand, he held a red cloth. 'I will place these on the front of the castle, if the enemy can take one of these they will win, if they do not, the people of Sanctuary will win. The game of war will last two hours.'

Pip shook her head. 'That sounds too easy.'

Iguchi held up a finger. 'I have not finished. There will be no weapons, and the gate will remain open.'

Pip shoulders slumped as she pictured people flooding through the gate.

*****

Zachary had led his army into Turtha in the late afternoon. Tensions among the Khilli were not too high, and he was glad they took the path they did. They had spent the past two nights sleeping in the plains, and he looked forward to a warm bed.

An escort of forty soldiers and the sheriff rode out to greet the kingdom army five miles from the town. Zachary was impressed, and he hoped this treatment would continue.

As they rode, the sheriff invited the king and two hundred of his men to dine with the mayor. Zachary knew this was a polite way of asking for the army to make camp outside the walls.

Zachary brought his agent, the royal guard, and archers into town with him. Once inside, they were met by the mayor. Zachary took an instant liking to the man. He was an old sergeant from the army. He was broad-shouldered, devoted to the king, and disliked the mayor of Covedon.

After the king and soldiers were shown their accommodation, the mayor sat and spoke with Zachary.

'You know we march for Sanctuary,' Zachary said, 'and we need more soldiers.'

The mayor stood and saluted the king. 'We have three hundred and forty men. All of them are at your disposal, my king.'

Zachary's eyebrows rose at the mayor's words and attitude. This man was eager and willing to help. Then the agent said it was only a day and a half until they reached Sanctuary.

Zachary asked the mayor about the wagons that brought supplies to the west. He was told that this had been happening over the last few months. They would tell people they were from small farming communities.

Zachary thanked the mayor for his help and said his army would be leaving at dawn. The mayor said everything would be ready for him by then.

At dawn's early light, the kingdom army left Turtha. The agent had been busy questioning people through the night and found that two farms had been assisting the people of Sanctuary. These farmers had previously lied to the agent.

Zachary looked forward to meeting these people.

A few miles out of Turtha, the kingdom army came across the first farm. The farmer and his wife stood at the front of the house, eyes wide with fear. The army had come in through the only road, destroying some crops in the process.

Once the army had surrounded the farmhouse, they remained quiet and motionless. Zachary sat on his horse in front of the couple and stared at them intently for a whole minute.

Then the king forced a smile. 'Good farmer, I pray that you are well on this fine day,' Zachary said, waving to the blue sky above. 'You have heard that people from all over the kingdom have gone missing. Have you, by any chance, seen them, or know where they might be?'

The farmer and his wife looked at each other before quickly shaking their heads.

Zachary began to laugh softly, but it was without humour, and tension built in the air. 'First you lie to my agent, then you lie to your king.'

Several soldiers dismounted, walked over, and grabbed the couple.

Zachary looked at the pair with fury in his eyes. 'Do you know what the punishment is for lying to your king?'

The farmer and his wife were pulled apart, and they looked around for some means of escape.

Zachary smiled. 'You will watch your farm burn before being sent to Gullytown.'

Both farmer and wife screamed as they struggled in the grip of the soldiers. Zachary ordered a dozen soldiers to stay at the farm while the rest continued their march.

Zachary heard the couple screaming in the distance as he rode to Sanctuary. He looked back with a smile as thick plumes of smoke rose from the farm and crops.

Zachary pictured himself standing at the walls of Sanctuary— the people and the Lord of Sanctuary were all on their knees begging for mercy.

Zachary was pulled from his daydream when they came upon the other farm which had helped the people of Sanctuary.

A single horse bolted from the farm, its rider holding on for dear life. Zachary looked behind once more to see the smoke in the distance. This rider had obviously seen his doom.

Zachary sent two royal archers to kill this farmer and gave orders for this farm to be razed to the ground as well.

A message must be sent to the people. Do not lie to your king.

***

The town of Sanctuary was quiet. Everyone was resting after the games of war. The people had practised for two days.

On the first day, the enemy made it through the gate to take the red cloth from the castle wall. Tactics and strategies were discussed on how they would fix their defences.

On the second day, the attackers made it into the passageway, but they were unable to reach the courtyard. By the end of the day, both groups were exhausted. Iguchi knew they needed rest.

'A skilled man who is tired will always be beaten by an unskilled man who is alert,' Iguchi explained. Shigar and the druids worked on potions to help the people recover quickly.

Ramulas spent time in the throne room going over battle plans with Iguchi, Rygar, and Owain, and then his mind began to wander. He needed a break.

As he walked out, Oriel appeared next to him. 'Ramulas, it is time. Your king has left Turtha. The time to rescue the Khilli families has arrived.'

Ramulas was instantly alert as Iguchi and Rygar looked at him. Thoughts of what he needed to do raced through his mind.

'We need Pip, Shigar, the hell hounds, and the Khilli.' Then Ramulas turned to Iguchi. 'And we need the Fallen Angels.'

Iguchi bowed. 'Lord of Sanctuary, I will return with my Angels.'

As the small man left, Oriel said, 'I have summoned Shigar.'

'I'll bring ye the Khilli,' Rygar said before walking away singing a dwarven song.

Ramulas went to his quarters, where he found Pip playing with Emily and his girls. Both hell hounds lay near the girls.

'Pip, we need to leave. We're rescuing the Khilli.'

Pip's green eyes flared as she stood in a fluid motion. Ramulas communicated with the hell hounds, and they came to his side. Ramulas and Pip said their goodbyes before they went to the throne room.

Rygar entered the room with the Khilli and Thomas.

'Welcome, my friend,' Ramulas said to K'ayden. 'Today, the women and children of your people will be free.'

The Khilli became excited as they spoke in their own tongue. As Thomas jumped for joy, a quick burst from K'ayden silenced them.

'The time of happiness will be when we are with our families,' K'ayden said.

Iguchi arrived with the Fallen Angels. Each wore a serious expression and was eager for battle.

Shigar entered adjusting his robes. 'The way into the castle is through my chambers. When you are ready, I will lead the way.'

Ramulas nodded and they followed the magician. Once in his chambers, Shigar walked to an outline of chalk drawn on a wall. He placed his hand on the wall while chanting, a moment later a door appeared, and Shigar opened it.

He smiled as everyone gasped in shock. 'I knew that when I left the city of Keah, I would not be able to take all of my things,' he said, waving to the shelves of books through the door. 'So, I left a rear door.'

'Have you used it before?' Ramulas asked.

'A few times, but it was too risky for me to take much. Today is the day I reclaim all my things.'

The magician walked through the doorway and Ramulas turned to those behind him. 'What we are about to do is rescue the Khilli families. We need to be careful—if word reaches those guarding the families, they will be killed. We must ensure that they are not harmed. There will be no mercy shown for those who would hurt women and children.'

Ramulas looked to the Khilli warriors. 'We will follow these men. They know the castle better than anyone.'

K'ayden turned to Thomas, who was eager to free the women and children, and placed a hand on his shoulder. 'I am sorry, my brother, but you must stay until we return.'

Thomas stepped back in shock. 'But why? I want to help. I want to bring them home.'

K'ayden slowly shook his head and gestured to the other warriors. 'We have been together since birth and know each other very well. We do not know your movements in battle, nor you ours. One mistake could mean tragedy for us. Be here to welcome us when we return.'

Thomas' shoulders slumped as he sighed before giving a slight nod.

The Khilli led the way into the castle. Everyone gathered in Shigar's old chambers as K'ayden checked if the hallway was empty.

He signalled the way was clear. Ramulas and Pip led the way with the hell hounds. Rygar, Iguchi, and the Fallen Angels were close behind.

They had travelled two hundred yards without incident, and then they came to a intersection. The Khilli froze, K'ayden looking back at Ramulas, waving him forward.

Ramulas and Pip crept to K'ayden. They heard voices. Pip lay on her stomach and slid forward until she could see. After a moment, she pulled herself back and stood.

'There are three soldiers twenty yards down the hall; they will see us. Is there another way to your families?' she asked K'ayden.

He shook his head. 'We are many, and eventually, we will be seen. This is the best way.'

Ramulas and Pip looked at each other and two soldiers came out of an opposite door. Both soldiers froze, eyes wide in shock. The group from Sanctuary did not move a muscle.

It was a standoff.

Ramulas' mind raced, knowing if the soldiers called out, the three around the corner would raise the alarm. That was the last thing he wanted.

Then Fenris barked, and the spell was broken.

'Intruders!' one of the soldiers shouted as he ran away.

The response was instantaneous.

The remaining soldier screamed in fear as he drew his sword and charged Ramulas, and Pip threw one of her knives, hitting him in the eye—the soldier was dead before hitting the ground.

The three soldiers skidded to a halt at the junction. The one in the middle pointed a loaded crossbow at the group.

'No!' was all Ramulas could say before the crossbow fired.

A warm sensation exploded in the pit of his stomach, flowing up to his right hand, which he held out before him. An arc of purple energy leapt from his hand, knocking the bolt aside and hitting the soldier and burning a hole in his breastplate. The soldier fell to the ground screaming as his hair burst into flame.

Ramulas was awestruck at the power of the spell. A fragmented memory of his past life came to him and left just as quickly.

The two remaining soldiers ran back to where they came from, screaming for help. Several Angels ran by giving chase.

'Alive,' Ramulas called. 'I need them alive.'

As the Angels gave chase, Ramulas saw one of the original soldiers run into a room and close the door.

'Pip,' Ramulas said pointing to the door.

She raced off as the sounds of a scuffle could be heard. Iguchi and Rygar walked up to Ramulas as the Fallen Angels walked around the corner with the two soldiers. They were both battered and bloody.

'Where are our families?' K'ayden asked.

One of them looked around fearfully. 'Spare us, we were only following orders.'

Ramulas placed a comforting hand on K'ayden's shoulder. 'Easy my friend, we will find them.'

The Khilli stepped back and Ramulas looked at the soldiers. 'You have one chance to see the sun rise tomorrow. Tell us where the Khilli families are.'

'They are not in the castle. They have been moved, but I know not where,' the soldier said looking to his companion, who nodded.

Pip's eye's flashed bright emerald as he spoke. 'Lies. The other one bolted the door. I could not enter, but heard him tell a group to go to the ballroom and kill the Khilli.'

Thoughts raced through Ramulas' mind at the news. He had offered an ultimatum, and they had lied. He needed to keep his word. By lying, they had forced his hand. Soldiers were on the way to kill the Khilli. Ramulas needed to move.

'K'ayden, take us to the ballroom,' he said before turning to the soldiers. 'Iguchi, Rygar, they lied—take care of them.'

Rygar leapt up, slamming his helmet into one of the soldier's faces; blood exploded from his broken nose as he screamed. As the dwarf came down, he swung his axe, splitting the soldier's skull and silencing him.

Not to be outdone, Iguchi's curved swords flashed through the air as the Angels released the soldier. Both arms were severed at the elbows. The soldier screamed in shock, and then Iguchi lunged forward, his swords puncturing his armour and heart.

Then the group from Sanctuary ran through the castle. Ramulas knew their element of surprise had been lost. All that mattered now was reaching the Khilli before the soldiers.

They encountered a few servants, who jumped out of the way. Worryingly for Ramulas, they had not seen any other soldiers.

They finally reached the ballroom doorway. K'ayden placed a hand on the handle.

'K'ayden, wait,' Ramulas called. 'Pip, check the ballroom.'

The former thief placed her hands on the door while her eyes glowed. A moment later, her hands fell to her sides and she looked defeated.

'The women and children are inside. They are on the ground floor, but archers patrol the balcony. They will see us enter.'

Ramulas' mind raced for a solution, and then Fenris nudged him. Ramulas smiled as an idea came to him.

Turning to the group, Ramulas lay out his plan. Once he had finished, everyone knew their role, and the door was opened slowly.

The two hell hounds raced upstairs to the balcony.

As soon as Ramulas heard the panicked screams, he opened the door fully. Iguchi, the Angels, and Pip ran into the ballroom. Ramulas and the Khilli followed.

Ramulas saw the chaos on the balcony as the hell hounds attacked the archers. The Khilli women and children, already scared of the hell hounds, screamed as the Angels entered the room.

Pip lifted her arm and shot her gauntlet crossbow into the balcony. The archer's eyes widened as the bolt appeared in his chest.

Iguchi threw two of his silver stars, killing another two instantly.

The screams of fear from the women and children turned to shouts of joy when they saw the warriors. The women and children surrounded the warriors, hugging and kissing them.

Looking up at the balcony, Ramulas saw the hell hounds circling the two remaining archers. They took turns to dart in and attack, powerful jaws tearing through armour as if it were hardened paper.

Within seconds, both archers were dead, and Ramulas called the hell hounds to him.

He saw the Khilli were still talking excitedly. 'K'ayden, we need to leave. There is still danger.'

K'ayden rapidly spoke in his language and the room went quiet. The women and children began following the warriors out of the ballroom, and then the rear doors burst open. Thirty screaming soldiers swarmed into the room.

Aleesha stood at the doorway, screaming for all the Khilli to be killed.

'Get them out now!' Ramulas shouted to K'ayden before running at the soldiers.

A warm sensation exploded within him, and fragments of memories returned to him. A familiar energy flowed through his body.

The energy flowed into his battle axe and war hammer, covering them in purple flames. Each of the soldiers carried a sword.

Four throwing knives spun past Ramulas, cutting into the front line, he stopped six feet from the soldiers and threw his battle axe, which flipped a soldier in the air.

Ramulas jumped toward the enemy with his war hammer overhead, magical energies coursed through his body and into his weapon. He landed amongst the soldiers and brought his hammer to the ground.

An explosion of purple energy lifted several soldiers into the air. Rygar raced into the enemy swinging his axe while singing a dwarven war song. The hell hounds were now next to Ramulas, tearing through the ranks.

The use of magic drained Ramulas, and all he wanted to do was rest. He tried to fight the dizziness but found himself collapsing.

Then Iguchi and the Fallen Angels surrounded their lord and swarmed over the soldiers. A few soldiers managed to escape out the rear door, dragging Aleesha with them.

Before Ramulas knew what was happening, the fighting had ceased. The battle was won. He looked to see that the last of the Khilli had left the room.

By an act of pure will, Ramulas gathered his weapons and stood. 'Return to Sanctuary.'

The group ran through the halls with the Khilli warriors and half of the Angels leading and the remaining Angels protecting the rear.

They encountered small groups of soldiers along the way, but these quickly disappeared. Near Shigar's chambers, there was a score of soldiers behind a barricade. The Fallen Angels leading the group pulled out their swords and shields and began to sing in Iguchi's language as they slowly marched forward. The Angels at the rear joined in the singing.

The soldiers turned pale and began to back away. Even Ramulas was puzzled at how the singing sent a chill through him.

The soldiers lost their resolve, turned, and ran. The group quickly made their way into Shigar's old chambers. The magician stood by the open door with a smile, showing the Khilli the way to a new life.

Once everyone walked into the door, Shigar stepped through and chanted. The door vanished, and only a faint outline could be seen.

28

The mayor of Turtha received word that a message had arrived from Covedon. After previous dealings with the fat mayor, he did not look forward to reading it.

When he opened the letter and read the contents, his eyes widened in shock and his heart pounded like a drum. A force had attacked the castle in Keah, killing a score of soldiers and freeing the Khilli.

He re-read the letter several times. There was something not quite right. The letter said the castle was attacked before midday. It was now two hours after dawn. The attack had happened the day before, and the letter had arrived at Covedon the previous night.

The mayor called for his fastest horse. King Zachary needed to be told of this.

He raced towards the Devil's Ridge Mountains, he hoped he would reach the kingdom army before they arrived at Sanctuary.

***

Ramulas led the procession of Khilli from Shigar's chambers to Sanctuary's great hall, where they spoke in hushed tones.

Iguchi touched Ramulas' arm. 'I will take my Fallen Angels to wash away the blood.'

As he walked away, Ramulas looked down and saw that he, too, had blood on him. He wanted to wash before returning to his family. A quick estimate told Ramulas there were approximately six hundred women and children. Thomas had entered the hall and was being introduced to the women and children.

He took a deep breath. 'Welcome to Sanctuary,' he said in a voice that carried across the hall. 'You are now a free people.'

The Khilli cheered. Ramulas waited for them to quieten. 'Your warriors are coming here with the king's army. When they arrive, I have a plan to bring them into Sanctuary.'

Shouts of joy erupted throughout the hall as the Khilli jumped around hugging each other. For so many years they had dreamed of freedom, and now it was a reality.

A lone Khilli child walked to Ramulas. He gasped in shock when he saw who it was.

'Ch'oak,' he said, dropping to his knees and holding out his arms.

She ran and engulfed him in a hug, and then she began to cry. Great sobs shook her body as she whispered 'thank you' over and over.

Ramulas felt a lump forming in his throat and his eyes filled with tears. He was surprised at how the girl's raw emotion affected him. He pulled himself away from her and held Ch'oak at arm's length.

'You are going to make me cry,' he said. 'The Lord of Sanctuary cannot be seen crying.'

K'ayden walked over accompanied by a tall Khilli female who carried herself in a way that spoke of royalty. When she smiled, all of Ramulas' worries were swept away.

'My husband and daughter spoke of you often. We shed many tears when word came to us of our four warriors had fallen. Now our hearts swell with joy—our warriors have returned, and soon all of the Khilli will be free once more.'

Ramulas smiled. 'For the rest of the warriors to return, I will need your help.'

She nodded and Ramulas told her of his plan and the part she would play.

Over the next hour, Ramulas spoke with the Khilli women, finding ways to improve his plan. Once he had finished, Ramulas knew he needed to introduce the Khilli to the people of Sanctuary.

Jacqueline and his daughters were the first to greet the Khilli and welcome them to their new home. He soon found out that rumours of the Khilli had already spread throughout Sanctuary. Several people had come into the castle and spoken to them.

One thing puzzled Ramulas: Oriel was nowhere to be found.

***

The next morning, Ramulas walked into the throne room to Oriel waiting for him.

'Hello, Ramulas. You have returned with the Khilli women and children—you have done well.'

Ramulas nodded, trying to voice the feelings he had inside. 'I am feeling happy, yet sad and confused.'

'Why?'

'Where were you yesterday when I brought the Khilli into the castle?'

'Appearing before you every day drains my magical energies. I needed to focus on being ready. The tunnel is getting deeper, and I need to be ready for when I am freed.'

Ramulas sighed. 'I have freed the Khilli, but soldiers were killed in the escape. I wish there was a way we could have done this without bloodshed.'

Oriel walked forward and placed her hands on the sides of Ramulas' head. She saw through his eyes what had happened, removed her hands, and smiled.

'I have seen what you needed to do to free the Khilli. If you had not acted that way, many women and children would have been killed.'

Ramulas shook his head. 'I wish there had been another way.'

'You were attacked first in the castle. You offered to talk, and they chose violence.'

'Now all we need is for our plan to bring back the warriors to work,' Ramulas said.

Oriel's expression grew serious. 'That time is coming very soon. The kingdom army has entered the forest. Tilly is searching for you.'

***

The dryads had been following the kingdom army as they slowly made their way into the forest. They had not shown themselves or interfered in any way. If the soldiers did not attack the dryads, they would be left alone.

Eady turned to Tilly. 'Ramulas needs to be told.'

The sprite flew into the trunk of a tree and came out of another near the wall. Her wings hummed as she flew into the courtyard.

Once again, people gathered below Tilly in awe as she called for Ramulas. A few moments later, he walked out of the castle and followed the sprite into the clearing.

Several dryads waited for him, and Eady stepped forward. 'The army is in the forest.'

'I know. Take me to them.'

He was led to a nearby tree and closed his eyes. He felt the sensation of being pulled down a narrow passage and was assaulted by a thick foliage smell. Then he felt the open air as he stepped out of the tree. The sound of horses, wagons, and marching greeted Ramulas. Eady touched his arm and pointed to his left. He turned to see the column one hundred yards through the trees.

He stood transfixed for several moments, and then he saw the machines of war. It was time for him to return.

'Take me back to Sanctuary.'

As Ramulas stepped out into the clearing, he turned to Eady. 'How long until they arrive?'

'They will be here within a few hours.'

Ramulas nodded his thanks before entering Sanctuary. His mouth was dry and his palms had become sweaty. His heart felt like a horse raced through his chest. After all this time training, he was not sure that they had done enough.

The battle was only hours away and Ramulas felt sick.

Pip saw Ramulas in the courtyard and knew that something was wrong. 'What has happened?'

'Zachary and his army will be here soon.'

He saw Pip's body stiffen at the mention of the king. An expression of pure hatred flashed in her eyes before she pushed it away.

'I need to prepare the people for battle,' he said.

They made their way to the throne room where Oriel, Iguchi, and Rygar waited.

'These two have both seen many battles,' Oriel said, waving at the pair.

Ramulas looked at the grim expressions and was reminded of the stories they previously told, of the tales of war—there were always losses on each side.

Ramulas knew with a heavy heart that in this coming battle, some of the people of Sanctuary would die. The duo had told him that was the way of wars and battles.

He could feel the awakened magic flowing within him and knew it would not be enough. He still only knew fragmented parts of his past and could not fully understand how to make use of it. Oriel was still regaining her power and was of no use outside of the castle.

'We need to organise the people.'

Oriel nodded. 'The army will be here in two hours.'

'I must prepare my Fallen Angels,' Iguchi said before bowing and leaving.

The dwarf winked at Ramulas. 'Don't ye be worryin'. Yer people will be ready when yer king comes.'

'What of the women and children of my people?' K'ayden asked as he walked into the room.

Ramulas shook his head. 'They will stay in the castle with Oriel, with Shigar and the druids watching over them.'

'We wish to fight with you.'

This statement was like a knife in the chest for Ramulas. He had just saved the Khilli women and children. He would die if anything happened to them or the four Khilli warriors.

'I am sorry, but you and your warriors will stay as well. You told me that your people hold family above all. Be with your people and let us fight.' He saw that K'ayden wanted to argue the point. 'Please. I will be losing enough of my people—it would break me if some Khilli died as well.'

K'ayden struggled with internal conflict for a moment before smiling. 'You have given my people something we have dreamed of for many years. I will grant this wish to you.'

Ramulas breathed a sigh of relief, and then Thomas walked into the room, and his appearance caused Ramulas to gasp. He wore only trousers and was covered in dark grey paint from his chin to his wrists.

He stared at Ramulas and K'ayden. 'The songs of my ancestors fill me with joy. Now is the time to show I have a warrior's heart. I will fight alongside you Ramulas to free our people.'

Ramulas shook his head gesturing to K'ayden, but the warrior spoke. 'Ramulas, it is Thomas' time. The rest of the warriors will stay with the families, but Thomas is being led by the old ones. His way is sacred— allow him to do this.'

Ramulas was torn with internal emotions. He had just told K'ayden that he couldn't fight, and Thomas wanted to join him in freeing the Khilli. His decision was made when he saw the absolute certainty in Thomas' eyes.

'Thomas stay close to me when we go into battle.'

K'ayden gave a cry of joy while Thomas seemed to float with pride.

***

Emily walked along the road away from Sanctuary. Three scouts from the kingdom army rode around the corner. They saw the young girl and slowed their mounts and glanced to both sides of the road for any potential ambush.

When they discovered that she was alone, they moved their horses to within ten feet of her.

'What are you doing out here?' The centre scout asked.

Emily looked at the men, seeming to notice them for the first time. 'You don't belong here. Leave my home.'

The three laughed at Emily and looked at each other in disbelief.

The centre scout climbed down from his horse. 'This brat could be taught some manners.'

He walked to Emily, pulling out a leather thong. The other scouts laughed and called out encouragement. They were eager to see this young girl punished.

With malicious intent, he stood before Emily, ensuring she could see the leather thong in his hand.

Emily ignored him, looking off into the distance. This angered him.

'Where is Sanctuary?' he asked.

'It is where I live,' she said absently, 'but you will not live to see it.'

The soft tone of her voice caused the scout to pause for a second, and then anger exploded within him. The brat would pay. He brought the thong above her and swung with all his might.

Emily looked up at the scout, her face a mask of primal rage. The irises of her eyes turned dark as a strong wind came from behind her.

The thong struck her across the face and the scout howled in pain. He dropped the thong and held the side of his face, where blood seeped through his fingers. He was confused and shocked. He had hit her—why was he injured and she unharmed?

Emily stepped to the scout, placing a hand on his breastplate. He threw his head back and screamed in agony for a second before flame burst from his mouth and eye sockets. His hands clawed the air as he burned from within.

She released him, and he fell into a burning heap. Behind him, Emily saw the two soldiers frozen in horror. She raised her hands toward them, and they gave a shout as their mounts suddenly stopped moving.

The sound of crackling could be heard beneath them. They watched in terror as their horses began turning to glass from the ground up.

Before they could react, their feet and legs soon turned to glass. They screamed in both pain and sheer horror. Within a second, both horses and riders were glass statues.

Emily walked back to Sanctuary, singing a song not heard in over five hundred years.

***

People hurried through Sanctuary, but Ramulas noticed that none of them was panicking. There was a feeling of excitement and anticipation in the air.

He stood on the balcony overlooking the courtyard with Pip, Rygar, Iguchi and Oriel.

As the people went to their positions, Iguchi turned to Ramulas. 'Lord of Sanctuary, how do you feel knowing that the enemy is close?'

'I feel sick,' Ramulas said, wishing the butterflies would leave his stomach.

'That is good,' Iguchi said, drawing an incredulous look from Ramulas. 'There are two types of men before battle—those who are afraid, and those who are liars. Do not worry, you will win this fight.'

'He's right, milord,' Rygar said. 'I still get a little jumpy after two hunnerd years o' fightin'.'

'I must go to my Angels,' Iguchi said as he left.

'The women and children,' Ramulas said.

'They are being gathered by Jacqueline and Jenna as we speak. They will all come into the castle.'

Ramulas and Pip walked out into the courtyard and saw companies forming along the wall. The passageway was open, and they could see out to the clearing.

Oriel had explained the workings of the maze to them. The passage would stay open for the people of Sanctuary until they returned to the courtyard. But when the enemy entered, it would close and become part of the maze. The passage was to be open to allow the Khilli warriors to enter Sanctuary.

Ramulas and Pip walked up to the top of the wall, where they saw Owain standing near a pot hanging above a brazier. It was one of twenty pots filled with iron ore from the tunnel.

Rygar said it would take an hour for the ore to melt and explained that when even the smallest drop of liquid metal touched your armour, it stuck like mud and would burn.

'Hello, Owain,' Ramulas said. 'How goes your preparations?'

The blind man smiled. 'My archers are ready, and we have plenty of supplies,' he said, waving to the barrels of water, food, and arrows that lined the wall.

Owain walked along the walkway, which was wide enough for four men to walk abreast. Ramulas and Pip saw young boys standing near the supplies. These boys would act as runners, bringing food, water, and arrows to the archers.

The ledge of the wall was three feet high and acted as a partial cover from those below. The blind man walked ahead as he clicked his tongue. He had told Ramulas how this helped him see his surroundings; however, it was still impressive to see him navigate around objects and people.

An archer stood every few yards with a bow resting against two quivers full of arrows. Each gave a slight nod as their lord passed.

'And ye have the same below,' Rygar said, pointing into the courtyard.

Ramulas and Pip followed his finger and saw several areas where barrels of water, food, and supplies had been placed in readiness. Everything seemed to be falling into place; the only thing to do was wait for the kingdom army to arrive.

***

Iguchi waved his hand slightly and then pointed at Michael, Miles, and Benji. The trio stepped forward, materialising out of the forest. The Fallen Angels had run silently through the forest until they came to the enemy.

As the trio came forward, Iguchi saw the rest of the Angels waiting patiently. With their camouflage, they were almost invisible against the trees.

The king's army marched twenty feet from Iguchi. He led the three to the roadside near some trees, and then, with painstaking slowness, the four of them moved to the roadside. As Iguchi had already explained, people only see what they wish to see.

They stood within arm's reach of the passing soldiers. Line after line of weary men marched by, eyes looking forward, only thinking about placing one foot in front of the other.

Then a wagon came down the road pulled by two horses; the driver stared blankly ahead.

Iguchi looked at the three Fallen Angels and nodded.

As the wagon passed, the Fallen Angels exploded into action.

Benji leapt onto the bench next to the driver, sliding his sword between the man's ribs and puncturing his heart. Michael flipped in the air behind the horses and cut the leather traces. He landed and slapped both horses on the rump with a shout. The horses bolted, running over shocked soldiers before them.

Miles charged into the line of soldiers following the wagon. He led with his shield, hitting the closest and knocking him into the next. The move was so unexpected and the force so great that five soldiers ended up entangled in the dirt. He slashed his sword at the startled soldiers in the next row before running back into the trees.

He glanced back to see Michael and Benji following.

As soon as the three Fallen Angels ran into the forest, Iguchi delivered a side-kick to the wheel of the wagon, snapping it in two. The sound of wood splintering echoed as the wagon fell to one side.

As soon as Iguchi disappeared into the trees, the kingdom soldiers screamed and gave chase.

Orders were shouted as the soldiers gave chase. Only a score of soldiers had seen what had happened. These were the ones who followed Iguchi and the Angels.

Once Iguchi, Benji, Miles, and Michael reached the other Angels, they turned and waited. To the soldiers, the Fallen Angels were almost invisible. One soldier stood in the middle of the camouflaged Angels and could not see anything.

'Where did they go?' he asked his companions, who stopped behind him.

The soldiers searched the trees, feeling confused. One moment they were chasing men through the forest, and the next they had vanished.

A loud voice could be heard as the sergeant made his way to them. 'You motherless curs,' he said. 'Who gave the order to leave the caravan?'

'The wagon was attacked,' a soldier said.

The sergeant spun and pointed a finger at the soldier. 'I don't give a damn. You were to wait for orders—'

The rest of the words were caught in his throat. All the kingdom soldiers faced him, and none of them saw the Fallen Angels materialise out of the forest.

The group were oblivious to the danger that surrounded them.

The soldiers began to scream in shock and pain as swords cut their arms and legs. They were given no chance to fight back—each of them had a hamstring cut or their sword arm slashed.

The sergeant stood in shock as his men were cut down in the blink of an eye by ghosts. He turned to run back to call for help when Iguchi's sword took his head from his shoulders.

Iguchi heard people running towards his position, and saw several Khilli enter their small grove. These were not to be harmed. He led the Fallen Angels into the trees.

The Khilli arrived a moment later to find the wounded soldiers and the dead sergeant. No trace of the attackers could be found.

***

Zachary heard a commotion behind him. He turned in his saddle in curiosity, and then men began shouting before it became frantic. Several horses raced toward him, kicking up clouds of dust.

One of the men yelled. 'We're under attack!'

Zachary was pulled from behind and landed hard on the path. Before he could abuse whoever dare touch him, he saw Lucas standing above him with his sword drawn. The rest of the royal guard followed their captain's lead, forming a human wall around their king. They looked into the trees for any enemy.

Zachary sat up when he heard screams cut through the air. Men and horses raced toward the scream. Lucas gently pushed the king back into a lying position on the ground.

'Stay low, my king. You will be safer there.'

Zachary bit back a retort, knowing the captain of the royal guard was only concerned about his safety; however, it was extremely hard for him to lie on the ground with people running around.

After a few moments, Lucas helped Zachary to his feet. The screaming had died down and news of the attack had reached them—two men killed, a wagon damaged, and over a score of men injured.

The royal guard escorted Zachary back to the damaged wagon. The soldiers made way as their king approached.

The wagon lay on its side and several men in front and behind the wagon lay injured. Zachary was led into the forest, where a score of soldiers had their wounds tended to. Once their wounds were seen to, they would be sent to wait in Turtha.

Lucas questioned everyone about what had transpired. When he had finished, Lucas told Zachary explaining that four men in camouflage attacked the wagon, killed the driver, and then a group followed these men into an ambush.

The Khilli followed but could find no traces of the attackers.

The soldiers were all on edge over the brazen attack, constantly scanning the trees. Lucas ordered the wagon to be pulled to the side of the road and for the soldiers to continue towards Sanctuary. By the time Zachary arrived at the front of the men, Lucas expressed his concerns over missing scouts.

A few minutes later, a soldier raced down the road as if he had seen a ghost. Lucas rode over to him and spoke with the soldier. As they spoke, Zachary noticed a grim expression on the captain's face.

The soldier was sent to the rear and Lucas went to a nearby wagon retrieving a hammer. 'My king, please come with me. There is something down the road I wish to show you.'

As they rode, Zachary wondered why Lucas needed a hammer.

Within a few minutes, the pair rounded a corner to see two life-sized statues of soldiers riding horses. The most amazing thing to Zachary was that they appeared to be made of glass.

Who made these, he wondered, *and why were they placed here in the middle of the road?* He could not fathom how much skill it took to make the statues so life-like.

He saw the burnt corpse near the statues, and the reality hit him—they were his soldiers. 'How is this possible?'

'My guess would be magic, my king,' Lucas answered.

'Shigar,' Zachary spat in disgust.

The captain of the royal guard swung the hammer, hitting the first soldier's hip. Both horse and soldier shattered, and large glass fragments littered the ground.

'Lucas, what are you doing?' Zachary asked in shock.

'The men do not need to see this; I will have the mess cleaned before they march past here.'

***

Ramulas walked through Sanctuary with Pip. This would be the last inspection before he took to the wall.

'The people are ready,' Pip said.

Ramulas was about to ask how she knew this, and then he saw her eyes glowing a fierce emerald colour. He knew that she was able to see into the people's hearts, but knowing the people were ready did nothing to alleviate his nerves.

Then Pip grabbed Ramulas by the arm. 'The dryads are coming out of the trees.'

He looked down the passage to see several coming out of the trees. Pip followed him into the clearing to meet the dryads.

Eady smiled as she walked up to the pair. 'The king and his army are very close.'

'How close?' Ramulas asked.

'They will be here within minutes. We must not be seen by the king's men.'

Eady and the other dryads melted back into the trees, Ramulas and Pip walked into the passage and closed the heavy gate and pulled the iron bar across. Ramulas fought to hold the contents of his stomach down. He wanted to recheck everything but knew he was out of time.

At the top of the wall, they were met by Owain, who stood next to the dragon's scale. Ramulas watched in awe as black shapes swam within.

'Greetings, lord,' Owain said, waving to the scale. 'The scale can only be used once. You told me that you will need this for when the legion comes, but it is here if you become desperate, and then we will show your king the dragon.'

'We will be fine,' Ramulas said.

As he walked along the wall, Ramulas was confident that he would not need to use the scale, and then he saw Pip staring out over the forest with her glowing eyes.

'What do you see?'

'They are almost here.'

Ramulas did not need to ask who 'they' were. He turned and waved his arms above his head. Rygar and Lodi returned the wave. The people of Sanctuary would be ready.

Pip looked out into the trees and saw dryads disappear into the trees. Wildlife moved away from the mass of men marching through the forest, and then she saw a company of knights coming through the trees.

They were followed by more of the king's army. Iguchi and the Fallen Angels flanked the knights as they came into the clearing. Looking past the knights, she could see a very long line of soldiers moving her way.

29

Ramulas and Rygar stood on the wall next to Pip, who showed them where the Angels were, and then Zachary's army started to come into the clearing.

One hundred knights on warhorses rode in with their polished suits of armour, which shone in the midday sun. They were followed by three hundred Khilli warriors. Royal lancers rode in, holding their lances high.

The cavalry, infantry, and finally Zachary entered with the royal guard. The wagons and machines of war remained down the road.

Ramulas felt Pip become tense next to him, he glanced down and saw an expression of pure hatred on the former thief's face, and her eyes glowed fiercely.

'Pip, we need clear heads to win this battle.'

Along the wall, all the archers sat with their backs against the three-foot ledge next to their bows. It appeared that only Ramulas, Pip, and Rygar were on the wall.

Iguchi had told them earlier, 'Appear weak when you are strong; appear strong when you are weak. They will expect archers on the wall—when they see none, they will think you are not ready for them.'

The kingdom army moved its way across the rear of the clearing into formations. The men in the front rank were one hundred and fifty yards from the wall.

The trio on the wall waited for the kingdom army to make their first move. It was plain to see that there was confusion in the clearing. Zachary could be seen talking to members of the royal guard while pointing up at the wall. After a few moments, Zachary rode to the wall with a score of the royal guard holding a flag of truce.

'Yer king wants to talk to ye,' Rygar whispered.

Ramulas waited until the group was fifty yards from the wall, and then he held up a hand. 'That is close enough.'

The group stopped, and Zachary looked up at Ramulas with a cold smile.

'I sent word that we were to be left alone,' Ramulas said. 'Why have you come here with your army?'

'I am your king!' Zachary exploded, pointing a finger at Ramulas. 'I travel where I wish in my kingdom.'

'This is Sanctuary, and from the edge of the forest to the mountains is my home. You are not welcome here.'

Zachary visibly fought to control himself before looking up at the trio on the wall. 'Two of my men were murdered and a score attacked in the forest. Your people attacked a patrol outside of Bremnon as they were stopping a group from coming here, and I believe you are the one who escaped from the tombs. What have you to say?'

A myriad of emotions ran through Ramulas, and he felt dizzy. Then he calmed himself before speaking. 'You killed my horse in front of me, and threatened my family.'

Zachary shook a finger at the wall. 'Everyone in Sanctuary will be punished for your insolence.'

Ramulas shook his head and smiled. 'The people of Sanctuary are under my protection. They do not wish any more of your tyranny.'

'You do not plot against your king without punishment,' Zachary said. 'Everyone in Sanctuary will be sent to Gullytown.'

'Bastard!' Pip yelled as she pointed her gauntlet crossbow at Zachary.

The dwarf bumped into Pip as she fired, sending the bolt wide.

Zachary and the royal guard moved back twenty yards as Ramulas looked at Pip, who knew she had done wrong and would not meet Ramulas' eyes.

'You have one chance!' Zachary called out. 'There is no-one on the wall—the people of Sanctuary must be hiding in fear of my army.'

'Owain,' Ramulas said.

The blind archer stood and whistled.

Two hundred archers swiftly stood, nocked their bows, and aimed at the clearing. Zachary's eyes widened, and the royal guard escorted him back behind his army.

'It does not have to be this way,' Ramulas called. 'We are prepared. I do not want anyone else hurt.'

Zachary looked at Ramulas in rage. 'Where is the traitor Shigar?'

Ramulas shook his head. 'Leave now.'

Zachary nodded to Lucas, who began calling orders. Machines of war were pulled out into the clearing on platforms—two trebuchets and a ballista. Behind them came a large battering ram pushed by a score of soldiers. Covers made from leather and wood protected those pushing the huge machine.

Ramulas sighed. 'They have made their choice. Prepare for the Khilli to join their families.'

Pip waved a red flag in the air, and Ramulas saw his old friend Thomas run down the passage with another man. They were to open the gate, allowing the Khilli to enter Sanctuary, then close it once they were inside, and then Thomas would join Ramulas.

Ramulas smiled, thinking how much his friend had changed since leaving Bremnon. He had never seen the man smile so much. He spent most of his time with the Khilli, connecting with his lost heritage. This was his chance to show his warrior spirit.

Once Ramulas saw that everyone was ready, he knelt down and arranged for what needed to be done.

A moment later, he jumped up with a high-pitched scream, holding a long spear in his hands. Everyone in the clearing focused on him. The spear had several pieces of coloured cloth tied to it. They swayed as he began to dance.

As Ramulas danced he looked to the sky calling out the words that no-one understood.

No-one except the Khilli.

They were the only ones who did not think Ramulas had gone completely mad. The Khilli warriors watched as the Lord of Sanctuary danced and weaved, stabbing the spear at imagined enemies.

After a minute of dancing, Ramulas stopped and threw the spear into the clearing. It buried itself fifty yards from the wall.

Then Ramulas spoke in the Khilli language once more. After he was finished, Ramulas pointed to the spear.

One of the younger Khilli warriors ran forward and picked up the spear. After inspecting it closely, he became very excited and took it back to the rest of the warriors.

They gathered around the spear, pulling at the pieces of cloth and smelling them. They were almost in a frenzy by the time the captain of the guard rode over on his horse.

'What did he say on the wall?' Lucas asked the Khilli. 'And why did he throw the spear?'

One of the elder warriors stepped forward. 'He spoke of bad things about our people, he said that we fight like women, and one hundred of his men would best our three hundred warriors. Please allow us to fight them—it will restore our honour.'

Lucas looked at the archers along the wall and then at the Khilli. He would encourage such a contest; it would boost the morale of the kingdom soldiers. The Khilli could best four times their own number.

However, he was worried about the archers—they could wipe out all of the Khilli. 'The archers on the wall will cut your men down before you reach the wall.'

The elder Khilli nodded before walking out into the clearing. He stopped fifty yards from the wall.

He pointed up to Ramulas. 'You wish to challenge our warriors with archers on the wall. Send them from the wall and we will face your hundred men.'

The elder kissed his fist before pounding his chest twice and pointing to Ramulas. He walked back to his warriors.

Ramulas could not believe how stupid he was, he was so worried about translating something the wrong way that he forgot how the Khilli would come into Sanctuary—now the elder had shown him a way.

Lucas was in deep conversation with Zachary when the elder approached.

'… the Khilli will crush the men of Sanctuary, and that will send them a message. We need to strike the first blow.' Zachary turned to the Khilli elder. 'Your women and children are in Keah. I want you to kill everyone who comes out of the gate. Then your families will be rewarded.'

The elder smiled. 'Do not worry my king, there will be much killing,' he promised before returning to his warriors.

Lucas watched as the elder spoke to the warriors. A few younger men cried out in protest before they were calmed. He became curious as seven elder warriors stepped back as the rest of the Khilli walked forward in formation.

The elders pulled out their throwing disks, rings of polished steel a handspan wide with a handle through the centre of the ring.

They looped a thong of leather through the handle and walked behind the royal archers.

***

Ramulas bent down to pick up the spear, hoping that he correctly remembered the moves and phrases he had been taught. He knew that one word or move out of place could mean an insult.

Everything was going well until the lone Khilli came to accept his challenge.

Oh no, Ramulas thought. *What have I done?*

Then the elder pounded his chest and pointed to him. He had seen K'ayden do this several times with the other Khilli. When Ramulas asked about this, he was told this was the Khilli way of calling someone 'brother'.

The Khilli's acceptance of the challenge was only for the king's benefit.

***

Lucas walked over to the elders, who stood behind the royal archers. 'Why are you here?'

'This is an old battle tactic of our people. We will stay and sing to our ancestors, giving our young warriors strength,' he said proudly.

Lucas nodded, pretending to understand. Something was bothering him, but he could not put a finger on it. Then he saw Zachary nodding for the Khilli to attack. He gave the order for the attack and walked back to his king.

The elder smiled at what the Lord of Sanctuary had called out. He had danced in the old tradition of the Khilli and then spoken words that no Khilli thought they would *hear: 'For too long, your people have been kept from your true home. Today, the Khilli will be free. Your women and children are safe behind this wall. Come join them.'*

Then the warriors had inspected the spear thrown from the wall. The cloth had come from the women's clothing.

The seven elders knew that sacrifices needed to be made in order for their people to be free once more. The leader saw the gate open slightly, and he gave a shout for his warriors to run.

As the warriors shouted in reply and raced for Sanctuary, the elders watched with hopeful eyes, willing them to run faster. The hearts of the elders soared as the gate fully opened when the warriors were fifty yards away, showing an open passage into Sanctuary.

***

When the gates opened, Lucas knew that he had been tricked. The archers appeared on the wall, yelling encouragement to the Khilli.

'It's a trick!' he shouted. 'Kill the Khilli!'

The royal archers recovered from the initial shock and nocked their bows just as the elders began to swing their throwing disks.

The archers screamed as razor-sharp disks cut them from behind. A score of archers lay dead or dying in the first second. All of the elders were covered in blood splatter.

Lucas looked at the gate in shock. 'The gate! Rush the gate while it's open!' he shouted.

The infantry broke formation as they sprinted forward. The cavalry soon overtook them on their mounts. Royal archers on the flanks began firing at the elders. The first elder fell with an arrow to the chest.

Then all hell broke loose at the rear lines.

Shouts of surprise preceded sounds of fighting; Lucas turned to see a commotion near the trees. The rear line was under attack by a small group. Confusion reigned as soldiers were torn between running for the gate or meeting the attackers.

The attackers began to sing loudly in a foreign language. Lucas was surprised at how, even at this distance, it sent chills through him. He looked at Zachary and saw that the royal guard had surrounded their king.

'To the rear!' he shouted. 'Repel the attackers!'

The sound of the ballista firing one of its giant arrows made Lucas jump.

***

Ramulas smiled when the Khilli shouted and ran for the gate. He called down for them to run with the archers. He looked back to the king's army to see some of the Khilli had stayed behind. They had just begun to attack the archers.

A sense of sadness came over Ramulas as he watched the elder's sacrifice. He quickly pushed those negative feelings away. The Khilli warriors were almost at the gate and would soon be reunited with their families.

Kingdom soldiers gave chase just as Iguchi and the Fallen Angels attacked from the tree line. The knights and royal archers raced to the wall, chasing the Khilli.

A loud crack echoed across the clearing as the ballista fired at the gate. A dull thud sounded as the large arrow hit the wooden gate.

Ramulas focused on the warhorses, trying to communicate with them, and was met with a wall of hate. There would be no persuading them to throw the knights.

Ramulas did the next best thing—he planted an image of a green dragon landing at the base of the wall. The leading four warhorses panicked and turned into the path of the dozen that followed.

The archers on the wall fired the first wave of arrows.

The infantry ran forward holding shields above their heads.

Owain clicked his tongue rapidly and saw what they had done.

'Throw the pots!' the blind archer called.

The archers used cloths to pick up the bubbling pots. They were thrown over the wall onto the kingdom soldiers below. The pots broke, sending their contents splattering amongst the men. Howls of agony were heard as soldiers dropped their shields and pulled away smouldering pieces of armour.

'Shoot them!' Owain cried.

Wave after wave of arrows peppered the infantry. Scores fell dead and injured. However, many more soldiers ran at the wall with shields held high. These were joined by the knights and royal lancers, and then the royal archers began firing at those on the wall.

The arrows fell a few feet short, hitting the wall below Ramulas. As Ramulas looked down, he saw a sight that chilled him to the bone.

It appeared as if the enemy were entering the gate, but how could that be? Thomas and a soldier were supposed to close it after the Khilli entered Sanctuary.

He looked over the rear of the wall to see the last of the Khilli entering the castle, and just below him, a score of kingdom soldiers ran down the passage.

A bolt of cold exploded inside Ramulas—the gate was open, and the soldiers were swarming in. He had never felt so helpless before.

***

Iguchi silently climbed the tree at the edge of the clearing with the agility of a cat. He watched as the kingdom army came before him and formed into columns.

With the Fallen Angels below him, Iguchi knew they would attack once the Khilli were free. After the attack, he would lead the Angels to hide in the forest.

Iguchi knew this would be a testing time for the Fallen Angels. They would need to remain patient and calm until the battle began. He began his breathing exercises. Breathing in, he would bring both hands slowly to his chest, when breathing out, he would push them away. Iguchi smiled when he saw the Angels were doing the same.

They would be ready when the time came.

The Khilli had almost reached the gate when Iguchi heard an order to kill the warriors. Iguchi dropped to the ground, slashing the air with his swords. Two kingdom soldiers fell as their heads rolled away. So clean were the cuts that blood did not come straight away, and then a spray of blood startled kingdom soldiers at the back line.

The other soldiers turned to see the Fallen Angel materialise out of the forest like vengeful ghosts. They began to slash and hack at the rear lines while singing the words Iguchi had taught them.

The soldiers were frozen in shock as the Fallen Angels tore through them. With economic movements, the Angels attacked vital unprotected areas. Once their swords found their marks, they moved to the next victim.

Within two seconds, over one hundred soldiers lay dead.

The Fallen Angels had now formed a semicircle as the kingdom soldiers recovered from the initial shock.

Three of the soldiers rushed at Iguchi, attacking with wild slashes. The small man made a show of laboured breathing while parrying the blows.

The sound of thundering hooves could be heard over the battle. Iguchi glanced up to see a company of cavalry coming towards them. The infantry opened up their ranks, allowing them through.

It was time to go.

'Back to the forest!' Iguchi called as he made a miraculous recovery.

His two swords blurred as he turned from side to side. In an instant, the kingdom soldier's swords and shields were pushed out wide. Iguchi launched a rapid combination of thrusts, and the three soldiers fell.

He ran into the trees with scores of angry soldiers in close pursuit.

***

Miles and Benji heard Iguchi call out for them to return to the forest, and then the cavalry burst through the tree line, gaining on the Angels.

Miles suddenly stopped, his expression going blank, and his eyes glazed over; he was having another vision. This was the only time he was unable to defend himself.

Benji turned in time to see his friend hit by a horse, which sent him flying into a nearby tree. Miles bounced off a large oak and hit the ground gasping for breath. Half-a-dozen soldiers ran to his position with swords ready.

Benji screamed as he rushed to the aid of his fallen friend. The noise turned the attention of the six soldiers to Benji.

He raced ahead without thought into the six kingdom soldiers. A combination of anger and sheer recklessness saved Benji amid the enemy. He ploughed into the group with new-found strength.

Whipping his sword from side-to-side, Benji mortally wounded four of the soldiers. The remaining two ran back the way they had come.

He offered Miles and hand, helping his friend to his feet. 'This is no time for a rest,' he said in his best Iguchi impersonation.

'I had another vision,' Miles said in a worried tone.

'What was it?'

'The Lord of Sanctuary will be shot down on the battlefield.'

Benji looked at the scores of soldiers running toward them. 'We cannot help him.'

The two friends ran deeper into the forest.

30

'Owain!' Ramulas called out. 'They're coming through the gate.'

As Ramulas raced down to the courtyard, he heard the blind bowman order three groups of archers to fire into the passage. He saw the companies of Sanctuary's soldiers. Ramulas would need them to help push back the enemy, and then he could close the gate.

Halfway down the stairs, he communicated with the hell hounds and Rufus; they would be waiting for him at the entrance of the passage.

The people of Sanctuary watched as he raced down the stairs,

'The enemy is in the passage. With me! Push them back out.'

He climbed onto his warhorse, and Pip jumped off the stairs to sit behind him and wrapped her arms around him.

Ramulas raced down the passage toward the enemy pouring through the gate. The hell hounds ran next to them, and the people of Sanctuary shouted as they followed.

Arrows still rained down on those entering the gate. Half-a-dozen knights on their armoured warhorses were unaffected by the arrows. They led more soldiers toward Sanctuary.

The knights formed a line as they raced down the passage. Ramulas knew that the combination of knight and warhorse would cause heavy casualties for his people.

He needed to even the odds.

Ramulas entered the minds of the three warhorses on the left, showing them large boulders falling into the passage, the warhorses instantly veered away, into the other warhorses. The knights cursed as they were pushed together, and two of them fell to the ground.

Ramulas had more fragmented visions of his past life as the symbol on his cheek began to burn. He seized onto one of the memories and held out his hand to the knights twenty feet away.

Tendrils of purple energy reached out to caress the armour of the four knights still mounted, and then deadly arcs of energy coursed through their bodies.

The knights spasmed and fell as the warhorses screamed and ran into Sanctuary. Ramulas quickly looked back and saw his people make way for the warhorses. He turned and focused on the open gate and the soldiers pouring through. Thomas was supposed to shut the gate, what had happened to him?

Then Rufus was hit by a wave of infantry.

Pip yelled as she jumped off the warhorse with a knife in each hand. She was a woman possessed, ducking, weaving, and slashing. Ramulas swung from the warhorse with his war hammer and battle axe. Even though he was doing damage, a part of him wanted to fight on the ground.

A score of his people had surrounded the two knights that fell. The rest rushed to help repel the enemy.

Ramulas called out to Pip as he jumped down next to her. He communicated for Rufus to stay close to the hell hounds and attack the soldiers.

Ramulas and Pip fell into a pattern of fighting back-to-back as they slowly turned. Their time training together was paying off.

The people of Sanctuary stood on either side of Ramulas and Pip. The tide was slowly turning. Curses and shouts of pain could be heard over the clashing of metal.

The sounds of the hell hounds growling intensified as they ran into the soldiers, sending a ripple of fear into the enemy. Terrifying screams told Ramulas where the hell hounds were.

A gap opened around the hell hounds. 'Push them back!' Ramulas shouted.

Ramulas found that this was unnecessary, as his people were already surging forward. As Rufus moved with the people, Ramulas was careful to avoid the dead and injured on the ground—one wrong foot could mean falling and opening himself to an enemy's blade.

Ramulas and Pip fought three soldiers as he dropped to one knee and swung with his battle axe. He cut through one soldier's knee and followed up by cutting the next through the breastplate. Blood fountained out as he moved forward.

He saw Pip grapple for a soldier's sword while kicking another in the groin, and then she thrust one of her knives under the soldier's chin, killing him instantly.

Orders from both sides were called out. These were mixed with shouts of pain, anger, and curses. The sounds of the hell hounds were welcomed only by the people of Sanctuary.

'Sanctuary!' Ramulas shouted, holding his war hammer high.

'Sanctuary!' his people called back as they renewed their effort.

Ramulas stood strong and proud amid the enemy, striking down any who dared come near. The people of Sanctuary saw this and drew strength from their lord. He chanced another look at the gate twenty yards away. Kingdom soldiers continued to enter. Arrows rained down upon upturned shields and several arrows found their mark, but still they came.

The sound of rolling thunder came up from behind Ramulas. The soldiers looked past Ramulas in fear. He turned to see the people make way for Lodi, who ran down the passage.

The giant swung his huge club as he ran. Rygar sat on Lodi's shoulder holding on for dear life. Shouts of panic flowed through the enemy lines; they began retreating out of the gate.

A great cheer went up as the soldiers were pushed out into the clearing. Ramulas communicated for the hell hounds and Rufus to return to his side.

Lodi came bounding past as Ramulas climbed onto his warhorse. The dwarf dived headfirst into a group of kingdom soldiers while Lodi sent some flying with his club. Fear helped push the soldiers through the gate.

Then Ramulas saw something that broke his heart.

His friend Thomas sat propped up against the gate with a giant arrow through his chest. His friend had died allowing the Khilli to enter Sanctuary. Emotions of sadness and anger flooded through him while thinking of his friend.

A warm sensation exploded in Ramulas' chest and quickly spread throughout his body. A feeling of pins and needles covered his skin.

'Aaaaargh!' he shouted, focusing on his magical abilities.

He communicated for his warhorse to charge the enemy as purple flame covered his body. The people of Sanctuary cheered and followed their lord.

The kingdom soldiers saw Ramulas covered in magical flame and charging his warhorse towards them. Next to him was the giant swinging his club as a man would swat flies.

Purple arcs of energy leapt out from the flame touching any kingdom soldier close enough. With a crackle of energy, they were sent flying through the air.

The remaining soldiers in the passage hurried into the clearing.

Before Ramulas knew how far he had come, he and Lodi had charged through the gate. The clearing was littered with the dead and dying.

Then he felt a surge from behind pushing him forward.

Several hundred of Sanctuary's people poured out of the gate to face the thousands of kingdom soldiers, they were at a fever pitch, allowing emotions to control them. The kingdom soldiers were momentarily stunned and formed defensive lines.

Ramulas knew that his people would suffer if they did not return to Sanctuary. Someone from the kingdom army gave the order to charge, and a sea of screaming soldiers charged the people of Sanctuary.

Ramulas turned to see the people of Sanctuary still coming through the gate eager to join the fight. The realisation that many of his people were about to die dawned on Ramulas.

'Oh no,' he said. 'You need to go back inside.'

Then a roar brought Ramulas from his thoughts. He turned towards the sound and saw four royal lancers riding away from Lodi. The giant pulled a broken lance from his leg and ran after them.

A shout brought Ramulas' attention to the tree line, where the ballista was loaded and aimed at Lodi.

Without a second thought, he willed Rufus to ride to Lodi as fast as he could. Ramulas yelled, trying to get the giant's attention. Just before he reached Lodi, there was a loud crack when the ballista fired.

At the last moment, Ramulas saw the giant arrow speed across soldiers' heads before it hit him, throwing him off the warhorse. He hit the ground and slid ten yards before hitting the base of the wall.

Ramulas lay very still, looking like one of the many dead in the clearing.

***

The sounds of battle echoed through the castle. Jacqueline looked around the throne room to see hundreds of nervous women and children. This was but one of many rooms where people waited for the battle to finish.

Her girls were doing the best they could to calm the other children, and then Jacqueline noticed something different with Kate. Her eldest daughter stood like a statue with a faraway expression, and then a look of determination came over her.

Kate raced to the wall where a few ceremonial swords hung. At the same time, Grace stood, and her eyes shone a fierce green. She followed her elder sister.

'Girls, what are you doing?' Jacqueline asked.

Kate turned to her mother, who almost flinched at the change that had come over her daughter.

'We must leave,' Kate said in a hollow voice. 'Father is in trouble, and he needs us.'

Grace nodded. 'We need to help Da.'

Jacqueline gasped as she saw Grace's hands surrounded by purple flame. 'Girls, you stay with me.'

Kate shook her head and walked towards the door. 'We must help Father.'

Jacqueline felt helpless as she watched her two girls reach the door. She had never seen them act this way and knew there was no way she could stop them.

Then a blue translucent wall appeared in the doorway, blocking the girls' retreat. Kate ran into it and fell back while Grace tried to use her magic-covered hands to get through the barrier.

Oriel laughed. 'Your father would not want you two out there.'

The sisters turned in disappointment, knowing they could not exit the room. Kate gripped the sword while staring at Oriel for a moment, and then the sword fell from her hand as Kate returned to her normal self.

Grace giggled as she clapped her hands and was devastated when the purple flame vanished.

***

Benji and Miles raced through the forest with what sounded like the whole kingdom army on their heels. The friends headed south near the mountain range. They had run this way many times during their months of rigorous training.

They could keep this pace for hours, and then they saw familiar signs around them and knew the time had come.

Benji and Miles stopped before looking at each other. Benji held his right side, his face a mask of pain. Miles dropped his sword and shield and placed both hands on his knees. He made a show of fighting for breath.

Within moments, they were surrounded by scores of angry kingdom soldiers.

'Can we talk …' Benji said as he winced, 'about this?'

Miles nodded. 'You've caught us—now we're your prisoners.'

'There won't be any prisoners today,' a sergeant said with a cruel smile.

The circle of kingdom soldiers closed in with their swords drawn. Benji made a quick recovery while Miles retrieved his sword and shield in a fluid motion.

'We were hoping you might say that,' Benji said with a smile.

Angered at the deception, the kingdom soldiers closed in on the friends, and then the surrounding forest exploded as the Fallen Angels burst from their hiding places.

Benji and Miles stood back ready for anyone who would come at them; however, the kingdom soldiers were busy fighting off the rest of the Angels.

As the Fallen Angels cut their way through the enemy ranks, Benji noticed something strange. He saw Michael fighting two soldiers; he wounded each with a cut to the sword arm, a nonlethal blow, and then he came behind other soldiers cutting hamstrings.

Benji knew that this had saved their lives, because they were no longer a threat, and would live. Out of all the Fallen Angels, Michael was the only one Benji had not seen kill anyone.

Within moments, all the kingdom soldiers were down at the Angels' feet.

'Our lord is in trouble,' Miles said to Iguchi.

Iguchi slowly shook his head as he looked to Sanctuary, where the sounds of battle could be heard.

'We are too few,' the small man said. 'We played our part in helping the Khilli enter Sanctuary—now we must follow the plan for the next part of the battle.'

He led his Fallen Angels toward the mountains.

***

Ramulas woke as both hell hounds licked his face. His whole body hurt, and he was confused as to where he was and how he came to be lying on the ground.

Then the sounds of battle reached him, and his memory returned. When he saw the ballista, Ramulas focused his magical energy, wrapping himself in a magical shield, which took most of the blow before shattering.

Turning, he saw the tree-trunk legs of Lodi as the giant stood protectively over him. With a groan, he pushed himself to his feet to see the people of Sanctuary sorely pressed against the kingdom soldiers.

It was too late to order a withdrawal into Sanctuary without too many dying. Another wave of arrows rained down from the wall. Ramulas knew that would not be enough.

He shouted for Owain, but he could not be heard over the noise of the battle. He needed to use the scale in order to save his people. It was their only chance.

Turning to the giant, Ramulas came up with an idea that might kill him if it did not work. 'Lodi, I need you to throw me to the top of the wall, are you strong enough?'

The giant's smile looked like that of a child. 'I can throw you to the clouds in the sky.'

Before Ramulas could give him any instructions, he was picked up and thrown at the wall. Ramulas turned in mid-air, trying to gather his bearings, and knew this was a bad idea.

At the apex of the throw, Ramulas was a few feet from the top of the wall and threw his hand up in desperation, his fingers grabbed hold of the wall as his body smashed against the wall, and Ramulas knew he could not hold on for long.

He hung by one arm unable to breathe properly or call out. Then, with agonising slowness, one by one, his fingers started to lose their grip.

He had no strength to lift himself up, he looked down at the carnage in the clearing and wished it had been different.

A strong hand grasped his wrist and Ramulas looked up to see one of the archers smiling down at him. Several more appeared and pulled him over the edge.

Ramulas landed on his back, as weak as a kitten fighting for air.

After a few seconds, he pushed himself into a sitting position. 'Owain.'

The blind archer appeared next to him.

'We need to use the scale, or many of our people will die.'

The blind archer gave him a stern look. 'You must be sure—this can only be used once.'

Ramulas grabbed him by the sleeve. 'Do it now,' he ordered.

Owain nodded before walking to where the scale rested against the ledge. He removed the cloth, and Ramulas was again transfixed with the dark shapes swimming within.

'Hold arrows,' Owain called.

Along the wall the archers placed their bows by their feet, with help from a couple of archers Ramulas was helped to his feet, and he looked into the clearing.

The people of Sanctuary continued to pour out to meet the kingdom soldiers, but he could see that they were overwhelmed.

Owain held the black scale above his head. 'I will throw this into the air. On my command, each of you will fire an arrow at it.'

The blind archer turned in a slow circle before throwing the scale off the wall. Ramulas watched as it seemed to float over the clearing. As it spun, Owain clicked his tongue.

As it began to drop, he shouted, 'Now!'

Two hundred archers released their arrows as one. They hit the scale, which shattered in a clap of thunder. A thick, black cloud appeared in its place. Orange and yellow explosions could be seen within. These, along with sheets of lightning, helped the cloud expand.

Everyone on the wall and in the clearing watched the growing cloud. Magical energies flashed within as a low rumbling sound could be heard. The sound grew louder as the cloud began to take shape and definition.

The cloud dissipated revealing a huge black dragon with a wingspan of one hundred feet. It roared down at the humans below in rage and fury. Its last memory was one of betrayal and its death by the green dragons.

It blamed this attack on the king of Keah and his magician—they would be the first to die. It scanned the battlefield below and could not find the one it was looking for.

Then it saw the symbol of the black eagle on red.

The dragon had found Zachary. He would be the one to pay.

***

Zachary thought the assault on Sanctuary had been going well. After the debacle of losing the Khilli warrior, and then being attacked at the rear lines, the person closing the gate was shot, the way into Sanctuary was open, and his soldiers flooded through the opening.

Then his army was pushed out into the clearing by the giant and the Lord of Sanctuary, who was bathed in purple flames. Lucas also saw the giant and gave orders for the ballista to be fired at it. However, Ramulas was shot instead. Zachary thought the fight was won.

His hopes were shattered a moment later when the giant threw the Lord of Sanctuary to the top of the wall and then a black disk was thrown into the air before it exploded and turned into a black dragon, which hovered above the clearing. Men from both sides were transfixed by the creature.

Memories of the Shangri-La story came back to Zachary as he felt the dragon's eye single him out. He looked for a place to hide as the dragon dropped from the sky.

Men ran screaming in all directions, and the battle was quickly forgotten.

'To the forest!' Lucas ordered.

The royal guard formed a human shield around Zachary and ran for the trees. No-one dared look back.

The ground shook as the creature landed, giving a mighty roar as it sent a spray of acid into the sky.

This was followed by screams of pain and sheer terror.

The dragon had begun to feed.

***

Those on the wall watched in fascination. Owain called for the archers to drop their bows. Kingdom soldiers ran for the trees, and Sanctuary's people ran to the passage.

Owain explained that if the people of Sanctuary did not attack the dragon, they would be safe, and then the creature began to feed.

With movements that reminded Ramulas of a bird eating insects, the dragon's head would snake down to grab a soldier with an audible *crunch* and toss it into the air before catching it in its great maw.

Two quick bites and the soldier was swallowed, and then it went for another. Ramulas was repulsed at the sight, but he could not turn away.

Some soldiers died instantly while others screamed for mercy as they were eaten. Royal archers fired arrows at the creature from the safety of the trees. This proved futile as the arrows broke on contact.

After a minute of feasting, the dragon's head snapped up and looked to the north. The lower half of a body hung from its maw. It finished the meal before throwing its head back and roaring. The sound seemed to shake the wall Ramulas stood on.

It lowered its body and spread its huge wings. With a single beat, the dragon was in the air. It roared once more before flying south along the mountain range.

Ramulas turned to Owain in confusion. 'Why did the dragon leave?'

The blind archer smiled. 'Because it knows the green dragons are coming.'

'But it was larger than the dragon I saw in Shangri-La.'

'There are many greens coming. The black knows it will be killed.'

'Why are they coming here?' Ramulas asked.

'The black dragon is their most hated enemy, and they felt its presence. The black knew they were coming and would lose the fight with so many. When the greens arrive, they will feed on the dead in the clearing. We need to gather our people and bring them inside.'

Ramulas looked down at the clearing in shock. Hundreds of dead and injured from both sides littered the clearing. A heavy burden weighed on Ramulas' shoulders as he saw the still forms wearing Sanctuary's uniform.

'It's not your fault,' Pip said as she came up to him. 'Do not blame yourself for this.'

Feelings of helplessness and despair threatened to overwhelm him, but he pushed those feelings aside. The people of Sanctuary needed a leader—there was still work to be done.

'We need to bring our people inside,' Ramulas said walking to the stairs.

As Ramulas walked into the courtyard, he found it odd that Pip did not accompany him. The people looked expectantly as he came down the stairs.

'We need carts to bring our people in from the clearing,' Ramulas said as he held back the bile in his throat. 'Green dragons are coming to feed on the dead—our people deserve better.'

He was not sure how many people would want to help after hearing about the dragons, but he was surprised at the response.

A caravan of carts made their way down the passage, bodies of the kingdom soldiers were moved to clear a path, and then Ramulas came upon his dear friend Thomas and he almost broke down and cried. His chest felt as if it were being crushed in a vice. He needed to be strong for his people.

Thomas was laid gently on a cart. As the people entered the clearing to collect the dead and injured of Sanctuary, Ramulas felt waves of pain in his consciousness.

One of the hell hounds had been injured and called for him. He looked to the left and saw Fenris sitting near a still form one hundred yards away. Ramulas raced to his hell hounds.

Fenris wagged its spiked tail as Ramulas approached. He saw a long-ragged cut along Valkyrie's side. Her mouth was open and her tongue hung out. Ramulas knelt beside her, and she attempted to move.

She whined softly and he knew she was close to death. Anguish cut through Ramulas, and then a shout came across the clearing.

Ramulas stood and heard that one of his people had been found alive, and then another and another.

The people looked to him for direction.

'Hurry, bring the injured to Oriel. She will heal heal them. Bring the dead into the courtyard.'

The people of Sanctuary doubled their efforts and Ramulas watched his hell hounds. Then a thought came to him. *Where is Rufus?*

Focusing his magical ability, Ramulas reached out for his warhorse. In a few moments, he discovered Rufus had run into the trees when the dragon landed.

Ramulas called the warhorse back as he gently picked up Valkyrie. With Fenris by his side, he walked down the passage with the carts of injured.

***

Ramulas walked into the throne room holding Valkyrie as if she were a child. He saw Oriel's concerned expression, and his girls were shocked.

Grace ran to him. 'Da, what happened?'

Seeing his daughter upset was the final straw. Ramulas collapsed to his knees holding the hell hound to his chest as tears flowed freely down his face.

'Don't cry, Da,' Grace said softly. 'I can make it better.'

Grace's eyes glowed fiercely as her hands reached out for Valkyrie. As she touched the hell hound, purple energy flowed from her hands into the ragged tear.

Before Ramulas' eyes, the wound began to knit itself together. Within seconds it had healed, and Valkyrie had fully recovered. The hell hound wriggled out of Ramulas' arms and licked Grace over her face and hands. Grace giggled trying to keep the hell hound at bay, and then Fenris jumped over Kate and Jacqueline in excitement.

Ramulas remained on his knees looking at his youngest daughter in shock. Valkyrie had been close to death, and he thought Oriel could help her. If someone had told Ramulas earlier that Grace had such magical power, he would not believe them.

Yet he had just witnessed a miracle.

'Ramulas,' Oriel said, 'you are needed outside.'

He stood and wiped the tears from his eyes as the first person was brought before Oriel.

'Can you help the injured?' he asked Oriel.

After she nodded, Ramulas made his way into the courtyard, where he saw people gathering the dead and wounded. K'ayden joined him as he walked down the passage.

The Khilli thanked Ramulas profusely for helping his people and offered to help him. They passed carts coming into Sanctuary, and Ramulas gave nods of thanks to the people helping.

There was a noticeable difference in the clearing. The area near the wall was clear of bodies and the last cart had gone through the gate. Ramulas slowly scanned the clearing looking for any more of his people.

'Ramulas,' Pip shouted from the wall, 'over there.'

He followed where she pointed and found one of his people with the kingdom bodies. With K'ayden by his side, Ramulas ran to the soldier and found he was still breathing.

He was unconscious but still alive.

The injured kingdom soldiers called out for mercy. He pushed away any feelings of sympathy—his first duty was to his people.

'Ramulas, hurry!' Pip yelled as he lifted the Sanctuary soldier. 'The green dragons are coming.'

Ramulas looked to the East and saw several dark shapes in the sky. A jolt of fear hit Ramulas and knew that they needed to get inside Sanctuary.

'K'ayden, run inside.'

The Khilli shook his head. 'I will not leave your side.'

The two carefully carried the injured soldier to the gate, the kingdom soldiers began to panic as they saw the dark shapes growing in the sky. With fear in their voices, they begged to be taken into Sanctuary.

As hard as it was, Ramulas ignored their pleas. He knew there were far too many people in the clearing. The frantic shouts told him that the green dragons were close.

Twenty yards from the gate, Ramulas looked to the east, and what he saw chilled him to the bone.

A score of greens began dropping into the clearing. Ramulas and K'ayden rushed through the gate and stopped to catch their breath.

Pip shouted out a warning.

A green dragon landed in front of them in the passage. K'ayden gasped in shock as he backed away. Ramulas used his magical ability to communicate with the dragon. *We have no fight with you. We want to take this injured man inside.*

He is food. Drop him and leave, the dragon replied.

'No,' Ramulas said out loud. 'He is one of my people.'

A wall of rage hit Ramulas as the dragon lowered its head and opened its mouth. With Ramulas holding the injured soldier, he knew there was nowhere for him to go.

The feelings of the dragon changed from rage to fear, and it pulled its head away from Ramulas. He was confused—what could put fear into a dragon?

The hair on Ramulas' arms raised a moment before Emily came next to him. Her eyes were completely dark and her hair danced as dark energies crackled around her.

'You are a bad dragon,' Emily said.

The dragon cowered and seemed very afraid of the small girl. Emily walked up to the dragon and slapped it. The dragon roared in pain as a shower of multi-coloured sparks came off its scales.

With a beat of its wings, it flew over the wall. Without another word, Emily turned and walked into Sanctuary. Ramulas and K'ayden exchanged astonished looks before following her.

Reaching the courtyard, Ramulas saw that all the dead had been laid out in front of the castle. K'ayden took the injured soldier to Oriel as Ramulas looked over the brave who had fallen.

A crowd had gathered around the bodies and made way for their lord. He counted twenty-eight who gave their lives for Sanctuary. Everyone except for Thomas had loved ones mourning for them. He could not find any words that would comfort them.

The sounds of the kingdom soldiers begging for mercy as the dragons ate them cut through the air.

Ramulas led the people into the castle, not knowing what he would do next.

31

Pip stood on the wall and watched in awe as the dragons fed. After a few minutes, they had eaten almost half of the bodies on the field.

They made a game of stalking and playing with the wounded. It reminded Pip of cats when they caught a mouse before killing it. A wounded soldier would be thrown screaming from one dragon to another.

Once the dragons had fed, they filled their mouths and claws with bodies before flying east. This continued until the clearing and passage were clear of bodies.

The clearing was littered with swords, arrows, and shields from both sides. A dozen wagons had been left by the army, but Pip saw the machines of war had been taken.

Then she saw movement in the southern part of the forest, and then she relaxed seeing it was the Fallen Angels. Iguchi waved to her as they came into the clearing. Pip walked down the stairs to join them in the courtyard.

Iguchi nodded. 'Hello to you, thrower of knives. We must see the Lord of Sanctuary. There is work still to be done.'

They walked into the castle to find Ramulas in a large room on the ground floor, the twenty-eight who had died lying before him in two rows.

Lost in his own thoughts, Ramulas did not hear them enter. With the weight of their deaths, he could not think of a proper way to honour them.

'Hello to you, Lord of Sanctuary,' Iguchi said.

Ramulas slowly turned, and Pip gasped seeing his torment.

'This is good,' Iguchi said. 'The fallen will stay here until the celebration.'

'Celebration?' Ramulas asked.

'Yes. We must talk of how they gave their lives so that others could live. This is a time where happiness or sadness is born—you need to choose.'

Ramulas nodded and pushed away the feelings of self-pity. 'Find K'ayden and Rygar and tell them to meet me in the throne room.'

***

Zachary held up his hand at the edge of the forest. The survivors stopped and Lucas came over to him. Their shadows stretched out as the sun dropped.

'We make camp here and move on at dawn,' Zachary ordered as he looked back at his men. 'How long will it take us to reach Keah?'

Lucas took a deep breath. 'We will reach Turtha tomorrow, two or three days to Covedon, and then five days to Keah. The men are tired and shaken from seeing the dragons. A lot are close to breaking—we could have mutiny on our hands.'

Thoughts of a mutiny fuelled the rage which already burned within Zachary. This had started when he lost the Khilli. His men would never defy him; however, he silently agreed with Lucas.

Orders were given to make camp; soldiers set tents and corralled the horses. Zachary smiled thinking of what he would do to the Khilli women and children. He would make them suffer.

Men sat around their fires eating and singing bawdy songs. Lucas had encouraged this to boost morale. An hour after sunset a sentry called out of someone approaching the camp. The royal guard quickly rode out to meet this person.

They returned a few moments later, and Zachary was surprised to see the mayor of Turtha gingerly climbing down of one of the royal guard's mounts.

'What are you doing here?' He asked the mayor.

'I received a message that a small force of soldiers had entered Keah's castle. They freed the Khilli women and children, and a score of your men are dead. I rode as soon as I could. My horse threw me during the day when it broke its leg. I have been walking ever since.'

Zachary had stopped listening after he heard about the Khilli. He wanted to know how such a thing could happen. Things were going from bad to worse. He wondered what else could go wrong.

***

Remus stood in front of the golden arch watching a continuous wave of flux moving through it, the red wizards had said the passage was almost ready and word had been sent to the First Legion.

The three captains of the legion had arrived with the legion and supply wagons within minutes.

Minute white lights began to dance within the arch, spinning in tiny circles. After a moment, they slammed together in the centre. The passage appeared with the sound of rushing air. A red wizard smiled. 'The way to Oriel is open.'

Remus walked up to the arch and looked into a passage filled with mist. The mist along the walls and ceiling moved as if blown by a strong wind.

Remus nodded and stepped into the passage with the red wizard. The other warlords and a dozen other red wizards followed, and then came the First Legion, slaves pushing wagons, and scores of mountillo.

The holes along the walls were covered in mist and long, dark shapes could be seen swimming just below the surface. The red wizards had warned of this, saying that as long as no-one attacked the shapes, they would remain safe.

After a few minutes of walking, the floor shook slightly, followed by a faint rumble behind them. Remus ordered two warlords and four red wizards to investigate.

They waited to see what the problem was; the floor shook once more and the shapes beneath the mist grew in number.

'We need to keep moving,' a red wizard said. 'Our number is too much for the passage to handle.'

Remus glared at the red wizard before ordering the legion to continue. A few moments later, they could see into Oriel's new world.

***

Jankt sat in her crude wooden shack watching the pretty crystal as the coloured light danced inside. She had been banished from the Clan of the Bear six weeks ago for refusing advances from the chieftain's son.

The fellow Symiaks ordered her to live on a small rise five hundred yards away from the camp. Part of her punishment was to live alone while looking over her former tribe.

They would accept her back once she married the chieftain's son. However, since finding the pretty crystal, Jankt did not care that she was an outcast. More and more of her time was spent gazing into the crystal—she had no need for company.

A moment ago, the colours had intensified in the crystal. Awestruck, Jankt leaned closer to the crystal, and then it exploded in her face, killing her instantly.

The crystal rapidly grew to form a golden arch ten feet in diameter. It punched through the roof of the hut, causing it to collapse.

The Symiaks looked up to see the legion walking out from the golden arch.

***

Remus and the red wizard walked into the new world to be greeted by cold winds on top of a mountain range. They stood on a plateau that was bare and rocky. A small village lay below them. Around two hundred strange creatures watched as the legion came out behind them.

Remus used his magical ability to inspect the creatures. They were slightly larger than the men of the legion, broad across the shoulders and muscular. They wore animal furs. The one thing that stood out was the two tusks protruding from the bottom jaw.

Reckoning appeared by Remus' side, and he turned to the captain. 'Come with me and meet the locals. I want to buy some time so the legion can come through.'

Remus walked to the village, knowing that Reckoning was sending telepathic instructions to the other captains.

The creatures became excited as the duo walked towards them. They grunted and snarled while waving crude spears and clubs.

They stopped twenty feet from the creatures as weapons were thrust at them. Remus knew he could kill the whole village with a thought. However, he knew that he needed allies on this strange world. He slowly spread his hands out to show he was not holding any weapons.

A row rumbling growl came from the large hut in the centre of the village. The creatures parted and began to chant. The animal hides that served as a door was pushed aside as another creature stepped out.

He was a full head taller than the others. He wore leggings and was bare-chested. As he strode over to the newcomers, Remus noticed the creature wore a necklace of human skulls. It held a huge, spiked club with ease.

'Why is you come through light?' it asked menacingly, pointing to the golden arch.

Remus casually turned and was happy to see the legion slowly coming out onto the mountain. The rocky terrain made it difficult to come into this world quickly. He did not know how many of these creatures were in the mountains—he needed to buy time.

Turning back to face the creature, Remus smiled while murmuring a simple spell under his breath. It was to search for Oriel. He felt a faint vibration far to the north. She was a long way from where he was.

'I seek someone north of here,' he said in a calm tone.

'You come from Keah city?' the creature said, lifting its club with a snarl. 'Symiaks crush humans from Keah.'

Remus' mind raced to calm the creature. He felt Reckoning readying himself for a fight, and then several creatures disappeared over the edge of the mountain.

'We are not from Keah,' Remus said as he fought the rage which threatened to explode. 'We come to ask for help. We do not like those who live in Keah.'

The creature pointed its club to the ridges surrounding them. 'Lots more Symiaks come to smash humans from Keah.'

Remus did not need this. 'We also hate humans of Keah!' He said in a loud confident voice. 'We come with gifts to help you smash them. We have heard great tales of how mighty you are from our world.'

The creature puffed out its chest with pride. 'What you hear?'

'That you are the mightiest of all the Symiaks—that is why we come with gifts.'

'What is "gifts"?'

Remus gestured to the golden arch. 'When all my men come through, I will show you gifts.'

'What is gifts? Grunch want see gifts.'

'Wait for my men.'

'Hurry. Bring men and gifts.'

Remus and Reckoning walked back to the arch as the Symiaks chanted Grunch's name.

'Start bringing the legion down here,' Remus said, noticing they were running out of room on the plateau. 'Keep them away from the creatures for now. We don't want any problems.'

Reckoning nodded as Remus walked to the arch. The columns of soldiers made their way down towards the lower ground. He stood before the red wizard, who monitored the golden arch as more of the legion came through.

'How many have come through?' Remus asked.

'Just over six thousand. The portal should hold until the rest arrive.'

Then blue arcs of energy moved along the borders of the arch, accompanied by a shower of sparks.

The red wizard looked absolutely terrified.

'What is happening?' Remus asked.

The red wizard placed his hand on the arch and closed his eyes for a moment. When they opened, Remus knew something was very wrong. 'The atmosphere of this world is affecting the passageway. The arch is about to collapse under the strain. I am not strong enough to hold it.'

Beads of sweat could be seen forming on the red wizard's brow as his body began to shake. Remus looked at the seven other red wizards and two warlords. 'Help him.'

They rushed over to lend assistance. Soldiers coming out of the arch knew something was wrong, they came out faster than those before them.

After a minute of the warlords and red wizards trying to stabilise the arch, large cracks formed on its surface. The red wizards and warlords let out screams of pain before the arch exploded, the pieces sucked into a small vortex.

Then it vanished with a *pop*.

Remus looked at where the arch had been in disbelief.

The red wizard looked at him with pain in his eyes. 'It has gone. I have lost all contact with the other side.'

'Where is the rest of the legion, my warlords, and the red wizards?' Remus said in anger.

The red wizard held out his hands. 'I do not know. With the arch gone, there is no way to communicate with them,' he said before falling unconscious to the ground.

Remus ignored the still figure before him. 'We now have no choice. We must find Oriel; she is our only way home.'

Remus quickly counted the columns that had come through. One hundred per column, and there were seventy-one columns. He had the three captains, Omega, and Beta, eight red wizards and the slaves and supplies.

He wanted more to retrieve Oriel.

He smiled as hundreds of Symiaks swarmed over the ridges around him. He needed to find a way to persuade these creatures to join his cause.

***

That night, over three thousand Symiaks had come from across the mountain ranges from various tribes. They were very curious to find out why the legion had come into their home.

Remus walked over to Grunch. 'Is this all of the Symiaks on the mountains?'

The chieftain shook his head quickly. 'Many and much more come. Hundreds and hundreds come,' he said, waving a hand at the mountain range.

Doubting the creature knew how to count, Remus posed a question. 'How many are here now?'

Grunch puffed out his massive chest. 'Hundred.'

Remus balked at the word. If Grunch thought three thousand were one hundred, how many would hundreds and hundreds mean? He wanted these creatures with him for Oriel.

He knew that Oriel would have called many to her cause.

Remus knew that he only had one chance. He organised for the six new chieftains and Grunch to meet with him in one of the legion tents.

Once they were all seated, Remus stood and, with a flourish, tipped the contents of a pouch onto the carpeted floor. The creatures stared in awe at the shiny stones and softly grunted in approval.

Grunch stood holding his club. 'This is gifts for Grunch?'

Remus smiled while looking at all the chieftains. 'Yes, and there are more gifts. The person I seek has these gifts in the north. When we find her, you will have gifts.'

The creatures stared hungrily at the gems on the carpet.

Grunch nodded. 'After snows, we get gifts from person.'

The other creatures grunted and nodded in agreement.

'Snows?' Remus asked.

Grunch shook his head. 'No walk in snows. After snows, hundreds of Symiak come to get gifts.'

The red wizard leaned in and whispered to Remus. 'We have cast spells. The climate here is much colder than on our world. Winter is coming, and it will be very difficult to travel with such a large number.'

Remus was not happy with the news, but he would use this time wisely.

After winter, he would march to find Oriel.

***

Ramulas stood in front of his throne with Oriel and Pip on either side. Gathered in the throne room were Iguchi, K'ayden, Shigar, the druids, the Earth elementals, and the families of those who had fallen in battle.

The people who were injured had been healed with Oriel's magic. However, Ramulas knew that the mental scars would take longer to heal. This was the first time most of the people of Sanctuary had ever been in a battle.

Training had been stopped for three days so they could recover. Iguchi, Rygar, and Owain had come up with a way for the dead to be remembered.

The Earth elementals, Oriel, and Ramulas worked most of the day on honouring the fallen soldiers. A wall of mist was placed in front of the work at the rear of Sanctuary.

The people of Sanctuary had gathered in anticipation, knowing that something special had happened. Once the work was finished, Ramulas walked through the wall of mist and waited for everyone's attention. The streets were filled, and there were even people on the rooftops.

He smiled and raised his hands. 'We are now ready to honour those who bravely gave their lives for Sanctuary.'

He looked up at Oriel on the balcony of the castle and waved. The wall of mist disappeared.

A chorus of gasps came from the people. The fallen soldiers were lined up along the face of the cliff, they had been covered in a thin layer of stone, giving them the appearance of statues.

They stood strong and proud. No wounds were visible. They wore new armour and held their sword and shield at the ready.

In the centre of the twenty-eight statues was a small altar with a magical flame floating above it. Images of the flame danced in the open eyes of each of the statues.

The families of the fallen were overcome with joy, they ran up to inspect the statues closely.

Ramulas looked over the crowd. 'We have lost twenty-eight of our brothers, but that does not mean that a part of them is not with every one of us. Know that with everything you do, they will be watching over us, lending the people of Sanctuary strength. Do not mourn their passing—celebrate their lives and honour them with your training.'

'Sanctuary!' the Fallen Angels shouted.

'Sanctuary!' the people replied, punching their fists in the air. This was repeated two more times before Ramulas waved for the people to walk past the fallen soldiers.

He remembered what Iguchi had said to him after he took responsibility for their deaths. 'Blaming yourself will not bring them back to life, so why do you do such a thing? The people of Sanctuary need a place where their spirits can be lifted.'

Another strange thing was that Oriel had said the flame appeared above the altar without her powers—the ancient magic of Sanctuary was awakening.

***

Remus stood on the precipice looking to the north. It was the legion's second night in this strange world. Another thousand Symiaks had come to the mountain, agreeing to march with the legion. More tribes would come after the snows.

A cold, biting wind came in from the north, blowing Remus' red robes around. He knew that this weather would suck the life out of the legion if they were travelling now.

He could feel Oriel's faint magical energy to the west. It would take weeks for the legion to reach her. A cruel smile formed thinking of when they would be reunited once more.

'Oriel, my dear, I am coming for you,' he whispered to the wind as he cast a spell.

***

A cold wind blew into the throne room, sending a shiver through Oriel.

Ramulas saw a worried expression on her face. 'What's wrong?'

She looked at Ramulas, her eyes filled with fear. 'Remus is here with the First Legion.'

'What!?' Ramulas said in shock. 'Here at Sanctuary?'

She shook her head. 'Where you dropped the crystal in the mountains.'

Ramulas thought about the battle with the kingdom soldiers and how close they had been to defeat. The First Legion had thousands more soldiers and they were better skilled than soldiers of the kingdom army.

'We are not ready for them,' he said, thinking of the dragon's scale they used.

'He cannot come until after the snows. You should hope for a miracle.'

Ramulas looked at Oriel. 'What kind of miracle?'

'Anything.'

***

Michael felt the rage and anger of his brother's scream. He knew something was wrong. He walked to the tunnel, where he saw a crowd of people gathered near the entrance.

Floating in the middle of the crowd were his brother's weapons. The sword and gauntlet had left the tunnel and were searching for new owners.

Shigar and the druids arrived just as people jumped up to try to grab them.

The gauntlet danced away from people's hands as if pulled by a string. People who tried for the sword quickly pulled their hands away. They rubbed their hands, fighting off the intense cold. The crowd laughed at the spectacle; it was the first time they had laughed since the battle.

Then one of the workers from the tunnel walked over to the sword. His hand opened as he reached for the blue scabbard, and then everyone gasped as it floated into his hand.

He grunted in pain as soon as the sword touched his hand. His body went rigid. People stepped back in alarm as the ground beneath him turned to ice.

Shigar rushed forward to inspect the man. 'Quickly,' he called, 'tell me his name so that I might help him.'

'Jason,' someone said.

'Jason,' Shigar said, clicking his fingers. 'Come back to us.'

The ice beneath Jason's feet cracked as his body relaxed. He opened his eyes to reveal blue crystals for pupils. 'Jason is no more,' he said, pulling the sword from its scabbard. 'We are known as Heaven's Reign.'

Both Michael and Shigar knew that the spirit of the sword had possessed Jason.

A wall of thick mist fell from the blade of the blue crystal sword. An aura of power emanated from Heaven's Reign.

'This cannot be good,' Michael whispered.

Acknowledgements

Being an author, you spend a lot of time writing by yourself, but outside of the actual writing there have been so many cool people who made my dreams come true, like Sarah Kate Ishii.

I would love to thank my family for allowing me to get lost into my own world, my beautiful partner for being my rock, knowing when to encourage me and knowing when I need a break.

A massive thanks goes out to the people in the online writing community who all support each other.

But most of all, I would love to thank the fans of fantasy who are willing to step into another world and forget about life for a while. Everything I do is for you guys.

About the Author

Adam has been a fan of fantasy his whole life and has always been happy immersing himself in another world. He has attempted to write his own novels several times over the years, but without success. It wasn't until he lost everything that the way to writing novels came to him with the characters of his fantasy series, The Ramulas Chronicles.

Outside of The Ramulas Chronicles, Adam has written the concepts of fourteen other stand-alone novels and is planning on releasing the first one soon.

He lives at home with his son and is enjoying this journey that writing is taking him on.